Praise for Marie Sutro

M000215308

"Marie Sutro's debut novel, *Dark Associations*, may just be this generation's *Silence of the Lambs*. Erotic and frightening, it keeps the reader guessing until the last pages."

—STEVE ALTEN, *New York Times* bestselling author of *The Meg* & *The Loch*

"*Dark Associations* is a crime thriller extraordinaire that offers a deviously devilish mix of madness, murder, and mayhem. Marie Sutro's finely tuned and polished debut effort channels the best of Thomas Harris ... Grisly without being gratuitous, *Dark Associations* strikes like a literary battering ram, as relentless as it is riveting."

—JON LAND, *USA Today* bestselling author of *Strong Cold Dead*

"*Dark Associations* is a wickedly compelling debut by Marie Sutro, who presents us with a great cast of characters and a villain who's as sadistic as they come. This one will keep you guessing right up till the end."

—SPENCER KOPE, author of *The Special Tracking Unit Series*

"... dark, gripping, tense, and filled with deep and interesting characters ... so blown away by the author's skill at creating tension and complex plot to keep the reader guessing right until the end ... A great book, deserving of five stars and my highest praise."

—K.J. SIMMILL, award-winning author of *Darrienia: The Forgotten Legacy Series*

"All the more impressive when considering that *Dark Associations* is author Marie Sutro's debut as a novelist, *Dark Associations* is a deftly crafted, inherently compelling, page-turner of a novel from beginning to end ..."

—*MIDWEST BOOK REVIEW*

DARK OBSESSIONS

A Kate Barnes Thriller

DARK OBSESSIONS

Marie Sutro

PISMO
PRESS

PISMO PRESS
AN IMPRINT OF PISMO PUBLISHING
CALIFORNIA

DARK OBSESSIONS
Published by Pismo Press
An imprint of Pismo Publishing
San Ramon, CA 94582

Cover design by Kelly Clark

ISBN: 978-1-7357488-1-8

Printed in the United States of America

Acknowledgements

The chance to formally express my gratitude to all who contributed to the creation of this book is one of the best parts of the road to publication. Whether through technical knowledge, skills, or support, so many have shined along the journey to bring this story to life. I am humbled by their abilities and kindness.

I must start with the wonderful folks who sacrifice so much to serve as community stewards for the magical part of the world known as the Olympic Peninsula. Sergeant Kevin Miller of the Port Angeles Police Department graciously stepped in to salvage my research quest, providing wonderful insights into the nuances of law enforcement and inter-regulatory collaboration in the region. The Park Rangers (including one special individual, who at the time we met, was stationed at very same Storm King Ranger Station featured herein) kindly shared insights into the amazing local topography and jurisdictional distinctions.

When it comes to inspiration, the wonderful cabins at the Hobuck Beach Resort in Neah Bay, allowed me to experience the singular natural glory of the Olympic Peninsula in ways I will forever cherish. In Port Angeles, the exceptional hospitality at the Olympic Lodge made me feel right at home.

Back in California, I owe thanks once again to Joy Viray of the Sacramento County Crime Lab, as well as a broader thanks to all her colleagues who work tirelessly to bring meaning to the word justice.

On the technical side of things, I am so grateful to have the talented Tim Schulte's creativity and industry expertise pushing to elevate my work. As ever, I remain awed and greatly appreciative for the glorious contributions of eagle-eyed editing maven, Barbara Becker.

I also remain grateful to Steve Alten for his numerous contributions to my writing journey and for thoughtfully guiding me through the early challenges of writing this story.

Long before anyone sees or hears a word of what I write, my husband patiently reads every chapter and doggedly participates in unending hypothetical discussions about alternate character development and plot twists. I am deeply grateful for his fortitude and commitment to my passion.

I also want to extend deep thanks to the multitudes of people who work tirelessly across the globe to help victims of violent crimes reclaim their lives and their voices.

Finally, a special expression of gratitude for all those who invest the time to read my stories and have supported me along the way. Without your imagination and interest, there is no magic.

To The Survivors of Violent Crimes.

Your Strength Is Our Hope.

"He came silently down the glen,
  Ever sing hardily, hardily.

It was there he met with a wounded doe,
  She was bleeding deathfully;
She warned him of the toils below,
  O so faithfully, faithfully!"

—Hunter's Song, Sir Walter Scott

Chapter 1

THE DEAD WOMAN'S HOUSE had a sunny quality to it. Set back a respectable distance from the street, the two-story craftsman was painted mint green with white trim. It was a color combination better suited to the sandy beaches of Southern California than to the small plot of land nestled under the leaden skies of Eagle's Nest, Washington.

Without breaking stride, Kate Barnes stole a furtive glance at the residence as she jogged along the opposite side of the street. Fit and attractive, the thirty-two-year-old brunette moved with a lithe confidence that was as much attributable to her athleticism, as it was to the small caliber pistol strapped to the small of her back.

Her gaze narrowed upon the large ceramic pots sitting on either side of the front porch. Once spring reached its zenith, the containers would overflow with a colorful array of pleasant blooms.

The thought turned Kate's stomach. Cheerfulness should not abide in the dwelling—not after what the dead woman had done. In addition to being Kate's mother, Chloe Barnes had also been a corruption of nature. She was a mother who had not given a damn about her two daughters—a mother for whom prescription drugs had trumped maternal instinct.

Indifferent to the frigid bite of the afternoon air, Kate picked up her pace. Icy bitterness pumped through her veins, spurring her to put as much distance as possible between herself and the residence. Turning left at the next corner, she approached a black Jeep.

1

She briefly considered looping around for one more pass before climbing inside. As soon as the door shut, she deposited her gun in the glove compartment. Dropping back against the seat she closed her eyes. Anger, uncertainty and a slew of other conflicting emotions washed over her in arctic waves.

It took a few minutes before the tide finally began to ebb. Starting the engine, she headed for home. As she neared the highway, the manicured landscape of the town's most recent residential development gave way to the wild, dense stretches of forest which made the Olympic Peninsula a favorite among nature enthusiasts.

Kate rolled down her window, treating herself to the heady aroma of dampened spruce and pine. As the miles rolled by, her mind wandered back to the house and its deceased owner.

Though very much alive, Chloe Barnes had been dead to her eldest child for years. Kate wished her mother could have stayed dead. In hindsight, it was shocking the addict had been allowed to raise two young girls, let alone one with a degenerative bone disease. But fate had conspired to turn a blind eye on the cruel pattern of neglect and abuse.

As a result, Kate's little sister, Candace, had never lived to see adolescence. The delicate ten-year-old to whom Kate had been best friend, nursemaid and co-victim had succumbed to a wretched end—choking to death on her own vomit. Had thirteen-year-old Kate not chosen that night to try to escape by drowning out the world with a set of earphones, she may have heard Candace's cries for help and been able to save her. It was a mistake for which Chloe had never forgiven her. And more importantly, one for which Kate could never forgive herself.

Her parents had divorced not long after the funeral, her father immediately setting off for parts unknown. As soon as Kate had been old enough, she had followed suit. But it was not until she had endured five more years of daily, drug-fueled, vitriolic rants from her mother.

Kate had worked through her past, the only way she knew how. She had buried the losses and channeled her energy into helping those who could not help themselves. With single-minded determination, she had pursued a career with the San Francisco Police Department. Up until six weeks ago, Kate had been an active-duty detective with the Special Victims Unit. It was a rank she had worked hard to attain—one which had come at the cost of her personal life.

It had been a price she had been happy to pay. Until the January day when her young protégé had posted a video of one of their conversations on social media, effectively tearing the foundation she had built for herself from its moorings. Cavalierly opining on a topic she had known very little about, Kate had provoked the ire of a notorious serial killer known as the Tower Torturer. Her uninformed assessment of how psychopaths operate and her belief they all deserve capital punishment had made her the object of his obsessive fascination and contempt. Taunting and tormenting the rookie detective, the cruel mastermind had killed her protégé, then began targeting other young women in Kate's world in a macabre game of cat and mouse.

She had triumphed in the end—at least, that was what the department and the media had claimed. But she had crossed some lines to get there.

The Tower Torturer had exploited Kate's weakness, ensuring the death of each successive victim compounded the loss of her sister. The experience had left her feeling shattered, rudderless, and unsure whether she wanted to remain in the profession she loved.

After weeks of intensive therapy, the department's psychiatrist had recommended she address the deep dysfunction of her child-hood with the woman who had created it. Unable to emerge from the traumatic quagmire, Kate had followed the doctor's advice. She had taken a leave of absence from the SFPD and hired a private investigator to track down her mother. A week ago, she had made the trip north to confront Chloe.

Today was the first time she had dared set foot on the street where her mother now resided. During her previous five visits to the neighborhood, Kate had remained in her car, arriving at varying hours of the day and night. The surveillance was unnecessary, but it was all she could bring herself to do—until today. The bit of progress did nothing to alleviate the feeling she had slipped into a pattern akin to those of the unbalanced stalkers she often brought to justice. She glanced at the glove box, wondering what the good doctor would say about her new habit of taking her weapon everywhere she went.

A siren wailed behind her. Kate watched in the rearview mirror as a sheriff's department SUV raced up to her bumper. Her eyes dropped to the dashboard. She was proceeding at a modest eight miles an hour over the speed limit.

With one last glance at the blazing lights, Kate activated her turn signal and eased off the gas. Pulling to the shoulder, she parked the car and awaited the inevitable. As the seconds ticked by, irritation bubbled to the surface of the emotional caldera in her stomach. Her anger sought succor in a dark well, devolving to conjure images of Hollywood stereotypes for small town law enforcement.

If her side view mirror was to be believed, the uniformed man hopping out of the SUV didn't fit any of them. Tall and trim, he strode confidently toward the passenger side of the Jeep. Kate rolled down the window just as his face appeared across from her.

His dark eyes, dimples and chiseled features would prompt most women (irrespective of their relationship status) to smile in return. Fighting the impulse, she met his penetrating stare with a blank gaze.

"Good afternoon. Would you like to tell me how fast you think you were going?"

"No."

He waited for her to expound. When a full ten seconds had passed in silence, the smile began to falter. Finally, he repeated the question.

She let another long moment pass. "Why don't you ask me how fast I *know* I was going?"

"Excuse me?"

"Asking me how fast I *think* I was going implies I might not know how fast I was *actually* travelling, thereby implying you possess facts I don't."

The dimples disappeared. "Look, I think we're getting a bit off track here."

Instead of responding, she reached into her purse and retrieved her ID and Police Credit Union card. Her badge was still at the precinct with Captain Singh, but taken together, the bits of plastic proved the point. Raising her chin defiantly, she thrust the cards in his direction.

He glanced down briefly before meeting her eyes again. "SFPD? Nice. I have an ID, too. Now, back to my original question. Would you like to tell me how fast you think you were going?"

Before a parade of expletives could march from her lips, Kate inhaled deeply. The last thing she needed to add to this ill-fated visit north was a ticket. Shaking off the frustration, she forced a shy smile.

Hoping to sweeten the pot, she added a little laugh. "I'm sorry. It's been one of those days. The gauge read eight miles over the posted limit. I guess I assumed you Washington state guys would offer the same ten-mile-an-hour window we do in California."

"Usually I do. But when you slowed for that last curve, I also noticed your left rear brake light is out."

"So it's a fix-it ticket, not a speeding ticket?"

"It's neither. Just a friendly warning. You were getting close to the danger zone on your speed, and you need to replace your taillight." He started back to his vehicle but paused after a few steps. Reappearing at the window, he asked, "By the way, were you at Beans of Mine the last two mornings?"

Kate immediately recognized the name of the hipster coffee shop on Main Street. She vaguely recalled seeing the police vehicle parked in the nearby vicinity both days. She also recognized the new sparkle in his eyes as he looked at her. Barely suppressing a smile, she asked, "Are you going to warn me about getting coffee, too?"

"Not at all. I wanted to run over and introduce myself but ..."

The dimples returned, reminding Kate of a boy whose hand has been caught in a bowl of raw cookie dough.

"*But* I'm the county sheriff *and* I'm single, which makes me a subject of unending speculation and gossip. Getting shot down asking a woman out on a date not only risks public humiliation, but a redoubling of matchmaking efforts by the local women's clubs and church groups."

Despite herself, Kate began to laugh. "Are you serious?"

"Cross my heart. My name is Tony—Tony Luchasetti." He looked up and down the highway, then back at her. "No one's in sight ... What do you say?"

She held his gaze for a full eight seconds. "Women's clubs *and* church groups?"

"They're good people, but relentless." The smile returned. "So, do I get a yes or a no?"

For one of the few times in her life, instinct leapt ahead of prudence. "It's a yes from Kate Barnes."

"Okay, Kate Barnes. How about dinner tomorrow night?"

Regret and shame from a whole separate set of circumstances

muddled her thoughts. "I don't know. Actually, I ..."

"Crap. It's weird because I pulled you over, isn't it? I'm always lecturing my team about sticking to the rules, and I broke one of the most important ones. I'm very sorry." He offered her the most dead-on sad puppy face she'd ever seen.

Smiling and shaking her head at the same time, she began reciting her telephone number. Looking as if he'd just received the security code to King Midas' treasure vault, the sheriff typed the digits into his phone. Seconds later her phone vibrated in the cup holder.

He gestured toward the device. "Now you've got my number. But I still feel guilty about asking you like this. It's the first time I've ever asked a woman out while on duty ..."

The radio affixed to his shoulder erupted with a loud clatter of static. Kate could not quite make out the details but watched intently as his easeful expression clouded. Wincing apologetically, he turned away from the window.

Kate took the opportunity to add the new number to her contact list, along with the name, *Sheriff Tony*.

A minute later he reappeared at the window. "I've got to run."

"No worries."

"I'll text you tonight with some ideas for tomorrow. Okay?"

"Sure."

"All right then. Bye." He paused, appearing anxious to leave but equally anxious to stay. Making up his mind, he offered a quick wave then jogged back to his vehicle. He waited for her to pull onto the highway before heading off in the opposite direction.

Kate watched in the rearview mirror until his vehicle had disappeared around a bend before shifting her gaze back to the road ahead. She had pulled off the highway and onto the narrow stretch of asphalt leading to her rental cottage when she realized her lips were transfixed in the same smile she'd worn since he had said goodbye.

Tentatively, she pressed a finger to the corners of her mouth. The feel of the expression and the emotions which had prompted it had become entirely foreign to her over the past month. The realization triggered unwanted memories of the Tower Torturer—macabre images and smells from crime scenes assailed her senses.

Using a newly acquired breathing technique, she rolled down the window. Feeling better, she pulled into the driveway and turned off the engine. She congratulated herself for getting out of the ticket; now all she had to do was get out of the dinner. After all, Kate had not come here to date. She had come here to deal with the dead woman.

∨

Intermittent rustling sounds accompanied the man as he trampled the broken branches, fallen leaves and other bits of detritus carpeting the forest floor. A thin blade of light sliced through the darkness as he swung his flashlight from left to right.

He had not planned on tracking tonight. Wearing jeans, a charcoal gray hoodie and a black baseball cap, he certainly was not dressed for it. Typically, he preferred to pursue his quarry during the daylight hours. Tonight, he was after something much higher on the evolutionary ladder than deer.

Sweeping the light up and across the branches of a nearby tree, he searched intently for clues. After a moment, he cut the beam back across a lower branch whose edge hung at a forty-five-degree angle. Within seconds he descended upon it, seizing hold of the fractured limb. He stroked his thumb over the moist yellowish pulp, which lay exposed beneath the bark. Satisfied the damage was fresh, he straightened and started off in the direction of the break.

He picked up his pace, confident she was nearby. The certainty was undermined by a raging frustration which had accompanied him since the start of the journey. Emotional control was paramount. He could not afford any distractions. The goal was to get the little bitch back in her cage as soon as possible.

Upon learning of her escape, he had not bothered to change into hunting attire. He had figured she had about ten minutes on him, so he had only paused to grab the essentials. While her bare feet would likely slow her progress, he did not have one second to spare.

A crunching sound off to his left brought him to a sudden halt. His nerves burned with anticipation. She was so close now he could feel it.

With Zen-like patience he remained motionless for a full six minutes before his prey finally broke cover and fled frantically into the forest. Breaking into a sprint, he dashed into the darkness behind her. She made a glorious run of it—leaping over fallen logs and ducking under branches. Age and size gave her an advantage in the dense woods, but his flashlight made up for it in the end.

Just as he feared losing sight of her, she darted around a massive pine, then seemed to hang frozen in the air ahead of him. Suddenly she dropped out of view amid a cacophony of rustling and grunting.

Approaching her location, he slowed and flashed the light across the ground. The beam illuminated a steep, six-foot drop. Huddled face down and mewling at the base of the steep hill was his prey. He scrambled down next to her, the commotion compelling her to struggle to find her feet again.

"Oh, no you don't!"

The command did not stop her, but his weapon did. A static crackle filled the air and she fell into a paroxysm. When she hit the ground, he depressed the trigger on the stun gun once more. A grin of satisfaction spread across his dark countenance as he watched her body seize again.

Certain the electrical voltage had rendered her immobile, he thrust the gun securely back into the holster at his waist. He regarded her critically for a moment, noting the scantily clad, pale form covered in mud and bruises.

Reaching over, he gently brushed the dark hair from her deeply furrowed brow. Her delicate Asian features seemed permanently carved by excessive physical torment. On some abstract level it seemed a shame to him that one so young should have experienced such pain. But in the grand scheme of things, these shots from the stun gun were the least of what the young teen had experienced.

He bound her wrists and ankles with zip ties, then hefted her up and over his shoulder. As he made his way through the forest, he solidified his plans for her punishment. In the end, it would exceed any torment she had heretofore endured.

Chapter 2

April 26

DEPUTY JENNA WHEATON slammed the door of the patrol car shut. The sound bounced off the walls of the abandoned quarry, doubling and trebling before finally fading in the late afternoon stillness. Spinning on her heel, she cast a final warning glare at the two teenage passengers huddled in the backseat. Exhaling, she turned toward the abandoned warehouse which stood across from the edge of the vast mining pit.

The setting sun reflected off a narrow row of windows running above the structure's main entrance, lighting the surrounding forest ablaze in a fiery glow. Averting her gaze, she strode toward the set of stairs leading up to the double door entry. Bits of gravel crunched softly under her boots as she walked, amplifying the overall sense of desolation.

Jenna's shadow kept pace with her as she moved—exaggerating her lean, lanky, features topped off by a shoulder length mop of blonde hair. Exuding the air of a woman not to be trifled with, she remained convinced she was on a fool's errand. There was no way the old warehouse would yield the unimaginable find the teenagers had reported when they had burst through the doors of the sheriff's office over an hour ago.

She had been finishing up a domestic violence report on the other side of town when the call had come in. The DV complaint had been a farce—an adolescent attempt to punish a parent for failing to buy a new cell phone.

Jenna had finally convinced the ill-mannered fifteen-year-old daughter to apologize to her overworked mother when her radio had come to life, recalling her to the station. Once there, two more teens had been dumped in her lap. There was every reason to believe the two wanna-be skater boys sitting in her patrol car were fueled by the same adolescent angst, wayward hormones and abject stupidity.

Foregoing the rusted railings on either side of the stairs, she jogged up to the porch. The right-side door stood open; a broken chain dangled from the handle—the padlock still intact. Beyond the first few feet of the doorway, darkness pervaded.

She unholstered her flashlight and stepped up to the threshold, glad she had taken the time to lock the boys securely in the car. The last thing she needed was for the miscreants to pop up from behind and scare the shit out of her—just their way of passing a boring Friday afternoon.

Truth be told, she could not really blame them. Eagle's Nest was high on nature but low on things to do. Other than the bowling alley downtown, there was little going on within the town limits. It was a reality she knew all too well.

Divorced at thirty-eight, with a nine-year-old son in tow, Jenna had ached for a change from the predictability of life in small-town America. She had been about to accept a position with the Seattle PD when a sudden heart attack had prompted Sheriff Selby to retire early. With no local candidates for the position, the town had been forced to look elsewhere.

After three months, they had found a unanimous favorite. Far more handsome than any of the local singles, Sheriff Luchasetti, who was only a few years older than Jenna, had immediately infected her with some form of Disney-esque brain fever. Abandoning her senses, she had turned down the Seattle offer.

In hindsight it had been a ridiculous move. After a few months of intense flirting on her part, Tony had made his disinterest clear by turning down Jenna's invite for a nightcap at her place. He had claimed he could not risk his new position by fraternizing with a deputy. But Jenna knew better. Any man who made it to forty-four without signing a marriage license or siring a child, had no sincere interest in either one.

Swallowing past the year-old frustration, she stepped over the threshold into the cavernous space. Her right hand settled on the butt of her Glock as she entered, evidence of good training and experience rather than anticipation of actual trouble.

The beam from her flashlight was not strong enough to reach the back of the building, but she moved ahead anyway. Had she even partially believed the boys' outlandish story about finding a dead body in the concrete pit up ahead, she may have proceeded with more caution.

She had only made it about five feet before a vile stench— reminiscent of a cross between motor oil and animal fat—hit her like a semi. Steeling herself against the aroma, Jenna focused on the goal ahead. If the boys had seen something, it was certainly nothing more than a sick animal which had sought refuge here in its final moments.

As she continued, the rubber soles of her shoes squeaked softly against the dusty concrete. Arriving at the fifteen-foot-square opening in the floor, Jenna pointed her flashlight down. Her eyes tracked the circle of visibility as it travelled down the opposite wall of the shaft.

A moment later, the light revealed a pale arm. As it swept over a mutilated breast, then worked its way across the rest of the slender human form, the deputy staggered backward. Her right hand clawed at her shoulder, grasping for the radio affixed to her uniform. When her fingers finally closed around the device, it took an entire minute before she was confident she could speak without shrieking.

V

The sheriff's office occupied a small block at the north end of town. After six decades of service, the concrete, single-story structure still seemed to be holding up well.

Pulling into an empty spot across from the entrance, Kate ignored the spark of dread in her stomach. She snatched her umbrella from the floor of the passenger seat and climbed out into the chilly night air.

During the fifteen-minute drive from her place, the skies had opened up, releasing the day's pregnant hold on the clouds. She picked her way across the well-lit parking lot, navigating a maze of puddles.

Tony had texted her three times since yesterday, providing ample opportunity for her to cancel. Despite her resolve after their initial meeting, she had waffled back and forth, eventually allowing loneliness to win out over common sense.

It was the unusual care she had taken with her appearance in preparing for the date that had finally tilted the scales in favor of prudence. Somewhere between the eyeliner and the finishing touches of mascara, she had suffered a series of flashbacks featuring her recent sexual misadventures. Mommy-issues notwithstanding, she had been forced to admit she was in no condition to be dating at all. Even if she were ready to date, a member of law enforcement was by far the worst possible option. For now, the plan was to get in, beg off with the sexy sheriff, and get out.

Inside, the beige entry was empty—yet another difference between Eagle's Nest and San Francisco, where police precincts were usually jam packed and buzzing with activity. Kate crossed to the far wall where bulletproof glass separated the front desk from reception.

The layout was a vestige of the post-911 hysteria. It now served the darkly ironic purpose of protecting the sheriff's department employees from the very public it had sworn to protect.

On the other side of the glass, a florid-faced sheriff's deputy peered through wire-rimmed spectacles at a computer monitor. The edge of a black plastic mouse protruded from his pudgy left hand.

Kate waited for a full minute before he turned to look at her. The man sat up and nudged his glasses higher on the bridge of his nose.

Getting a good look at the new visitor, his hand flew back to smooth what was left of his rapidly receding ginger hairline. "Hi there. I'm, uh, I'm Deputy Flaherty. How can I help you?"

"I'm here to see the sheriff."

"The sheriff's busy. But I'll be happy to help you." The watery smile implied he would be happy to do whatever she desired.

A sudden shout sounded from somewhere in the back. Instead of turning to respond to the call, the deputy yelled, "What's up?"

His boss appeared at the edge of Kate's field of view. The sheriff was in the process of shrugging into a thickly padded coat. "The state lab guys called. They're almost done at the scene. I've got to get back over there ..."

His voice trailed off as he recognized his date through the transparent divide. Frustration clouded his expression. Tony glanced from his deputy to Kate and back again. "Flaherty, I need you to mind the store until I get back."

The deputy's eyes narrowed. "But Wheaton has been out at the scene for hours. Why don't I go relieve her? She can come back and cover the desk."

"I've got every available person at the scene. I need you here."

Flaherty slumped back in his seat. "Fine."

Without another word, Tony opened a wide metal door and joined Kate. "Hi, I am so glad to see you." The words were issued in little more than a whisper.

"Thanks, but it sounds like you've got something more important going on."

Tony glanced pointedly at the deputy. The ginger crown immediately snapped back in the direction of the computer monitor. Reaching for Kate's elbow, the sheriff guided her outside in silence.

The rain had ebbed into a light sprinkle. Tucked safely under the protection of the roof's overhang, the sheriff explained, "You're right. And I need to ask for a favor."

Convinced he was about to cancel their date, Kate beamed back at him. "Sure."

"As you heard in there, I'm short-staffed at the worst possible time. Eagle's Nest just got its first homicide case in over twenty-seven years."

"No problem. I understand."

"No, you don't. The victim is a young teen and there are certain circumstances … All I'm asking is for you come take a look and give me your take on it."

"My take?" Deep furrows formed in her brow.

He nodded somberly. "You are the Detective Barnes who brought down the Tower Torturer, right? I realize this might be small potatoes to you, but I'd really appreciate your help."

Betraying none of the shock she felt, Kate looked off into the night. It should not be surprising he had looked her up. It was Dating 101. But why did she suddenly feel as if she were a twenty-first century Hester Prynne, with a scarlet letter searing her breast?

This case was right up her alley, but that wasn't the point. She had come here to find her mother and put the past to rest. Was she ready to jump back in the saddle right now? *Did she even want to?*

The questions fell with the rain, pooling into murky puddles which yielded no clear answers. A moment later, Kate's eyes met the sheriff's. "Look, I don't know what you read about me, but I'm not some kind of super detective. I can take a look and give you my thoughts, but I can't …"

He held up his hands. "Hey, I don't expect you to solve this thing in five minutes. I'm only looking for another set of eyes. And, of course, our dinner date. I promise to pick up the tab. You look spectacular, by the way." The charming dimples reappeared, causing a fleeting smile to grace Kate's lips.

The truth was, the moment she had heard him say the victim was a young teen, a familiar hook had snagged her heartstrings. Turning a deaf ear on the choir of inner voices warning her against getting involved, she nodded at him and asked, "Why don't you drive?"

∨

A row of black and yellow barricades spanned the width of the unmarked road. As an added deterrent, an official looking, dark green pickup truck stood sentry in front of the line.

The last vestiges of rain disappeared as Tony eased his SUV to a stop alongside the second vehicle. Studying the blue shield affixed to the door of the truck, Kate noted the variety of nature-related images depicted in its center. "The Department of Fish and Wildlife? I thought this case was in your jurisdiction."

The sheriff began rolling down his window. "It is, but this is a small county. We don't have the resources to handle a case like this on our own. Around here we all help each other out."

He turned to address the uniformed man who was stepping down from the truck. "Hi Mike, any problems?"

"Nope. Been quiet since you left."

"Exactly what I wanted to hear." He waited until the younger man had pulled the end of one of the barricades clear, before offering a genial wave and proceeding down the dark road.

Kate watched in the side view mirror as the officer returned the barricade to its rightful place before speaking again. Flaherty had given them little chance to debrief on the way over. He had called the moment they had climbed into the car, launching into an impassioned appeal to join them.

Tony had hung up when they had reached the barricade. Kate still had no idea what she was about to walk into.

"Who called this in?" she inquired, as the forest closed in around them.

"Two local kids came into the office reporting they'd discovered a body out here. They were pretty shaken up."

"Did they know the girl?"

"Claimed they've never seen her before. I released them to their parents after taking their statements."

"You believe them?"

He glanced at her briefly, before his gaze settled back on the road. "My gut does."

"Any ID on the victim?"

"No."

The woods suddenly opened into a vast clearing. Up ahead a large, faded sign leaned precariously on two aging supports. Kate strained to read the faded blue letters.

"This is the old granite quarry." Tony explained. "Keating Mining ran it from the late 1960s until the early 80s. Since then it's been vacant, but Keating still owns the land. Once in a blue moon, they send a rep out to inspect the place. Then we usually get a follow-up call complaining about graffiti or some other nuisance."

Tony passed through an open gate and turned onto a gravel road. For a moment, the SUV's headlights illuminated part of a massive pit up ahead. Sheer rock faces descended into the earth below, accompanied by intermittent flashes of flora which had seeped down into the scarred walls from the surrounding forest. Though she was in the midst of the Pacific Northwest, the old quarry reminded Kate of a jungle scene from Tarzan.

"It's always been a magnet for petty vandalism, small time

B&E," Tony continued. "But nothing like this has ever gone down out here. And this is pretty fucked up."

"How so?"

"You'll see." Slowing, he pulled the car into the last remaining spot between a slew of other vehicles whose doors were adorned with various law-enforcement logos.

Glancing briefly at the building up ahead, Kate exited without responding. Instead of heading directly for the main entrance, she walked back across the road toward the quarry. Wet gravel crunched beneath her feet as she strode ahead.

Tony trailed noisily behind her, watching silently as she paused at the rim and surveyed the area. Nature had decided to side with her. The storm clouds had parted enough for bright moonlight to spill through to the earth below.

A full minute later, she turned to him and asked, "Is this rim road the only way in and out?"

"Yes."

"What about neighbors?"

"Nothing for a few miles to the east. The north and west sides are bordered by state forestry lands. And as you saw, the south side is bordered by the highway."

Kate nodded and started toward the building. As they hurried up the stairs, Tony was addressed by a state trooper who stood outside the entrance. "They're about to pack it up in there. Time to pull the body."

"Good. Thanks again for the help." Tony opened the door and directed his next comment at Kate. "I'm glad you got here in time. Photos can't capture the feel of this scene."

A deep grunt issued from the trooper's throat. Kate wasn't sure if it conveyed an affirmation or a warning. She regarded the trooper for a moment before deciding it was a little bit of both.

Stepping over the threshold, her attention was immediately

drawn to the center of the building where all activity was centered on a brightly lit area surrounding an opening in the floor.

Kate identified the state crime lab technicians by their apparel. Wearing matching Tyvek suits, the two men stood off to the left talking with another state trooper. The taller tech was rigged up in what appeared to be a climbing harness and was busy pulling a breathing apparatus over his head while the shorter one looked on.

Shrewdly inspecting the layout as she proceeded, Kate fell into step alongside Tony. Within two strides, a foul scent unlike any she had ever come across assailed her senses. It almost stopped her in her tracks, but she forged ahead.

A short woman in her late fifties stood to the right of the tableau, talking in hushed tones with two men and another woman, each of whom wore uniforms identical to Tony's. As the new arrivals drew near, the female officer looked up.

Relief, and something Kate could not quite name, flashed briefly in the woman's pale blue eyes at the sight of her boss. "Hi, Sheriff. We're about to bring her up."

"I know." Tony replied.

The sheriff inclined his head toward his guest. "This is Special Victims Unit Detective Kate Barnes from the San Francisco PD. Washington State Patrol couldn't spare any detectives on such short notice, and she's agreed to help us out.

"Detective Barnes, these are my deputies: Carson, Lloyd and Wheaton. And this is our County Coroner, Mildred Gellert."

She shook each person's hand in turn. Split second impressions hit her as she moved down the line. Carson smiling slyly down at her from under a ridiculously bushy dark mustache; bald-headed Lloyd barely holding eye contact; Wheaton clamping down on Kate's hand with a vice-grip; the coroner, professional, but brief. Dropping Kate's hand, the woman turned to the sheriff and fired off a question about interdepartmental investigation procedure.

Uninterested in Washington state red tape, Kate strode toward the rim of the pit. With each approaching step, she gained another foot of visibility into the shaft. All too soon, she arrived at the very edge. What lay below waged an all-out assault on her senses.

Standing above the source of the stench, it took every ounce of self-discipline for her not to swoon, vomit or both. The scene below was almost as bad as the smell accompanying it. Fourteen feet down, a thick brown sludge filled the bottom of the concrete vault. Partially submerged in the liquid was the battered body of a slender Asian female, clad only in sheer neon green panties.

The corpse lay at an improbable angle across the far wall of the pit. It would have slipped completely into the soupy miasma below, but the upper right shoulder had caught on one of three long hooks protruding from a wide steel bar, which ran along the back wall.

The hook had impaled the frail shoulder, suspending the body like a side of beef in a butcher shop. Where bovine carcasses typically hung vertically, this cadaver lay at almost a forty-five-degree angle because the left leg had caught between the wall and a second steel bar mounted right above the liquid. Thus secured, only the lower extremities had disappeared below the surface.

The badly abused face was visible only in profile as it slumped against the chest. The eye socket appeared to have been crushed, leaving the dark, bloody eye to appear out of place within the surrounding folds of loose skin.

Kate's gaze slid down from the victim's shoulder over a patchwork of massive bruises. Mentally cataloging the damage, she tried to approximate the possible impact required to elicit such injuries.

Her eyes fixed on the mangled remains of breast tissue before traveling up a waterfall of dried crimson up to a massive gash in the throat. The vicious wound ran from one side of the neck to the other.

Kate resumed her inspection, noting the torn fingernails, smears of dirt and evidence of various minor abrasions. She looked back at the face one final time. Thirty seconds later, she nodded, (a movement so slight it was almost imperceptible) before walking around to the left side of the opening and then circling back to the right. From the side views it was apparent whoever had slashed the victim's throat had done so with gusto.

"The lovely aroma we're all enjoying is the effect of the sodium hydroxide." The flatness of the tone sucked the mirth from the intended sarcasm.

Kate turned to find the shorter crime scene tech watching her from her original vantage point.

He waited until she stood beside him before continuing. "See how it looks like she's partially submerged in the pool?"

Turning her gaze back on the cadaver, Kate nodded.

"Well, she's not. Anything below the brown sludge is gone."

She looked at the odd angle of the body, noticing how the brown liquid crept up as high as the knee of the corpse's right leg, but only to mid-shin on the left leg. "Are you saying the UNSUB cut off her extremities to fit precisely against the liquid?"

"No. Like I said, it's sodium hydroxide. You probably know it's more common name—lye."

Kate raised an eyebrow. Suddenly, the purpose of the noxious liquid became vividly clear. "The killer was trying to dissolve the body?"

"Yeah, and it would have worked, if she hadn't gotten snagged on that hook when he dumped her in here."

The second technician joined them as the state trooper and Deputy Carson set about establishing a redundant system for belaying the unlucky volunteer into the nightmarish hole.

"See what I meant earlier?"

Kate spun around toward the sound of the voice behind her.

She met the sheriff's gaze before he turned his attention on the tragedy below.

"This is pretty fucked up."

Chapter 3

April 27

THE MACHINE TOILED OVER its task, indifferent to the pain inflicted by its agonizingly slow pace. The moment Kate thought she had reached the point of no return, the barista turned off the espresso machine and added steaming milk into her mug.

"Rough night?" Fiona, the fifty-something owner of Beans of Mine, inquired as she poured out the last of the liquid. The woman, whose speech still carried traces of her early upbringing in Jamaica, wore a black-and-white-striped, high-neck shirt and black leggings. A short crew cut completed the beatnik look. It was a perfect match for the décor which featured numerous pictures of Audrey Hepburn from *Funny Face*.

"All that and then some." Kate had not left the crime scene until after two in the morning, and here she was only four and a half hours later. She watched as Fiona scooped the last of the foam from the metal cup and deposited it in a pretty little dollop on top of her latte. Accepting the oversized mug with a smile, Kate dropped a few extra dollars into the tip jar before grabbing her pumpkin walnut scone and turning back to the seating area.

Tony stood as she took her seat. It was a simple gentlemanly gesture, but it prompted a rush of hormones nonetheless. Seeking a distraction from her wayward instincts, Kate scanned the empty shop. At the painfully early hour, it was all but deserted.

She had insisted they meet here as soon as Fiona opened. The last thing she had wanted was another visit to the sheriff's office. The sooner she cut ties to this investigation, and the sheriff, the better.

"Do you always look this good after only a few hours of sleep?" Tony inquired.

Knowing the hasty ponytail, eyeliner and lipstick fell far short of last night's presentation she shot one eyebrow skyward. "False platitudes will get you nowhere."

"As will being skeptical of other people's sincerity."

"We're cops, skepticism is in our DNA."

"Only as far as the job is concerned. In my personal life, I try to give everyone the benefit of the doubt. Especially when they pay me a compliment."

"Point taken." Kate took a sip of her drink. "So, you've got a nameless victim and a violent perp who is big on grand schemes, but not so big on follow-through."

"Right on both counts. The IAD will run what details we have through their system to see if our guy has done this before, but it may take a while before we get any hits. As of now, you know everything I do about this case. What do you think?"

His professional persona had sprung back into place so rapidly, it felt as if the physical distance between them had increased by a few feet.

"Assuming those boys are correct about the victim not attending the town's one and only high school, we have to presume she was brought here for a reason."

"Do you think he lives in Eagle's Nest?"

Kate nodded. "Either in town or nearby. I'd check all the high schools in a fifty-mile radius. And don't forget to check for home-schooled kids. Remember, there's no signage on the highway for the quarry and the forest hides the entire property. He'd had to have known it was there and had to know it was a place unlikely to have any visitors."

Tony took a bite of banana bread as he considered her words.

"I also think he feels overly confident he won't get caught, because he was planning on coming back."

"How do you know?"

"Did you see the damage he inflicted on her? Evidence of serious rage. Whether at her specifically or because she was supposed to be a stand-in for someone else. Still, he had to take it a step further. Going for the ultimate punishment he went to the trouble of using lye to erase her existence altogether. Someone so hell bent wouldn't just dump her and take off. He'd want to wait and watch her disappear."

"Maybe time was an issue. He could have a wife, a kid, some kind of night job. Maybe he knew he'd been gone too long and figured he could leave her there as long as he needed to before coming back to make sure it was done."

"Maybe ..." Kate took a sip of her drink, reveling in the feel of the hot liquid as it warmed her from within. The espresso seemed to have an immediate effect on her, parting the clouds from her sleep-deprived mind. "In hindsight it might have been more prudent to have erected your barricade line closer to the quarry rather than out at the highway. You basically created a big neon billboard warning him to stay away."

The sheriff winced. "Yeah, major league fuck-up on our part."

"Don't worry about it. I've made more than my share of mistakes." Her gaze fell upon her mug, dragging her mood down with it.

Tony took a long sip of his coffee, waiting another fifteen seconds before twisting his features into a comically stern expression. "If you give me the 'it's not about how you start but how you finish' line, I may have to wring your neck."

Kate's eyes found his. Her contemplative expression was replaced with a shrewd one. "You already have one homicide in this town. It's not going to help your popularity if you double the number in less than twenty-four hours."

He smiled. "You're right. Back to our perp."

"Start with the most obvious places. This guy went after a minor; pull up all the registered sex offenders in the immediate area."

"Maybe it doesn't have to be a local."

"I think it does. There was no blood evidence found anywhere but in the pit of the warehouse, so she had to be killed somewhere else. That pit was literally a dumpsite and I can't imagine a warehouse in Eagle's Nest is on any perp's top ten list. Consider the number of options he had to choose from. A good portion of this part of the Olympic Peninsula is undeveloped, with massive amounts of federal forest and private land. Places so remote the body wouldn't likely be discovered until the next ice age. Before you go chasing down every long-haul trucker with a route through town, start with the locals."

Tony chugged down the last of his coffee, watching over the rim of his cup as Kate finished her last bite of scone. "Exactly what I thought. Let's go."

"Go where?"

"I pulled the list of local registered sex offenders before heading over here. If we leave now, we can catch a few of them before they leave for work."

"Wait a minute. I told you I'd give you my thoughts and I have done so. My part in this is over."

Tony jerked his head back as if avoiding a blow. "Oh, okay. I thought you'd ..." The words trailed off into a silence, which Kate chose not to fill.

He looked at her for a full ten seconds before trying again. "I'd hoped you'd stick with me a little longer. I don't know how long you spent talking to my deputies last night, but none of them have the background to add much to this investigation. And you know the IAD can't offer us any help right now."

Kate's gaze dropped to the polished concrete floor. She stared at the mottled hues of grey, battling the familiar and all-too-insistent pull from the arms of justice. There were so many reasons she should walk away.

Prepared to turn him down, she looked back toward the sheriff. Unbidden images of the young victim's desecrated corpse flashed before her mind's eye. Blinking them away, she opened her mouth, but the words would not come. After all, what words could ever justify Kate's personal needs above finding justice for that poor girl? She closed her eyes, knowing she had to impose some sort of limit.

Raising her index finger toward the ceiling, she opened her eyes and glared across the table. "One day. I'll give you one day, but only one."

Tony's hand grasped hers, enveloping it in a genial shake. "Deal."

Kate pursed her lips, trying to ward off the smile threatening at the corners of her mouth. She rose and headed for the door, keenly aware of the fact that if the simple touch of his hand could prompt such a response, one day might be one too many.

∨

The slam of the car door echoed through the small pine meadow. For the first time since Kate had arrived in Eagle's Nest, the sun reigned supreme in the late morning sky. Despite the star's dazzling brilliance, the air was crisp and cold. Joining Tony at the front of the SUV, Kate surveyed the layout before them.

The single-lane road continued for another ten feet, eroding away into a gravel path which led up a slight incline to a nondescript, double-wide trailer. The residence squatted in isolation amid a sea of tall green grasses. A new model black pickup was parked about five feet from the concrete steps leading to the front door.

About forty feet behind the residence, the forest stood as implacable as a roman legion surveying a soon-to-be battlefield.

Unlike the other three properties they had visited, this one, while dated, was at least well maintained. It also had the distinction of being even more remote and isolated than any of the others. The smell of damp grass permeated the air, contributing to the sense nature owns the land and man may only rent it.

Tony glanced at Kate, who nodded in reply. They started toward the house, separating to approach the vehicle from opposite sides. Before proceeding to the cab, they paused to scan the truck bed. It was empty. Other than a faded green canvas satchel in the passenger footwell, the leather trimmed passenger area was equally unremarkable.

A few moments later, they were standing on the tiny concrete pad which served as a front porch. Tony knocked soundly on the front door, prompting a sudden rustling from the lush grasses behind Kate. She turned, in time to spy the emerald sea part as some unknown creature scurried away.

"Who is it?" a muffled voice demanded from within.

"Mr. Delford, this is Sheriff Tony Luchasetti. I'm hoping you can help me."

After a long pause, the door opened and a man stepped into the doorway. Standing at five-eleven, Rick Delford was a few inches shorter than Tony. He gazed briefly at the sheriff before his eyes darted over to Kate and back again.

"What do you want?" The words issued from the midst of a thick, well-trimmed brown beard which matched a narrow set of eyebrows. His head was immaculately shaved and the hint of a gut drooping over his waistline was well concealed beneath an untucked plaid shirt.

According to his rap sheet, Delford was a three-time loser. At thirty-nine, he'd been picked up twice for solicitation of a minor before doing an eight-year stint for unlawful penetration of a minor. He had been released four years ago and had lived in Eagle's Nest ever since; purportedly without further incident.

"Mr. Delford, a girl's body was discovered last night. We're reaching out to the community for help in identifying the victim."

The last word sent him skittering back into the house. "You're talking to the wrong guy. I'm not like that anymore." He reached for the door handle and yanked it after him.

Kate stepped into the rapidly closing aperture, wedging her foot securely against the door. "Please, Mr. Delford, she was an innocent young girl. We only want to know if you've ever seen her. I have some pictures to show you."

She paused, waiting to see if he would take the bait.

Delford's eyes searched her face, probing her features for signs of falsehood. She could see the quiet desperation in his expression. He looked like a recovering cocaine addict, trying to convince himself one little snort would not hurt.

Kate ignored the momentary twinge of conscience before pressing further. "The picture is on my phone, but my battery died. May I plug my phone in for a minute so I can show you?"

Delford clenched his jaw.

Sensing she was losing ground; Kate upped the ante. "Please Mr. Delford." She pulled out her phone, holding it up for his inspection. "This girl has been murdered. If you'll just give us a few minutes of your time."

Delford's eyes darted to the sheriff, then fixed on the phone. "Alright. You can come in, but he has to wait outside."

Before the sheriff could protest, Kate raised a hand in his direction. Her gaze remained fixed on the ex-con. "The sheriff will wait here. Thank you."

Delford stepped aside, allowing barely enough space for Kate to enter. The moment she set foot in the small, neat living room, her host closed the door firmly behind her.

Taking in the dark walnut paneling and thrift store furniture, she strode briskly across the thin magenta carpet, past the couch, to the dining table.

"Where the hell are you going? There's an outlet right here."

Indifferent to his warning tone, she skirted around the table, pulled a charger from her purse, and plugged it into a nearby outlet. Facing the open area, she tapped the screen a couple of times, then pushed the device back toward Delford.

He shifted his weight for a moment before making up his mind. Hurrying over to the table, he snatched the phone with his calloused hands.

Kate scanned the room behind him. Two local colleges waged a mute battle for basketball supremacy on the ridiculously large 75" television dominating the opposite wall. The unit, as well as the numerous sound system components concealed in the heavy oak console beneath it, appeared to be state of the art. Her glance flew to each corner of the room, where sleek black speakers had been mounted near the ceiling.

"Never seen her before." Delford held the device up in the air, clearly indifferent to the rough condition of the dead girl's face and neck.

"Are you sure?"

"Yes, I'm sure. I'm also sure this phone already has forty-eight percent power. Now get the hell out of my house."

Kate retrieved the phone, her fingers brushing against his during the transfer. "Okay, I thought it might be a long shot, but thanks anyway." She dropped her gaze to the floor, slowly unplugging the charger and making her way back around the table.

Delford turned to lead her back toward the door. Without taking her eyes from his back, she deftly lifted the lapel of a dark blue canvas jacket which hung over the back of a nearby chair. She dropped it a second later, sneaking up behind her host as he reached the door.

Spinning on his heel, he glared at Kate and yanked the door open.

She began to slip out but paused in midstride. "Nice to have the day off today, huh?"

His lids opened wider for a split second, before morphing into a sneer. "Get out."

"Thank you again, Mr. Delford."

Her gratitude was rewarded with a burst of air as the door slammed soundly behind her.

Noting the frustration and anxiety in Tony's gaze, Kate spoke loud enough to be heard through the thin walls of the trailer. "Mr. Delford has never seen her. Let's move on."

Tony's brow pulled tight, but he followed her down the steps without question.

It was not until they were both back in the sheriff's vehicle and were headed back out on the one lane road that Tony began to speak. "For someone who doesn't want to be a part of this investigation, you had no problem taking charge back there."

Kate regarded him for a moment before responding, trying to determine if the chastising tone was evidence of a bruised ego or merely a response to her brash approach. Deciding it was more likely the latter, she drew in a long breath. "According to the books, he's been on government assistance since his release from prison. But he's got an entertainment center in there rivaling the screening rooms at Lucas Arts. And you saw the truck."

"Think he's running drugs?"

"No. There were callouses on his hands. I think he has a job."

"Which is why you asked him about having a day off. What kind of job could a convicted sex offender get around here making that kind of money?"

"There was a jacket in the house with a security badge clipped to the front pocket. The logo on the lapel looked familiar, but I can't recall where I've seen it before."

"What did it look like?"

Kate pulled up the note app on her phone. She made a series of strokes across the display with her finger and turned it toward the sheriff. "Do you recognize this?"

Tony pulled his eyes from the road. The moment he saw the crude drawing, his head jerked. "How the hell could that be?"

Kate turned the display back toward her, studying her rudimentary reproduction of a sun shining above an Egyptian pyramid. "You know what this is?"

"Yes, I do. And I know where you've seen it. It happens to be one of the last places which would employ a guy like Delford."

"Why, what do they do?"

"I'll show you." Tony pulled onto the highway and sped south back toward town.

Chapter 4

SITUATED NORTH OF TOWN and comprised of eighteen acres of pristine forestland overlooking the mighty Pacific, Aaru was truly one of a kind. Unlike other resorts that relied upon exorbitant prices to keep the less desirable elements of society from darkening their doors, Aaru was more exacting in guaranteeing its claim of exclusivity. Here, guests were admitted by invitation only.

According to local gossip, inspiration for the property had struck the developer during a visit to nearby Cape Flattery five years earlier. The moment he had emerged from the dense forest and climbed up to the wooded lookout point set above a series of small ocean inlets, he had been struck mute. The water was so transparent, and varied so greatly in hue, it was almost impossible to accept it was located at the northwestern-most tip of the contiguous United States, rather than in the tropics.

In the distance, he had beheld Tatoosh Island standing its ground amidst the relentless onslaught of the seas. The abundant sights and sounds of marine life had combined with the salty tang of crisp ocean air to complete a sense of other worldly magic. But the beauty of Cape Flattery was not for sale. The land was part of the Makah Indian Reservation. Visitor access was granted by permit only, forcing the developer to settle on a building site to the south.

Fifteen months before, after years of planning and negotiation, the resort had finally opened its doors. The largest structure housed the full-time staff. Guest accommodations consisted of one-to-three story custom villas, which varied in size between fifteen hundred and three thousand square feet.

Each home was uniquely decorated and had been constructed

with the finest materials. The one unifying theme was the emphasis on the views. Occupying one-acre lots, every structure boasted floor-to-ceiling-glass windows providing uninterrupted vistas of the ocean. The distance between buildings and the omnipresent forest between them ensured a natural privacy barrier. Providing the perfect mix of peace and beauty, the resort had been aptly named Aaru: the ancient Egyptian name for heaven.

Recreating heaven on earth was not easy. Among other things, technology was a necessary ingredient, and Aaru's budget was large enough to buy the best of the best.

A series of well-hidden, high-definition cameras tracked the sheriff's SUV as it progressed along the winding road leading from the highway to the resort. Each device whirled in fluid succession, picking up the task of observing the passing vehicle before handing it over to the next one in the chain.

The on-site landscape team was tasked with the never-ending goal of allowing nature to flourish, while maintaining optimal visibility. Keeping the peace between the security and the landscaping teams was one of the many responsibilities which fell firmly on the shoulders of Hyland Fairbourne.

At fifty-three, Hyland was enjoying the peak of a long career in the hospitality industry. Over twenty-five years earlier he had started out as a night clerk in one of the big hotel chains. Being a stickler for details with an uncompromising personality, he had been a natural fit for the luxury world. Before landing at Aaru, he had served at the helm of a preeminent resort in the Florida Keys. Despite its alleged cachet among the ultra-elite, the Trade Winds could not compete with his new assignment.

The resort's general manager was every bit as well-groomed as the grounds. He had a standing monthly appointment to tint his precisely cut graying hair into an eye-catching shade of silver. Workout, manicure and spray tan regimens were also a strict part of his required routine.

Raising one of two perfectly tended eyebrows, Hyland glanced down at his phone's display. The camera feed showed the SUV slowing to a stop in front of the main gate. Tucking the device into the front pocket of his blazer, he coaxed his Rolls Royce over the resort's fifteen mile-per-hour speed limit.

As the car approached a wide turn, he eased off the gas. Moments later, he spied the main gate up ahead. The sight of it evoked a familiar tingle of pride. A model of ornate craftsmanship, the iron structure stood over twenty feet high. At its center, the metal had been crafted into an exact replica of Aaru's signature logo; a pyramid with the sun shining brightly above it.

On either side of the ironwork, two large limestone pyramids anchored the structure in place. Hyland stopped in front of the one on the right. It was one of two security checkpoints guests had to clear before being admitted to the facilities. He motioned to the guard inside. The iron sun gently slid from its moorings as one half of the gate opened before him.

He exited and pulled even with the driver's side window of the sheriff's SUV. Offering one of his warmest smiles, he regarded the driver and female occupant. "Hello Tony, what brings you out here today? Nothing wrong in town, I hope?"

"I'm going to need a few minutes of your time."

Aware the sheriff had chosen not to answer the second part of his question, Hyland nodded. "Certainly. I'm on my way to Seattle for a meeting with corporate. Can it wait until I return tomorrow?"

"No, it's important."

"Okay, let's swing by Fiona's place for an Americano before I head out. I'd like to get on the road before the traffic gets too ugly."

"Sure. I'll turn around and follow you."

Hyland took his foot off the brake and gestured to the guard. Three seconds later, the second half of the gate opened. The SUV eased between the pyramids and executed a U-turn. As the vehicle fell in behind him, Aaru's general manager breathed a sigh of relief. Keeping up good relations with the local community was an important part of his job. Still, the last thing he needed was to be late for his meeting because of some inane town issue having nothing to do with him or with Aaru.

∨

Beans of Mine was only one block from the main plaza in the center of town. Tony and Kate had made two trips up and down the street before one of the diagonal parking spots opened up on the near side of the square.

Kate had no sooner exited the vehicle and climbed up onto the curb before her heart leapt into her throat. She tore her eyes from the couple who had just exited the clothing boutique on the corner. Both in their early sixties, and both dressed incredibly chic by Eagle's Nest standards, the man and woman laughed quietly between themselves as they turned and headed for the crosswalk to the plaza.

"I can't imagine why Hyland would allow someone like Delford to work at Aaru." Tony's statement fell on deaf ears.

Eyeing the couple, Kate straightened her shoulders and reached for Tony's arm. "I have to make a call. Why don't you go on ahead and I'll join you in a few minutes?"

Tony frowned. "You need to make a call ... right now?"

She glanced toward the crosswalk, where the man and woman were waiting for the light to turn.

"Yes." Aware the retort was louder than necessary, Kate let go of his arm and lowered her voice. "I'm not on the clock here, remember? I'm a volunteer, not your subordinate."

Looking contrite, he nodded vigorously. "Of course! I'll stall Hyland."

Kate watched as the crosswalk indicator light turned green. "Give me a minute and I'll catch up with you." Making a show of pulling her phone from her purse, she turned her back toward him, and stepped off the sidewalk onto the grass.

"Okay." Tony called out, his tone less than certain. "I'll meet you there."

Kate kept her back to the sidewalk and put her phone to her ear. Even if she really had been making a call, she doubted she would have heard a thing. Her pulse had increased to a manic pace, blocking out all sensory input.

In the rush to track down their new lead, Kate had momentarily forgotten why she had come to Eagle's Nest. There was no forgetting now. The reason was rapidly walking toward her.

Inhaling deeply, she focused on the simple task of steadying her breathing. The last time she had looked, the couple had not seemed to have taken any notice of her. Besides, no one would expect to find her here.

Heart still pounding, she cut briskly across the open expanse to the small, ivy-clad, white gazebo tucked against a grove of trees in the back-right corner. She bounded up the short set of stairs. The aged wooden planks sighed in exasperation under her feet.

Once inside, it took her eyes a moment to adjust to the sudden dimness. A determined ivy plant had completely enshrouded one half of the structure—cutting off the natural light, and completely blocking two of the four exits.

She dropped her phone back into her purse. The whirlwind of pain, regret and hatred was overwhelming. Determined to regain her composure, she began to pace. This was what she had come here for—the chance to talk to her mother. Yet here she was, running and hiding.

She began to mentally recite the list of things she had told her psychiatrist she wanted to get out of a meeting with Chloe. He had called them 'takeaways." Right now, Kate wished she could take herself as far away from Eagle's Nest as possible.

One breath, two breaths, three breaths, four ...

The wait seemed to go on for hours. A full two minutes later, her pulse began to slow. The couple had to be on the far side of the block by now.

She stood in the opening which served as the back exit. Closing her eyes, she raised her face upward, enjoying the feel of the sunlight trickling through the thick tree canopy overhead. For a brief moment, she considered retrieving her phone and placing a real call to Dr. Wissel in San Francisco. Pride stopped her. There was no point getting into an hour-long session with the psychiatrist merely to explore why she had chickened out.

"Kate ...?" The name was issued in the barest of whispers, but the voice was as familiar as her own. She spun around.

There, standing in the entrance to the gazebo, was Chloe Barnes. Sunlight illuminated her from behind, bathing her in a flattering glow.

It took Kate a moment to swallow past the surprise and sudden resurgence of emotion. "Hello, Chloe."

The use of her mother's given name was a first for both women. Chloe's mouth tightened a bit at the corners, but her passive expression remained otherwise unchanged.

"It's nice to see you, Kate." She did not take a step toward her daughter, but merely waited in the pregnant silence.

Kate regarded her mother, striking down each of the highly argumentative retorts which sprung up in rapid-fire succession in her head. She had role played through this moment with Dr. Wissel. Her goal was closure. Pettiness and acrimony would only derail her effort.

Exhaling the emotion, she finally replied. "Thank you."

The ensuing silence stretched for a full forty seconds. Aware they were standing at opposite ends of the structure, each waiting for the other to make the next move, Kate was reminded of a main street standoff between wild west gunslingers. Banishing the thought, she tried to let go of all the equally antagonistic feelings associated with it.

Instead, she focused on the changes in her mother's appearance. Despite the intervening years and the ravages of prescription drugs, Chloe's blue eyes sparkled youthfully from a relatively unlined face. Her hair, although much shorter than when Kate had last seen her, set off her features in a sophisticated way. Even the additional fifteen pounds helped; softening the harsh angles in ways most people would consider to be attractive.

"You look well, Chloe."

The tightness reappeared at the corners of her mother's mouth, but this time her muscles relaxed into the semblance of a smile. "Thank you, Kate. You ... you look absolutely beautiful."

Kate pursed her lips and glanced away. Addressing the maze of vines clinging to one of the white support posts, rather than her mother, she responded evenly. "Thank you."

Another thirty seconds passed before Chloe spoke again. "I don't want to bother you, but I was so surprised to see you here in Eagle's Nest. I couldn't help myself from at least saying hello ..."

After another extended silence, she tore her gaze from her daughter and turned to leave.

"Wait!"

When she turned back toward the sound of her daughter's voice, Chloe's eyes were filled with tears, and something approaching hope. "Yes?"

Kate took an awkward step forward. "I came here to talk to you." She looked meaningfully around at the small space. "This isn't really the time or the place, but if you're willing, I think it's time we both get some closure."

The hope in Chloe's eyes was replaced by acceptance. "Of course, Kate. You're welcome to come to my house any time you like." She opened her purse, retrieved a pen and paper, and jotted down a set of numbers followed by two words. Holding the paper out in front of her, it appeared as if she was offering a bit of fish to a feral cat. "Here's my address."

Kate opened her mouth, and promptly shut it again. She strode toward her mother and took the proffered paper. The next question flew out before she could determine whether she wished to utter it. "How about tomorrow night at six?"

A slight frown creased her mother's brow. "Tomorrow, I ..." She waved her hand dismissively before her. "Never mind, tomorrow night will be fine." Chloe took a step toward Kate but stopped when her daughter retreated two steps in response.

"I'll see you tomorrow."

"Okay, tomorrow." With an odd little wave, Chloe turned and walked out into the sunlight. Kate watched as she made her way back to the sidewalk where Jacob Gresham was patiently waiting for her.

Kate had learned his name from the private investigator she had hired to track her mother down. He was a few years older than her mother and had been married to her for the last three years.

Chloe spoke briefly with her husband before turning and waving to her daughter once more. Kate raised her hand for a moment before letting it drop. Jacob put his arm around his wife's shoulder and led her away.

As the two continued down the street, an unbidden memory popped into Kate's head. The sound of the Tower Torturer's mocking tone was as clear as if he were actually standing next to her. "*... one might only go so far in torturing the human body, but the mind— that is a world of endless possibilities.*"

The gazebo seemed to melt away around her. She could feel

the unyielding white tile beneath her knees, and the handcuffs biting into her wrists. Shaking off the terrifying sensations, she started down the steps. Grudgingly, she admitted there was one thing she and the Tower Torturer agreed upon—mental torture was the worst possible kind.

∨

Hyland Fairbourne was the type of person whose heart did not quite meet the hype of the body it was packaged in. Kate's eyes narrowed as she regarded him from across the small table in the back booth of the coffee shop. It was not the man's obvious narcissism, his dismissal of her, or any misplaced feelings of animosity toward her mother. It was about how he responded to the news of the murder.

Lowering his voice to a whisper, the general manager leaned toward the sheriff. "Please tell me you're not serious. A murder, in Eagle's Nest? There hasn't been a murder here in over …"

Tony cut him off. "Twenty-seven years."

"This is not going to be good for Aaru. Part of our appeal is the safety of the community, we can't have …"

"Hyland, I know it's your job to see this through the Aaru perspective, but it's my job to see it through the victim's."

Abashed, Hyland leaned back in his seat and took a sip of his drink.

"I need information on one of your employees."

Kate watched as the older man struggled to keep from spewing his Americano all over Tony.

Forcing the liquid down his throat, Hyland placed his cup on the table, and worked his features into a mask of calm. "You can't seriously believe one of our people is mixed up in something like this."

"Hyland, this is not about Aaru right now, it's about the victim.

Doing what is best for the victim, is the best thing for the resort. You understand, don't you?"

He glared at Tony, but eventually nodded. "Of course. But this was the last thing I ever expected to happen here. There is only so much I can say because of human resource laws, but I'll do whatever I can to help."

"Tell us about Rick Delford."

Noting the sudden tightening of Hyland's jaw, Kate jumped in. "How long has he worked at the resort?"

Apparently unimpressed by Tony's earlier explanation that she was a special consultant to the sheriff's office, Hyland directed his response to the other man. "Rick Delford works in our landscape department. His record has been exemplary."

Kate jumped back in. "He also has a record with law enforcement. Were you aware of that Mr. Fairbourne?"

The question earned her a side glance before he turned to Tony once again. "I am aware of Mr. Delford's past. Community outreach is an important part of our corporate mission. One of the local church rehabilitation programs had recommended him. We fully investigated his records as well as his release evaluations. The state doctors assured us he was not likely to reoffend. We even enlisted a private psychiatrist and received similar assurances.

"Given our property is adults only and knowing his duties would not require him to interact with guests, we relied upon the advice of professionals and offered Mr. Delford a second chance. Part of the agreement was he must attend ongoing counseling, which he has done faithfully since he started working for us last year. If you need to know anything more, you will have to contact our human resources department." He pulled out his phone and began typing. "I texted the contact to your personal cell."

Tony nodded. "Good. What about Delford's schedule? Was he supposed to be working the last few days?"

"The landscape crew is …" Something shifted in the man's demeanor, but he continued smoothly. "The landscape crew is *under* the supervision of Miles Hastert. He can provide details about Mr. Delford's schedule."

"Fine. I'll swing back by the resort and talk to him."

"Miles is out on vacation, but he's supposed to be flying back to Seattle tomorrow morning. I'll arrange for you to talk to him as soon as he arrives." He typed another text, then made a show of looking at his overly embellished watch. "Now I am sorry, but I must get on the road."

The two men stood. Tony genially clapped the resort manager on the shoulder. "Thanks, Hyland, we really appreciate your time today."

"You're welcome, Tony." Hyland gave Kate the briefest nod before snatching his drink from the table and hurrying toward the front door.

One of the compartments in Tony's belt gave two quick chirps. He retrieved his cell phone and checked the screen. When his eyes found Kate's again, they were guarded. "Preliminary autopsy results are in. If you've still got the energy, we can head over there now."

"I did say you could have one day. Might as well make it one full day."

Some of the warmth from Tony's smile melted through the tangle of emotions left over from her meeting with Chloe.

Kate stood and hitched her purse onto her shoulder. Flashing him a tight smile, she continued dryly, "During the drive, you can tell me why that man has your personal cell phone number and whether you agree he's hiding something."

Chapter 5

THE WORLD OUTSIDE the car window passed by, seemingly indifferent to the exchange playing out between the driver and passenger. A defunct strip mall came and went, followed seconds later by a series of ramshackle industrial buildings. They appeared like malignant blemishes amid the natural beauty of the woods, but the condition of the commercial zone was the least of Kate's concerns.

She was still trying to wrap her mind around the revelation Tony had just made. Flashbacks of the recent conversation with her mother were weaving through his words, forcing her to ferret through a minefield of emotions. Finding no assistance from the world outside the window, she pursed her lips and turned back to the sheriff. "I really don't see you and Hyland as poker buddies."

Tony tore his glance away from the road long enough to note her conflicted expression. "Come on, Kate. It's not like we're actual friends. Besides, Hyland rarely shows up, and when he does, he doesn't exactly fit in with our group." A hearty chuckle erupted from his chest. "You should see his face when he tries to drink our cheap beer. And I've never, ever seen him dip a hand into a community chip bowl."

"He does seem like a high maintenance guy." Kate's mouth stretched into a weak smile.

"But here's the thing, for as much as Hyland can come off as a tight-ass, he's also a really good person."

"Are we still talking about the same guy?"

"The same guy who donated a kidney to a total stranger."

"Seriously?"

Tony nodded. "His little brother died of liver failure when he

45

was eight. They couldn't find a donor in time. As soon as Hyland turned eighteen, he registered to donate one of the few vital organs he could spare. He still gets Christmas letters from the children of the woman who was saved by his sacrifice. And he still donates blood and bone marrow as often as he can."

"Wow."

"That's the word for it." The sheriff turned into the driveway of a faded red, single-story building, tucked in between an auto repair shop and the county impound lot. An incongruously sleek steel sign identified the building as the county coroner's office. The structure seemed to be sinking in a quagmire of potholes and loose asphalt.

Tony pulled in behind the building and parked near a metal door adorned with brightly colored biohazard warning signs. Two security cameras gazed down from the eaves of the roof as he pressed the intercom button.

Mildred Gellert's disembodied voice boomed from the small speaker. "I'll be right there."

Less than a minute later, the door opened and the coroner greeted them with a smile. The moment they were inside, Kate was confronted with a tablet.

"I'll need you both to sign in before I can share my results."

Kate did as instructed. Passing the tablet to Tony, she noted the coroner's gray hair had been pulled into a tight ponytail and she was outfitted in blue scrubs. Leveling Mildred with a direct stare, she warily inquired. "Your results? *You* did the autopsy?"

Kate wanted the coroner to say no, hoping the body had been sent to a medical examiner. The county coroner's role (prevalent in most small communities nationwide) was an elected position, which often required no medical expertise. In many cases, eligibility was only predicated upon being old enough to vote and having no felony convictions. Often, candidates did not need to be a medical professional, nor did they need to have any formal education in human anatomy, biology or chemistry.

Mildred stared evenly back at her. "I am a certified forensic pathologist with over thirty years of experience. I moved here from Sacramento, California twelve years ago."

She continued in the wake of Kate's chagrined expression. "I'd had my fill of never-ending reams of red tape and limited resources at the state capitol. Thanks to a generous inheritance from my uncle, I took an early retirement and relocated here to pursue my other passion." Mildred gestured to a nearby counter where an almost ethereal blue ceramic vase sat upon the immaculate surface.

"But you missed your old career?" Kate guessed.

"Absolutely not. I bought a five-acre property outside of town and built my very own kiln. It was our previous sheriff who had other ideas. He explained the coroner's job was only a part-time gig in this county. That, and the fact the incumbent's sole medical knowledge was derived from his veterinary practice, suckered me in. I threw my hat into the election. When I won, I donated a good portion of my inheritance to convert this building for my use."

Impressed by the woman's dedication, as well as the equanimity with which she had handled the uncomfortable inquiry, Kate smiled. "Sounds like the county couldn't be in better hands."

Tony passed the tablet back to the coroner, who led them to a door at the back of the open receiving area. They followed her through a short hallway and into a drastically different chamber. While nowhere near as vast as the medical examiner's facilities Kate was used to in San Francisco, the space was no less well appointed. The specific standards to which it had been configured, as well as the meticulous organization, spoke volumes about the coroner's professionalism and work ethic.

Mildred proceeded directly to the teen's body, which was laid out upon a stainless-steel table toward the rear wall. Kate and Tony came to stand side-by-side, across the table from the coroner.

Having been removed from the pit of lye and cleaned, the body was less noxious than it had been at the quarry. Despite the improvement, the building's ventilation system still seemed woefully inadequate to the task of proper air exchange. Or maybe there was nothing wrong with the system. Maybe it was the white tile adorning the floors and walls. Thick invisible tentacles seemed to lash out, seizing Kate and dragging her back to a similarly decorated space—one forever tainted by ghostly tortured screams.

Mildred peered at her keenly over the remains of the victim. "Are you okay?"

"I'm fine. Let's get started."

The coroner stared at her for a few extra beats before donning a pair of blue latex gloves.

"Given the amount of skin damage, it was virtually impossible to close the upper thoracic." She reached over the cadaver and pulled back the sheet, exposing the chest.

With the thick veil of blood removed, each wound stood out in vivid detail. The tendrils tightened around Kate as she recalled another autopsy review—one she had heard from the San Francisco medical examiner.

Inhaling sharply, Kate forced herself to stare at the dark hair hanging limply on the table. The very fact it was not blonde helped drag her back to the present.

In addition to the gaping wound bisecting the victim's throat and the numerous slashes in her chest, Mildred's investigation had left two new deep trenches which met in a great chasm in the upper part of the corpse's abdomen. Mercifully, a series of large black stitches closed the vertical incision; the sheet shrouded the rest.

The coroner's voice was clear and distinct. "We have an Asian female in her mid-to-late-teens. Deceased approximately two days."

The estimated age stabbed at Kate's heart. She resisted the sudden and irrational urge to reach out and touch the lifeless juvenile.

Unaware of Kate's internal turmoil, the older woman continued. "The cause of death was exsanguination from the neck wound. The weapon was likely a single-bladed hunting knife, between five and six inches long. Based on the shape and direction of the wounds, the killer was right-handed.

"There are numerous lacerations to the chest which vary in depth. Most cut deep enough to slice through the pectoralis major and minor." She pointed a gloved finger at the cross section of muscles exposed in one of the wounds.

"Only two went deep enough to impact the costal cartilage. One glanced off a rib, another barely nicked the body of the sternum." She pointed to one of the wider wounds where a yellowish-white bone was visible.

"Relevant because ...?" Tony inquired.

Mildred tilted her head to the left. "Because taken in the context of how many times the victim was slashed, and the number of overall contusions, it implies a level of restraint in the midst of what appears to be a moment of complete rage."

"He went wild carving up her chest, but regained control in time to stop short of the organs?" Tearing his gaze from the body, he looked at the coroner. "Meaning he didn't intend to kill her?"

"Maybe. If so, he must have changed his mind shortly afterward. The throat wound was incurred not long after the damage to her chest. No doubt about intent there." She gestured to the wide opening at the neck. Two tubes protruded at awkward angles from either side of it. "He cut through both carotid arteries, all the way through to the C4 vertebra."

Tony crossed his arms over his chest. "If he did consider her a stand-in for another victim, maybe the chest was practice work. When the dry run was over, he killed her."

Kate frowned. "Or maybe it was about delayed gratification."

Mildred thought about it for a moment. "Could have gone either way. The lye is an interesting twist. Most perps who've ever tried get it wrong. The use of the pit was smart—not as ideal as fully pressurized containment, but he still deserves points. Chemical agents can be a very effective way of disposing of remains."

"Yeah, let's hope it doesn't catch on," Tony scoffed.

Mildred's face remained impassive. "Actually, the notion of using lye equivalents to dissolve bodies has been gaining traction across the country. The alkaline hydrolysis process has become a political hot button over the past ten years or so. Many people think it is the future of disposing of human remains."

Tony rolled his eyes skyward. "Tell me you're kidding."

"I'm not. A number of states have legalized the process. While no mortuaries have actually processed remains with alkaline hydrolysis yet, there are two medical facilities operating in the United States who are using it."

Tony blanched, "Why?"

"There are arguments on both sides. On the pro side is the reduced environmental impact. The body is inserted into a pressurized capsule, which is heated for approximately three hours. When it's done, all that remains is the same soupy mixture you saw in the pit. There is also some calcium residue and bone fragments which can be ground up, much like cremains, for the family to either inter or keep in their home.

"The liquid doesn't contain any toxic chemicals, so there are no special protocols for disposal. On the con side, others feel it is disrespectful to wash human beings down the drain and into the sewer. In fact, when they tried to legalize the process in New York, opponents labeled it *Hannibal Lechter's Bill*. By associating it with the psycho from *Silence of the Lambs*, opponents put a macabre and gruesome spin on it."

Neither the sheriff nor the coroner noticed Kate stiffen at the mention of the word psycho.

"What do you think of it, Mildred?" Tony was not ready to let the topic drop.

She glanced back down at the cadaver. "Death is the hardest thing for us to accept. I think people should do whatever brings them personal peace."

Following her gaze, Tony relented. "Anything else we should know?"

"She spent some time out in the woods before she died. There are numerous small lacerations to her skin and I found some bits of leaves in her hair. I also pulled traces of soil and other organic material from some of the scratches on her legs and from under her fingernails."

"Any links to a specific location?"

"Nothing in those samples stood out. But this does ..." The coroner pulled back the sheet, revealing a burn mark on the right hip. "While there is extensive soft tissue damage elsewhere, this is the only place where it was caused by a burn."

"Thoughts on how it got there?"

"A partial thickness burn with a secondary hematoma? Probably an electrical source. Take a closer look."

Kate and Tony leaned in, spotting two small dots in the middle of the affected area. Both nodded, recognizing the obvious shape of contact points from a stun gun.

"Based on the slight overlap in burn radius, I'd say he used it on her more than once."

Kate leaned back. "If her trek through the woods had been unauthorized, he may have had to use it to subdue her."

"Could be. It will still be a while before I'll get the results of the tox-screen back from the lab. And there was something else I found which may help with the victim ID." Mildred turned and walked over to the large computer monitor sitting atop a nearby metal desk. A dental x-ray filled the screen.

She gestured to the upper jaw, and then the lower. "See those screws? They make up over forty percent of the teeth in her mouth."

"Implants?" Kate frowned.

"Yes. And by my guess, they weren't going to hold up for very long."

Kate recalled the litany of complaints she had heard around the precinct from those who had opted for implants. From desk sergeants to detectives, all had regaled her with some problem or another relating to the process. "Improper implantation?"

"Oh, no. They were properly implanted, but they shouldn't have been implanted at all. See these almost transparent pockets in the maxilla and mandible?" Mildred traced her finger over the upper and lower jawbone.

Both investigators nodded.

"Those are areas where her bone mass is thinner. No medical professional ever should have considered this girl a candidate for implants, especially not this number of them."

"So, we're looking for a disreputable dentist?"

"Ideally a team should have been involved in this kind of procedure. Dentist, oral surgeon and maxillofacial surgeon," Mildred corrected. "And it's not only about the implants, it's the cause of those thin areas of bone. Based on the lack of bone density and a variety of other factors, I'd say this girl suffered from prolonged malnourishment during her early development. The good news is I should be able to identify the manufacturer. From there, I should be able to track down whoever did the work."

She paused for a long moment. "And then there's the heartbreaking part."

Kate lifted an eyebrow, curious to hear what more it took to tip Mildred's scales to "heart-breaking."

The coroner sighed wearily and leaned her hip against the

nearby counter. "There is massive scarring to her genitals. Based on the variation in scarring and tissue damage, I'd say this girl had been sexually abused for a prolonged period of time."

"Weeks?" Tony inquired.

"A lot longer. And the abuse wasn't exclusively sexual in nature. I found evidence of multiple recently healed fractures in her arms and legs. I was able to collect some semen samples, which I sent to the lab with the tox screen." Mildred let the information sink in for a long moment before finishing.

"And one more thing." She reached out and tapped a finger against the monitor. "Based on the rate of healing around the dental implants, they're recent. That work was done no more than a few months ago at the most."

April 28

Thunder crashed in the skies overhead, startling Kate so badly she almost lost her death grip on the wooden board above. Feeling every bit of the earth's gravity leveled against her, she strained her muscles for the fortieth time. Slowly, her body began to creep upward.

Her forehead cleared the exposed pine board first. Eventually her eyes rose up and peeked over the wood. She did not stop until her chin came parallel with the board. Satisfied, she lowered herself until her arms were fully extended. Then she let go and dropped the remaining distance to the ground.

Just as her feet met the concrete, the skies opened up, releasing a deluge that chased her through the wooden maze. Making her way through what would eventually be a family room she sprinted across the expansive yard to her rental cottage.

Kate hustled up three short steps to the shelter of the narrow porch. Indifferent to the water trickling down her face, she placed her hands on her soggy hips, and started to pace. It was not an ideal cool-down, but it would have to do. Ever since moving here, she had been using the neighboring home construction site as her personal strength conditioning gym.

While fitness had always been a part of her life, her run in with the Tower Torturer had increased her dedication to it. It had also prompted her to seek out the expertise of an ex-navy seal in San Francisco. Weeks in his studio had helped improve the hand-to-hand combat skills she had first learned in martial arts classes at the age of nine. The investment had yielded obvious results, further defining the contours of her muscles and elevating her endurance levels.

The improvised gym next door had its own complex past. The would-be dwelling was the last in a smattering of widely spaced houses at the end of a private road. Located on the same parcel of land as Kate's cottage, its progress toward returning to a domicile was impeded by a fierce legal battle.

Her landlord had been fighting with her insurance company since the previous summer, putting the project on indefinite hold. She regarded the skeletal structure, watching the sheets of rain coat the wood, as it likely had throughout the preceding months.

In the short time Kate had lived in Eagle's Nest, the sun had been a reticent host. On those few occasions when it had been front and center, its rays had barely penetrated the thick tree canopy which perpetually shaded the property.

If the landlord ever did get the remaining funds from the insurance company, Kate would not be surprised to hear malignant mold had snuck in and infected the new house.

She placed her left foot on the porch rail and began to stretch. Exhaustion made each movement more of a fight than necessary. With only three hours of sleep, it was a miracle she had been able to put in a full hour and a half of lunges, incline sit-ups, lumber lifting, pushups and pullups.

During the drive back from Mildred's office the day before, Kate had been struck by the extent to which the memories of the autopsy had affected her. By the time Tony had dropped her off at her Jeep, Kate bid him good luck with the case and told him she planned to leave Eagle's Nest within forty-eight hours.

After a brief appeal, Tony had abandoned the professional track and tried the personal one. Ignoring the nagging pull of attraction between them, Kate had firmly rejected his proposal for dinner. The parting had been heralded by a stilted handshake and a sincere yet disappointed extension of gratitude.

Glad she had finally ripped off the bandage, but schizophrenically wishing she had not, she had headed back to the rental cottage. In search of a distraction from the persistent thoughts of the handsome sheriff, Kate had immersed herself in a series of blog articles to help prepare for the meeting with her mother.

The never-ending stream of opinions about how to find closure with recovering addicts filled the hours until the first muted rays of light had signaled the arrival of dawn. By then, she had been drowning in a vast pool of do's and don'ts.

Looking for an anchor, she had turned to the ancient television. Forty-five minutes later, she had finally dozed off in the midst of a documentary about the preservation of the ancient Greek city of Akrotiri.

With her last reserves of strength fading, she bent for one final stretch against the railing. Her gaze was drawn to the peeling beige paint along the length of splintered wood. Since she was on leave from the SFPD, money was tight. The one bedroom, one bath cottage was miniscule, but she had gotten it for a steal and the financially strapped landlord was extremely flexible about her start and end dates. The only real downside was the dated exterior, and forty-plus-year-old décor.

After putting her muscles through a few more paces, Kate let herself inside. Kicking off her shoes, she hurried down the short hall to the bathroom and began peeling off her clothes.

A poignant realization hit her as she stepped into the shower; the meeting with her mother was less than eight hours away. Desperate to ward off the sudden chill accompanying the thought, she cranked the old chrome faucet to the highest setting. As the hot spray hit her skin, she reveled in the knowledge that by this time tomorrow she would be preparing to be free of both her mother and Eagle's Nest. Although where she might go from there was anyone's guess.

She squeezed an overgenerous portion of shampoo into her hand and began lathering her hair. The invigorating scent of lemongrass filled the steamy air. Determined to keep the weighty questions of what her future entailed at bay, she immersed herself in the task at hand.

Emerging from the shower fifteen minutes later, Kate wrapped herself in a towel which looked as if it had been dyed in old coffee grounds. She grabbed a smaller version to dry her hair and headed back to the bedroom. No sooner had she crossed the threshold, than her temporary peace was shattered by the sound of her cell phone vibrating against the surface of the oversized walnut dresser.

The name on the display shook the moorings of the boundaries she had erected the night before. Struggling to control her irritation, she snatched up the device.

"Hi Kate! Bet you didn't think you'd be hearing from me so soon." A sense of urgency lay beneath the pleasantry.

"Tony, I made it clear yesterday ..."

He bulldozed past the protest. "I met with Delford's boss. He claims the guy is one of his stars; good attitude, always reliable, does a great job ..."

The image of the young teen lying on the stainless-steel table popped into her head, reigniting the familiar spark of responsibility in her chest. Despite her better judgment, she let him continue.

"But it's about what Delford's girlfriend does in her spare time." He let the pause sit for a few extra beats. "She tours the craft fair circuit, selling homemade specialty *soaps*."

The last word struck its intended target. Kate's grip on the phone tightened. Memories of the grisly pit and its noxious odors assailed her senses, reminding her of the lye, and the fact that other than its use in drain cleaners, its most common household use was in making soap.

One after another, Mildred's descriptions of the unending abuses the young victim had suffered throughout her short life trotted through Kate's mind. Without thinking, she said, "I can be ready in fifteen minutes."

"Great. We've already brought him in. I won't start until you get here."

Chapter 6

WHITE FLAKES DRIFTED DOWN onto the oak tabletop. The sound of steady grating accompanied the flurry, adding to the generally unpleasant atmosphere in the interrogation room.

Indifferent to the result of his handiwork, Rick Delford dug his jagged thumbnail across the surface of an empty Styrofoam cup. Immersed in the idle task, the ex-convict seemed entirely unaware of the two-way mirror in the opposite wall, or the camera mounted near the ceiling.

The solitary door opened for the first time in the thirty minutes since he had sat down at the table. Kate entered and took a seat across from him.

Tony followed, carefully closing the door behind him. "Hey, Rick. Sorry about the wait."

"Why am I here?" He stared at the cup like a modern-day Michelangelo trying to decide how to free a pious Madonna from a block of marble.

The sheriff placed a close-up picture of the victim's face on the table. "You need to tell us what you did to the girl."

The scratching abated for a fleeting moment. Keen eyes scanned the picture then settled on Kate. "Who the hell are you anyway?"

"I'm Detective Barnes, with the San Francisco Police Department."

"Why does the San Francisco ..." Looking as if he had just caught himself in the midst of starting down a rabbit hole, he began again. "This is a load of shit. You've got no reason to suspect me."

The sheriff responded. "Your rap sheet gives us plenty of reasons."

"I don't make those choices anymore. Ask my counselor. I've

never missed a meeting." He placed the cup on the table before him, signaling the end of the conversation.

Leaving his spot by the door, Tony stopped less than a foot from where Delford sat. Settling back against the edge of the table, the sheriff responded, "We did talk to your counselor. You call in once a month for a fifteen-minute bullshit session so you can keep your job. What I want to know is why'd you kill this girl?"

The suspect pushed his chair backward across the linoleum floor, increasing the distance between them. "I don't know what you're talking about."

"Fine. Let's start with the sodium hydroxide."

"Sodium-what?" He tore his gaze from Kate and riveted it on the sheriff.

"Deputy Wheaton talked to your girlfriend a little while ago."

Delford slumped back in his chair, his brow pulling into a tight frown.

"She's been using sodium hydroxide for the past few years in her soap business. She said you picked some up for her last month when she was running low."

"Yeah, I helped out my girlfriend. Is that a crime?"

"No. But kidnap, rape, torture, murder and trying to dispose of a body to cover up a murder are."

"I already told you, I've never seen the girl before."

Kate cut in. "Your girlfriend was shocked to hear about your past with young girls. Deputy Wheaton said the poor woman got physically sick when she learned about your prison sentence and the reason for it."

Delford snatched the cup off the table. The last of the Styrofoam crumpled beneath his fingers. Rage simmered in his eyes as he turned his attention back to the sheriff. "You had no goddam right to do that! I already told you, I'm not into that shit anymore!"

Tony lunged forward, coming nose-to-nose with him. "Really,

Rick? I find that hard to believe. You didn't stop after the first little girl complained when you were nineteen. And you didn't stop after the next one reported you when you were twenty-three. Do you really expect us to believe you've lost your appetite for kids?"

Leaning back, Delford cocked his head to one side. "Fuck you."

Undeterred, Kate jumped back into the fray. "You had access to enough sodium hydroxide to dissolve a body in a pit. You are a convicted pedophile. And ..." She paused for emphasis before reciting the news Tony had shared with her when she had arrived. "And, you are one of the few people in town who had regular access to the dumpsite."

"Bullshit!"

Tony sighed. "We talked to your boss at Aaru. Before getting hired there, you used to freelance hauling away trash. Keating Mining used to pay you to take care of illegal dumping at the quarry."

"So?"

"So that's where you dumped the girl." Kate finished for him.

"I didn't dump anyone, anywhere. No matter what I did in the past, I never tried to murder anyone."

"But enough hardcore child porn was found in your apartment at the time of your last arrest to prove you do fantasize about getting rough with kids. Face it Rick, you're screwed. We tried to give you a chance to confess, but you want to keep lying to us. Once the lab results are in, it will be too late."

Delford clenched his jaw. Searching Kate's face for truth, he demanded, "Lab results?"

"The victim was a mess. If the lye had done its job you wouldn't have had to worry, but as it is, you probably left your DNA all over her. Because of your prior offenses, you're already in CODIS."

Delford's eyes widened at the mention of the FBI's national DNA database. He glanced from Tony to Kate and back again. A split second later, his right leg began to bounce up and down under the table. His next words spilled out in an almost indistinguishable mumble. "I didn't do it."

Kate's tone softened. "Look Rick, we only want to find out what happened. If you can help us understand, we might be able to help you. Unlawful penetration of a minor only got you eight years. For felony murder, you can bet you'll die in prison."

"Help from the cops? Fuck that!" He crossed his arms over his chest and stared at the table.

Tony mirrored the movement. "I can only imagine how hard those inmates are going to make it on you, Rick. At the moment, Washington state has a moratorium on the death penalty, but it could always change. If it doesn't, jailhouse justice for pedophiles is a shitty way to spend the rest of your life."

After a long pause, the suspect dropped his arms. He reached out and began idly fingering the pile of shavings on the table. Finally, he exhaled deeply and looked at Kate. "What if I ..."

The door swung open. A somber-suited man in his mid-thirties entered with the recklessness of a flash flood. He was followed by Deputy Wheaton whose apologetic look hardened into an icy gaze when she spotted Kate across the table.

The new arrival's brown hair was slicked back by copious amounts of product. From his designer clothes to his ridiculously expensive leather briefcase, he exuded a big-city aura. The attorney announced Delford was his client before launching into the standard rebuff, informing the sheriff his client would not answer any further questions outside of his presence.

Puzzlement flashed across Delford's features. The expression was immediately replaced with bravado. "You better let this drop, Sheriff. I already told you I had nothing to do with this."

Ignoring Delford's threat, Kate studied the self-aggrandizing barrister, thinking there had to be a special type of sociopathy to a person who would defend a convicted child molester and suspected murderer. More importantly, she wondered who had called the guy on Delford's behalf.

∨

A bell chimed somewhere on the other side of the front door. Kate removed her finger from the button. In the ensuing silence, the memory of an incident during her college years resurfaced.

Her mother had shown up on Kate's doorstep, trying to scrounge up money to fuel her drug habit. Kate had not given Chloe any quarter, finally casting her out by shouting at the top of her lungs she hoped her mother would die. It had been the last thing she had said to her, until yesterday.

The muffled sound of approaching footsteps could be heard on the other side of the door. Before Kate could properly prepare herself, the door opened and her mother appeared. Dressed in peasant blouse and slacks, the older woman looked simultaneously relaxed, yet entirely uncomfortable.

"Hi, Kate. I'm so glad you made it."

"Me too."

"Please come in." Chloe showed Kate through the small, but well-appointed foyer and into a living room with a distinctly modern flair. Sitting down on a cream-colored loveseat, she waved her hand toward the large couch across from her.

Ignoring the directive, Kate bypassed the couch and went directly to one of the rose-colored chairs near the fireplace. Before sitting, her eyes swept across the framed photos decorating the mantle.

Chloe and Jacob smiled back from distinct moments frozen in the past—their wedding day; a trip to the Eiffel Tower; an exotic jungle hike and an outing at a horse farm. Two other photos featured Jacob with a twenty-something woman who resembled him too much to be anything but a daughter. The final photo featured all three together at what appeared to be a Christmas celebration in the same room in which Kate now stood.

Mounted to the wall above the photos, was a cross carved out of ebony. A ceiling light bathed it in a soft yellow glow. Without comment, Kate pulled her purse from her shoulder, spun around and dropped onto the chair.

"My husband, Jacob, is upstairs. He will respect our privacy."

"Your husband knows about me?"

"Of course he does." Chloe straightened her shoulders. "After my stay in rehab, I enrolled in an outpatient program in St. Helena. One of the counselors there loved to talk about her childhood in a small town in Washington state. Her stories about life there reminded me of a Norman Rockwell painting. It all sounded so simple, so easy. Life had never come easy for me.

"One day, she introduced me to her cousin who was visiting from her hometown of Eagle's Nest. I became friends with Jacob and eventually fell in love with him. But it was another two years before I trusted him, or myself, enough to get married.

"So, yes, he knows about you." Chloe gestured grandly, but her voice cracked around the next words. "He knows about everything. And somehow he still loves me."

"You got clean and started a new life."

Uncertainty clouded Chloe's expression. "Yes, but I …"

"Let me guess, you thought about Candace and me every single day, right?" Kate glanced toward the ceiling then fixed her eyes back on her mother. "No, that can't be right. Because if you felt that way, you might have tried to reach me, but you never did. Oh, and of course, Candace was dead so there was no reaching her."

The demure veil dropped to the floor. "You were very clear

63

about how you felt when we last spoke, Kate. If I recall you told me never to talk to you again *and* made it clear you would have preferred if I had died instead of Candace."

Kate's cheeks flushed as the familiar rage exploded in her chest. She leaned forward and opened her mouth, happy to trade closure for retaliation, but Chloe cut her off.

"You were right. She was such a sweet, innocent soul, and I was the exact opposite. I could say it was the drugs. That is the out the counselors give you, but they also remind you to own the devastation you've caused."

Chloe began smoothing the fabric on a nearby pillow. "I would move heaven and earth if it would erase what I did to you girls … but it's not in my power."

She paused, then inhaled slowly. "In the beginning, I was so convinced you were right, I tried to even the scales."

Turning her palm upward, she offered it to Kate. "After a few failed attempts with pills, I tried twice with a razor." Pulling the sleeve of her blouse upward, she revealed a series of garish scars.

Kate inspected the damage, then riveted her gaze back on Chloe. "Many people make the same mistake. They cut horizontally instead of vertically. If you had opened up the length of the vein upward toward your elbow, you'd have bled out before anyone could have saved you."

Something akin to horror flashed across Chloe's features, then she nodded and placed her hands in her lap. "I didn't show you because I wanted you to feel sorry for me."

Buzzing pierced the quiet. As the sound reached Kate's ears, so did a familiar smell—her mother's beef stew.

The memory was an ancient one. Chloe's preoccupation with addiction had prompted her to give up cooking when the girls were young. The tangy aroma taunted Kate now, luring her salivary glands into the enemy camp.

Chloe rose. Her next words took her daughter completely off guard. "I thought it might be easier to talk over a meal. I hope you haven't eaten."

Kate was about to decline when her stomach decided to take a stand. There was no masking the grumbling sound from her mother.

Nodding, she stood and trailed Chloe into the kitchen. Over the next few minutes, they worked in relative silence, plating salads and pouring red wine. When Kate finally sat down at the dining table, she paused to still the rage simmering inside her.

The feelings were far more powerful than she had anticipated. Dr. Wissel had warned this might happen. If she did not get a better hold on her emotions, the only thing she would take away from this encounter would be more bad memories.

As Chloe took her seat across the table, Kate grabbed her glass and took a generous sip. She had picked up her fork and was about to spear a particularly ripe tomato when movement from across the table caught her attention. Chloe had bowed her head and began to pray over their meal. Kate placed the utensil back on the plate and waited.

When the amen came, her mother picked up her fork but did not make any move toward the contents of her plate. "You came here for closure. What do you need from me to get it?"

Kate regarded Chloe for a moment, begrudgingly respecting the older woman's straightforward approach. The practicality of the question momentarily quelled the inner turmoil.

Matching her mother's even tone, Kate answered. "Honestly, I'm not sure. I hired someone to find you, then traveled here to resolve my past. But how we do that ... I have no idea."

"I understand. I've spent so many hours debating what I would ever say if I had the chance to talk to you again. Now you're here and I'm at a loss."

Kate popped a forkful of salad into her mouth.

Chloe regarded her thoughtfully, then decided to change tactics. "You should be very proud of catching the Tower Torturer."

A clump of lettuce caught in Kate's throat, prompting a coughing fit. She reached for her wine glass, nearly emptying the contents before returning it to the table.

"Sorry, I didn't mean to upset you."

While the case had topped the headlines for weeks, her mother's mention of it felt like a trespass. When she could speak again, Kate fired back. "It's my job. I didn't do it for my pride, I did it because it needed to be done."

A shadow of sadness swept over Chloe's features. "Okay." She took a bite of lettuce. After a few more moments of silence, she inquired, "Are you here investigating the dead girl they found at the old quarry?"

Kate's fork froze in midair. Tony had not offered any information to the press. The sheriff's office clearly had a leak. "As I said, I came here to see you. Who was the victim?"

Chloe leaned forward, relieved to have found a path that led away from the ruins of their relationship. "An Asian girl. She had been dumped in one of the old treatment pits. Apparently, she was in very bad shape. I heard about it from a friend. Her husband's brother is a deputy."

"Really?" Kate moved the last of the salad around on her plate. "What else did she say?"

"No one seems to know who the girl is. She told me, and a couple of other members of our church, in confidence. It's incredibly sad. We would like to organize a candlelight vigil, but we were unsure because the sheriff's office hasn't said anything about it. Her brother thinks the sheriff is totally lost."

Lost was one of the last words Kate would use to characterize Tony. After Delford's lawyer ended the interrogation, they had gone directly to the Tony's office and called the county prosecutor for a search warrant. They had also placed another call to Mildred to see if she could push the state lab to expedite processing the DNA samples.

"Actually, I think it's a great idea."

Chloe brightened. "You do?"

"Absolutely. If the sheriff doesn't know who the victim is, the media coverage may help identify her."

"Okay, I'll start making calls tonight." Grabbing her near-empty plate, she stood and began to reach for Kate's when the doorbell echoed down the hall.

Chloe shook her head. "Jacob knows we're not to be interrupted. He can take care of it while I get our stew."

As her mother headed into the kitchen, Kate heard movement on the floor above. A minute later two male voices could be heard in the direction of the front door.

Chloe placed steaming plates of mouthwatering goodness on the table and took her seat as her husband entered the dining room. Wearing Washington State University sweats and a sheepish expression, Jacob addressed his wife. "Honey, we have more company."

"Jacob, Kate is here. I told you we …"

He gestured to their visitor, who was decked out in a navy-blue crew-neck sweater which clung a bit too snugly to the beginnings of a middle-aged paunch. The new arrival smiled affably at the two women. His goatee balanced a receding hairline, but his age was closer to Kate's than her mother's.

Chloe jumped out of her seat. "Oh, Pastor! I'm so sorry! I completely forgot to call and cancel our meeting."

"It's no problem. If you and Jacob have other plans, we can always reschedule."

"It's simply that I haven't seen my daughter in a very long time, and we really need to talk."

"Your daughter ...?"

Chloe gestured across the table. "Pastor Brian, this is Kate."

He offered his hand. "It is a sincere pleasure to meet you."

Finding no trace of the judgment she had expected, she shook his hand. "It's a pleasure to meet you, too, Pastor Brian."

He turned back to Jacob. "I can try to call the other members of the council ..."

Chloe jumped in. "No, it's alright. I know how hard it is to coordinate everyone's schedules, especially yours. Kate and I can finish eating upstairs in the library."

The notion of adjourning to a more intimate area of Chloe's house while a group of strangers assembled downstairs was too much. Placing her napkin on the table, Kate stood and addressed her mother. "It's fine. We can reschedule."

Her lips pursed for a few moments before Chloe finally relented. "Okay. But, at least let me pack up your dinner."

Another rumble from Kate's abdomen ended the burgeoning argument. "Thank you."

Chloe's eyes glistened with frustration as she snatched up the two bowls and hurried into the kitchen. Jacob left to change, promising his wife he would return shortly.

Kate was left with the Pastor, who came to stand beside her. "Your mother told me how proud she was of your work on the Tower Torturer case. It was a horrific situation, but thanks to you, he will never harm another young woman."

He handed her a business card. Reading it, she raised an eyebrow at the fact her mother had abandoned her Catholic faith for an evangelical one.

He forged ahead, "Sometimes people don't realize the toll a such a case can have on even the most seasoned officer. I'm sure your department has offered you counseling, but if you ever wish to talk, please feel free to call me. I served in Afghanistan in my twenties. I understand the many forms trauma can take."

"Thanks, but I don't think that will be necessary."

"Fair enough. The offer remains open anyway. And understand, it comes with no strings attached. I'm not going to try to convert you or ask for a donation."

Kate smiled, good naturedly admitting it was exactly what she was afraid of.

Chloe arrived at her elbow holding a plastic container in one hand and her daughter's purse in the other.

"This is my cue. Goodnight, Pastor." Kate nodded as she retrieved the items.

"Likewise." His dark eyes twinkled back at her. "And remember, no recruitment and no donations required."

"I will."

Her mother led her through the hallway and into the foyer. Approaching the door both women were seized by a painful awkwardness akin to the final moments of a first date.

Chloe pulled a slip of paper from her pocket and handed it to Kate. A phone number was scribbled beneath her mother's proper name. With a quick good-bye, Kate opened the door and hurried down the porch stairs to the Jeep. She had meant it when she had said their conversation could wait.

Pulling away from the curb, Kate began dialing Tony's cell. He needed to know about the leak and the vigil.

Chapter 7

April 29

A BEVY OF WIDE-EYED CREATURES gazed down upon the public assembly, seemingly immune to the pall of sadness which hung over the evening's proceedings. Carved into the concrete roof of the bandstand at the west end of the town square, the collection of ravens, eagles, bears and orcas were a permanent reminder of the values of the native peoples who had long inhabited the lands of the Pacific northwest. The townspeople had gathered in the frigid cold to mourn the most recent desecration of those values.

Kate's gaze swept over the bandstand, and the small group of community leaders who sat in a single-file row of folding chairs upon it. Clad in a padded jacket and clutching a candle, she stood alone on one of the muddy, tree-topped knolls enclosing the open plaza. The muck clinging to her boots was a small price to pay for both an unobstructed view of the proceedings and a reprieve from the overwhelming press of the crowd.

Despite the short notice, Chloe had proven an adept event planner. Hundreds of people filled the open area, each holding a candle identical to Kate's. The sea of soft light served as a visible representation of the town's empathy for the loss of the girl no one had ever met.

On stage, the high school's star soprano finished a haunting rendition of *Amazing Grace*, then ceded the podium to Pastor Brian. Kate set her jaw, preparing for a slew of false platitudes and bible verses.

The familiar voice resonated clearly over the speakers. Without preamble, he began by acknowledging man's capacity to commit acts of evil, then promptly segued to the importance of healing that can be found through mercy and love. No deities were mentioned, nor were any scriptures.

Despite her predisposition for skepticism, the man's plain-spoken approach and lilting cadence breached Kate's defenses. Gazing at the crowd, it was evident his words had a similar effect on the assembly, planting a seed of hope in the face of senseless tragedy.

For a moment she wondered whether it could be so simple. *Could fiery rage be extinguished by the cool embrace of forgiveness?* Tightening her grip on the votive, Kate turned her attention on Chloe, who stood with her husband to the left of the stage. Old memories came surging back, stoking the fire once again.

As Pastor Brian turned the podium over to the Mayor, Kate swallowed past her emotions and turned her attention back to the stage. Tony sat at the far end. While his posture exuded a quiet confidence, the relentless way his eyes scanned the crowd spoke volumes.

Over the past forty-five minutes, Kate had been similarly engaged. Vigils drew murderers like open flames drew moths. Killers rarely missed the opportunity to bask in the attention.

While Kate had not seen any sign of Rick Delford, she also had not identified any other attendees exhibiting telltale signs of unusual interest or attempting to insert themselves into the proceedings. Although all signs seemed to be pointing to the convicted sex offender, she had learned how dangerous it could be to develop tunnel vision from circumstantial evidence. Following Tony's lead, she resumed scanning the massive crowd.

Fourteen minutes later, the Mayor solemnly brought the evening to a close, parroting the plea Tony had made in his opening remarks—for anyone with information about the crime should report it directly to the sheriff's department. He repeated the hotline number and wished everyone a good evening.

Kate glanced down at her watch as the throngs began to dissipate. The event had lasted an hour. Back on stage, Tony had joined the Mayor in quiet conversation. As she watched, the sheriff clapped the politician on the arm, then turned away to take a call.

Two minutes later, Kate's phone vibrated in her jacket pocket. It was Tony.

"Hi. Where are you?"

"Small hill on your left, in front of the spruce trees."

He glanced in Kate's general direction. With a curt nod, he began making his way to the stairs. "Mildred just got a hit on the DNA samples she ran through CODIS."

Kate remained silent, praying the circumstantial case against Rick Delford was about to transform into a concrete one.

"Delford's DNA was a match."

"Great." Kate began picking her way down the slick hill toward the stage.

"Not entirely."

Kate stopped short. "Meaning?"

"I said Delford was a match ..." He jogged down the short set of stairs. "But his wasn't the only profile they found."

"Please don't tell me ..."

"I won't—until we get somewhere private. My car is on the street. Meet me there?"

"On my way."

Tony ended the call and began working his way through the masses of people flowing through the nearest exit. Without slowing, he exchanged fleeting remarks with some of the townsfolk. Kate followed him out to the SUV, which was parked in the closest stall.

No sooner had she climbed inside and closed the door behind

her than Kate demanded, "How many profiles?"

"Two. Both male."

"Tell me they got a match on the second sample."

"No. And what's worse is where they *didn't* find Delford's DNA." He watched as Kate's frown deepened. "Only one profile was identified in the rape kit—and it wasn't Delford's."

Kate's gaze narrowed. "That doesn't mean Delford is innocent of murder."

"Right, and whether he killed her or not, we do know he came in contact with her body after she was murdered. DNA confirms a strand of his hair was found in her chest wound."

"Begs the question ... was UNSUB number two an accomplice, or a client."

"Client?" Tony frowned.

Kate reflected on the variety of twisted perpetrators she had come across working sex crimes in the Special Victims Unit. "All the technology in his home entertainment center cost more than he'd make working as a landscaper at Aaru. Perhaps Delford found someone willing to pay for the opportunity to rape her."

Tony started the engine and turned on the overhead lights. The crowd responded to the visual cue, parting in the streets like the waters of the Red Sea before Moses. "I already called the county prosecutor. Deputies Lloyd and Carson will stay here on crowd control until everyone clears out. Wheaton is going to meet me at Delford's place. By the time we get there, we'll have a search warrant as well as an arrest warrant. Want to join?"

Kate leveled him with an even stare. "Rhetorical questions aren't worth asking."

V

Deputy Wheaton's cruiser was parked outside of Delford's house when the sheriff's SUV arrived. Tony parked a few feet behind her bumper.

He left the overhead lights on, washing the house in an unending kaleidoscope of reds and blues. A faint glow spilled out from around the corners of the dwelling's front window softening the bright palette of color.

Kate opened the door and hopped out, blinked past the pungent smell of wet grass, a leftover from the rain which had fallen earlier in the day. Their determined footfalls fell upon the gravel driveway violating the peaceful silence of the still night air as they made their way to the deputy's cruiser. Wheaton got out and joined them at the front bumper.

"Is he in there?" Tony inquired.

Wheaton nodded. "Looks like it. Someone closed the curtain over the window when I pulled up seven minutes ago. I'm parked behind his truck, so there's no getting out, unless he goes through us."

"You mean there's no *driving* out." Kate corrected. "The forest is only twenty yards behind his house. He could have already slipped out the back." She did not bother to hide the irritation in her voice.

Eyes wide, the deputy turned to the sheriff. "I'm here by myself. I couldn't cover the front and the back. Besides, I …"

"Save it." Tony's gaze remained fixed on the house, but Kate noted the hurt expression on the other woman's face. "We'll take the front. Wheaton, you head around back."

The deputy pursed her lips. Biting back a retort, she pulled her flashlight and began dutifully making her way along the narrow, unpaved path that snaked around the right side of the building. By the time they arrived at the front door, she had disappeared into the darkness.

They waited for a few moments in silence before Tony raised his left fist to rap on the door. His right hand remained at his belt, resting upon the butt of his weapon, as the sound thundered through the air.

After twenty seconds, the sheriff knocked again. His tone was deep and commanding, "Sheriff's Department! We need to talk to you Rick!"

Silence for another ten seconds.

Tony resorted to shouting. "Rick open up now, we ..."

His shoulder radio suddenly sprang to life with the sound of Wheaton's troubled voice. "Delford's coming out the back ..."

Kate and Tony's eyes met as he reached for his radio. "We're on our way."

They bounded down the stairs as muffled shouts resounded from the rear of the domicile. Tony unclipped his flashlight from his belt and pulled his weapon. Kate's Glock was already in hand.

The beam from the flashlight bounced across the path as they sprinted toward the rear. An edge trimmer, which had fallen sideways across the path, provided a momentary barrier. Kate followed a step behind Tony—leaping over the tool like competitors in a steeplechase.

As soon as they arrived in the open clearing, the shouting stopped. The beam from Tony's flashlight cut manically across the yard before fixing upon the fallen forms of Wheaton and Delford. The two were locked in a wrestling match on the ground.

Kate and Tony tried to train their weapons on the suspect. Getting a line of sight between the struggling forms was impossible.

Tony shouted, "Sheriff's Department! Hold it, Delford! We ..."

The single report of a gun tore through the night. The ensuing echo was joined by frenetic rustling in the nearby forest as creatures of every stripe fled the commotion.

The prone figures froze for a moment, then fell apart from one another. Tony and Kate approached cautiously as the sheriff began calling out a series of instructions.

As they neared, the beam from Tony's flashlight traveled up over Delford's head, exposing the missing front corner of his skull. Tony fell silent, then cut the beam back toward a blood-soaked Wheaton, who was struggling to rise into a sitting position.

Her hair, which had previously been pulled into a no-nonsense ponytail, was now adorned with bits of bone and flesh. Her face was frozen in an expression of both complete control and abject incredulity.

Kate recognized the familiar contradiction as the onset of shock. Sheathing her weapon, she went to the deputy and helped pull her to her feet.

"Are you okay?"

Wheaton turned toward her, her wide-eyed stare reminding Kate of the animal carvings at the town plaza. "Yes, I …"

"Good, now tell me what the hell happened." Tony's words were as steely as the bullet which had just ended Delford's life.

"He ran at me. I warned him to stop, but he kept coming. He grabbed for my gun and …"

"And you shot him." Kate finished gently.

Without another word, Tony began dialing the state police. A bleak expression took up residence in the sheriff's features as he spoke. His broad shoulders slumped as the seconds ticked by.

Kate could empathize. Losing a chief suspect in a murder investigation was bad enough, but an officer involved shooting was a guaranteed ticket to a real shit show. At least this time, she was not the ringmaster.

Chapter 8

THE TEQUILA WAS AS UNDESIRABLE as the bartender. With her badly dyed black hair pulled into a plastic clip, the woman attempted to flash a glimpse of her ample cleavage to both of the broken-down bikers seated at the end of the bar. Fifteen years ago she might have had some decent takers, but with two missing molars and leathery skin looking like it had been repurposed from a saddlebag out of a John Wayne western, Myrna was not likely to get lucky tonight.

Kate turned away from the sad spectacle. She regarded her glass dolefully before slamming a shot of the noxious alcohol. The syrupy liquid lit her throat on fire, temporarily distracting her from Delford's death and the avalanche of consequences about to befall the investigation.

Tony had promised to meet her at the roadside honky-tonk, but he had not shown yet. She regarded the remaining contents of the glass, deciding she had about two good shots left. If the sheriff failed to show by then, she was leaving.

Kate glanced down at her cell phone lying on the scarred wooden bar. On the screen was an earlier text from Chloe suggesting a new time to meet. Wincing, she snatched the device off the bar and shoved it in her back pocket.

Raising her gaze, Kate stared at the mirror behind the bar. Her eyes drifted across the reflection, until she spotted the randy band of patrons seated at the table behind her. The four men were a few years younger than Kate. They were accompanied by a pixie-faced, younger woman whose haunted eyes had been camouflaged under layers of black eye makeup.

When the group had arrived twenty minutes ago, the girl had appeared wary but willing to please. She was completely enamored with the loud-mouthed blonde Neanderthal sitting beside her. Sporting a T-shirt featuring a cartoon dog lifting its leg over the words, "Women's Rights," he presided over the table like a Viking king holding court after a bloody conquest.

Since arriving, he had treated the girl as a spoil of war, repeatedly goading his minions into trying to grope her. At first the girl had gamely laughed along, playfully swatting away their greedy hands.

But the attempts were becoming more insistent. The thinnest of the cretins, whose hair resembled a soiled prison mop, bellowed as the sting of his latest rebuke echoed over the house music.

The ruling beast's hand snaked out and seized the girl's wrist where it still hung in midair. In a flash, he bent her slender arm backwards. The girl yelped out in pain. Teetering on her chair, she promptly fell to the floor. He sprang from his seat and loomed over her.

Kate closed her eyes. The anticipation of another meeting with her mother crashed down like a landslide, mingling with haunting images of the unknown female victim. In the next second, her mind was assaulted by a chorus line of autopsy scenes headlined by the Tower Torturer's victims. Impotence and fury rocketed up through her abdomen. Suddenly, she was no longer sitting in the bar, but was on her knees in a tiled room, her hands cuffed and tethered to the floor—the sounds of a woman shrieking in the background.

Kate's eyes opened wide, then narrowed. She swiveled around in her seat in time to see the Neanderthal draw his right leg back and stomp his heavy boot down between the pixie's legs. The girl screamed and drew herself into a ball.

The act brought cheers from his companions. The nine other

patrons sprinkled about the room cast uneasy glances in the group's direction, but quickly looked away.

Placing both hands on the bar, Myrna called out, "Hey Boyd! Don't start nothing in here tonight. Leave the kid alone, huh?"

He pointed back at her in return. "Shut your fuckin' mouth! Unless you want to trade places with her?"

Kate rose from her stool, slammed the last of the tequila and placed a twenty-dollar bill on the bar. In a voice loud enough to be heard at the neighboring table, she said, "I will."

Myrna opened her mouth, looked from Kate to Boyd and back again, then shut it. She pocketed the currency and waddled back to the bikers.

Boyd turned on his heel, appraising Kate from head to toe. "You will, *what?*"

She walked over to him, pulling up close enough to smell the sour beer on his breath. "I'll trade places with her." Without another word, she strode to the front door.

Boyd looked to his cohorts who laughed and hooted as they climbed out of their chairs. Grabbing his beer bottle from the table, the bald one with bad skin yelled, "Go get her Boyd! She wants it."

"You bet your ass she does!"

He headed for the door without another look at the girl writhing in pain on the dirty concrete floor. Myrna came out from behind the bar. Looking as if the fates had unfairly conspired to force her into sainthood, she bent over to help the girl up.

Outside, the four men spotted Kate standing at the far end of the lot. The branches of the encroaching forest cast deep shadows around her.

Boyd stopped about five feet from her. His companions flanked him as they vied over who would get seconds. He stilled their yapping with a murderous glare.

Kate raised her chin, regarding each of them in turn. "So, who

79

wants to be first?"

Boyd took a step closer. "They're going to need a sewing machine to put you back in one piece, bitch."

Kate took a step closer. "Funny, I was thinking the same thing about you."

He smiled at his companions then reached backward and pulled a hunting knife from his waistband.

Kate raised an eyebrow. A slow smile spread across her face.

Boyd growled then charged at her, thrusting the blade toward her throat. A split second before the blade made contact, she ducked and punched him squarely in the stomach. Air whooshed from his lungs as he doubled over.

Kate spun around, allowing his weight to fall across her back. She jabbed her left elbow backward where it connected with his face in a sickening crunch of bone. Blood and teeth erupted around her arm while the force of the blow sent him careening backward.

Without hesitation, Kate wheeled back around and delivered a powerful kick to his stomach. He crumpled to the ground, as mop-hair grabbed her from behind.

"You fucking whore!!! You think you can get away with that?"

She clawed at the chokehold, unable to loosen the pressure on her windpipe.

His friend snatched the knife from the ground near Boyd and gestured between her legs. "You're gonna bleed, bitch!" Non-plussed by her ambivalent expression, he stepped toward her.

Before he could reach her, his head snapped forward like an overzealous Pez dispenser. He stumbled forward to regain his balance, allowing Kate a glimpse of the man in jeans and a Seattle Mariners jacket standing directly behind him. The new arrival had delivered the jarring blow which had prompted the thug to spit pieces of his teeth into the gravel.

Backlit by the lights from the bar, Kate recognized the new

face. Tony nodded at her before turning to face his adversary, who had finally righted himself.

Becoming desperate for air, Kate dropped her right hand and reached behind her. The moment her fingertips brushed against his crotch, she squeezed her fingers together like a vice. She did not relent, compressing his testicles until her thumb and fingers almost touched. His ensuing howl nearly split her eardrums.

She turned away to the left as he doubled over. A savage kick to the side of his kneecap prompted another crunching sound. A dark crimson stain blossomed across the knee of his tan pants, followed by a high-pitched wail and the sound of his body striking the ground.

Kate turned back toward Tony, watching him feint away from the advancing blade. Before she could offer assistance, the bald guy stepped between her and the sheriff. Holding his beer bottle high, he swung it down toward her head.

Her hands shot into the air. She crossed them above her head, bracing them in the form of an X, just in time to block his wrist in midair. The rage etched into his features melted into surprise.

Reaching over with her right hand, Kate wrenched the bottle from his stunned grasp. She whipped it backward then slammed it across his head. Glass shattered across his temple, tearing open his flesh.

Glaring at her through a wash of blood, he shifted his weight. Kate stepped forward, balancing her weight in anticipation. A split-second after his foot left the ground, she caught his ankle and held it suspended with her left hand. Her right fist shot forward, delivering a crippling punch to his exposed crotch. The ensuing scream echoed into the night. Unimpressed, she dropped his extended leg. He crashed onto his back and rolled across the gravel.

Panting, she turned back to check on the sheriff. Tony swung around and delivered a sound left-right combination to his opponent's kidneys. Pulling a short, black baton from his waistband, Tony brought it down against the side of the man's skull.

Tucking the baton away, the sheriff bent over the prone figure and plucked the blade from his open hand.

Kate regarded the weapon. "Little boys shouldn't play with knives."

"From what I saw, little boys shouldn't play with grown women."

"Thanks for the help."

He looked at each of the bodies on the ground then smiled. "I'm not so sure you needed it, but you're welcome."

Adrenaline still coursing through her veins, Kate strode over to him. With the same single-minded determination she had used on her adversaries, she raised her right hand up and snaked it around his neck. Her fingers worked their way into his hair, and her lips were on his before she could think better of it.

His eyebrows shot skyward. A split second later he responded in kind, slipping his tongue inside her warm mouth. Delighting in the electric sensations dancing across her nerve endings, she accepted it readily, teasing the side of his mouth until she had prompted the desired response.

Enveloping her in his arms, he drew her in tight against his taut body. When she finally pulled away warmth had begun to pool between her legs, turning them to gelatin.

He ran his tongue across his lips, then asked, "Tequila?"

"Yes."

"Enough that you shouldn't drive?"

She stepped out of his embrace. "My reflexes are fine."

He glanced at the fallen band once more. "I know. But I'm the sheriff and if you're over the legal limit ..." He watched her open her mouth to protest, and continued before she could say a word, "... then I'll have to drive you home." The huskiness in his tone was a clear invitation.

The dueling voices of responsibility and better judgment started to nag at the edge of her consciousness. Knowing they would persist until they grew into a wailing siren in her head, she decided to take the easy way out. "How about one more drink before we go?"

"Sounds good to me. Carson is on duty tonight. I'll get him out here to round these fools up."

"Not necessary." Kate took a few steps back toward Boyd, who had struggled to his knees. "I don't care what you need to do, Fuck-Face, but I want you out of here by the time I leave. Understand?"

He nodded miserably without meeting her eyes.

"And don't you ever touch that girl, or any other, again. Because if I find out about it, I won't be so friendly next time." She punctuated the threat by kicking loose gravel in his face, then followed Tony back inside.

∨

Kate's back slammed against the front door of the cottage, closing it against the cold night. Reaching around Tony's arm, she thrust the lock into place.

He pulled his mouth from her neck and glanced over at the lock. "You take security seriously."

"I don't like to be interrupted."

"Why don't you tell me what you do like?" His eyes sparkled with challenge as he rubbed his crotch suggestively between her legs. His jeans barely contained the pressure from his erection.

Something dark flashed in her expression. "I'm not sure you really want to know."

"I want to know everything about you."

Cocking her head, Kate frowned, then placed both hands on his chest. "I hope you don't."

Looking sheepish, the sheriff dropped his hands and stepped away from her. "Did I kill the moment?"

A wry expression contorted her features, "I just need to be clear; I'm not looking for anything serious."

He backed up a few feet and sat on the tiny loveseat which served as the couch. "I understand. I merely wanted you to know I'm open to it."

"Open to it, and hoping for it, are two entirely different things."

He stared her straight in the eye. "Believe me, I know." Humor sparked in his eyes, then he laughed softly.

"And that's funny because …?"

"Because this is the first time I've been on the receiving end of this conversation." The sincerity in his tone belied any trace of ego.

"Well, as long as we're clear …" Kate pulled her sweater over her head and walked toward him.

Tony inhaled sharply at the sight of her nipples through her sheer black bra.

The tequila pumped through her veins, keeping her better judgment at bay. "You wanted to know what I like and now I'm going to show you." She dropped her sweater over the nearby lampshade, diffusing the room's only source of light.

Standing before him, she unzipped her jeans, and slid them to the ground. His gaze trailed the denim as it moved down between her thighs and past her calves. As soon as she stepped out of the garment, he raised his eyes upward. Her panties were a wall of solid lace, revealing nothing of what was contained within.

Kate slid them down, then kicked away the pile of discarded clothing. As he reached for her, his cell phone buzzed to life in his back pocket. They both went still.

He began to shake his head, but Kate was already backing away from him.

The fire in her eyes had been reduced to embers. "Go ahead and answer it."

He yanked the device from his jeans and checked the screen before stabbing a finger at it. Raising the phone to his ear, he watched as Kate pulled her sweater back on. She settled onto a worn plaid lounge chair across from him, drawing her legs up underneath her.

Deputy Flaherty's annoying whine filled his head. "Hi, Sheriff." The younger man launched into a pitched fit about how Deputy Carson was reneging on covering a second shift. With his attempts to placate falling upon deaf ears, Tony stood and began to pace. Finally, he agreed to come back in and cover the second shift himself.

When he hung up, Tony turned to find Kate standing by the doorway. She was completely dressed. "Sounds like you better get back in there."

He rubbed the back of his neck. "In case I haven't told you, being the boss in a small town sucks."

Kate shrugged. "I'm sure it has it perks, too."

He smiled wryly. "At the moment, none of them seem worth it."

Reaching into her pocket, she pulled out a black band and pulled her hair into a ponytail. "Honestly, I think we're better off. Let's consider it a bullet dodged."

"I can promise you *I'm* not better off. But I understand. It's probably better to keep it in the friend zone." He crossed the room and gave her a chaste peck on the cheek, then he was gone.

Shaking her head, Kate made her way back to the dark bedroom. She fell onto the bed and lay awake atop the covers for the next few hours. Intermittent splashes of regret threaded the minefield of her thoughts, serving as erstwhile paladins to keep her demons at bay.

Chapter 9

THE BLUE FILE CONTAINED a life's work, or rather, the skeletal outline of one. Nowhere in the collection of documents was an accurate depiction of the blood, sweat and sacrifice which had defined a career in public service.

Tony paused in the doorway to the conference room. The acrid smell of reheated coffee washed over him, souring his stomach enough to match his mood. He cast one last look down at Jenna Wheaton's personnel file before calling out to the chamber's sole occupant. "Here it is."

Derek Samuelson, the exceptionally slender, fifty-two-year-old Washington State Patrol investigator sat at the table. Appearing to be in jeopardy of disappearing beneath the massive stacks of paper surrounding him, he glanced up from the report he was reading. "Thanks, you can leave it on the table."

Last night, Samuelson and his team had descended upon the crime scene with pinpoint precision. Over the past few years, the citizens of Washington state had made it clear they were not about to allow the fox to guard the henhouse. Regulations required local law enforcement to cede authority of investigations to oversight agencies such as the WSP.

Whether Tony liked it or not, Deputy Wheaton, and by extension Tony's entire department, was now the subject of an investigation. Samuelson had taken the reins last night without exercising undue ego or engaging in false flattery. The approach had earned him Tony's respect.

Watching a shortage of resources for an unknown young girl turn into a veritable bounty of resources for the death of a convicted pedophile had rubbed Kate the wrong way. After submitting to a seemingly endless barrage of questions about how the attempt to arrest Delford had turned into a homicide, she had been more than ready to accept Tony's invitation to go out for drinks, as well as everything afterward. While their parting had not been unpleasant, her drastic change in demeanor had made it appear last night's offer was a one-time deal. He hoped like hell that was not the case.

The taste of her kiss still lingered in his mouth. It had teased his senses on the brief ride back to his place, rising to almost unbearable proportions when he jumped into the shower before heading back in to relieve Flaherty.

As much as he wanted her body, what he most needed from Kate was her help. Although he hated to admit it, he would not be surprised if the added layers of bureaucracy and public scrutiny sent her running. He couldn't blame her. As much as he had originally wanted the sheriff's position, there had been a split-second last night when poor Wheaton had squinted up at him through the blood and bits of Delford's brains when he had almost taken off running himself.

Pushing all thoughts of the hot detective and his beleaguered deputy from his mind, Tony placed Wheaton's file on the table. "When I came on board as sheriff, I wanted to make sure everyone in this department understood the gravity of walking around with a gun strapped to their hip. I instituted mandatory quarterly training classes. You'll find all the certificates of completion in here."

Intelligent blue eyes settled on Tony's. "I reviewed the footage from Wheaton's body camera. It's like a textbook training video."

"That's a credit to Wheaton as much as to the training."

The investigator's expression remained impassive. "When I complete my investigation, I'll forward my findings to the county prosecutor who will review the evidence and decide whether there is cause to proceed with charges."

"I understand. The last thing I want is any appearance of a rush to judgment. This department has had a squeaky-clean record and I don't want it to change."

"Perception is important. We're going to hold a joint press conference with the Mayor this afternoon. The Governor plans to make a statement afterward and we'll want you to be there. Wheaton's name will be made public."

Tony winced. "I assumed as much. It's the right thing to do for the sake of transparency, but it's going to suck for her son. The poor kid is going to know people are questioning whether his mom is a hero or simply a bully with a gun."

For a moment, Tony thought Samuelson's features were about to morph into something approaching sympathy, but the man merely nodded and resumed his reading.

Without another word, Tony headed back to his office. Retrieving his coat and hat from the row of hooks behind his door, he walked to the front desk where he endured a full three minutes of Deputy Flaherty's impassioned protests to what he considered Samuelson's excessive use of the coffee machine.

Taking a minute to back the younger man off the emotional ledge, Tony emerged into the parking lot and jogged through the light rain to his car. Starting the ignition, his heart rate climbed by leaps and bounds. He smiled, unsure whether the increased pace was a response to who he was about to see, or what he was about to find out.

∨

Familiarity with the route made the trip to the coroner's office seem much shorter than it had been on Kate's first visit. She took a sip of the latte Tony had presented when he arrived at the cottage to pick her up fifteen minutes ago. Mercifully, the drink came with no strings attached. There'd been no reference to the previous night's tryst, only a brief smile and an invitation to be on their way.

During the drive, he had briefed her on his interactions with Samuelson. He had almost finished when they were interrupted by a call from the Mayor. Kate had listened as he fielded round after round of questions. With every passing mile she learned in addition to being an exceptionally promising lover, the sheriff was also an exceptional gamesman.

Finally, Tony ended the call. Shaking his head, he relaxed his grip on the steering wheel and glanced at her. "I want to tell you how sorry I am for getting you caught up in all this. You know I won't blame you if you want to call it quits."

The last statement was directed toward the windshield, but Kate responded to it anyway. "I may regret it, but with Wheaton on administrative leave, Lloyd busted down to desk duty for leaking like a sieve and your entire department the target of a state investigation, I don't see how I can walk out on you now."

She glanced out the window then fixed her gaze back on his profile. "So, I'm staying on to help for the next few weeks. But you have to promise to keep me out of the spotlight."

Letting out a long sigh of relief, he turned back to her. "You've got it. By the way, has anyone ever told you how awesome you are?"

"Only the people who desperately need my help."

"I never thought I'd be happy to be considered desperate, but here I am." Something wicked sparked in his eyes as he gazed briefly at her.

Kate let the words hang in the air. A few moments later, Tony pulled into the lot. Mildred Gellert greeted them at the back door. She had exchanged her blue scrubs for jeans and a knit sweater adorned with cats in various stages of repose.

After completing the check-in process, they followed her into a small office adjoining the autopsy suite. The workspace was as immaculate and organized as the rest of the facility. An artful display of ceramics incorporated the coroner's artistic nature into the decor.

"I take it you heard what happened last night?" Tony asked.

Stepping behind her desk, Mildred settled into a chair which was more like a cast off from a chic dining room table than something one might find in a typical office. "The Mayor called me first thing this morning to tell me WSP is taking over Delford's autopsy. I reminded him playing with political grenades is not my thing. Anyway, let's get to the reason I called you over here—Jane Doe's implants."

"I hope you've got something good." Tony mumbled, as he and Kate dropped into matching black task chairs.

"I wouldn't have called you if I didn't." Mildred winked at him as her fingers flew across a wireless keyboard.

She turned her monitor around to face them. The display featured the homepage for a corporate website. "They were part of a run of conical connection implants Gerterre Industries manufactured late last year. This particular set had been exported to an oral surgeon in Malaysia."

The coroner tapped her mouse, bringing up another window. The website was replaced with a mugshot of a southeast Asian man in his late forties. Excessive wrinkles and a deeply furrowed brow implied a history fraught with adversity.

"This is Bujang Nik. Forty-eight years old, single, and until recently, the sole practitioner in his struggling business. He was arrested two months ago in Kuala Lumpur." She brought up another window alongside the picture; it contained an arrest record.

Kate scanned the document but could not decipher a single word of the Malay language. She raised an eyebrow. "For?"

"Accessory to human trafficking. He was getting hefty sums from a sex ring dead set on making over their teenage girls with perfect cover girl smiles. During a visit, a girl slipped an SOS note to one of his assistants. The woman made an excuse to leave the room then called the police."

"Did he talk?" Tony asked.

"He admitted knowing the girls were sex slaves. Apparently, he was required to work under the strict supervision of a handler who was also arrested at the scene. Six other girls had sat in that chair before the last one had the guts to risk reaching out for help."

"Did he give them anything else?"

"No. He committed suicide two days after he was arrested. To this day, the handler has refused to say a word."

Kate recalled the horrific sex trafficking cases she had encountered in the Bay Area. She had seen everything from traumatized little girls and boys squirreled away in building heating and cooling machinery spaces, to adults strapped to beds in perpetual states of drug-fueled delusion.

When she spoke, her voice conveyed none of the turmoil the memories evoked. "Those rings are one-stop shops. They procure victims, break them in, and have vast networks for getting them into the United States."

The facts fell into place like pieces in a puzzle in her mind. "Most of these rings operate on sheer volume. Slaves are forced to turn upwards of thirty to sixty tricks per day. Usually, it isn't so much about the slave's looks as their abilities. But if these guys are investing so much cash to make sure their girls look perfect, they must be appealing to a higher caliber clientele with more discerning tastes."

Tony's cell phone clamored to life. He glanced at the screen. "It's Samuelson."

"Go ahead and take it, I've told you all I know." Mildred grabbed a nearby cup of tea and exited the room.

Tony waited until the door closed to accept the call. He was on the phone for no more than thirty seconds before he suddenly stiffened. Pulling the device from his ear, he began tapping at the screen. Nodding to no one in particular, he resumed the call and ended it a few seconds later.

When he turned to Kate, it seemed as if the air around her was tingling with electricity.

"One of the state techs found a hidden stash at Delford's place. He was searching the bedroom, when he spotted excessive wear on the screws in a heating vent. He pulled the screws and looked in the duct. Inside was a strong box full of child porn photos. They also found a flash drive laden with digital porn, along with one other file. Samuelson emailed it to me. He wants us to watch it right now."

Tony turned his phone sideways and propped it on the desk in front of them.

Steeling herself, Kate looked at the screen. A frozen, grainy image of a concrete slab appeared with a white triangle in the center of it. Tony tapped the white play icon, prompting a low hissing from the device's speakers.

"Where are you?" The disembodied voice carried a faint echo, as well as a note of familiarity.

The image began to bounce up and down, making it appear the world was tilting on its axis. The movement became increasingly frenetic, making it impossible to discern anything in the field of view.

In the next moment, the world stood still. "Okay, there you are." The cadence and tone tickled Kate's memory while souring her stomach.

The camera had settled on a blue tarp, which had been neatly wrapped into a long, thick bundle. She leaned forward, peering intently at the screen.

In the background, she could just make out the outline of a deep pit cut into the concrete nearby. She recognized the warehouse she had visited days before, immediately recalling the putrid stench which had seared its way into her olfactory senses.

"Hold on a second, we have to be able to see you." A hint of exasperation accompanied the voice. The image went blurry again for a moment then stilled.

Instead of the floor, the camera was now fixed on the ceiling. A gloved hand and part of a white sleeve appeared. The appendage moved back and forth with steady determination. A crackling sound, reminiscent of cats running through a crinkle tunnel, blasted through the speakers.

"There you are." The exasperation in the mystery voice's tone was replaced by triumph. The arm rose, revealing a gloved hand for a split second before the image flipped again.

Delford, who Wheaton had shot the night before, appeared looking alive and well. He wore white plastic coveralls. A spark of defiance lit his eyes as he gazed directly into the camera.

"This video is my insurance policy. You better not dick with me down the road because I've got a lot more than this, I've kept other stuff—things that can prove what you're up to if you ever try to fuck me over."

The view shifted once more, sweeping down across the floor and over to the bundle. The entire tarp had been unwrapped, exposing Jane Doe's battered corpse. Copious amounts of blood streaked the sides of the plastic around the dead girl's torso.

Kate's gaze trailed down the body to the cadaver's feet which had not yet been devoured by sodium hydroxide. The only betrayal of the roiling cauldron of rage and revulsion inside of her, was the breathless release of the words, "Son of a bitch."

Delford brought the camera back around to face himself. "Remember—I know everything. Not only where you keep the girls here, but how you got them into the country and what you're doing with them. Bottom line ..." He pulled the phone closer to his face, filling the screen with a menacing glare. "DON'T … FUCK … WITH … ME!"

A spray of spittle accompanied the warning. In the next second, the intense expression was replaced with the original still image of the concrete floor.

The sheriff sat back in his seat and looked at Kate. "That's all there is."

Kate turned from the screen to look at Tony. When she spoke, her expression was downright stony. "He mentioned girls—*plural*."

"He also confirmed someone else is involved. *And* that those girls are being smuggled into the country. No wonder the victim didn't show up on any missing persons lists."

Kate nodded. "Did the WSP find anything else at the property?"

"Samuelson said there was nothing significant. But based on the video, he's going to rush the lab results for every sample they collected out there."

"So, Delford was either bluffing about having more evidence, or he split it between more than one hiding spot. Either way, this has turned into much more than a simple murder case."

As soon as she said the words, Kate felt as if reality shifted. The same internal clock which had mercilessly counted down every moment of powerlessness during the Tower Torturer investigation, suddenly rumbled to life deep inside her.

Tony sat back in his seat, casting a forlorn look at the framed topographical map of northwestern Washington hanging on the wall behind the coroner's desk. "He said the girls are being kept *here*. How many? And how long before they end up like Jane Doe?"

Recognizing the sheer size of the challenge before them, Kate decided to grasp it by the throat. "Every second that passes is another second lost. We need to go back to Delford's girlfriend. We also need to pay another serious visit to Aaru."

She narrowed her gaze. "At least we won't have to go it alone anymore. We have reason to believe the girls are the victims of human trafficking. That expands the case beyond your jurisdiction, Sheriff." Anticipating the inevitable trajectory of the dominos which had begun to fall in her mind, Kate pulled out her cell and began dialing the one phone number her recent experiences with the Tower Torturer had made her hope she would never use.

"Who are you calling?" Tony mouthed as she waited for the line to be answered.

"Someone who owes me a favor. Let's hope I can collect enough on it to keep this case from slipping through our fingers." Steeling her stomach against the sound of each successive ring, she stood and headed outside. An audience was the last thing she needed for this particular conversation.

Chapter 10

KATE STRODE THROUGH A VEIL of diamond-shaped shadows. The dizzying effect was the result of late afternoon sunlight spilling through the exterior walls of the Central Branch of the Seattle Public Library.

Comprised of five separate platforms cantilevered in an alternating pattern, the ultra-modern, eleven-story building sat poised upon one of the many hills in downtown Seattle. A steel outer frame inlaid with glass panels encompassed the entire structure, giving it the feel of an extraterrestrial greenhouse.

Kate was not looking forward to the meeting she had scheduled. Throughout the four-and-half-hour trip from Eagle's Nest, she had come up with every conceivable excuse to cancel. Yet every time she had decided to turn around, snippets of Delford's video replayed in her head, reaffirming her resolve.

Tony's investigation was stalling out and he could no longer claim absolute jurisdiction. Meanwhile, every moment was another one of torment for the captive girls. For as many personal reasons she had for wanting to avoid the FBI, she was desperate to secure their assistance.

The fact she'd been able to negotiate neutral territory was a small consolation. A mere half block up the street from the communist-esque, concrete monolith which housed the Federal Bureau of Investigation's Seattle Field Office, the library was still too close for comfort.

She boarded an elevator and soon found herself outside the designated conference room. Inhaling sharply, she opened the door into another airy space with amazing views of the surrounding buildings.

Sitting alone at the far end of a banquet-size table was a red-head whose milky white complexion was ideally suited to life under the metropolis' perpetually gray skies. She stood as Kate walked over to join her. The utilitarian hairstyle, nondescript navy-blue pantsuit, finely pressed white collared shirt and highly shined black loafers all screamed FBI.

Shrewd blue eyes catalogued every detail of Kate's face. The woman thrust her hand forward. "Hello, I'm Special Agent Blake Clayton."

"Thank you for meeting me." Kate returned the firm hand-shake as well as the scrutiny.

"The Special Agent in Charge of the San Francisco office is convinced you are a fantastic cop."

Kate took a seat. "I do my job."

"Well enough to have earned you an offer to join the Bureau. I was instructed to remind you the offer is still open, by the way."

"I appreciate it, but I'm not here for a recruitment drive. I was told you could help me."

Clayton sat back down. The decided grace with which she crossed her legs contrasted sharply against her straightforward demeanor. "Quite a bit of animosity, Detective. But understandable given your recent experiences."

Without waiting for a response, she retrieved a manila envelope from a black satchel laying on the table. "Coroner Gellert sent over a forensic facial reconstruction of your victim. Normally, it's impossible to identify girls abducted from third-world countries. You happened to luck out."

Unclasping the envelope, she retrieved a letter-sized photograph and laid it before Kate. "We obtained this from *Break the Chains*. They are a Malaysia-based human rights group working tirelessly in poverty-stricken regions throughout the third world. They try to educate families to keep them from falling prey to traffickers and help repatriate the few lucky kids who have been rescued. Some even raise money to buy the kids out of bondage."

Kate studied the stunningly beautiful image of Jane Doe as she had appeared before being beaten, murdered and tossed in a pit. Proudly wearing a school uniform consisting of a plaid skirt and white Peter Pan collar shirt, the girl sat at a rustic desk in a classroom with wooden walls and dirt floors.

"Her name is Haryati binti Tan. She disappeared from a small village in the Malaysian region of Borneo two years ago. She was sixteen at the time."

The softness in the girl's dark eyes hinted at a sweet disposition. The more Kate studied the image, the more it seemed to change. First the bone structure around one of the eyes collapsed in on itself, then the entire face washed over in blood.

Kate tore her eyes from the photo. Ignoring the constriction in her chest, she leveled her gaze on the FBI agent. "Did the local authorities have any leads?"

"According to *Break the Chains*, the traffickers used a common ploy—a handsome young man from the big city, promising a rich dowry ..."

"Her father was happy to turn her over, but the dowry never came." Kate finished.

"Exactly. According to the video you provided, Rick Delford knew Haryati was not the only one who had been brought here."

"Correct. We have no idea how many more there are or where they are being held." She chose her next words carefully before uttering them. "Which is why Sheriff Luchasetti is glad to have help from the FBI."

The agent winced. "Seattle is a port city and the sex trade is as robust as it is in San Francisco. It is a serious problem. Sadly, it's not our only priority. Since World War II, our proximity to the Boeing aircraft company has kept counterespionage at the top of the list. Include the occasional white supremacist groups and eco-terrorists, and I'm sure you can appreciate we do not have many resources to spare."

Watching Kate's features harden, she added, "I'm not saying we will fail to act. I am saying our resources are severely limited so do not expect things to proceed at the pace they did in your last case."

Kate placed her forearms on the table. "Let me be clear, I don't want this to proceed in any way remotely similar to my last case. I'm not asking for the FBI to take over this investigation. We need intel and support."

Agent Clayton placed a hand on the envelope and leveled Kate with a leaden stare. "Jurisdiction dictates which agency will head the investigation from the point, Detective Barnes." She waited for the statement to penetrate before continuing. "As it is, our lack of resources and your popularity with the powers that be may allow you to get your wish—for a while."

When the deep furrow in Kate's brow disappeared, the woman picked up the envelope once again. "There is something else you'll want to see." She pulled out a second photo.

Kate reached for the picture. It took a moment to pick out the subtle features distinguishing the new lovely visage from Haryati's. Most notably, it was the way the girl's smile did not carry quite the same sense of lightheartedness.

"Zamira binti Tan, the victim's younger sister who disappeared the same night. Haryati had left a note saying she was running off to marry her suitor, but there was no mention of Zamira. She may very well be one of the additional girls to whom Delford was referring."

Kate had heard each of the words Clayton said, but only one stuck in her head and clutched at her heart. Haryati had not been able to save herself, let alone her younger *sister*. Kate knew exactly how it felt to fatally fail a younger sibling. She forced her eyes to hold the agent's gaze while raw pain tore at her soul.

The agent continued. "Detective Barnes, the Bureau owes you, and I've been told to pay off the marker. Please do not prove my faith is misplaced."

Kate laid the photo on the table and stared at the woman. "I take my job very seriously."

The redhead raised an eyebrow. "But that's just it. This is not your job. You are involved in an investigation which has nothing to do with you or the SFPD."

"Justice has nothing to do with organizations or self-interest."

"I knew I'd like you. Can you stay in Seattle for a couple of nights?"

Kate leaned back in her seat and nodded. Despite her protests, Tony had insisted she book a cheap hotel room on the south side of the city rather than tough through the epic round trip.

"Good, for starters we will have you …"

A loud knock sounded from the hallway. Kate turned in time to watch a tall Latino man, at least ten years her senior, walk into the room. The canvas duffle bag slung over his shoulder clashed violently with his pinstripe suit.

"It's a pleasure to meet you, Detective Barnes."

She stood. "I'm sorry, you are?"

Depositing the bag on the table, the man cast a wary look at Clayton, who announced, "This is Special Agent Fuentes."

Placing his hands on his hips, he smiled broadly. "So, you're going to be my date for tomorrow night?"

"Your what?" Kate demanded.

"She doesn't seem to know much, does she?" Gesturing to Kate, Fuentes shot a disapproving look back at the redhead.

Clayton stood. "I haven't briefed her yet." She turned to Kate. "Like I said, we cannot spare the immediate resources this case demands. At this point, Agent Fuentes will need to rely on local resources to aid in the investigation. Meaning you will report to him and follow his direction. Understood?"

Kate folded her arms over her chest. "Looks like I will be working for the FBI whether I want to or not."

Clayton shrugged. "This is the best offer you are going to get. Were the circumstances evenly remotely different, I can assure you a San Francisco detective who is on personal leave would not be allowed anywhere near this investigation."

She turned back to Fuentes. "I trust you can bring her up to speed in time."

He cast a critical eye on Kate. "If not, she'll find her ass on the first bus back to San Francisco."

May 1

Kate sat in the white Escalade doing her best to ignore the painfully repetitive series of rudimentary beats blaring through the speakers. The incessant barrage had persisted for the entire twenty-minute ride. She decided Agent Fuentes was either an aficionado of patently offensive rap lyrics or he was eagerly immersing himself in his undercover persona.

Shifting in her seat, Kate tugged at the red spandex dress, which clung mercilessly to her body. Despite the fact it was barely long enough to cover her crotch, she gamely tried to manipulate the garment down between her derrière and the leather upholstery.

"Having problems?" Fuentes inquired from the driver's seat.

"I'm still trying to decide if this is actually a dress or a glorified cocktail napkin." Glancing down at her chest, she spotted the upper rim of her nipples cresting above the red fabric. Frowning, she continued to fight with the material.

"Well, all you need to do is look good, and you certainly do."

The words were issued as a statement of fact, rather than an opportunity to demean.

Stilling her hands, Kate studied his profile in the reddish glow from the dashboard. "Thanks again for letting me tag along."

"As long as you don't fuck anything up, I'm happy to have you."

Kate accepted the words at face value. Fuentes' briefing on the deal about to go down tonight had been detailed and meticulously delivered. He had been working this case for the past eleven months and had every reason to be concerned about adding a new face at the last minute. Over the past twenty-four hours she had pored over his case notes, making every possible effort to avoid fucking it up.

"We're here," he announced without fanfare. He pulled the Escalade into a parking spot in front of a dumpy warehouse. A sleek sports coupe and two other high-end SUVs occupied spaces nearby.

He cast one last look at her. "Remember, we're going in unarmed, without backup. This guy is merely a link in the chain, and I've got my sights set much higher. Play your role, keep to the script, and don't fuck it up. As I told you, this guy is one of the biggest players in the market and he deals exclusively with higher-end clientele. His buyers' tastes are a bit different, but if we're lucky, we may walk out tonight with a clue to what is going on in Eagle's Nest."

"Got it." Kate grabbed the ridiculously expensive leather tote bag Fuentes had provided her. It contained the standard female fare, including a wallet with a legitimate looking Washington state driver's license proclaiming her name was Brenda Foyle.

She stepped down from the high running board, carefully holding onto the door while testing her four-inch stilettos out on the badly cracked asphalt. Once sure of her footing, she shrugged into a black faux fur coat and slammed the door shut. The Puget Sound lay a few blocks to the west, its salty aroma punctuating the bite of the chilly night air.

"Come on, Chica! I got shit to do tonight!" An unfamiliar, thick Hispanic accent weighted Fuentes' words as he made his way to a scarred door about ten feet from the vehicle. The single industrial light above him gave an ethereal glow to his pricey turquoise blue suit, and the string of gold chains, which hung from his collar in place of a tie.

Hitching her bag over her shoulder, Kate tossed her carefully straightened hair over her shoulder then sashayed over to the door. "I'm here now, okay?"

"Don't disrespect me, *puta*!" He grabbed her left arm and twisted it back painfully for the benefit of the cameras above the door and those at either corner of the building.

"I'm sorry, baby." She tried to lean in to kiss him, but he pushed her away roughly.

"Why the fuck do I keep you around?"

Forcing a simpering smile, Kate remained silent as "Hugo" knocked on the door three times. The door opened a moment later, spilling bass-heavy club music into the air.

A bear of a man stood inside the threshold. A Heckler and Koch 9mm pistol was strapped securely in the shoulder holster worn over a tight gray T-shirt. He looked over each of them, before grunting something resembling a Russian accented invitation to enter.

No sooner had they entered the 1990s era reception area, than the door slammed shut behind them. At the far end of the room two other goons guarded an open doorway. Each had an AR-15 slung over their shoulder.

Kate's coat and purse were stripped from her. The contents of the bag were dumped on the nearby reception desk. A second later, the Russian's massive hands were on her body, fingers probing every intimate curve. With a final pass up and down her thighs, he waved her away and started in on her companion.

When he was finally satisfied the couple posed no substantive threat, the burly man titled his head toward the open doorway. "Take your things and go."

Kate snatched up the unfamiliar items. Fuentes made a show of straightening his jacket, as if setting his clothing to rights could remove the indignity to which he had been subjected. Grabbing Kate by the upper arm, he glared at the Russian one final time before ushering her toward the guards.

Emerging on the other side of the doorway, they found themselves in another world. Dimly lit by floor lamps and softly colored strobe lights, the intimate area had the vibe of an upscale nightclub. Heavy gold brocade curtains hung from the ceiling, and oversized white leather couches flanked a small marble-topped bar. Except for the underlying scent of dust and mechanical fuel, it would be easy to believe this was a downtown hotspot.

A well-built man in his early forties sat at the bar. A small group of people had gathered around him. Dressed in an impeccably fitted suit, he politely held a hand up and beckoned to Fuentes.

Kate immediately recognized Maksym Belovol from the dossier photo she had received from Fuentes. According to the file, the well-connected Ukrainian had been at the sex trafficking game for a long time—having started decades earlier with his own sister.

"And here we go." Her companion murmured in her ear as he ushered her to the bar.

"I trust you came ready to buy?" the Ukrainian asked in a heavy Russian accent laced with German undertones.

"If the product is worth the hype." Fuentes accepted a glass of vodka from a lovely young Nordic bartender whose transparent white halter top left nothing to the imagination.

Appraising his guest over his drink, Belovol nodded. "We only offer the very best for our clients." His gaze slipped over to Kate, trailing from head to toe. Finally, he rose from his barstool and reached for her hand.

The moment their fingers connected, he whipped her arm up over her head and spun her around. Completing the inspection, he released Kate, then turned back to Fuentes. "I admire your taste, although I would have something done about the hair color."

Kate resisted simultaneous urges to wipe the man's touch off on her cheap dress, and to kick him in his testicles. Instead, she reached for a second glass of vodka being offered by the bartender.

"Now that all parties have arrived ..." Belovol circumnavigated the group and stood in front of an overlapping section of the curtained wall. "... the bidding will commence."

The material parted, revealing a wide hallway lined by more gold curtains. Soft LED floor strips illuminated the path, reminiscent of those reserved for emergencies on commercial planes.

Kate and Fuentes exchanged a brief look, then followed their host. About twenty feet in, Belovol stopped and turned to his right. On cue, the drapes parted to reveal a thick plexiglass wall, through which the contents of a dimly lit chamber could be seen.

Complete with an elephant tusk poster bed, mosquito netting, safari props, and a zebra rug, it resembled a hotel room in an African safari theme park. Belovol waited while the rest of his guests jockeyed for position. When he was confident everyone had a prime view, he knocked soundly against the clear wall.

The beat of tribal drums filled the air. A few moments later, a figure rose up from the mass of fur blankets on the bed. Clad only in a leopard print bikini, which barely contained her ample breasts, the woman came to her knees. Her waist-length, blonde hair had been teased out to resemble a lion's mane. Inches of wickedly sharp black acrylic nails adorned her fingertips. Staring at her audience with a carnal magnetism, she ran the faux claws over her body with unbridled ferocity.

As the drum rhythms increased, she slid down from the end of the bed and crawled toward the assembly. She moved like a jungle animal, coming close to the wall before wheeling around to offer an unobstructed view of the upper portion of her thong which disappeared neatly between her firm buttocks. Casting a glance over her shoulder, she snarled at the audience and began to bounce up and down with the music.

Belovol's voice rang out above the sound. "Option 1: Twenty years old; five foot, seven inches; trained in aerial acrobatics. Excellent health with exceptional anal, oral and vaginal skills. Equally skilled at pleasuring men and women."

Spinning forward once again, the young woman placed her hands against the barrier. She locked eyes with each of the potential buyers in turn before she straightened and began a slow but determined striptease.

Hooking a thumb into the straps on either shoulder, she pulled aside the bikini top. Two potential buyers leaned forward to get a better look at the set of intricately crafted claw tattoos encircling her areolas. Casting off the material, she untied one corner of her bottoms, then reached for the other side. The open mouth of a panther, similar in artistic detail to the tattoos on her breasts, had been inked around her vagina.

Seizing the fabric from behind, she tugged upward, pulling it into the cleft between her legs. She whipped the material around with a flourish, then caught it into her mouth, where she sucked greedily on that which had just traveled between the intimate folds of skin.

"One hundred thousand U.S. dollars." Belovol stated simply, before turning and walking away. The music ended abruptly, and the curtains swung closed.

Fuentes grabbed Kate's arm, propelling her behind Belovol. They proceeded down the hallway, stopping periodically before five more chambers. From an outer space cosmonaut, whose naked body was adorned with phosphorescent body paints, to a paramilitary soldier whose nipples and clitoris had been pierced with bullet-shaped jewelry, Kate had stood outside the wall of each young woman's cell as they debased themselves in the simple hope of pleasing their potential new owner.

As Belovol called out each new set of selling points, Kate felt as if she were listening to a livestock auctioneer in the 4-H corner of the state fair. By the time the curtain opened on the final room at the end of the hall, Kate was practically vibrating with the compulsion to slit the throats of each and every one of the potential buyers in her group.

It did not help that, like the Tower Torturer's victims, every girl was blonde. By the time she gazed into the last room her rage was almost uncontainable. Decorated in varying hues of pink and white, the chamber was adorned with artwork designed to appeal to a toddler.

An oversized playpen stood between the canopy bed along the far wall and the room's occupant. Hair parted into two long braids; she was dressed in a high-collared, ruffled dress which did not quite cover her bare bottom. Instead of interacting with the audience, the young woman merely sat upon the floor, licking a ridiculously large lollipop. The gentle lisp of a child's voice reciting nursery rhymes was the only accompanying audio track.

Unable to control his interest, one of the men standing behind Kate pushed her aside and placed a hand on the plexiglass. She stepped aside willingly, backing up against the curtains on the far wall. Belovol had just begun to speak when Kate's eye was drawn back to the start of the hallway.

The guard who had patted her down was there with a slender,

bald man. The new arrival gestured to Fuentes, then retreated back from where he had come. The gargantuan reached for his handgun and started down the hall. Kate looked back at Fuentes whose eyes were locked on the vile display.

She turned back to the Russian. Despite his size the man moved with the speed of a cat. He had already made it down the hall and was only a few feet from the agent.

Kate made a move toward him, but she was too late. The guard had placed the barrel of his pistol against Fuentes' temple. The lights went out in the nursery and the audio track ceased.

Their host turned and raised an eyebrow. "Do we have a problem, Alexei?"

"Facial recognition confirmed this man is FBI!" The guard snarled.

The rest of the guests backed away as if the acronym was a venomous snake. Belovol turned to reach for Kate but was met with a punishing punch to the jaw. Momentarily dazed, he offered no objection when she reached into his jacket and pulled out the gun she had noticed when he had spun her around earlier.

Ducking behind Belovol, she held the gun to his head. "Okay, Alexei. Put your weapon down."

The guests rushed for the exit, jamming the doorway where the other two guards were now trying to enter.

"I said, drop it!"

He looked from Kate to his boss and back again.

"Do as she asks Alexei. Do not worry, they will not be leaving here alive."

"Of course, sir." He lowered his weapon, allowing Fuentes to pluck it from his grasp.

"Now get out." Kate warned, shoving the muzzle hard against Belovol's temple.

The two other guards had finally made it into the hallway. A short hand gesture from their leader sent them scurrying back from where they had come. As soon as Alexei disappeared, Kate glanced upward. A series of cables hung from the ceiling, suspending the curtains in their current positions.

"What is this place?" she asked her captive.

"It is the place you will die. There is no way out, except through my guards."

"Fuck you, scumbag. Fuentes, try the curtains."

Nodding, the agent grasped a handful of brocade hanging between the toddler theme cell to his right and the cosmonaut cell to his left. He jerked downward, tearing the material from its moorings to reveal the dark emptiness beyond.

"Glad I came along?" Kate asked the agent.

"Jury's out. Come on!" Fuentes ducked into the opening.

"Move!" she hissed, shoving Belovol ahead of her.

Coming to the end of the cells, Fuentes backed up against the wall on his left. He peeked around the corner but was greeted with a flurry of automatic gunfire.

He snapped his head back, leveling Kate with a wide-eyed glare. "Shit!"

The gunfire stopped as abruptly as it had begun. A loud clanging sound rang out, then the entire world was suddenly ablaze in stark white light. Between the cells, Kate glimpsed the vastness of the open warehouse.

Belovol smirked. "You will not survive this."

Before she could draw a breath to respond, the entire building came alive with gunfire. Each new spray of bullets added to the echoes of those preceding it. Kate winced, unsure whether her eardrums would begin to bleed before her heart exploded in her chest.

The torture continued for a few more minutes, before ebbing to a gradual halt. Ears still ringing, Kate almost missed the new voice calling out through the emptiness.

"We've neutralized four hostiles. You okay, Fuentes?"

The agent brightened at the sound of the familiar voice. "We're fine, Clayton!"

"Good. Hold tight, we're on our way to you!"

Visibly relieved, Fuentes turned and grinned at Kate. His dark eyes softened when he noticed how violently the gun trembled in her hand.

Kate scowled back at him. "You said we were going in without backup."

His wink was laced with mischief. "I had to make sure you were properly motivated."

Chapter 11

THE PLASTIC FBI VISITOR'S BADGE swayed like a pendulum against Kate's front shirt pocket as she hurried down the hall behind Fuentes. She was running on fumes, having skipped breakfast to ensure she would arrive at the requested time.

The debrief with Agent Clayton had ended a little more than six hours ago. Kate had barely returned to her hotel room, stripped off the insipid red dress and slipped into bed before she had been awakened by a call from Fuentes. Belovol's attorney had requested a conference to discuss a potential plea deal.

The immediacy of the request implied Belovol placed more faith in the U.S. judicial system than he did in whoever pulled his strings. Apparently, the federal prosecutor was equally as anxious. She had rearranged her schedule for the ten o'clock meeting.

Kate had been invited to listen in. The offer was a further extension of the FBI's good will. She had no intention of making them think twice about it. After a five-minute shower, she pulled her damp hair into a ponytail and headed over to the FBI building.

Fuentes stopped at the door to the observation room and opened it for her. Kate followed him inside, coming to stand before a long rectangular window that looked into the adjoining interrogation room.

Peering through the glass, she studied each of the three people seated at the black wooden table. Belovol sat next to a gray-haired man who had the unmistakable polished veneer of a well-paid defense attorney. The Ukrainian sat slouched in his chair. An intricate web of wrinkles, softened by the dim light at the warehouse, now stood out in vivid detail under the harsh overhead lights.

Kate's glance shifted to the federal prosecutor who sat across the table from the two men. Short, dark hair graying at the temples, framed the slender woman's exceptionally narrow face. She appraised Belovol from behind thin black rimmed glasses.

Fuentes flipped a switch mounted to the right side of the window. A second later, the prosecutor's controlled tone filled the room.

"The United States government is not inclined to treat your client with any lenience, Mr. Sayers."

Belovol's attorney did not miss a beat. "On the contrary, I think you are very interested, Ms. Prescott. You need information from my client … it will only be given with an assurance of both witness protection and full immunity."

The prosecutor raised an eyebrow. "Those are a big asks, Mr. Sayers. Your client hasn't even been in custody for twenty-four hours, yet here you are ready to make a deal. Why should I believe anything coming out of his mouth?"

He glanced at Belovol whose eyes bore into his. "Let's say my client is aware of the considerable aversion his employers have to the fact he has found himself in your custody. Upon my advice, he believes a deal would benefit both parties, but only upon those conditions."

In the ensuing silence, Kate and Fuentes exchanged a glance. The agent opened his mouth to speak, but the sound of the prosecutor's voice cut him off.

"I will not consent to anything until I know what you're offering."

Belovol leaned forward. "I don't talk until you guarantee immunity and protection!"

The prosecutor narrowed her gaze. "Mr. Belovol, need I remind you we picked up four young women last night who you were seeking to sell at an auction? We have also recovered your security video and the accompanying audio tracks. In the meantime, we have executed warrants on your condo. We now have access to your phone; computer, and both of your safety deposit boxes. You hold no cards here."

Sayers placed a hand on Belovol's shoulder and whispered into his ear. After a brief but heated exchange, he turned back to the prosecutor. "Mr. Belovol can provide names and contact information for all buyers over the past five years."

"Not good enough." She pushed away from the table, preparing to stand.

"Wait!" Belovol's miserable tone prompted her to drop back in her seat. She crossed her arms over her chest.

Belovol ran a hand through his hair. "If I give you the people above me, there will be consequences—ones which will not stop at the bars of your jails. I will give you everything you need, but you must guarantee my safety."

The prosecutor stared at him intently before nodding. She listened as he drew an outline of the shadowy world of money, power and vice. By the end of the narration, he had painted a vivid picture of an insidiously diverse organization which had burgeoned from the seeds of a drug trafficking network. It had grown to traffic female and male sex slaves, as well as labor slaves obtained from ex-Eastern bloc countries.

Kate's lips compressed into a tight line.

As if sensing her disappointment, Fuentes whispered, "Don't worry, she'll get to it."

On cue, the prosecutor inquired. "Did you ever import girls from Malaysia?"

Belovol frowned for a moment before his eyes widened. "I have some knowledge of the Pacific markets."

Kate stepped closer to the glass.

"Can you elaborate?"

Belovol glanced at his attorney then settled back into his seat. "The world is a big place. Why do you ask about Malaysia?"

"We have another investigation …"

"The brunette!"

"What?"

"The brunette from last night. I want to speak with her."

"You are speaking to me, Mr. Belovol, and I am the one who will determine …"

Kate did not hear the rest of the sentence. She had already turned on her heel and headed into the hallway. Fuentes hurried after her, grabbing her arm just as she began to turn the handle of the door to the interrogation room.

"Kate, stop …"

She wrenched her arm from his grasp and entered the room. A sadistic smile spread across Belovol's face. His eyes greedily appraised her, as if she were still wearing the spandex dress rather than a flannel shirt and jeans.

"And here she is …" Belovol leered triumphantly at his attorney.

Ignoring the waves of hostility emanating from the prosecutor, Kate took the empty seat next to her.

"What do you know about girls being brought in from Malaysia?" Kate asked.

"I know you should follow the advice I gave you last night and change the color of your hair."

The prosecutor practically jumped from her seat. "Mr. Sayers!"

The attorney placed a hand on his client's arm and whispered in his ear once again. Belovol tilted his head left then right, and finally nodded.

"Okay, FBI lady, what do you want to know?"

Kate did not correct the false assumption. "Who is importing the Malay girls, and who is buying them?"

"My clients are not interested in the Pacific markets."

"But you do know who is importing them?"

He stared at her from a long time before responding. "I do not know exactly, but I was approached over a year ago."

"By whom, and for what?"

"A man of little consequence. He came to me through an associate, offering a fee to import his inventory. My employers are not interested in comingling resources. I refused the offer."

Kate sat back in her chair. "But you made a counter?"

"For a fee, of course. I referred him to another man of little consequence—one whose debts might make him more open to obliging in such an operation."

Kate reached for the prosecutor's notepad and pushed it toward Belovol, who stared at her for a long moment, before borrowing his attorney's pen. He scribbled a few lines on the paper.

"As far as I know, they came to a mutually beneficial arrangement." He pushed the pad back toward Kate.

She glanced at the information before raising her gaze to his once more. "And the name of the man who requested the information?"

"You know, it might take longer than usual to beat the fight out of you, but it would be worth it. You would bring top dollar." He smirked at his attorney, who had the good sense to look away.

Kate lowered her voice to a controlled whisper. "Funny, because it wouldn't take me long to beat the fight out of you. Now answer the goddamned question!"

Belovol chuckled deeply. "No, you would break as easily as the rest. The actual time it takes varies from female to female, but you would break eventually. All of you do." Noting the fire rise in her eyes he decided to end the game.

"I told you, he was a man of little consequence. A man named Rick Delford."

∨

The unincorporated community of Sekiu stretches along the western edge of Clallam Bay. Beyond the inlet waters, the mighty currents of the Straight of San Juan de Fuca provide a natural barrier between Canada and the United States. First settled in 1879, the tiny fishing village melts easily into the surrounding landscape, with the exception of one notable oddity.

Having been both lauded and reviled by visitors, the statue known as Rosie, waited in solitary vigil at the entrance to Sekiu. Looking as if she had been rescued from a 1920's freak show attraction, Rosie was neither fish nor fowl—or more precisely, neither fish nor human. Her enormous glassy eyes, gaping mouth and upper torso were undisputedly those of the former. Yet, from the waist down she drastically transformed into that of the latter.

Despite the physical impossibility of Rosie having mammary glands, she wore a pink bra over her flat, scaly chest and a matching tennis skirt over her athletic, pale legs. Completing the ensemble were a pair of pink socks and pink running shoes. She had been sculpted in midstride, doomed by the artist to an eternity of perpetual departure without any hope of arrival.

Exhausted after the long drive from Seattle, Kate sped right by the Front Street turnoff from Highway 112. A split second after the wash from her headlights illuminated Rosie's gaping grin, Kate hit the brakes and made a U-turn.

The sheriff had told her to keep an eye out for the oddity, but his basic description had failed to do it justice. Perhaps it was the way the car's headlights bounced off the unusual features, or maybe it was the fact it had been less than twenty-four hours since Kate had attended a human auction. Either way, something about the statue struck a discordant inner note as she wound her way along the bay front road to the marina.

The sheriff's SUV was one of few vehicles in the marina parking lot. Soft lights spilled from the boats moored in the small harbor, reflecting on the water in orange blurs. Kate parked the Jeep and hopped out. The clean saltwater air filled her lungs, while the gentle splash of boats bobbing gently alongside the docks teased her ears.

Tony stood at the entrance. His gaze swept up and down her body as she jogged toward him.

Whatever his thoughts on her appearance, he confined his comments to the task ahead. "*The Foul Rudder* pulled in about twenty minutes ago."

Kate nodded. Upon leaving the FBI offices, she had called Tony to brief him on the meeting with Belovol. During the intervening hours, the sheriff had dug up crucial intel on the name the Ukrainian had provided. According to Washington state records, Nevil Wyman was a thirty-nine-year-old fisherman who happened to be the registered owner of a large boat dubbed *The Foul Rudder*.

According to Tony's sources, within the past eighteen months Wyman had lost his house and his family due to the vice grip of a methamphetamine addiction. The boat was all that remained of what had once been the life of a well-respected member of the community.

Tony scrutinized Kate's tired expression. "Are you sure you are up to this? You've been running hard for the last few days. I can handle this if you want to get back to Eagle's Nest."

"I'm fine."

Despite the concern in his expression, Tony headed for the dock. "Watch it," he warned a few moments later, as he stepped onto the floating structure.

Something in his tone made her nerves stand on edge, but she followed without comment.

Moored in the last slip at the end of the dock, *The Foul Rudder* rocked softly along with the current. Built in British Columbia more than sixty years earlier, the thirty-six-foot trawler looked ready for duty. While the wheelhouse was enshrouded in darkness, enough diffused light spilled from corners of the windows in the main cabin to cast a romantic light on its fading paint and rusty rigging.

Tony approached the aft of the boat and called out. "Nevil Wyman?"

Silence ensued.

Increasing his volume, the sheriff repeated the call. A soft scraping sound could be heard somewhere below the water line. Ten seconds later, the rear door to the main cabin opened, spilling light onto the deck.

"Who wants to know?" Clad in a sweatshirt and jeans, with a black beanie pulled low over his furrowed brow, Wyman peered into the darkness.

"I'm Sheriff Luchasetti and this is Detective Kate Barnes. We'd like to come aboard and ask you a few questions about your boat."

The man looked back inside as if he were about to retreat but seemed to think better of it. Turning back to Tony, he dropped his head to one side. "What kind of questions?"

Kate rubbed her arms over the sleeves of her jacket for effect. "Please Mr. Wyman, I've driven all the way from Seattle and it's freezing out here. May we explain inside?"

He gave them an additional once-over. "All right. But I don't have long."

"Thank you." Kate put her right foot onto the gunwale and extended her hand.

Wyman paused to wipe his hands on his jeans before taking hers and helping her aboard. Letting the sheriff fend for himself, he motioned for Kate to precede him inside.

The space was cramped, with a small kitchen to the right and a built-in table with bench seating on the left. A framed photograph of a natural-looking blonde flanked by two smiling kids was tucked into a built-in shelf above the counter. The metal on each side of the frame was worn exactly where two hands might fit were it to be clutched tightly for excessive periods of time. Straight ahead a series of steps disappeared into the darkness below.

Ignoring the crusted-on relics of a least four different meals dotting the gray plates strewn around the table, Kate took a seat at the end of one of the benches. Tony entered the cabin behind her but remained standing as the boat's owner closed the door against the night.

Turning away from the exit, Wyman stood and stared at the other man's uniform as if it were an unwelcome guest. "So, what d'ya want to know about my boat?"

"Why don't you sit down, Mr. Wyman?" Kate asked.

"Yeah, sure." He adjusted his beanie with his right hand then crossed the small distance and took a seat across from her.

"We understand you are an associate of a man named Belovol."

The fisherman's gaze flew toward the stairs before coming back to Tony. "I run a fishing business. A lot of people come through here—crew members, charter fares. I can't remember all their names."

"You were in debt to this man for large sums of money related to your drug habit. Does that help jog your memory?"

Wyman's gaze fell to the floor. Eventually he nodded. "Yeah."

In the following stillness, Kate's eyes returned to the photo. Before she glanced away, something about the child on the right drew her eye. Recognition flashed.

For a split second, Kate thought of her partner back in San Francisco. Tyler Harding was one hell of a detective, and it was not only due to the fact he was more seasoned than her. He had a more natural way of connecting with people that put them at ease.

Doing her best impression of her partner, Kate started quietly. "Mr. Wyman, sometimes we do things we would never do because of the people we love. And sometimes those people, no matter how wonderful they are, can be very hard to love."

Wyman's lips tightened into a line. For a split second he looked as if he might cry.

"Your daughter suffers from an illness?" Kate prompted.

The fisherman stared at the floor, then nodded almost imperceptibly.

"My sister suffered from a degenerative bone disease. She died at ten. I understand how much you just need to get away from it all sometimes. The meth helped at first, didn't it?"

"Yeah," he choked. "At first it gave me a little reprieve from the constant worry and pain. But then …"

"Then it started causing more worry and pain." Kate finished for him.

"I swear I never would've gotten involved with those bastards. I knew it was wrong, but the medical bills were piling up and my ex-wife, she lost her job, and …"

"And you needed more meth …" Kate whispered.

"Yeah, yeah, I needed more meth."

"So, Belovol set you up with Rick Delford."

Tony jumped in. "Here's the deal, Wyman. Belovol is in FBI custody and Delford is dead. We know everything about his activities." The truth and the lies comingled effortlessly.

"Look, ya may not believe this, but I still have no idea exactly what was in those boxes. All I did was take Delford out to the shipping lanes to meet the freighter."

"How did they get the boxes on board?"

Wyman swiped a hand across his mouth. "They winched 'em

over and dropped 'em into the hold. Transfers at sea can be very dangerous. These waters'll take your ship faster than ya can say help. It's why I got paid so well." He shot a wayward glance at Kate. "I needed the money—I owed Belovol a lot, and he said he knew a way I could make enough to pay him back. There was the medical bills and I didn't ..."

"You didn't have a choice," Kate offered.

The fisherman sighed. "That's the bitch of it. I did have a choice. I never should've started with the fucking meth in the first place."

Kate sat back, momentarily stunned by the parallels between this conversation and the one she had had with Chloe last week.

"You really expect us to believe you didn't know what you were hauling?" Tony demanded.

Before the fisherman could respond, Kate laid a reassuring hand on his arm and asked, "Can you show us where you put the boxes in the hold?"

Wyman thought for a moment, then nodded. Wordlessly, he led them down the stairs, along a narrow hallway, and through a tiny door. He flipped a light switch and made way for them to enter behind him.

The cramped space stunk of the sea and dead fish. Wyman gestured to an area about three feet ahead, where metal brackets dotted the floor. "Once they were offloaded from the freighter, I secured 'em in here."

"And you never looked inside them?"

"No. Delford showed up at the agreed time. He didn't talk much the whole trip. All he told me was to strap 'em in, then winch 'em out back on land."

"You brought them back here?" Kate asked.

His mouth curved into a wry smile. "'Course not." He gestured toward the door. "Didn't ya see all the buildings on the hill out there? This marina sits under the eyes of practically everyone in town. We dropped 'em off at a dock on the Straight."

"Where?"

"About thirty miles east. Somebody's private property I think."

"Can you take us there?"

"Not by boat. The waters out on the straight will chew us up tonight."

"Then we'll drive." The sheriff's tone left little room for debate.

Chapter 12

AS THE ODOMETER CLIMBED, so did Kate's anxiety. With each passing mile, they were getting closer.

Up ahead, the sheriff's blue and red lights flashed in the darkness, magnifying the sense of urgency. Kate clenched her teeth against the jaded voice of experience whispering in her ear. *It might already be too late to save the missing girls.* Each time the thought had resurfaced in her mind, it sprouted new claws and tore at her heart.

In response, she recited one of the many positive affirmations Dr. Wissel had taught her. *"You're doing your best, and it's the best you can do."*

Tony's right turn signal joined the palette of blazing lights, dragging Kate up from the depths of the dark ruminations. Barely tapping her brakes, she trailed the sheriff onto a narrow driveway that veered northward.

The Jeep bounced along the increasingly pock-marked road for another two hundred feet before emerging into a clearing. A one-story, blue and white Victorian sat at the far end of the open space. Elaborate lace curtains diffused the warm light spilling from the windows.

To the right, a period-era shed squatted in the darkness. The paint was badly faded and the small windows on either side of the front door looked like they had not been washed in over a decade. Branches encroached on all sides, giving the impression the small structure had already resigned itself to the inevitability of being devoured by the surrounding woods.

Peering around, Kate was glad they had taken the time to offload Wyman. Before leaving the marina, Tony had insisted he show them the location on a map. Then he had called the neighboring sheriff in Port Angeles to make the necessary requests for support and clearance in the neighboring jurisdiction. The custody exchange with a PA deputy hadn't eaten too much time off the clock.

Kate eased the Jeep alongside the sheriff's SUV and cut the engine. Willing the veil of professional detachment firmly back into place, she retrieved her Glock from the glove compartment. Seconds later, she joined Tony on a short march toward the shed.

Weapons pointed at the ground, they approached from the right, careful to stay out of sight from the windows. Placing his shoulder against the wood paneling, the sheriff raised his flashlight to the grimy glass. The dim beam cut across three dusty old saw-horses, and a well-used workbench mounted to the far wall. A few rusty old handsaws hung from the ceiling, but otherwise the space was empty.

The blare of headlights reflected off the windows, drawing their attention back to the driveway. Holstering their weapons, they turned to find two PA patrol vehicles pulling into the small clearing.

Tony nodded to each of the male deputies as they exited their vehicles. "Thanks for coming out. Detective Barnes and I will …"

"Excuse me, Sheriff," the younger deputy with black rimmed glasses interrupted. "I know we need to move fast, but I want to make sure you know whose house this is before we go knocking on the door."

"The records say it's owned by Celia Verson."

The deputy winced. "I went to school with her. Verson is her married name, but she was divorced two years ago, so she's back to using her maiden name—Mayhew."

Tony looked at Kate. "Well, I guess it makes sense Delford would use his girlfriend's house. I was supposed to meet with her tomorrow to see if she could remember anything else that might help us. Now is better than later." He motioned for the second deputy to take a position alongside the shed. Kate fell into step with the sheriff behind the younger man.

The moment they reached the porch, the sexy chords of an old jazz standard crept across the night air. Kate and Tony strode up the steps behind the deputy and waited while he rapped on the front door.

"I'm coming!" The voice bore a slight tremor. A second later the music abruptly ended, immediately replaced by a shuffling sound near the front left window. A hand clenched one side of the curtain and pulled it aside. A pair of pale blue eyes scanned the porch. They belonged to a face which looked as if it had recently weathered a horrible storm, one which had nothing to do with the elements.

The curtain fell back into place. The shuffling sound resumed, then drew nearer to the door. Kate listened to the sound of hardware flipping back and forth before the door finally swung inward.

"Hello, Nolan." The greeting was directed at the deputy from a woman who stood no taller than five feet. Silver clips neatly pinned back straight brown hair above each ear. Deep hollows under her matching brown eyes made her appear gaunt despite the extra twenty pounds padding her hips. Clad in a peach robe and matching slippers, she crossed her arms over her chest.

"Good Evening, Celia. Sorry to bother you so late. Sheriff Luchasetti here drove over from Eagle's Nest because he would like your help. But first, we need to know if you have anyone else here with you tonight?"

"Oh, God! What is it now? That monster is dead! Can't you please leave me alone?" Her lower lip vibrated.

Tony offered a disarming smile. "Please Ms. Mayhew, we really do need your help. We'd like to start by checking out your house."

Her features collapsed. "My home?" She cast her gaze about

as if hell's worst demons might be hiding in the walls. "Do you think he did something here? Oh God …"

Deputy Nolan stepped inside and laid a hand on her shoulder. "Don't worry, Celia, we'll just need to check everything out and make sure you're safe. No one is here with you tonight, right?"

Panicked eyes darted from face-to-face before settling back on the familiar one. "Yes, I'm alone. Is there some reason to think I'm not …?" The words trailed off as the deputy slowly guided her through a wide doorway on the right.

Tony and Kate hurried across the threshold into a tight foyer which opened into a short hallway. At the far end a door stood partially open, providing a glimpse of a white enamel stove standing alongside an ancient refrigerator.

To their left, Nolan was slowly escorting their host across a tidy living room toward a thickly padded recliner. Kate stepped into the room which was redolent with the smell of lavender.

A glance confirmed there were no other occupants in the room. Kate stepped back in the foyer and pulled her gun, keeping it pointed down while Tony gently closed the door to the living room.

"I'll take the hall," she murmured as the sheriff pulled his weapon.

Tony nodded and started toward the dining room across the way. Within minutes, they had searched the hall, dining room, kitchen and two back bedrooms comprising the fifteen-hundred-square-foot Victorian. Finding no sign anyone else was present, they holstered their weapons and rejoined Nolan in the living room.

Betraying no hint of disappointment, Tony smiled brightly. "All clear, Celia. Thanks for letting us take a look."

She looked up from where she sat perched at the edge of a recliner. "Sheriff, I still don't exactly understand what you were looking for. Can't you please tell me what this is about?"

Kate thrust her hand forward. "We are very sorry to have disturbed you tonight, Celia. My name is Detective Barnes. We'd like to ask you some questions about Mr. Delford."

The woman stared at Kate's hand as if it were a species from another planet. "I already contacted a realtor. I'm moving out of here—as far away from here as I can get. He was here ... in this house. I let him come here, I let him ..." The last words were lost in a series of choking sobs.

Kate retracted her hand, then took a seat on the oversized sectional across from Celia. Tony sat down next to her while Deputy Nolan remained standing near the recliner.

The sheriff waited until the outburst began to ebb then abruptly changed topics. "When was the last time your dock was in use?"

"My dock?" She glanced at Nolan. "I never use it. My ex-husband used to fish for Coho. He had the boat and he took it with him when he left. I've never used the dock since then."

"Did Delford ever ask you to use it?"

"No. He didn't have a boat. At least I didn't think he did. Obviously, I didn't know him very well." Her eyes found Kate's gaze and held it.

Kate had seen the look many times before. Celia was merely another in a long line of victims of sexual predators whose inner darkness had destroyed the light in those around them.

"Unfortunately for the good people, bad people lie well. I know you feel like your world has been torn apart Celia, but please trust me when I tell you, this had nothing to do with you."

The other woman's eyes filled with tears once more. Her words spilled out in a breathy whisper. "But how did I not know? Why didn't I look him up online before I dated him? There are sites. You can find out ... I didn't even try!"

Tony leaned forward. "Celia, there's something you can do now. You can help us."

127

"Help with what? The bastard is dead."

"We are investigating some other crimes he may have been involved with."

"Besides the dead girl?"

Tony stared at her evenly. "Celia, it is very important you tell us if there are any cellars, wells or other storage places on this property."

She used the cuffs of her sleeves to wipe away the tears before inhaling deeply. "No, except for the small unit out front."

"Did Delford have any places where he liked to go around here?"

"What? Like for hiking or ..."

"Were there any cabins he would go to or ..."

"No, we usually hung out at his place most of the time."

"Can you tell us about his friends?"

She shook her head and looked down at the carpet. "He didn't really have any friends. He said his parents died when he was young—he never learned to make friends easily."

Tony placed his elbows on his knees, hoping to catch her eye. "Is there anything at all you can tell us about him? Extended family? Anyone he corresponded with online?"

"No one I know of. My ex-husband was so into his buddies he never had time for me. I actually used to wonder if Rick was too good to be true." She winced but did not cry.

Kate folded her hands in her lap. "Do you have any of his personal belongings?"

Celia stood, prompting Kate and Tony to do the same. "After Deputy Wheaton told me what happened, I got so sick."

She glanced away. "I tried to go back to work, but my boss told me take the rest of the day off. So, I came straight back here and tore the house apart looking for anything that belonged to him. I boxed up all his crap and got it the hell out of this house."

As she spoke, she seemed to gather more energy. "It looked like a hurricane had torn through here. It took almost two hours before I got all the drawers and closets put to rights."

Kate glanced at Tony. "And you threw everything out?"

"Of course, I did!" Clutching at the neck of her robe, she continued in a softer tone. "Got rid of everything. Especially the ugly-ass bracelet he made for me. He told me I had to keep it forever. Even if he died."

Kate and Tony exchanged a glance.

"Did he have any reason to think he was going to die?"

She shook her head. "I told him not to say stuff like that. But he went on and on about it. Said he would never rest in peace if I didn't keep the bracelet."

"What else did you find?" Kate asked.

"Some clothes and a few other pieces of junk. All of it went to the trash." She turned on her heel and gestured toward the front window. "And I can't wait until tomorrow when the garbage company hauls it the hell out of here."

Tony took a step toward the hallway. "Celia, we'd like your permission to search the rest of your property."

"Look as long as you like. But can't you tell me what you're ...?" She was in the process of turning back to look at Tony when she realized he and Kate were already headed out the door.

∨

The world spun, not in the way a planet imperceptibly rotates on its axis. It reeled in the empty, surreal way it does when a human heart has lost its anchor.

Zamira lay on her side atop the rudimentary cot that served as her bed. LED lighting shone down from overhead fixtures, illuminating the small space which had been her prison for the last three months.

She stared straight ahead, not seeing the thick chain link walls of the eight-foot square cell or registering the persistent stench from the five-gallon portable toilets sitting nearby. The windowless room was home to ten other girls who shared identical accommodations. Like every other aspect of her environment, Zamira had ceased to acknowledge them.

Having been stripped of all hope, it was almost as if Zamira herself had ceased to exist. After she and her sister, Haryati, had been kidnapped from their village, they had been subjected to one atrocity after another. From losing their virginity in a gang rape, to spending days under the influence of mind-numbing drugs, she had prayed over and over again she might die.

Over the course of their imprisonment, she had been trained in every way imaginable to bring sexual pleasure to the human body. No act was too obscene, no fetish was off limits—including forcing the sisters into sexual acts with each other. With each passing day, she had felt as if she were transforming from a person into a human sewer, forced to receive any possible combination of bodily fluids excreted from the men she was forced to service. The punishments for failure had been unimaginably cruel.

Through it all, Haryati had begged her not to lose faith. She had insisted none of the things they had been forced to do could ever change the goodness in their hearts. Despite their captor's emphatic threats that their parents and family would be killed if they ever escaped, Haryati had promised they would be reunited with them one day. The conviction in her dark eyes had been enough for Zamira to retain a tenuous hold on hope.

After all, Haryati had always been a master storyteller. Zamira's best memories, which now seemed like fairy tales themselves, were of bedtime in their parent's house. Zamira would cuddle up against her sister on their mat, so tired from working in the rice fields she often dozed off long before Haryati finished telling her story.

Without fail, her sister would patiently retell the story during their long trek to the mission school which had been built a few miles outside of their village.

Those had been the good days. Since then, there had been nothing but bad days. The horrible abuses she had suffered over the last few years had taken so much from her she had not believed there was anything left.

Until they took Haryati away from her. It was not long after they had made the arduous journey across the ocean that her older sister had finally decided to make good on her promise to escape. Ten days ago, Haryati had been taken from her cell. She did not return for a very long time.

When she did, the overhead lights were turned on, and all the girls were roused from their cots. They were told to stand at the gates to their cells.

The soulless man to whom they had been delivered when they arrived from Malaysia, had dragged a wide-eyed, Haryati into the room. He had a large knife strapped to his belt. The bald man with the beard who had driven them from the ship to this new hell, had stood quietly beside him.

Without preamble, the soulless man announced Haryati had tried to escape. Unsheathing his knife, he had demanded the girls watch as he meted out the punishment for such abject disobedience.

Haryati had screamed to her little sister in their native tongue, imploring her to turn away. It was a request Zamira could not honor. Her sister had always been her light, even when they had descended into the darkness. She had no choice but to watch through all the screams and the bloodshed until her light was brutally snuffed out.

In the end, the screaming was joined by a second voice, one which persisted long after the life had left Haryati's body. Faces frozen in a mask of shock, the other girls had eventually returned to their beds, some placing their pillows over their heads to drown out Zamira's wails. In time, her strained vocal cords had quieted, emitting nothing more than a pathetic whisper.

The sights and smells of those moments had not left her mind for one second in the days afterward. They played on a continuous loop from which there was no reprieve.

Nothing could stop Zamira from reliving every second, not even the revelation that had occurred in the midst of them. In those final moments, while Haryati's life had been tortuously drained from her, she had made a final effort to save Zamira. What the soulless man and his accomplice had likely believed were native nonsensical ravings, had actually been Haryati's last gift to her younger sister.

Interspersed between her heart-wrenching screams, Haryati had managed to reveal what she had learned during her brief period of freedom. The information was Zamira's key to escaping and ensuring neither she nor her family would ever be hurt again.

The problem was escaping required both physical and mental strength. As it was, Zamira did not even have the emotional fortitude to rise from her cot. Besides, Haryati had always been the strong one. With her sister dead, there was no one else to save Zamira—there was only hell.

Chapter 13

MANEUVERING THE TANK TOP over her head was more difficult than it needed to be. The process would have been much simpler if Kate's toothbrush not been clenched between her teeth. Since it was well past two-thirty in the morning, she decided to forgive the lack of coordination. The last thing she needed was to heap more self-criticism on the evening's consecutive helpings of disappointment.

Slowed by the darkness, the search of Celia's property had taken the better part of two and a half hours. Despite their dogged efforts, they had found no sign of the girls. Kate had tried to salve the sting of disappointment with the knowledge they had at least acquired some new leads.

They had been forced to rifle through three-quarters of the devastated woman's trash before recovering three men's shirts, the stack of tax files, a Mariner's bottle opener, and the bracelet Delford had made for Celia.

For Delford's many failings as a human being, he had put together a decent bracelet. Thin brown leather straps joined six arch-shaped, ivory-colored medallions. Each was tapered on one end and had a pointy nub extruding from the midpoint on its outer edge.

Carved into the front-facing surface of the first five were the words "Somewhere Between Heaven and Hell." The last medallion bore a simple heart. A tiny pinwheel with a star in the center adorned the backside of all six.

Celia had pitched a fit when they had shown it to her. It had taken extensive handholding before she would even agree to look at it again. Ultimately, she had confirmed it was the one Delford had made, but she claimed to have no idea about what the little symbol on the back of each medallion represented.

Before relinquishing the item to Tony, Kate had taken multiple photos of it. Delford's insistence for Celia keep it in the event of his untimely death had aroused their joint suspicion that the piece of jewelry was the dead man's version of a breadcrumb in the insurance policy trail he had created against his co-conspirator.

As she had climbed up into the Jeep to leave, the sheriff had held the door open for a moment, quietly thanking her for the extraordinary efforts she had taken in Seattle.

With more abruptness than she intended, she had brushed him off telling him to hold his gratitude until they actually found Zamira and the other teens.

Finishing with her teeth, Kate waged a short battle with dental floss before turning off the bathroom light. She crossed the room and climbed wearily onto the bed. Instead of settling under the covers, she sat cross-legged on top of them and opened her laptop.

The same image carved into the backside of the medallions in Delford's bracelet was now visible on the display. It had taken a bit of searching before she had been able to identify it as a corporate logo.

Over the next half hour Kate immersed herself in the TekPharmaCel, website. The profile page painted the portrait of a massive global company which had expanded over the past fifteen years to include every manner of business. From farms to biotech, shampoo to candy—and seemingly everything in between—the company appeared to have a finger in every major market.

Kate studied a variety of other pages before settling on the biographies of the corporate officers. Reading through the litany of advanced degrees and corporate pedigrees, nothing stood out, other than the preponderance of photos featuring white males. At TekPharmaCel, ethnic and gender diversity clearly took a backseat to product diversity.

She was about to start running separate searches on the company's subsidiaries when her phone buzzed to life. Leaning over, she plucked it from the nightstand.

It continued to buzz as she stared at the familiar number. Until recently, those digits had dominated Kate's call log. Caught in a sudden rush of conflicting emotions, she wondered whether to answer at all. Finally, concern and another emotion she could not quite name, left her no choice but to answer.

"Hi, Barnes." The sound of Tyler Harding's voice strummed heavily on every one of her heart strings.

She feigned levity. "Hey, Harding. What's up?"

"Apparently you are, since you answered my call."

There might have been a faint slur to her previous partner's Boston-accented words, but Kate could not be sure. "Ha, ha. Very funny."

He chuckled softly. "I can be." He paused for a long moment then continued in a more somber tone. "Seriously, I wanted to see how you're doing."

"At two fifty-four in the morning?"

His voice dropped two full octaves. "We just picked up a dead twelve-year-old. Got the father in custody, but ..." He paused to take a sip of something, likely whatever had caused the now persistent slur in his speech. "I guess I needed to get my mind off things."

Kate knew exactly what he meant. Some bells you could not un-ring, no matter how hard you tried. "Nice to know I make a good distraction."

"You are my ultimate distraction." A deep and familiar note sounded in his voice, setting off alarms in her chest. It resonated with memories of the one night when she had made the epic mistake of allowing their relationship to slip from the confines of professional to intimate.

"Yeah, right. So, how's everybody at the precinct doing?"

He let out a defeated sigh then picked up the deflection thread. "Everybody's good. They all keep asking when you're coming back. Especially Captain Singh and Kevin. You know, I'm beginning to think the kid's got a crush on you."

"Kevin is only a few years younger than me. Besides, he's a tech genius. Leave him alone."

Another long pause. "I have been thinking about us a lot, Kate."

Unable to reciprocate the sentiment, she remained silent.

"Am I coming off like a dick?"

"A bit."

"Sorry. Let me start again. Hey, Barnes. How's it going? I really hope you're finding what you were looking for." The last sentence was heavily laced with emotion.

For a split second she considered lying to him. She could spin a tale replete with unicorns and rainbows, but after all they had been through lying to Harding was as pointless as lying to herself.

Unsure whether it was the exhaustion or the warm feeling his admission sparked in her chest, she felt the ice begin to thaw. Knowing she had never given him a detailed explanation for her departure, she decided to let the details spill through a very narrow sieve.

"I came here to make peace with my mom. A lot of crap went down between us when I was growing up—it needs to be put to rest. On an unrelated note, I picked up a consulting gig with the local sheriff's department."

"Our bailiwick?" He asked.

"Yes. One underage girl found dead in an abandoned warehouse. We believe there are others still out there."

"Shit, Barnes. You don't know when to quit. I thought the shrink told you to take some time to get your head straight."

"It's a small county without a lot of resources. It's been slow going, but at least we keep turning up new leads."

"How long are you planning on staying?"

"I don't know. These girls are pulling at me. I can't let go until I know they are safe."

"Meaning you didn't happen to be awake at this hour. You're working."

She glanced back at the computer screen. "Right again."

"I'm your partner. I'm always right."

"I'm on leave, so technically, you're not my partner. And you're sure as hell not always right." The sound of his laugh made her suddenly homesick.

"Come on, at least give me fifty-fifty. Anyway, how are things going with your mom?"

Her mind drifted to the three additional texts she had received from Chloe over the past few days. All remained unanswered. "They aren't at the moment. I've been too busy with the case."

"I know the work is important, but make sure you don't sacrifice your personal needs for professional ones. You and me, we've sacrificed far too much already."

"I know. Anyway, I better get back to it."

"Oh, okay. Well, thanks for taking my call. And I do miss you, Barnes. Despite the fact you can be a real pain in the ass."

"Right back at you, partner." Kate hung up, wishing she could take back the last word. There was serious question in her mind about whether she could, or should, ever work with him again.

Pursing her lips, she pushed away the confusing swirl of emotions. She pulled the laptop closer, determined to find something in the breadcrumb Delford had left for them. Her fingers flew across the keys. Site after site popped up on the screen as she conducted a series of separate searches on TekPharmaCel's subsidiaries.

Thirty minutes later, eyes dry from lack of sleep, she had to blink them several times before she could recall why one name near the edge of her screen had set off warning bells in her head. Finally, the answer emerged from her murky thoughts.

The name was one she he had heard recently. It had been spoken by Mildred Gellert. One of TekPharmaCel's subsidiaries was Gerterre Industries, the maker of Haryati's implants.

∨

The pen had not been imbued with any magical properties. No matter how fervently Kate wished it to be so, there was no way the tool would teleport Deputy Flaherty out of the sheriff's office.

She finished signing in, then shoved the tablet back across the counter to the deputy. It was not the procedure she minded. It was the haughty air the deputy took relishing in the miniscule amount of power.

A pasty white hand, dotted with freckles and the occasional red hair, snaked out and seized the tablet. After verifying she had indeed signed her name and listed the accurate time, he looked up at her with the same mixture of awe and desire Kate usually reserved for a slice of crème brûlée cheesecake.

"I don't believe the sheriff is expecting you." He reached for his phone. "If you let me know, I can …"

"Thanks." She volleyed the word over her shoulder as she strode toward the hallway to Tony's office. A string of indignant protests fell flat behind her.

Arriving at the sheriff's door, she rapped soundly. A few moments passed before it opened. Various expressions flashed across his features at the speed of a frenetic financial ticker.

"Detective Barnes ..." He stepped back, allowing her to see he had a guest. "I'm so glad you could join us."

Delford's attorney remained seated in a blue cushioned guest chair as Tony ushered her into the room and closed the door behind her. She took the empty seat next to the lawyer and waited while Tony returned to his seat behind the desk.

He looked to Kate, then back to his visitor. "Mr. Wells is here to register a complaint. His client's home has been violated."

Kate leveled a cold gaze on the attorney. "Your *deceased* client's house was processed as a crime scene in accordance with a legal warrant."

Disdain dripped from his voice. "I am not disputing the warrant, Detective. I am here to register a complaint for criminal trespass and vandalism."

Tony consulted the report on his desk. "Someone has been spreading the word about Mr. Delford's past. I'm guessing it was his girlfriend. In any event, Mr. Wells is here to register a complaint. Apparently, the words, 'fucking pervert' and 'rot in hell' were painted on the outside of the decedent's home and the interior of the house was tossed."

"That is unfortunate." There was no mistaking the disinterest in Kate's voice.

"Unfortunate!" The attorney surged forward in his chair and struck the desktop. "My client is dead! He was killed by one of your deputies, and now his entire house has been ransacked and desecrated. This does not look good for you Sheriff."

Kate jumped in before Tony could respond. "Mr. Wells, do you live around here?"

"What?" The corners of his lips dragged downward as if she had fed him something unpleasant.

"You are from Seattle, right?"

"Yes, but that has nothing to do with ..."

"I'm simply wondering why you would travel eight hours roundtrip to report a case of vandalism." She inhaled slowly, letting the moment drag out. "How did you know the house had been vandalized?"

"The same way you find out anything in the twenty-first century." He dug into the front inside pocket of his suit jacket and retrieved his phone. Placing it on the desk midway between Kate and Tony, he tapped the screen and launched a video.

Three men in ski masks appeared in the same living room where Kate had met with Delford. Two of the men swung a metal baseball bat, smashing four lamps and the large screen television before dropping them to upturn furniture. The third was busy spray-painting letters on a wall.

"A brand-new Twitter account called @ENStandsup posted it last night. The tweet included the three hashtags: #eaglesnest, #communityjustice and #makingitright. So, I'll ask you again, Sheriff. What the fuck is going on in this town? Is this what you do? Kill innocent people, then incite the community to destroy their property?"

Tony's voice took on a warning edge. "Let's get some things straight, Counselor. One: my department does not incite unlawful activity. Two: Rick Delford was not innocent. He was a convicted child molester whose DNA was found on the murder victim. Three: When my deputy arrived to execute a lawful arrest warrant, your client rushed her and tried to take her gun. The weapon discharged in the ensuing scuffle. Four: Evidence linking him to the subject murder has since been discovered at his home, as well as additional evidence linking him to ongoing crimes."

"I haven't heard anything about any ongoing crimes." Settling back into his chair the attorney's gaze volleyed between the two law enforcement officers.

Kate spoke first. "What did Delford tell you about the murder?"

"Mr. Delford assured me he had nothing to do with it."

"What about the disposal of the body?"

"He had nothing to do with the girl at all."

"Stop lying. We've already established his DNA was found on the body. We need to know whether he ever gave you anything to hold for him—documents, files, photos ..."

"He did not. Even if he did, it would be considered privileged."

"I should not have to tell you attorney-client privilege does not survive death, nor does it apply if your client was in the process of committing a crime. Why don't we try an easier question ... How did you come to be employed by Rick Delford?"

Wells' lips curled into a snarl. "He called me not long after you originally knocked on his door. He was alarmed you were targeting him because of his past. Given one of your deputies killed him, I would say his concerns were more than justified."

Kate remained silent, letting the incendiary language starve for lack of oxygen.

Tony picked up the thread. "The righteous indignation sounds good Counselor, but we know you're lying. Delford's phone records indicate you originally placed the call to him."

He held up a hand as Wells leaned forward to protest. "It is possible he called you from a different number. If that is true, we can easily verify it by getting a look at *your* phone records. It would help us with another fact we've been hung up on."

"Delford never asked for his attorney when we were questioning him. Yet you showed up anyway. With the exception of having a telepathic connection with your client, how you could've known we picked him up—unless someone else told you."

"You are out of your mind if you think I'm going to give you access to my phone records."

"We can subpoena them."

"You don't have any cause ..." His cheeks reddened.

"Listen, either you're in this up to your neck or you're simply an idiot who has gotten too far out in front of your skis. Either way, I'm going to make sure I find out exactly how you are connected to this."

The attorney stood. "I don't know what kind of game you are playing Sheriff, but you are playing to lose." The power of the words was diminished by the slight tremor with which they were delivered.

He strode toward the door with Tony on his heels. "I'm sure we'll be talking again, Mr. Wells. For now, I'll see you out."

"Have a nice drive back to Seattle." Kate settled on the parting jab in lieu of punching the prick in the face.

When Tony returned a few minutes later he closed the door and leaned against it. "He's clearly hiding something."

"Agreed. Hard to tell whether he knows about the other girls."

"My gut says he knows more than he's telling."

"He also refused to say why he drove all the way out here when a simple phone call would have sufficed."

"We're going to have to force it out of him. I'll request another subpoena. By the way, I finally heard back from the state lab. Would you be surprised to know all of Delford's devices had been wiped clean six hours before we went to serve the subpoena?"

"Seriously? We didn't even have DNA results until moments before we went over there. Were they able to retrieve any data?"

"It was completely wiped clean. The tech didn't think it was something Delford had done. Something about root access software ... I can only follow those guys to the edge of the forest. A few yards in and I'm lost."

"I'll bet whoever did it is a match for the second DNA profile. And on that front, I may have a lead for us." She stood and walked around his desk.

His heavy gaze traveled up and down her body as she moved.

Ignoring the electrical charge racing up and down her nerve endings, she dropped into his chair.

Her fingers raced across the keyboard. "Remember the pinwheel with the star carved into the back of Celia's bracelet? It's the logo for a company named ..."

"TekPharmaCel—a huge international conglomerate based out of Bellevue, Washington." Tony finished dryly. His face betrayed no sign of the desire which had burned there seconds before. "Early morning research."

"Did you look through their subsidiaries?"

"Some of them. I was still working on it when Dick Face came in and started screaming about Delford's house."

Kate navigated through a few more sites until she found the right one. "Remember these guys?" She pointed to the screen.

"The company whose shipment of implants were stolen?"

"Right, the same ones which showed up in Haryati's mouth."

Tony leaned a hip against his desk. "Can't be a coincidence."

"We need answers fast. The best way to start is at the top." Kate pulled up TekPharmaCel's list of corporate executives.

Tony stared at the screen, reading the name listed next to the title of CEO. "I doubt Martin Cruthers is going to come out here to see us."

"Of course he won't. That is why I am going to see him."

Tony's eyes flew open wide. "No way, Kate. Bellevue is farther east than Seattle. There is no way I can ask you to drive ..."

"We have been over this before. You're still short staffed here and ..."

"True, but you just put in a ton of miles. I can't send you back on the road ..."

"I'm not going until tomorrow. In the meantime, we need to keep checking under every possible rock. This afternoon would be perfect for paying another visit to Aaru."

With a half-smile, he pulled out his phone and showed her a reminder to contact Hyland at Aaru. "Great minds think alike. Let's dig a little deeper into how Delford got his job."

"Delford implied he had more evidence in the video. If Wells doesn't have it maybe he stashed it somewhere at Aaru."

Tony planted his hands on his hips. "By the way, how do you even know Cruthers will be in town tomorrow or that he'll agree to see you?"

Kate thought about the phone message she had left while on her way to the sheriff's office. "Because I know someone who can make things happen."

Chapter 14

HYLAND FAIRBOURNE GLOWERED at the video feed displayed on his computer screen. The sheriff's SUV was parked at the main gate ... again. Tapping out a silent rhythm on his imported marble desktop, he considered his options.

"Mr. Fairbourne, what should I tell the sheriff?" Through the speakerphone, the guard's urgent question sounded more like a recrimination.

"Tell him I'll meet him at the motor pool. Direct him to the path. I'll take it from there."

Hyland grabbed his overcoat and scarf and hurried out of his office. Announcing his intended destination to his assistant he picked up a set of keys from the rack mounted to the interior wall of her cubicle. She raised her eyebrows as he stalked out of the office, wondering what could coax her boss out when so much work awaited on his desk.

Outside he headed directly to one of two electric golf carts parked at a nearby charging station. Customized specifically for Aaru's guests, with heated leather seats and a Bose sound system, the vehicle was as well-appointed and expensive, as a midlevel Mercedes.

Oblivious to the elegance, Hyland climbed inside and started the motor. He drove along a paved, narrow pathway, making his way around the administration building in relative silence. Without heeding the discreet sign prohibiting guests from venturing further, he turned right at the first fork. Moments later the cart was enveloped by the woods. Hyland's eyes had barely adjusted to the dimness when the overhead canopy disappeared. He entered a small, clearing where a fleet of carts and various maintenance

145

vehicles were parked under a roof of solar panels.

At the rear of the open area stood a single-story, gray and white building. The structure's façade resembled a modern take on an eighteenth-century French barn. The front doors had been rolled apart, providing a glimpse into the mechanic's shop.

Hyland parked his cart and climbed out of the vehicle as the sheriff's SUV came into view. Tony waved curtly before pulling into the empty stall on his right.

He smiled as Tony emerged from the vehicle. The expression wavered the moment Kate came around the back bumper. He had looked her up after the meeting at Beans of Mine. The media coverage around the Tower Torturer case had set off alarm bells. Surrounded by such unsavory notoriety, she was exactly the sort whose association with Aaru might impinge on its sterling reputation.

Tony exchanged a few words with the brunette before the pair started toward him. "Thanks for making time for us, Hyland."

"You're welcome. But I'm really not sure why you're here. I understand you spoke with Mr. Delford's supervisor and I was told our HR department has been more than cooperative. After all, the man is dead, so …"

Tony held up a hand. "The case is not closed."

"But if Delford is dead …"

Donning the implacable expression which had bested Hyland more than once at the poker table, the sheriff cut him off again. "The investigation is ongoing. When we last spoke, you told us a community group had recommended Delford for this job. We never received their contact information."

"If Mr. Delford is deceased, I don't see any harm in disclosing it. Standby one moment."

Stepping out of earshot, he placed a call to Miles Hastert who answered on the second ring. A few minutes later Hyland turned around to find he had been abandoned.

The sound of soft laughter trickled out of the garage. Breaking into a jog, he pulled up short before the doorway. The pair stood inside shooting the breeze with the resort's mechanic. Hyland watched as Tony engaged the employee, while Kate milled about the area. The shrewdness in her eyes belied her casual demeanor as she seemed to mentally catalog every item in the building. Eventually they switched roles, the sheriff looking around while Kate took over the conversation.

"I have your information." Hyland's tone cut through the banter with the sleek efficiency of a samurai sword.

The mechanic excused himself and exited through a nearby door.

Hyland turned to Tony, "The recommendation came from ..." He consulted a text on his phone. "Wendy Jessland at Faith, Hope and Light."

"Pastor Brian's church?" Kate inquired.

"Yes. Well, if you don't need anything else, I really must get back to the office."

Tony responded for Kate. "There is something else. I know your people are busy with the big upcoming shindig, but we need to inspect all areas Delford had access to here at Aaru."

"*Shindig?*"

"Gates said you guys are sold out next week for some special event."

The general manager paused for a long moment. "Aaru's Oceana Week is not a *shindig*. It is a unique experience designed to rejuvenate, awaken and inspire our guests. It is the most important event we hold all year."

"All the more reason for us to look around now."

"Tony, if it were any other time of the year, I'd be happy to personally show you every blade of grass on this property. But we simply don't have the resources right now."

Tony stared at him, the expression around his eyes hardening. "I guess I'm a bit confused. Aaru has always been a friend of the sheriff's department. Last week, Miles Hastert allowed us to search Delford's locker and work areas."

"Corporate policy requires visitors to be escorted at all times. Miles took time from his other duties to escort you. Right now, everyone is pulling double overtime to make sure we're ready for Oceana Week. I truly don't have the resources to spare."

Tony frowned. "Then I guess you can let us go unescorted. I am the sheriff, not some random tourist looking for something to post on Instagram."

Hyland held his hands out at his sides, "I'm sorry, but if you insist on immediate access, you are going to have to get a warrant. It is the only thing our corporate offices will accept as an excuse for taking resources from Oceana week."

∨

Tony fumed as the SUV tore along the road. He glared at the rearview mirror where the ornate gate was closing behind them.

"I can't believe that little prick!"

Kate glanced at him. "Really?"

"You don't understand. Eagle's Nest isn't like San Francisco. We are a tight community. People don't walk around with sticks up their asses here!"

"You might want to share that sentiment with Hyland." She shook her head. "I still can't believe the county prosecutor didn't automatically include Delford's place of employment in the original search warrant. You were lucky they let you in last time. Sticks up our asses or not, we do tend to pay attention to the details in San Francisco."

Expression darkening, Tony opened his mouth to respond.

The words never came. It was not until they turned onto the highway and drove for another mile in silence before he tried again.

"Okay. My stupidity. No more city-to-town comparisons."

"Fair enough." Surprised by the vehemence with which she had defended her city, Kate relaxed into her seat.

Tony's phone broke into an insistent dance in its dashboard mount. Checking the display, he glanced back at her. "Mildred wants to video chat."

Kate nodded. The need to find out if the coroner had discovered any incriminating DNA on the bracelet Tony had submitted to her last night, triumphed over the desire to squabble.

Pulling to the side of the road, he cut the engine and activated the call. The coroner appeared on the small screen, standing next to the same examination table where Haryati's remains had lain. In the cadaver's place, was a small stainless-steel tray.

"Hey, Mildred. Pick up anything on the bracelet?" Tony asked.

"Hold on, let me switch to the overhead camera."

She stepped out of frame. In the next moment the image shifted from the lab view to an aerial view of the table. Celia's bracelet lay in the center of the tray.

Mildred spoke again. "I'll enlarge it ... there!"

The bracelet filled the screen, its brown leather straps and ivory medallions standing out in vivid detail against the reflective metal.

Mildred continued, "I recovered two contact DNA profiles from the band and the surface of the medallions. One matched Delford's DNA and the other matched the swab sample you gave me for Celia."

Tony sighed. "Crap. Can't we ever catch a break?"

"Don't be so ready to throw in the towel, Sheriff."

Kate leaned closer to the phone. "What else, Mildred?"

A black plastic pointer was introduced at the corner of the screen, it moved over each of the medallions.

149

"These intrigued me right off the bat. My dad was an avid sportsman. When he wasn't at his practice, he was traipsing around the Sierras hunting for deer. Watching him field dress his kills prompted my interest in forensics. When you dropped this off last night, I recognized them immediately as animal bone."

The coroner's words had taken on an increasingly ominous note. It crawled slowly up Kate's spine with the painstaking deliberateness of a child's fingers walking up the keys of a piano.

"What kind of animal?"

"The human kind."

The facts which had formed the foundation of her understanding of the investigation seemed suddenly inured to the force of gravity. Kate unconsciously tightened her hold on the armrest as if she too might rise up and drift away in an incomprehensible jumble.

Tony gave voice to Kate's feelings. "Holy shit! What the fuck was Delford into?"

Mildred responded with professional equanimity. "You tell me."

Inspired by the coroner's detached calm, Kate let her head fall back against the seat. "He wanted to leave evidence. The medallions are one half of it. The logo carved on the back was the second half. He gave it to Celia between the time Haryati was murdered and the time he was killed." She frowned suddenly, recalling the appearance of the cadaver suspended in the warehouse pit. "You never reported any missing bones during the autopsy ..." The temperature in the SUV seemed to drop five degrees with each word.

"Correct."

"But you said they were all human." Tony's vocal cords sounded as strained as his credulity.

"Right."

"Then, the rest are from another body?" Kate asked.

"Not from another body—from other *bodies*. Five other medallions from five other bodies."

A full thirteen seconds passed before Tony attempted a response. "Son of a bitch ..."

Mildred moved the pointer over the "Somewhere" medallion." "This came from our victim. I didn't find any missing bones or fragments during the autopsy. It's safe to assume he extracted this from her right foot before it was dissolved by the lye. Size is consistent with her hallux."

"Her what?" Kate asked.

"Sorry. Her big toe. A little more food for thought ... he would have had to use an oven of some sort to properly dry the bone before he could fashion it for use in the bracelet."

"He put a good deal of work into it, beyond the carving."

"Definitely. I called in a favor and sent the profiles to a friend at Washington State who specializes in anthropological DNA studies. Besides our original victim, she confirmed there are two Malays and four Scandinavians."

"The two Malay profiles—was either one close enough to ...?" Kate's tone increased with emotion as her volume trailed off.

The camera view changed once again. Mildred peered through the screen. "To be Haryati's sister? No. There was no mitochondrial match."

Kate exhaled. Zamira might still be alive. There was still a chance to do for her, what her older sister could not. She listened while Tony and Mildred finished the conversation. As they ended the call, she silently wondered whether six victims would be the complete count, or whether there were even more girls from whom Delford hadn't bothered to keep mementos for his sick insurance policy. The scale of the evil in Eagle's Nest was growing faster than her mind could comprehend.

"Do you think they were all sourced from the same sex

trafficking ring?" Tony asked.

Shaking her way out of the mental house of horrors, Kate responded in a quiet tone. "Who knows. For all we know, Haryati and Zamira were the only ones who were brought here from Malaysia. DNA only tells us about ethnicity not citizenship. The other girls might have been taken from towns inside the U.S. But if it is the same ring, its reach is much more global than we thought."

"Time to talk to Fuentes."

Kate began dialing the agent's number. "Maybe the increased body count will get the FBI to pay more attention." She issued the last words mere seconds before the Special Agent answered.

Letting Tony handle the morbid update, Kate's thoughts turned further and further inward, until she was barely aware of the animated exchange between the two men. Into that inner silence, she made a vow—one which she would make and sacrifice to fulfill. Wherever the investigation led, and whatever sacrifices it required from her, there would be no more corpses. Zamira would not end up like Haryati.

May 4

Occupying the majority of the landmass in northwest Washington, Olympic National Park is one of crown jewels in the federal park system. The magnificent expanse of ragged peaks had been formed thousands of feet below where they now stood. Time and tectonic pressures had uplifted and reformed the original sea floor, creating a diverse series of ecosystems, and making it one of the most breathtaking places in North America.

Situated almost at the epicenter of the park, glacier-crusted Mount Olympus presides over spectacular rainforests, gorgeous coastlines and a complex network of rivers. The mountain is the forest's namesake, as well as that of the state capitol of Olympia, which lays approximately sixty-five miles to the south.

Having traversed the same awe-inspiring landscape less than forty-eight hours before, Kate had difficulty focusing on the area's natural bounty. As it had during her last trip, fear for the girls stood like a wall between her and the magical effects of nature.

The number of victims had grown by a factor of five within less than twenty-four hours. The knowledge was as debilitating to sleep as it was disturbing to the soul. She had tossed and turned the night before as scores of desiccated female corpses, each one missing a critical piece of its anatomy, had chased her through the impossible realms of the unconscious. Skeletal fingers sharpened into talons, what remained of the girls had clawed at her for help, tearing her flesh from her bones until the violence of her own screams had awakened her from the hellish mental prison.

Thoughts in the waking world had proved little better than those in the unconscious. She'd stumbled from bed more than two hours before the sun had risen feeling as lost and uncertain as she had when the Tower Torturer had killed his third victim. It was not until she had headed for the highway hours later, that the increasing sense of hopelessness began to equalize against the weight of action.

With the exception of a brief stop at a gas station in Poulsbo, Kate had made great time. She had already made it all the way down Highway 16 to the Tacoma Narrows Bridge and had begun crossing Puget Sound. Taking the ferry might have spared a few minutes, but that assumed it would be running on time. She was not about to risk her appointment with the CEO of TekPharmaCel on public transportation.

During the last twenty minutes, two consecutive texts from Chloe had compounded her distress. Sitting so long in the car wasn't helping her physical disposition much either. Ignoring the angry nerve signals from her backside, Kate finished making her way across the breathtaking expanse and started toward Interstate 5. Minutes later, the busy port of Tacoma appeared on her left. She had just passed the slew of large white cargo cranes when her phone rang.

According to the display, Chloe had tired of waiting for a response.

"Damn!" Kate rolled her eyes before settling them back on the road. Setting her jaw, she stabbed a finger at the answer button. "Hello, Chloe."

"Hi, Kate. I'm so glad I was able to reach you. I don't know if you have received any of the texts I've been sending you. I definitely want to reschedule our meeting." The attempted exuberance in the mother's voice did nothing to improve Kate's mood.

"I did."

Chloe paused. "Well, although it meant the world to me to see you the other night, I think we can agree our last meeting was not very ... productive."

"Yes."

Accepting the one word as the only response she was going to get, Chloe continued, "I don't know if you are up for it, but I thought it might be helpful if we had a professional to help mediate for us. You know, help us navigate through all the pitfalls, so we can really communicate without, without ..."

Kate inhaled deeply. Chloe was right. Their last meeting had been a waste of time. There was no reason to expect the next one would be any different. "You think we need a referee."

Chloe's laugh was stilted. "Kind of. I think there is a lot we have to say to each other, but all of our history is hard to get around. I think we need a guide."

Kate's distrust of her mother remained somewhere in the stratosphere. Dr. Wissel had warned her a family therapist might be necessary. "Do you know anyone in Eagle's Nest?"

"Yes, I know the perfect person and you've met him, too. Remember Pastor Brian? He is a very well-respected counselor. Would you like me to set up an appointment with him?"

"I would prefer to do this without the religion angle."

"I understand. But it won't be a problem. Pastor Brian works with families at all stages of the faith cycle. Faith does not have to come into this at all."

Kate's stomach began to spin. Somewhere in Washington, a group of girls were in the clutches of a monster. She had made a vow to save them, yet here she was discussing family therapy.

Still, Dr. Wissel had warned her that until she could put the ghosts of the past to rest, she would forever be operating at a deficit. Those ghosts had distracted her in her battle against the Tower Torturer—the lack of focus had cost lives. Shaking her head to no one in particular, Kate replied through clenched teeth. "Fine. How much does he charge?"

"Don't worry about it. What day works best for you?"

"I guess the sooner the better."

"If we can get in as soon as tomorrow, could you join us?"

"Any time after six." A darker question followed but it never made it to Kate's lips. *If she had not found the girls by then, would there be anyone left to rescue?*

"Wonderful! I'll get it scheduled and send you a confirmation text. I'm really happy we're doing it this way. Thank you for agreeing."

"I can't imagine it'll be much worse than last time. I'll keep an eye out for your text." Kate ended the call without any further exchange.

She had only gone another five miles before her phone came to life again. A new text from someone she had not spoken to in a while. It was the one female who had ever come remotely close to resembling a friend in Kate's adult life. The message was limited to three lines:

> Confirmed for 1 p.m.
> Ask for Cruthers' Assistant—Trina Chen.
> Want credit for this against my tab. ;)

The reminder of the running joke about Maria Torres having a tab with Kate, prompted a smile. When she had first met the gorgeous journalist, Kate had immediately pegged her for a pampered viper out to make a name off the misfortunes of others. Yet, Torres had proved herself to be compassionate, highly competent and tough as nails.

The woman also happened to be the only person besides Kate who had survived the Tower Torturer's lair. And while Kate had ultimately been able to save both herself and Maria, the encounter had left the journalist with as many physical scars as emotional ones.

Torres was still trying to pay off what she called her tab. The first installment had been to recommend the private detective Kate had used to track down her mother. Coordinating this meeting with a high-powered executive, whose net worth was in the billions, was the second installment.

Kate drove on, silently praying Martin Cruthers would be able to open up the doors to help her keep her vow to Zamira and the rest of the girls.

Chapter 15

SITTING PRIMLY ALONG the eastern edge of Lake Washington, the city of Bellevue is a testament to the growth and prosperity to be found in the new millennium. The downtown district alone might double for the utopian dream setting of a science fiction novel.

Modern office towers soar to the heavens, carrying the intellectual aspirations of one of the country's most highly educated populaces. The gutters and sidewalks look as if they are steam cleaned daily.

In addition, Bellevue boasts the lofty status of being one of the most racially diverse cities in the nation. Antithetically, its origin bears the painful stain of prejudice—a stain the color of strawberries.

Prior to 1941, Bellevue had been a sleepy bedroom community known for its annual strawberry festival. The celebration of the bounty of nature was made possible by a hard-working and vibrant Japanese farming community. Yet global events were about to put a spotlight on a dark virus of hostility which had been quietly growing against the Japanese. The intrusive malignancy had silently begun to strangle the prospect for what might have been an idyllic life among the strawberry fields.

Following the Japanese Empire's attack on Pearl Harbor on December 7, 1941, the contagion flared out of control. Public opinion ignited against the immigrant community, as well as generations of American-born Japanese who had lived their entire lives as United States citizens.

In the face of legitimate intelligence from the Department of Justice arguing for the contrary, President Roosevelt approved an order requiring the involuntary removal and detention of all Japanese inhabitants of the West Coast. Within months, tens of thousands of American citizens and legal immigrants, were imprisoned behind the barbed wire topped walls of internment camps.

Undeterred by the shame of benefitting from ill-gotten gains, developers had swept into the void scooping up the strawberry fields for a song. In the intervening decades, people of good will and open minds eradicated the malignancy. Triumphing over its dark roots, Bellevue's successive generations had overhauled the city into a wellspring of diversity.

Sitting on a trendy orange couch beneath a massive wall-mounted bronze rendering of TekPharmaCel's pinwheel logo, Kate watched the diverse groups of employees coming and going as she waited for her appointment. The tallest in a cluster of modern high-rises, the company's headquarters made her feel as if she were back in downtown San Francisco.

"Detective Barnes?" The question came from a willowy Chinese woman in her late twenties. Her dark hair was pinned back into a tight bun, accentuating her delicate bone structure. The severe style stood in stark contrast to the flashy, low-cut magenta dress with matching platform heels.

Kate rose. "Trina Chen?"

"Yes. Welcome to TekPharmaCel." Red lips split into a warm smile as she gently grasped Kate's hand. "Please, follow me …"

The younger woman started off toward the far end of the expansive space, where a large bank of black turnstiles separated the elevator bank from the rest of the lobby. A contingent of armed security guards presided over the main entrance from a massive security desk.

"Is this your first time in Bellevue?"

"Yes. It reminds me of San Francisco."

Trina responded with an understanding smile. Pausing in front of the nearest turnstile, she waved her wrist in the direction of the card reader. A discreet plastic card dangled from a clip affixed to her ornate jade bracelet.

The turnstile released with a soft buzzing sound. They continued through the left bank of elevators, before emerging into the rear lobby. Beyond the glass exterior wall, a serene Japanese tea garden provided a stark contrast to the modern tower.

The younger woman strode across the cream-colored stone floor toward a wall-to-wall wood carving of the Puget Sound. Two more guards stood to either side of the artwork.

As she neared, Kate noticed another card reader discretely set to one side of the panel. Trina swiped her wrist before it. After a few beats the entire panel swung outward. Behind it, a stainless-steel elevator door silently slid open.

Inside the lushly appointed cab, Trina held up her wrist for another security reader.

As the machine began to whisk them skyward, Kate asked. "Executive elevator?"

Trina smiled indulgently. "Yes. Mr. Cruthers likes his privacy. And of course, security is an important concern."

"I would imagine so. By the way, how do you know Maria Torres?"

"I was a communications major at Boston U. Maria hired me to intern for her at WCVB. She is one of the most awesome people I've ever known." Her expression crumbled. "My heart broke when I heard about what happened to her."

Unbidden, Maria's heart wrenching screams echoed in Kate's head. She tightened her stomach against the sudden nausea, breathing slowly through the piercing memories until they mercifully began to fade.

Studying Kate's features, Trina laid a hand on her arm. "I'm so sorry! I never should have mentioned it. Maria told me how you saved her. It must've been so awful for you both."

A soft chime heralded their arrival. Swallowing back a bevy of responses totally disproportionate to the younger woman's transgression, Kate smiled tightly and followed Trina into a large vestibule. A narrow security desk dominated the space. From behind it, two additional guards nodded curtly at the women.

Trina stopped at a matching set of black double doors with an unusual matte finish. TekPharmaCel's initials were spelled out in a hammered bronze on either side of the entry. A discreet black camera was mounted in the wall on the right.

Raising her manicured hand, the younger woman knocked on one of the doors. A muffled sound from within prompted another swipe of the wrist.

Grasping both handles, Trina opened the doors into a room more appropriately sized for a receiving room in an Emperor's palace than a corporate office. The elegant décor looked as if it had been appropriated from the very same place.

Exquisitely delicate antique couches framed a seating area immediately to the right, flanked by a small bar to the left. The one nod to modern art was a large painting of what appeared to be a stylized stag's head. The unfortunate creature's skull hovered like an undersized afterthought beneath a massive set of horns. At the far end of the chamber, an expansive black desk with scrolling gold accents squatted grandly before a panoramic view of Lake Washington.

Trina escorted Kate to the monolithic antique, across from which Martin Cruthers sat poking his two index fingers at a keyboard. They waited in silence for at least two minutes before he paused to look up.

Trina's mouth curved into a simpering smile. "Mr. Cruthers, this is Detective Barnes."

The lineless face of the fifty-six-year-old, revealed he was no stranger to plastic surgery. While nowhere near as expensive as the medical ministrations, what remained of his thinning hair had been artfully dyed in natural shades of mahogany. A trendy, light gray suit with a bright pink tie stood as the last obvious bastions against the ravages of Father Time.

Appraising eyes flew up and down Kate's body as he rose to shake her hand. She responded in kind, noting the amount of time and care spent on hair and skin had not been extended to either a gym or a nutritionist.

He gestured to a narrow-legged guest chair. "A pleasure, Detective. Please sit down."

"Is there anything else you require before I leave, Mr. Cruthers?" The meekness in Trina's voice bordered on cartoonish.

Without glancing in his assistant's direction, the CEO gestured to a half-empty coffee cup sitting near the edge of his desk. "I'm done."

"Would you care for another, sir?"

"No. Get back to work."

Kate cringed inwardly as the young woman bowed her head, retrieved the cup and stole quietly out of the office.

"I understand you're here to request my help." An odd light shone in his watery brown eyes. "But before we start, I want to hear all about your last case."

"Excuse me?"

"The Tower Torturer case. They say you were the one who finally got him."

"Yes, they do. But that case is closed. I'm here for your help with a current investigation."

Irritation flashed in his eyes. "As important as the Torturer business?"

Kate leaned forward in her seat, as much to control her rising anger as to find a comfortable angle on the half-inch-thick seat cushion. "All cases are important, Mr. Cruthers."

"I'm sure they are." The retort dripped with sarcasm.

Recalling Tony and Fuentes' agreement to keep the revised victim count confidential, Kate chose her next words with care. "A young woman has been murdered. We believe she was one of a group of young victims who were brought into the country illegally."

"Illegal immigration is a serious problem in this country. If we could ever close our damn borders …"

Kate tuned out the ensuing diatribe, waiting patiently for the next five minutes before plowing into a brief opening between breaths. "I don't think you understand. These girls were brought here against their will."

His shoulders rose and fell with the hallmark insouciance of a teenager.

She chose not to rise to the bait. "We have uncovered circumstantial evidence linking one of your subsidiaries to the crime."

His expression darkened. "We employ hundreds of thousands of people worldwide. The law of averages dictates we will have a percentage of bad apples."

Keeping her face impassive, Kate fired back. "One of those bad apples may be holding minors against their will."

"You said the evidence is circumstantial." His eyes blazed with interest. "Unless you have more—a serious reason to believe we should be worried? Hopefully not someone who might be crazy enough to come in here on a shooting spree?"

"There is no reason to believe TekPharmaCel has been targeted in any way. The victims in this case are all believed to be minors."

He raised an eyebrow. "And they are all illegals, too?"

Bile tickled the back of Kate's throat. "Would it make a difference?"

He looked down at his keyboard, pursed his lips, bounced his head from side-to-side, then found her eyes once again. "I suppose not. As I said, TekPharmaCel is a large organization. Where did this murder occur?"

"The body was discovered in the Olympic Peninsula about four hours' drive from here. In a small town called Eagle's Nest."

His eyes shifted off to the right for a brief moment before finding her gaze once again. "I'm not familiar with it, but then I don't necessarily spend much time out in the sticks."

He stabbed at a small button on his phone. "Trina will put you in contact with the appropriate people so you can make some *discreet* inquiries. Of course, I highly doubt anyone in our organization is mixed up in this mess. But I do have a question before you go ... Isn't Washington a little out of your jurisdiction?"

"I'm working as a consultant for local law enforcement."

"Is that right?" His gaze cut with the precision of a scalpel. "Well, I'm sure you'll have this matter cleared up soon."

He stood and extended his hand. Kate rose and reached out, stopping short of making contact. "By the way Mr. Cruthers, do you happen to know an attorney named Herb Wells with Dalton, Soles and Trask?"

Other than a slight tightening in his jaw, his expression remained impassive. "No. Why do you ask?"

"He works in Seattle. I thought you might have heard of him."

The door to the office opened, drawing their combined attention. Trina entered and took a position a few feet behind Kate. Remaining mute, the younger woman clasped her hands behind her back.

Kate turned back to the CEO, who had since dropped his hand. "Trina will show you out. Good luck with your case, Detective. I expect if a TekPharmaCel employee is involved, you will keep it as quiet as possible. Bad press never helps sell products."

"Funny, I've always heard good products sell themselves."

"Touché, Detective. By the way, next time you find yourself in

Bellevue call Trina. I'm still dying to hear all about how you solved the Tower Torturer case." His gaze fell to her breasts. "I'm sure it would be a very enlightening evening."

Kate looked pointedly at the credenza behind his desk. The surface was crammed with framed photos of Cruthers arm-in-arm with foreign dignitaries, powerful politicians, famous athletes, and high-powered business moguls. Offset in one small corner were two photos featuring a redhead in her early thirties surrounded by a bevy of small children.

Kate inclined her head toward the familial images. "I'm sure it would be. Especially if your wife came along. Unfortunately, she doesn't appear to be the kind of woman who would enjoy hearing about the darker side of humanity."

Ignoring the thunderclouds threatening in his glare, Kate turned on her heel and headed for the door.

Trina escorted her silently back down to the lobby. Once they were through the turnstiles, the younger woman extended her hand. "It was a sincere pleasure meeting you, Detective Barnes." She cast a furtive glance around, before continuing in a conspiratorial tone. "I've got to give you points for the comment about his wife. The man is such a pig!" She plucked at the neckline of her dress. "Do you see anyone else around here dressing up like this for work?"

"Why not quit?"

"Believe me, I plan to. In seven months, I'll have been here three full years; enough to make my resume legit. Until then, I take his crap and bide my time."

Kate pulled out her cell phone and began typing. "Do me a favor? Don't go away quietly. Tell HR what he's been doing before you go."

"I will. And I plan to do one better. I'm going to blow his ass up on social media."

Kate laughed. "Good for you. And thanks again for making this happen today. Would you mind copying Sheriff Luchasetti on the contact information? I texted you his number."

"Sure, and if you talk to Maria again, please tell her I said hi."

The smile Kate offered in response faded the moment the younger woman walked away. Trina was right about one thing; Martin Cruthers was a pig. He was also hiding something, and Kate had the whole drive back to Eagle's Nest to try to figure out what it might be.

∨

During the drive across Puget Sound, the sun had been low in the sky, ensuring fantastic views from the ferry. In a little over an hour, Kate had arrived in Port Angeles where the only light in the night sky came from the few intrepid stars which managed to shine through the swiftly passing clouds scudding overhead.

With the Jeep's gas tank nearly as empty as her stomach, Kate decided to stop at the last available station on the way out of town. When the tank was full, she headed into the accompanying convenience store. She exchanged a few words with the clerk who was getting ready to close. Emerging minutes later with a bottle of water and two granola bars, Kate was struck by the immediate sense something was not quite right.

Feigning an undue interest in shifting the weight of her purchases between her hands, she surreptitiously scanned the lot. The pumps were empty, with the exception of one elderly man who was replacing the gas cap on a red Hyundai sedan.

Across the street, a black Chevy Tahoe was parked in front of a large hedge. Sitting far enough from the bright lights of the gas station, the vehicle's interior lay shrouded in darkness.

Despite the sense of unease, Kate marched confidently to her car. Keeping an eye on the SUV, she pulled back out onto the highway. The vehicle stayed put.

Having learned to respect her instincts, she watched the rear-view mirror for the next sixteen miles. With the exception of a handful of cars headed in the opposite direction, she had the tree-lined highway to herself. She was almost to Lake Crescent when the gentle twists and turns of the two-lane route were beginning to rock Kate into a semi-somnambulant state.

Blinking away the exhaustion, she turned off the car's heater and rolled down the window. Having driven the lakefront route earlier in the day, she knew it had its challenges. In spots, the route wound right along the water mere feet above the shimmering surface. The pull of centripetal force around some of the larger turns made for a white-knuckled ride. Angry locals added to the stress. No doubt wondering why she had been inching along at ten miles below the speed limit, they had ridden her bumper as if every moment wasted might be their last.

Whether it was the unearthly clarity of the water or the knowledge the lake was over six hundred and seventy feet deep, Kate had fought the urge to let the enchanting scenery pull her gaze from the roadway. It also might have been the vivid details Tony had shared with her about the Hallie Illingsworth case.

In 1937 the corpse of Mrs. Illingsworth escaped the rotted bonds which had anchored it in an underwater grave for three long years. Hallie had floated to the surface, her skin turned into what was described as "ivory soap." The moniker aptly described the skin's appearance in the wake of a long-term chemical reaction between her body fat and the lake minerals.

Hallie's abusive husband was eventually tried and convicted for the murder. As if the example of Kate's parents' failed marriage were not enough, the story added to Kate's disbelief in the viability of the institution. It also sat at the edge of her consciousness, mingling with all the dead bodies and grim horrors she had seen.

Gradually, the tree line on the right of the road began to thin. Within minutes it was gone altogether, replaced by a simple guardrail which separated her from the inky darkness of the lake. Kate inhaled deeply.

Reaching for the window controls, she shut out the icy breeze rolling in off the water. Up ahead the road curved, prompting her to ease on the brakes. As the Jeep began to slow, the rearview mirror came alive with the bright blare of headlights. Squinting against the glare, Kate swore silently to herself.

The jerk started flashing his high beams; driver's Morse Code equivalent for "my life is more important than yours, move out of the fucking way." Scowling as the vehicle drew dangerously close to her rear bumper, Kate stepped on the gas.

Clenching her teeth as tightly as the steering wheel, she sped into the oncoming curve. Despite the centrifugal force, the Jeep stayed upright. The car behind her remained firmly glued to her bumper as the road opened back onto a straightaway.

Determined to be rid of him, Kate edged as close as she dared toward the guardrail, an open invitation for the other driver to pass. The vehicle pulled alongside her, opting not to speed by, but rather to keep pace with her.

Venturing a look out the driver's side window, she prepared herself for a slew of obscenities and/or equally odious gestures from the other driver.

The first thing she noted was the car beside her was a black SUV. Before she could process the fact, a succession of new ones flashed through her brain.

The vehicle's passenger window was down.

The driver was wearing a black mask.

The barrel of a gun was pointed directly at her head.

Instinct taking over, Kate ducked beneath the window line a split second before the sound of a gunshot rocked the night.

Before she took her next breath, the glass exploded.

Her pulse pounding, she stood on the accelerator. Left hand locked in a death-grip on the steering wheel, she fumbled for her purse with her right hand.

The car bounced wildly as she listed onto the rumble strip carved into the shoulder of the road. On the passenger seat her purse, and the gun inside it, inched across the leather seat toward the floor.

Her right hand shot out, but it was too late. The bag fell into the footwell.

She risked popping her head above the dash to check whether another curve was imminent, but the SUV roared up alongside the car, forcing her back down. Kate had barely retreated before the front windshield exploded under the impact of several more bullets.

Her head was still down when the Jeep struck the guardrail at the next curve. The sound of tearing metal pierced the night.

For a surreal moment, Kate seemed to float in mid-air. She straightened up in her seat in time to feel the iron grasp of gravity dragging her back downward. Her headlights illuminated the impossibly clear waters of Lake Crescent for less than one full breath before the Jeep plunged toward their tranquil depths.

Upon impact with the water, the car's airbag engaged, sparing Kate from impaling her chest on the steering wheel. Momentarily dazed, she collapsed against her seat, choking on talcum dust.

Still coughing, she rolled to the side where the passenger window had once been. A torrent of water was pouring into the vehicle. A glance toward where the front windshield had been revealed the same. Lake Crescent was flooding in with the vigor of an open ocean tsunami.

The Jeep had already begun to sink. Splashing against her legs with determined pressure, the icy deluge shocked her nervous system, prompting her back into action.

She reached for the seatbelt release. Her fingers trembled violently amid the rising water, failing to open the device on the first try.

Gasping as the frigid water rose to her chest, she watched for a horror-stricken moment as the ceiling of the Jeep sank to within feet of the surface of the lake.

She peered down at the seatbelt. Water swirled up toward her chin. Dim blue light from the dashboard provided just enough visibility. Her thumb was slightly off target. Praying, she depressed the release button again.

Hope leapt in her heart when the harness came apart. The momentary high was replaced by terror as the water level swelled above her mouth.

She scrambled onto her knees. Sucking in as much air as she could, she closed her mouth and dove headlong through the open space above the dashboard.

The lake enveloped the Jeep, dragging it down into the darkness. Unwilling to release her from sharing its fate, the top of the windshield frame slammed across Kate's lower back.

Air whooshed from her lungs. For a few precious moments, the vehicle dragged her prone body with it. Watching the surface begin to float away, Kate kicked with all her might, finally freeing her lower half.

The vehicle was not done with her yet. As it plunged, it created a vacuum, sucking at Kate's limbs. Panicked, she pumped harder, desperate to avoid the same lonely grave to which Hallie had been condemned so many decades before.

Stroke after stroke, the pressure in her lungs seemed to multiply. Her thoughts began to slow as the beginnings of a headache teased her skull. Without warning, her body decided to mutiny. Her mouth opened, expelling all the air she had been holding.

With her body now reigning supreme, her lungs demanded

their due. In less than the blink of an eye, water flooded through her mouth and nose.

Her left hand shot into the night air. A split second after, head broke through. Coughing and sputtering, she hyperextended her jaw, intent on inhaling as much of the earth's oxygen supply as her body could hold.

It was a full minute before she remembered the man with the gun. Adrenaline and oxygen brought back her mental acuity in high resolution. Aware she must put as much distance between herself and the impact point as possible, she mustered the rest of her energy reserves and set off at Olympic pace.

She had only progressed seven strokes when she caught sight of the beam of a flashlight. All hope faded as the bright light stole over the surface of the water and settled fully on her face.

Chapter 16

THE WOMAN'S FIERCE EXPRESSION appeared feral in the bright beam. Before the guy in the boat could call out to her, she took a deep breath and plunged back under the water. Thanks to Lake Crescent's unusually low levels of algae-feeding nitrogen the water had a level of transparency akin to fresh tap water. There was no hiding beneath the surface.

Pulse pounding, he cranked on the boat's outboard motor and headed off after her. He closed on her submerged form within seconds. He cut the power to avoid overtaking her.

"Hey, lady! Lady!"

She finally breached the surface. With a full inhalation, she cut a determined stroke parallel to the shoreline.

"Aw, shit! Come on!" He jammed his hand through thick locks of unruly brown hair. His pulse pounded so hard it felt like his heart might explode in his chest. Watching her splash away from him, he gave in to instinct and rose to his feet.

Careful to keep his weight balanced in the fourteen-foot aluminum fishing boat, he spat out, "Shit, shit, shit!" Snatching a glow stick from his emergency pack, he dove headlong into the water.

He expected the cold to hit him like a brick wall. Instead, it hit him like a nuclear blast, seeming to obliterate his air supply before he could reach the surface. His jeans and tennis shoes hung like anchors around his lower half, requiring double the normal effort to move.

He managed to hold on until his head popped up into the night air. The aching cold had already seeped into his muscles, making every movement torture. He could only imagine how bad it was for the woman.

Within ten strokes he began to gain on her. Doubling his efforts, she was soon within reach. Her right foot splashed before him. He lunged for it.

His fingers had just closed around her ankle when she flipped back like a porpoise and landed a punch firmly against his jaw. She was free once again.

Momentarily stunned, he rapidly gathered his wits and tried to shake off the impact. His scream echoed over the sound of her splashing. "Shit, lady. I'm trying to help you!"

Either the cold was finally getting to her, or something in his tone made her reconsider. She stopped and turned around. Treading water, she studied his youthful features in the soft green light of the glow stick. Her eyes darted to the boat bobbing nearby.

Tenderly probing his jaw, he tried again. "I saw your car go off the road. I'm only trying to help you."

She looked back toward the highway. "Did you see what happened to the other car? The one that was following me?"

"It was all over your ass! He didn't bother to stop after you crashed, just took off. Can we please stop with the questions and get back in the boat? I'm freezin' my balls off."

The last comment sparked a wry smile. "Mine would be too, if I had them."

By the time they got back to the boat, she was too weak to haul herself up over the side. He climbed in first, then pulled her in after him. She collapsed onto the floor in a soaking wet puddle. After a few deep breaths, she started toward the seat beside his.

He lowered his arm like a security gate. "You don't want to do that. I'm going to haul ass to get us back to the dock. The wind chill is going to be a bitch."

"Fine." She propped her head against the side of the hull while he stared the engine. She called out over the ensuing roar, "What's your name?"

"I'm Kyle." He tapped a small camping lantern on the bottom of the boat. It brightened up the surrounding night with soft LED light.

"Thank you for coming after me, Kyle. My name is Kate, and I'm sorry for hitting you." Her words clattered out between chattering teeth.

Pulling a hand from the boat's controls, he fingered his jaw gently. "Anyone who thinks chicks can't throw a punch needs to meet you."

Her lips had turned corpse blue. "How old are you Kyle?"

"I'm almost seventeen." He pointed straight ahead toward a large wooden lodge nestled along the shore. Warm lights glowed from within, illuminating the picturesque grounds. "My parents run that B&B. Listen, can you do me a solid?"

"You saved my life. As long as it doesn't involve anything illegal or immoral ..."

He pursed his lips miserably. "I was sneaking over to my girlfriend's house when I saw you. My parents are going to flip shit when they find out I was on the lake at night, and I snuck out!"

"Don't worry about it. I'm sure when your parents hear you saved a stranger's life, they'll be more proud than angry."

His teeth had begun to chatter so violently she could barely make out his response. "You don't know my parents."

∨

Almost an hour later, Kate had showered and changed into a pair of ill-fitting sweats donated by Kyle's mother. Sitting alone on a small couch in the only vacant suite in the B&B, Kate pulled a brightly patterned, thick, fleece blanket closer around her. A warm fire crackled from within a wall of smooth river stones. She gazed at the flames, not really seeing them dance.

The moment she and her unexpected hero had arrived at the

backdoor of the B&B, the boy's parents had descended upon the two as if they were a pair of hatchlings who had fallen from their nest. The couple had insisted on calling an ambulance for Kate. She had talked them out of it, getting them to settle for calling the sheriff's department instead.

The reason for his son's forbidden foray onto the lake had elicited a disapproving scowl from Kyle's father. Watching the boy swat away his mother's attempts to dry his dripping hair, the serious violation seemed like a minor infraction. The most the man had been able to verbally muster had been a half-hearted rebuke. As Kate had anticipated, both parents had been extremely proud of their son.

A knot in one of the burning logs popped, sending a shiver down Kate's spine. Despite the hot shower, her entire nervous system seemed ready to explode. She grasped her hands together, willing them to stop shaking.

It had been three days since the shootout with Belovol. Her nervous system had barely recovered from that incident before she had come under fire and crashed into a lake. Add to it the preexisting trauma from fighting for her life in the Tower Torturer's lair, and it was no wonder she felt like she was on the cusp of an all-out meltdown.

Before she could stop them, maudlin thoughts began to cascade through her mind. Death had been persistently visiting her door. It seemed inevitable it would claim her soon.

She closed her eyes. The best thing she could do in the face of fear was to take control. Dancing around the effects of latent shock, she began trying to piece together what had just happened and why. Her mind started to race—speculating about the gunman's motives and his whereabouts.

A loud knock at the door almost stopped her heart. Relaxing her death grip on the blanket, she took a moment to steady herself before responding. "Come in."

Tony entered and closed the door behind him. She started up from the sofa, but he held out a hand. "Don't get up."

He walked to the sofa and knelt down before her. Concern etched his handsome features. "How are you?"

"I'm still in one piece if ..."

The kiss was unexpected. It radiated a warmth which seeped through her lips and throughout her body. She relished the calming effect but put a hand on his chest and pushed him away before it had a chance to transform into something more urgent.

Turning her head to the side, she breathed, "Professional relationship, remember?"

He forced a good-natured smile, then took a seat on the couch beside her. "What the hell happened, anyway? The last time we spoke you had finished crossing the Sound. Next thing I know, I'm getting a call saying you've been fished out of a lake." Sincere concern weighed down the lightness in his tone.

"Did you talk to Kyle and his parents?"

"The kid pounced on me the moment I got through the front door. He said he saw you go right through the guardrail. The Jeep sank and he thought you were done for, but then you popped up and started swimming for your life. He said you wouldn't let him help you—he basically had to wrestle you out of the water."

Kate smiled. "Did he tell you about his poor jaw?"

"He didn't have to. The bruise is already starting to show."

She winced. "I feel bad about that."

"Kyle said the other car practically ran you off the road. I hope you got his fucking plates because accidentally running you off the road is as bad as ..."

"The other driver didn't *accidentally* do anything. The reason I didn't accept help from Kyle at first was because I thought he was trying to kill me, too."

175

Anger blossomed in the sheriff's features as Kate recounted the details leading up to the crash. Try as she might, she could not keep the occasional tremor from her voice. Gradually, he reached over and placed a warm hand over hers, making it a little easier.

The longer she talked, the darker his countenance grew. When she finally finished, he sighed. "All we've got to go on is the car is one of the most popular makes, colors and models in Washington state."

"Sorry. Between ducking bullets and fighting to escape a sinking car, I didn't really have time to get his plates."

His face crumpled. "That sounded worse than I meant it."

She leaned away from him, huddling deeper into the blanket. "No, I get it. I definitely make a bad … witness." She stopped herself short of the word *victim*.

"You failed to mention how you still had the balls to bust the next guy you saw in the jaw." His deadpan expression hit something in Kate's funny bone. Perhaps it was a mere need to blow off steam. A high-pitched giggle escaped from her lips.

Suppressing his own smile, he shot back. "I'm glad you think this is funny, but we need to get you to the hospital in Port Angeles."

"What for?"

He ticked off fingers in succession as he spoke. "You hit the guardrail, then the water. You need to be checked for a possible concussion, and you may have hypothermia."

"I'm fine." She lifted her chin defiantly. "Believe me, I've been through a lot worse than this. All I want is to get back to my place and get to bed."

The challenge in her eyes made him feel as if he were preparing to attack the Great Wall of China with a toothpick. He exhaled loudly. "I'm not getting you into a hospital tonight, am I?"

"Absolutely not. But I have narrowed down my take on what

happened tonight into two possibilities. One of Belovol's buddies is helping him exact payback. Or the person behind Haryati's murder realizes I'm getting close, and he wants me out of the picture."

He winced. "There is a third option."

"Which is?"

"This has nothing to do with Belovol, or the case. You've been through a lot tonight. Don't you think it odd someone would wait and follow you all the way from Seattle when he could have taken you out on a variety of equally remote spots between here and there?"

"There are plenty of assholes out there who think it's fun to get liquored up and drive around shooting people's livestock from the highway. They drive Fish & Wildlife nuts all the time."

She raised an eyebrow. "He fired multiple rounds from a moving car which he was also busy driving. Pretty hard to do with a rifle."

"Then maybe you pissed someone off by driving too slow."

Kate leaned back. "Would have to be one severe case of road rage."

He looked away. "Not really, you should see how bad it gets over on Highway 112. The logging trucks scare the shit out of the tourists driving out to Cape Flattery. Some so bad they swear they'll never return."

Her demeanor cooled. "You're talking about logging trucks are bearing down on bumpers. They aren't using guns."

"Kyle didn't report hearing gunshots."

"I know. He said he was listening to music with his earbuds. He saw what happened, he didn't hear it." She thrust her hand forward. "Give me your phone?"

"Why?"

"Because I need to make a call and mine is in the lake."

He handed over the device. She placed a call and activated the speaker.

Seconds later, Special Agent Fuentes answered. "What's up?" His voice was slightly strained, as if he had spent the entire day lecturing.

Kate jumped in. "I'm here with the sheriff. Something's come up. We'd like to get your take on it."

"Fire away."

He remained quiet while she recounted the details of her misadventure. It was not until she finished that he asked, "No major injuries?"

"Nothing lasting."

Tony finally piped up. "She hasn't been checked out yet. I'm going to take her to the hospital in Port Angeles—at least get her screened for a concussion."

"Based on what I know of Barnes so far, good luck! Getting back to this attack. Who do you think was behind it?"

Kate interjected again. "Sheriff Luchasetti wants to believe it wasn't related to the investigation, but I disagree. At the very least, the timing is too coincidental."

"I'm with you, Barnes. You may have stirred up a potential hornet's nest at TekPharmaCel. I'll start digging a little deeper into them and their CEO. How many people knew about your meeting with Cruthers?"

"His personal assistant, Trina Chen and the security guards who saw me enter his office."

"Thoughts on her?"

"If I had to guess, I'd say she's one of the good guys. Cruthers, on the other hand, is pure corporate sleaze."

"Any reason he might want you out of the way?"

"He's involved. Or he's trying to cover for someone who is." Kate paused. "This may be a bit out of left field, but what about Belovol?"

Tony crossed his arms over his chest and leaned back against the couch.

"What about him?" Fuentes demanded.

"How tight do you have him locked down?"

"You think he ordered a hit on you?"

"Never eliminate anyone with motive from the suspect list until you have concrete proof they didn't do it."

"Agreed. Belovol took a special interest in you. He should have bigger problems right now, and we have him locked down tight, but a guy with those kind of connections … I'll check in with the safe house, maybe even pay him a visit to make sure you've moved off his radar."

"Thanks."

"You're welcome. Let me know as soon as you turn up any new evidence."

"So, you can sweep in at the last minute and take all the credit?"

"Barnes, you know I would be right beside you if I could."

Kate laughed. "Don't be so sensitive. I'm just giving you a bad time, Fuentes. Believe me, I've had more notoriety than I'd ever want in one lifetime." The laughter dried up. "Right now, I only want to find these girls. I don't care how or who gets the credit."

"You know, there's still a chance there are no other girls. Maybe it's all a distraction. Delford might've left a false trail in case he was caught. I mean the guy was a fucking pedophile—they're not usually the most reliable sources."

Kate's eyes raked over Tony, noting every detail of his body language, before turning her attention back to the fire. "Doesn't make sense. We know there was another DNA profile. Someone else is involved, he has more girls, and he doesn't want me digging any deeper. But that's not going to happen."

"From your mouth to God's ears. Stay safe Barnes and keep me posted."

"Will do."

The line went dead.

Tony studied her profile for a long moment. "I think it's time we get you home. While we're on the road, I'll call for a team to pull your Jeep out of the water. Hopefully, you went in close enough to shore so we can easily reach it."

She handed the phone back to him and nodded.

"But promise me if you start to feel dizzy or even feel the hint of a sneeze coming on, you'll let me take you to the hospital."

Still clutching the blanket around her, she stood and looked him squarely in the eye. "I appreciate your concern, but the only thing I need right now is to know who tried to kill me—and why."

May 5

The wind tore through the dense brush, enticing the foliage on either side of the highway to move with the undulating fluidity of a fantastical Chinese dragon. Immersed in the task at hand, Sheriff Luchasetti was oblivious to the ethereal display.

He had taken a knee in the middle of the eastbound lane. Port Angeles Deputy Nolan, who had been so adept at handling Celia a few days before, stood a few feet away snapping pictures of the spray of shattered glass before them. Since erupting from the Jeep last night, the tires of subsequent drivers had churned up much of the glittering mess, cutting two clear tracks through it.

A decades old German van pulled up slowly alongside them. The driver's curious face peered through the passenger window before he was waved on by another of the Port Angeles deputies who was directing traffic around the scene.

"Such fucking bullshit." Deputy Nolan lowered the camera and glowered at the yellow plastic markers he had placed about the debris.

"Yep." Tony stood and headed for the side of the road.

"I can't believe some shithead would fire on another driver! At some point we've got to find a way to build a breathalyzer lock into a rifle."

Tony stood and crossed over the white lane. "Right and while they're at it, they should add a mental competency lock."

The deputy turned and watched the sheriff as he began inspecting the trunks of the nearby trees. "You aren't trying to find the bullets in there are you?"

"The trees are tightly packed, if ..." He placed both of his hands on the bark of a nearby pine. Tilting his head to one side, then the other, he continued. "If I can find it, at least we'll know what kind of gun we should be looking for."

"Talk about a needle in a haystack." The deputy walked toward the edge of the highway. "Give me a second to stick the camera back in the car and I'll give you a hand."

Another thirty minutes passed while the two men traipsed about the roadside, inching deeper and deeper into the woods. Finally, Deputy Nolan's radio crackled to life breaking the relative silence. Tony listened with one ear while the retrieval team at the lake asked for Nolan and the other PA deputy to help them pull Kate's Jeep from the lake.

The moment the deputy signed off the radio, Tony called out to him. "Go ahead. I can finish up here."

Expression clouding, he looked away. "Sure, Sheriff, but ... I'm beginning to wonder whether this whole thing is a complete waste of time. I mean, it happened on asphalt so we can't even do tire track forensics. It was the same thing over at the guardrail. She didn't even brake before she hit it. The only physical evidence we have is the broken glass."

"You doubt Kate's story?"

Nolan's gaze shifted awkwardly behind his glasses. "Well, you have to admit it sounds a bit over the top. Why would someone go after her?"

Tony's gaze sharpened as it swept across the ground. "That's the million-dollar question. You better get over to the lake. We may recover bullets from the Jeep. Needle in a haystack or not, I'll keep searching here for a little while longer. If I happen to get lucky, I'll call for your ballistics gear."

Nolan nodded. "Okay. But if I don't see you, would you, um ... would you tell Detective Barnes I really hope she can shake this—whatever it was—off soon?"

"I will." Tony turned his attention to a nearby tree.

The deputy turned and walked over to his coworker. The sheriff remained lost in his work while the other two men reopened the lane to traffic. Eventually, they called out a farewell and took off.

Over the course of the next hour, he moved further inside the tree line. He was about to give up, when he spied a glint of metal wedged into the bark of a redwood. An identical piece was similarly embedded less than fourteen inches away.

Nosing closer to the first one, he noted the pristine shine on the alloy. While it had not rained last night, the area had received a good deal of precipitation over the last week. If it was a bullet, it had not been in the tree for very long.

Tony pulled out his phone and was about to call Deputy Nolan when his gaze was drawn back to the bullets. He would not know their exact caliber until he had pried them out of the tree, but he could tell they were not large enough to have come from a rifle.

The bullets had clearly come from a handgun. He could hear Kate's words from last night echoing in his head—passionately theorizing about Belovol and/or other unknown assassins.

Before he could catch himself, he offered a silent prayer to the cosmos. If Kate was right his small-town world as well as his duty to her had just become exponentially more complex.

It was a reality he had irrationally tried to reject last night. She had looked so uncharacteristically fragile wrapped up in that blanket. The unexpected impulse to protect her and her subsequent rejection of his overtures, had proven a toxic combination for his ego. Mixed with his pent-up frustrations with the case, it had resulted in a pathetic ostrich-esque attempt to retreat from events he had suddenly felt were becoming too much him to handle.

He stared hard at the bullets. Whatever the hell was going on, he had a duty to Kate and the community he served to face it head-on. And that was exactly what he intended to do.

Chapter 17

THE HOUSE REMINDED KATE of a taxidermy museum. Soulless glass eyes stared out at her from a variety of faces, some of which shared the distinction of being on the endangered species list.

Not wishing to dwell upon the existence of the vast display, or the impetus for it, Kate reached into her backpack and pulled out her wallet. The father and son duo sitting across the table stared back at her. The older man's mouth hung partially open, as if ready to devour her cash payment.

Pausing, she nodded toward the metal box lying on the table between them. "I'd like to take a look first."

Approaching fifty and having grown so obese no reputable casino in Las Vegas would lay odds he would make it to sixty, the father nodded. "Of course." He turned a narrow eye on his son. "Let her see it, Jack."

The straggly-haired twenty-two-year-old opened the box. Retrieving the Glock 43 9mm handgun, he passed the weapon to Kate with the same carelessness one might use to remove toilet paper from a roll.

Checking to make sure the safety was engaged, her fingers moved over the weapon with robotic precision. When she had completed a thorough field stripping, she asked, "Is there somewhere I can test fire it?"

"Sure, but let's make it fast." The pair led her through the kitchen and onto a back porch overlooking a vast stretch of open land, bordered by forest. "I've got a backstop behind the target." The father gestured to a bale of straw about fifteen yards away.

The setting sun cast lazy shadows across the terrain as Kate walked down a series of short steps. About twenty feet from the house, she turned around and asked. "Any neighbors I should worry about?"

"No, the backstop is there as a precaution."

Kate disabled the safety. Wincing through the stabbing pain of whiplash in her neck and shoulders, she raised the weapon and fired five times. The gun was a similar caliber to the one she had lost in Lake Crescent. Like the other weapon, it offered a smaller, more natural grip than the standard SFPD department issue. Removing the magazine, she reengaged the safety and walked back into the house. The father and son remained behind for a full minute, gawking at the tightly grouped bullet holes sitting dead center in the target.

Kate waited impatiently for them to join her. It had been a long day and it wasn't over yet. The morning had started with notification calls to her credit card companies, the car rental agency and her insurance company. Battling lack of sleep—and nerves that felt as if they had doubled for a set of Eddie Van Halen's guitar strings—it had not seemed like her day could possibly get any worse. To her surprise, Tony had taken steps to ensure it would.

On his order, Deputy Flaherty had knocked on her door after she had finished her last call. The doleful deputy announced he had been tasked with driving her to get a replacement rental car from Port Angeles.

The experience had ranked somewhere near the seventh level of hell in Dante's Inferno. When he wasn't grilling her about the circumstances around the crash, he was making pathetic attempts to hit on her. Mile by mile the impacts of the previous night's bouts of whiplash had begun to make their abuse known. By the time they had arrived at the car rental agency, she was practically clawing at the car door. Kate had murmured a brief thank you before slamming the car door shut on the deputy's offer to follow her back to Eagle's Nest.

The combination of a digital copy of her driver's license, a call from Tony, and one from her credit card company, convinced the agent to rent her a new vehicle. The four-door, white sedan stunk vaguely of clove cigarettes but otherwise seemed serviceable. After stops at the bank and a cell phone dealer, she'd made her way outside the city limits, to the house of taxidermy horrors.

Jack arrived back at the table first, his face brightening as he watched Kate lay the weapon back in the box. Kate pulled a wad of cash from her wallet as his father shuffled in behind him.

The older man sneered. "Jack was gonna miss rent this month, but this money'll keep a roof over his head. You know how it is when you're young and dumb." The father elbowed his son in the ribs, nearly knocking him to the floor.

"It worked out well for both of us."

In fact, it had worked out perfectly for Kate whose one reprieve from the Flaherty talk-fest had been a call from Tony reporting they had retrieved the Jeep and her purse, but not her Glock. With required background check periods in Washington averaging up to thirty days, double for out-of-state residents, Kate had used her new phone to search for a private sale. Not only had Jack posted an ad for the right make and caliber, but he'd also been available to meet within an hour.

Kate held the cash out to Jack. It was promptly snatched from his reach by his father who began counting the bills out loud.

Jack turned and started fishing through one of the kitchen cabinet drawers as Kate tucked her wallet into her bag. Withdrawing an extra box of ammunition, he held it out to her. "Want these?"

"I only brought enough for the one box."

Jack stuck his free hand deep into the pockets of his low-slung jeans. "Just take 'em. You're a way better shot with that thing than I'll ever be."

"Don't be stupid, son! You could get ..." A suddenly stormy look from Jack stopped his father in midsentence.

Kate placed both boxes in her backpack, thanked the men and hurried out. Before exiting the private driveway, she pulled to the side of the road and reloaded the magazine. Tucking the Glock into the open space at the base of the radio, she closed her eyes and allowed herself one deep, hopefully cleansing, breath.

She willed away the familiar creep of paranoia which had plagued her the previous night. Millions of real and imagined noises had conspired to keep her wide awake until the early morning hours. She had no intention of letting the feeling take control of her again.

Opening her eyes, she exhaled and headed for the highway. If the bastard who had run her into the lake came back to finish the job, he would find the task much more challenging than it had been last night.

∨

The Thunderbird Theatre rose majestically into the night sky. Over three quarters of a century had passed since the locals of Eagle's Nest had first donned their finest for the opportunity to watch Ginger Rogers and Fred Astaire glide across its silver screen. Since then, cultural values had drastically changed. In the modern world of compressed audio files and screens the size of watch faces, the Thunderbird had become functionally obsolete.

Pulling into an open spot in front of the main entrance, she leaned toward the windshield and stared up at the marquee sign. Rather than showcasing the name of a new blockbuster, it displayed two simple phrases:

**If not for the LIGHT, there would be no HOPE.
If not for HOPE, there would be no FAITH.**

Shooting skyward above the message, a vertical sign shaped like an upturned wing soared into the dark sky. The letters F, H and L, glowed in bright neon against the stylized backdrop. Faith, Hope and Light was not the first church to take over an old theater, but it was the first Kate had seen to take over this kind of a theater.

Turning off the engine, her hand went instinctively to the new gun. She picked up the weapon and stowed it in her backpack.

Outside the car, Kate paused for a moment to scan the street. The only vehicles on the road were a delivery van, a sports coupe and a sedan. Her gaze lingered on each of the two black SUVs parked nearby before turning to the facade of the two-story, art-deco building. Painted in a pristine coat of white paint with navy blue trim, it was clear the old relic was being fastidiously maintained.

She turned left toward an adjacent building which had been painted to match the theater. Unlike the Thunderbird, whose flashy neon sign could be seen for blocks, the smaller building's sole adornment was four simple black numbers matching the street address Chloe had texted her.

With a deep breath, she pulled open the door and ducked inside. The contrast between the unassuming exterior and the vibrant interior was striking. The airy reception space was lined with a series of pictures depicting volunteers of varying ages engaged in all manner of service. From grammar schoolers planting gardens at senior centers, to seniors serving at soup kitchens, to middle-aged people building houses in third-world countries, the room was a visual testament to the organization's good works.

Along the far wall, a pleasantly plump woman in her sixties was busy stuffing envelopes at a white farmhouse style desk. As soon as she heard Pastor Brian's name, the older woman smiled and led Kate down a short hallway to what resembled a cozy sitting room in a Cape Cod cottage.

White wooden bookshelves lined two of the four walls. The majority of the display space contained inspirational tomes; the remainder displayed a variety of photos and rural artwork.

Two settees faced each other in the middle of the room. A large navy-blue armchair stood between them, reminding Kate of a professional referee standing before two overly eager mixed-martial arts fighters. Beige knit blankets had been draped over the back of each settee, giving the impression guests were invited to make themselves at home. Despite the fact she had arrived ten minutes early, she was not the room's only occupant.

Chloe and Pastor Brian offered her welcoming smiles as the receptionist carefully pulled the door shut behind her. The pastor rose from the armchair and walked over to greet her. "Welcome, Kate. It is so nice to see you again." His handshake was as warm as his smile.

"It's nice to see you too, Pastor." She allowed him to lead her to the small couch opposite Chloe's. Kate sat down and carefully placed her bag on the oblong coffee table before her.

"Hello, Kate." Chloe's rigid posture appeared at stark odds with her light expression. "Thank you again for agreeing to meet with Pastor Brian. I really think this will be good for us."

Kate simply nodded in return. *After all, what better way did she have to spend her evening? Dodging more bullets?*

Chloe addressed the Pastor. "Thank you again, for fitting us in. We are very grateful."

"No problem. You know I am always happy to be of service." He stood before the armchair, regarding each of them in turn. "I want to start by telling both of you that coming here today is an excellent first step. It takes special hearts to be open to healing, especially after they have been deeply wounded."

Kate closed her mouth against the protest bubbling up in her chest. She had not come here as a first step; she had come here as the last step. Crossing her legs, she waited while the pastor took his seat.

"My role today is merely to act as a facilitator for communication. When relationships have been ravaged by addiction, old emotions often resurface. They can cloud our ability to express ourselves, as well as our ability to objectively receive information from the other party. Please remember I am not here to pass judgement or to offer personal opinions."

His gaze settled on Kate. "I understand you two have been estranged for a while. Why don't you start by telling your mother why you decided to seek her out now?"

Kate's gaze slid from the pastor's face to her mother's and back again. Trying to match the neutrality in his eyes she started slowly. "When I went to college, I had resolved never to see her again. At the time, it felt like I was slamming a door shut on my childhood. I thought as long as I moved on and avoided the choices she had made, everything would be fine."

"What kind of choices?"

"The obvious one was drugs ... but I wanted no part of her game." In response to his blank stare, she continued. "You know, the whole marriage and kids thing."

"And how did that work out?" The Pastor offered softly.

"I thought everything was fine. But lately I've realized I had slammed the door shut on a pigsty. Crap had been leaking out around the gaps between the door for years. All along it had been stopping me from ..."

"From living a balanced life?" he finished.

Kate thought about the occasional one-night stands, the lack of meaningful friendships and the pervasive loneliness which defined her adulthood. "From living *any* kind of life. I've got my job, but nothing else. It's the only reason I get up in the morning. Par for the course for me."

"How so?" the Pastor asked.

"It's the same role she forced me into as a child. I never really mattered—except to the extent I could be of service to others. The dark irony is it took the Tower Torturer case to finally open my eyes." She stared off into the distance recalling the serial killer's exacting psychoanalysis. "After Candace was born, every moment of my childhood was lived under a crushing sense of responsibility. As a child it necessarily came with a debilitating sense of powerlessness. Ultimately, I let that crap slip into my head. It distracted me—enough to guarantee I would fail with every one of those girls—like I did with my sister."

Chloe leaned forward. "Kate, I'm so sorry for the unfair burdens I placed on you. For God's sake, there are professional caregivers who struggle with the ups and downs of dealing with special needs children. You were not prepared nor equipped to deal with that. But please don't say you failed with the Tower Torturer. The entire country knows you're a hero!"

Kate regarded her mother ruefully. "A hero? For what?" The corners of her mouth turned toward the floor. "The Tower Torturer is in prison. But three girls are in their graves because they happened to know me. Three young women who will never marry, never know what it is like to grow old, because I could not save them. Just like Candace."

Chloe recoiled at the mention of her deceased daughter's name. Tightening her lips against the soft tremble threatening at the edges, she cast her gaze toward the floor.

The pastor intervened. "Those girls didn't have a choice about losing their lives. Kate. You do. It sounds as if you've made a series of choices designed to give yours away." He paused to let the thought sink in. "Why do you feel like you failed your sister?"

"Because I told her she did." Chloe's shoulders collapsed along with her features. "When we found Candace dead ... the anguish and the heartbreak ... it was so utterly devastating. From the first moment she'd been diagnosed, I lived in fear every moment. All the meds and the care ... her life and death hanging in the balance every day." Deep lines of anguish etched her face. "The pills were the only place I could find refuge. But when I saw her lying there that last night, there was no escaping the truth. It was all my fault."

"Candace was dead because I had chosen to hide from my responsibilities instead of facing them head on. Instead of admitting it ... instead of using it as an opportunity to sober up and start over, it was much easier to blame Kate." Chloe threw her face into her hands and began to sob.

Pastor Brian regarded her for a long moment before wincing sympathetically and turning to Kate. Noting her furrowed brows, he asked, "Is there anything you wish to say to her right now?"

Kate watched as Chloe pulled one tissue after another from a box on the coffee table. "It's about time."

Dabbing at her eyes, Chloe fixed the watery orbs firmly on Kate. "If I could, I'd tear open my soul so you could see how much the knowledge of what I've done to you kills me." She leaned forward, willing her daughter to look at her. "I swear to you, Kate! I've spent so many nights lying awake thinking about how horribly I treated you. Jacob could tell you. He knows how often I've said Candace got ..." Chloe choked on another sob.

Pastor Brian retrieved a handkerchief from his pocket and passed it to her. "You think Candace got what?"

"I *know* Candace got the better deal."

Kate practically leapt out of her chair. "What Candace got was death! How the hell do you call that the better deal?"

Pastor Brian laid a calming hand on Kate's arm, which she immediately shook off.

She was about to tear back into Chloe when she noticed something steeling in her mother's blue eyes. Taking a deep breath, the older woman straightened her spine and looked her daughter in the eyes.

"It was a better deal than you got, because after that final night Candace never had to deal with the misery of living with me. She had peace. But you had to live with a strung-out mother who laid your sister's death at your feet each and every day. I know you loved Candace more than anything in the world. You used to take such good care of her." Her voice broke into a near whisper. "Sometimes I resented you for mothering her when I couldn't."

The words, and the solemnity with which they were uttered, sucked the oxygen out of Kate's lungs. She stared quietly at the woman across from her. Unbidden, a question sprouted to Kate's lips. "Why did you decide to get sober?"

Chloe crossed her arms protectively over her chest. "After you left things got progressively worse. My addiction soon outpaced the alimony from your father. I sold the house. When the money was gone, I moved into a homeless shelter off International in Oakland."

"They kept warning me if I didn't stop using, they'd have to turn me out. I didn't stop and they kept their word. I found a spot to sleep near the railyards. I thought it was safe, until I realized it wasn't." Chloe's entire body went still as her gaze turned inward. "There was a gang of them ..."

Kate immediately recognized far off look in her mother's eyes and the way her body seemed to collapse in on itself.

"A railway worker found me two days later and brought me to a hospital. The doctors were surprised I was still alive after having lost so much blood. They were unsure whether I would live to see the next day. They had to sew me back together in the ..." She winced as if seized by a ghost of the pain she had once endured. "... in the front and in the back."

Kate blinked several times as her heart struggled to process a feeling she had never had for her mother—sympathy. In the next moment she slipped back into cop mode. "Were you able to report it to the police?"

Chloe's eyes flew open wide. "Oh God, no. I was so scared it would get back to you. After all the pain I caused you, the last thing I wanted to do was embarrass you like that." Her eyes dropped awkwardly to the floor. "Besides, you know how long my list of sins are. I deserved it."

One side of Kate wanted to raise a sword and hack away at her mother. The other saw a victim sitting before her—a badly flawed victim—but a victim, nonetheless. The thought was followed by another which came through with crystal clarity. Her mother's profound flaws had doomed her to a lifetime of victimization.

Chloe had not been endowed with the skills, nor the strength, to cope with the real world. That glaring shortcoming had led her to darken the doors of those who love to feed upon the weak. From greedy pharmaceutical companies to corrupt doctors who knowingly overprescribe, to the faceless gangs of brutes who haunt the streets at night looking for women to rape and kill, Chloe was simply another mark. The revelation did not come with forgiveness, but it did shine an unexpected light of understanding.

Pastor Brian continued to watch the two women for a long moment. Finally, he placed a hand on Chloe's arm. "I said I would not offer any judgements, but you have to believe me when I say you didn't deserve what happened to you." He turned to Kate. "How do you feel about what your mother revealed?"

She lifted a shoulder. "No one ever deserves that."

Chloe's voice sounded almost shrill in the small room. "Oh no, Kate. I did! The therapists have always tried to convince me I didn't. But we both know I did!"

Kate leaned forward, settling her elbows on her knees. "You are accountable for what you've done to Candace, to my father and to me. But no group of dirt bags raped a strung-out junkie because the universe made them into avenging angels. Rape is about a twisted quest to exercise power, not some galactic sense of justice."

Seeing the hope sparking in Chloe's eyes, Kate almost wished she could take back the words. Suddenly it felt like she was back in the Jeep, with frigid water spilling in all around her.

Kate tore her eyes from her mother's, letting her gaze fall upon the coffee table. Staring at the white wooden surface, she took several deep breaths. Finally, she turned her attention on the pastor.

Studying the thin line into which her lips had been pulled, he ventured, "Maybe this is a good time for a break?" He looked to Chloe who nodded miserably, then back at Kate.

"I think so."

"Good. Then let's call it for today. A lot came out of this session and I think you both need some time to process it."

Kate stood and reached for her backpack. "Are you asking us to come back and do this again?"

"It's up to you ladies. Do you feel you achieved everything you needed to today?"

Chloe clutched her hands together. "I'm sorry for falling apart, Kate. I completely understand if you're done. But, but maybe … maybe we can leave it open ended for now. After our last meeting, I never would've thought there was any way in heaven or hell we'd ever get this far."

Her mother's sentiments faded into the background as Kate's brain cut through the tangle of emotions, seizing instead upon the words her mother had just uttered, "heaven and hell." The same words Delford had etched into Celia's bracelet. The emotional turmoil fell away as her thoughts coalesced to solving a puzzle she hadn't realized was right before her.

"I'm sorry, but I really do need to go." She started toward the door, oblivious to the farewells called out behind her.

Outside, the bright lights of the marquee brought additional clarity. By the time she had opened the door to the rental she already knew exactly what she needed to do.

Chapter 18

CHUNKS OF GRAVEL PINGED against the undercarriage of the rental sedan as it sped along the rim of the quarry. The erratic sounds struck at Kate's nerves, like discordant notes in a frenetic symphony composed of anxiety and anticipation.

The warehouse appeared in her headlights. Relieved, she let go of the breath she had been holding and pulled in beside the sheriff's SUV.

Tony stood in front of the double door entrance. His flashlight was trained on the ground, where it cast a large arc of white light around him. She could barely make out the bright yellow crime scene tape which still hung across the entrance—a stark reminder of her first visit to the building.

Silently sending a plea for hope into the universe, she hurried up the steps and greeted the sheriff. "Thanks for meeting me here on such short notice."

Keys at the ready, Tony smirked back at her. "While I would normally jump at the chance for a late-night rendezvous with you, it'd be nice to know exactly what we're supposed to be doing here."

"We're looking for something Rick Delford left for us."

Tony frowned. "But we already found the bracelet."

"Delford might have been a sick son of a bitch, but he wasn't an idiot. For an insurance policy to work, it had to be kept secret. Think about how carefully he crafted the bracelet. It led us straight to TekPharmaCel. And, if I'm not mistaken, it was also meant to lead us right back here." Raising her eyebrows, Kate pointed toward the keys.

Tony unlocked the new padlock and chain, then carefully pulled away the tape. Holding the door open for her, he cast his light into the desolate space. "Yes, the carving on the back led us to TPC, but why would you think ..."

She strode inside. Tony followed, letting the door slam shut behind them. The sound echoed through the empty building. Kate spoke over the fading sound. "The TPC logo was carved into the back side, but remember what was carved into the front?"

He passed her the flashlight. "Yeah. 'Somewhere Between Heaven and Hell.' Celia said it was his dumb attempt at romance."

As if manipulated by an invisible puppeteer, Kate's head snapped in the direction of the pit where Haryati had been found. For a moment she was standing at the edge again—her senses assaulted by the sight of the savaged flesh and the accompanying rancid odor. Clamping her lips shut, she shoved the memories into a small box in the back of her mind.

Stone-faced, she turned back at the sheriff. "I have no doubt that is what he *said*." In the next moment, she set off for the north side of the building where a full height wall separated the open warehouse from the office area which ran along the entire length of the building.

Arriving at a set of blue doors, she turned back to the sheriff. "The explanation made perfect sense to Celia, but I think the words are meant to serve another purpose. I think they're another breadcrumb."

Kate reached for the door handle. The metal hinges protested as if they had been personally wronged.

"Pointing to what?" Tony asked as he followed her inside.

Dust tickled the saliva in the back of Kate's throat. Choking back a cough, she proceeded to the middle of the room. "Have you ever been to the old theater in the downtown?"

"The Thunderbird? It's not a theater anymore. Pastor Brian had it converted into Faith, Hope and Light Church about a year ago. Why?"

"It's the reason we're here." She cast the light in a wide arc, slowly spinning to illuminate the entire space.

Faded imprints in the blue threadbare carpet revealed the outline of where a long double-sided row of cubicles had once stood. Individual offices lined the perimeter of the space. The doors to each stood open, revealing the chambers to be as empty as the one they now occupied. All except for the first one which was occupied by a lone steel stool, as well as six tall gray shelving units that stood like abandoned sentries at each wall.

"How does a theater normally price tickets to a show?" Kate asked.

His eyebrows bounced at the sudden change in topic. "Orchestra, mezzanine and balcony. Orchestra is always the most expensive but I'm not sure how ..." He looked off blankly then caught her eye again. "Mezzanine?"

"Right. Somewhere between heaven—the good seats. And hell—the bad seats."

"Then why aren't we at the church?"

"Because they told you Delford never went there. He used the church to get the job at Aaru then dumped them when it suited his purpose. Have you ever wondered why Delford chose to shoot his video here?"

"Because this is the place where he left the victim."

"But wouldn't it have been more compelling to film at the actual crime scene?" The question had nibbled at the edges of her consciousness many times over the past few days, but she had never seriously sought to answer it—until tonight.

"Maybe the other guy was still there."

"Or he wanted to draw special attention to *this* warehouse. Before I called you, I got Flaherty to give me the phone number for your contact at Keating Mining. Mr. Turnal was still very distressed a body had been found on the property, but overall, he was very helpful."

"Is there a mezzanine here?"

Kate made her way to the first office, breezing past the discreet storage sign affixed to the door of the cramped space. Layers of dust lined the rows of empty shelves. "Originally the entire area above us was used as office space for upper management. There was a wall of windows that provided a perfect vantage point to oversee operations. According to Turnal, it was accessible by a metal staircase in the warehouse.

"Twenty-three years ago, plans to upgrade the facility stalled when the mezzanine didn't meet code. Rather than pay for the upgrades to make it code compliant, they simply demolished the staircase and walled off the area."

Kate shone the light on the ceiling. She swept it back and forth, finally settling on a wide gray panel near the rear corner of the room. "Turnal said they left this access panel so they could service the heating system."

Tony walked over to the set of shelves standing directly below the panel. "Bring the light over here."

Kate swept the beam up and down the dusty metal furniture. She steadied the light on a series of elliptical-shaped impressions dotting the sides of the frame.

"There."

She moved the beam over to the opposite side of the shelves. They were similarly marred. "Somebody has handled these recently."

"We're next." Tony pulled out his phone, set the flash and took a few photos of the affected areas. Tucking the device away, he reached into one of the utility compartments mounted to his belt and retrieved two sets of blue latex gloves.

"You came prepared." She accepted one of the proffered pairs.

"I always keep a box in the car." He pulled on the gloves.

Careful not to disturb the existing fingerprints, he lifted the shelves and carried them out of the room.

Kate tucked the flashlight into the waistband of her jeans then slipped her fingers into the latex. Picking up the stool, she positioned it directly under the panel.

"You really think there's something up there?" Tony asked as Kate climbed onto the stool.

"I hope so."

"Hold on," Tony warned as she began to raise her hands above her head.

He pulled out his phone and took a series of photos of the panel. With a final hopeful glance at the sheriff, Kate reached up and placed her left hand on the ceiling. She used her right hand to pull the thin metal lever mounted near the right edge. The door came open fairly easily, raining a generous amount of dust onto her upturned face.

Blinking furiously against the irritating particles, she swung the entire panel downward until it hung freely on three hinges.

Retrieving the flashlight, she shone it up into the dark space above. The light cut through the darkness, illuminating a series of exposed roof support beams identical to those visible in the warehouse area.

Hope began to pulse through her veins. Standing on tiptoe, she shoved the flashlight through the opening and placed it on the floor above. In the next moment, she reached up with both hands. In the same way she might pull herself up out of a swimming pool, she deadlifted herself up and into the mezzanine.

Pain screamed up through her shoulders and seized ahold of her neck. Gritting her teeth, she sat up just as competing currents of water welled up from her eyes and raced down her face. Pausing to fight back a sneeze, she surveyed the thick layer of dust on the ancient carpet stretched out before her. She pressed the back of her right sleeve against her face until her sinuses were calmed.

"Are you okay?" Tony inquired.

Dropping a hand back through the opening Kate offered the sheriff a thumbs up. She stood up, retrieved the flashlight, and swept it before her. A rustling sound sent her wheeling back in the opposite direction.

The light moved across an old desk and a file cabinet which appeared to have been disemboweled many decades before. A few feet away, she spotted the drawers stacked haphazardly against the wall.

There didn't seem to be anything ... The rustling sound again—behind her once more. She turned sharply. The little hairs on the back of her neck came to attention. She was being watched. Her free hand slowly reached up under the back of her shirt and grasped the handle of the Glock.

"All clear up there?"

The sudden sound of Tony's voice hit her with the voltage of a downed power line.

She moved the light in a slow circular pattern. "Give me a minute." Attention fixed on each new foot of illumination; Kate was barely aware of the words escaping her lips.

She began to back up against the stack of drawers behind her. Two more steps and she would have a defensible position. She never made it past the first one.

The shuffling sound stopped her cold. This time it came from directly behind her. Before she could turn around, a series of razors raked across the back of her right arm.

A high-pitched squeal pierced the silence as she wheeled on her assailant. The flashlight beam fixed on a fearsomely hellish countenance. Fiercely bared teeth flashed above a set of eyes with no discernable pupils. Taken aback by the unearthly reflective stare, Kate stumbled.

Her brain screamed the word *raccoon* in the same second the animal bared its teeth and lunged at her.

"What the fuck is going on up there?" Tony demanded from below.

Kate didn't respond. She was too busy diving out of the way.

Leaping from its perch atop the stack of drawers, the creature barely missed her. The sudden shift in weight sent the entire heap crashing to the floor as the bandit scurried off to the other side of the room.

Lying on her stomach, Kate raised her head from the musty carpet. She caught the retreating form in the light as it plunged into a hole in the drywall. From her prone position, she watched as three miniature ring-tailed acolytes appeared out of the darkness, following their mother into the world between the walls.

In response to the sounds of Tony trying to clamber up from the stool below she called out, "It's nothing—just some racoons."

Lifting the flashlight high above her opposite shoulder she shined it down over the backside of her upper arm. Craning her neck, she spotted a dark crimson stain spreading across the light gray fabric of her sweater.

"Shit." She muttered the word under her breath. In the next moment, her breath was taken away completely.

Beyond her arm, the toppled pile of drawers revealed two sickly white objects laying on the floor but a few feet from her. Her mind went blank for a split second. She had come here seeking answers, but what lay before her made her forget the questions. Dropping the light and her weapon, she scuttled sideways across the floor so fast the carpet burned her flesh.

"What is it? What's up there?"

Tony's voice hit her like a slap to the face. She squeezed her eyes shut, willing the moment of terror experienced by the woman in her to become a moment of discovery for the detective.

Praying the latter had entirely replaced the former, Kate opened her eyes and rose to her knees. Transfixed, she stared back at the objects illuminated by the abandoned light.

Two human skulls stared back at her. Freed of skin and tissue, their empty eye sockets seemed to gaze right through her soul.

Light glinted from one of the mouths. It shone from a small space near the root of the canine tooth. Steeling her stomach, she leaned nearer. Upon closer inspection the root of the tooth did not appear to be natural. It was affixed to the jawbone by a metal threaded screw.

Her response to the sheriff was uttered with dead certainty. "More victims."

∨

Ignoring the pain erupting from beneath the bandage Tony had affixed to her upper arm, Kate watched as Mildred made her way down the ladder. Stepping off, the coroner glanced up into the opening above and called out, "Pass it down please."

A small blue plastic bin emerged from the ceiling. Mildred accepted it and hurried out of the storage room to the open area where Tony and Kate stood.

"Crime scene techs will be here for another hour or so, but I found something I thought you should see." She led them over to one of the portable lights erected near the door to the warehouse.

Inside the box was a single, clear plastic evidence bag which contained a black flash drive. Kate and Tony exchanged a brief look.

"The same brand as the one found at Delford's house." Kate announced.

"The one containing his insurance policy video," Tony added.

Mildred nodded. "I found it under one of the skulls. I'll get started on examining them tonight."

"Preliminary thoughts?"

"I need to get them back to the lab to weigh and measure them. But based on the overall shape of the frontal bones, muscular ridges, eye sockets, superior nuchal lines, external occipital protuberance, etc., it's fair to say they're both females."

Kate scowled. "And those implants—they've got to be more victims." She didn't give voice to the fear that had seized her heart the moment she had first glimpsed them—the fear one of them belonged to Zamira.

Mildred's features seemed to collapse as if the laws of gravity around her head had suddenly increased ten-fold. "Since Eagle's Nest has never been known as a hotbed of murder and mayhem, that's another safe assumption. And because the skulls appear to have suffered a degree of chemical corrosion, I won't be surprised if they had been exposed to lye, too."

"Why only the skulls?"

Mildred shrugged. "Maybe he decided he didn't need full skeletons to prove his point. Sodium hydroxide works much faster on soft tissue. He probably fished the skulls out before they could be broken down. In any event, I probably won't be able to answer the question you most want—which is when they died. The next question for you two is how many more girls are out there?"

"And will we find them alive or dead?" Kate added.

Tony handed the box to Kate. "Hold this—I'll be right back." He turned and jogged from the room.

The women waited in companionable silence until Tony jogged back into the room clutching a black laptop. He set it on the stool they had pulled out of the storage room.

Kate and Mildred stood close beside him. The device came to life as soon as he opened the lid. Tony entered his password then turned to Kate. She opened the evidence bag and held it out to him.

He pinched it between his gloved fingers and plugged the drive into the laptop. A prompt appeared in the screen. There was only one file entry. It was a video.

"Come on, Delford. Show us where they are." Tony clicked the file and the screen filled with the frozen image of the forest floor. Another click and the woods bounced to life in series of herky-jerky movements. They settled into a progression of fits and starts, skittering across shrubs and tree trunks in a dizzying path to nowhere.

Accompanying the moving landscape was the sound of someone thrashing through the underbrush. The noise continued for ten seconds before the movement halted and Delford's voice boomed in the stillness.

"You think your threats can scare me? I don't give a shit about you or your pissant threats!"

A faint wind could be heard whispering in the background. The camera's progress resumed. It continued through the trees for the next two minutes. The elevation of the ground began to tilt at an increasing pitch, giving the perception of moving uphill.

Eventually, the dense forest opened up to a small clearing. Rock outcroppings climbed steeply up the mountainside in the background. The field of view went still.

Delford's voice boomed again. "I approached from this angle so I'd be outside of the camera range. I'm not as stupid as you think. Now, let's zoom in ..."

The image bobbed up and down for a moment before settling on a small group of boulders piled up toward the base of the hill.

Kate saw it first. "There's a door there!"

"Where?" Tony's eyes searched the screen.

Kate pointed to the middle of the pile. "See? It's been painted to match the moss as well as the boulders."

"I see it." He breathed.

Mildred nodded silently.

Delford spoke again. "I should have known the first time you asked me to come here ... I should have known you were full of shit! You promised I'd get my choice of girls, but you haven't let me have one taste, not one. All I get is fucking clean-up duty!"

The forest suddenly spun around. Rick Delford glowered down at the screen, framed by thickly leaved, large boughs through which thin slivers of blue sky shone. Rage contorted his features. "The cops are asking a lot of questions. They think I killed the last one, but I'm not going down for it."

Smugness softened the deep lines in his countenance. "I know what you have planned for the rest of those girls. I might decide to make my own deal with the cops before it happens. That'd really piss you off, wouldn't it?"

Inhumanity hollowed his laughter. "Like I said, don't fuck with me. You've got way more to lose than I do! And I've got all sorts of little mementos the cops would love to see."

The video ended and the original forest image returned to the screen.

Kate turned to Tony. "Do you have any idea where it was filmed?"

He shook his head, then turned to Mildred. "Do you?"

"How could I? There were no definitive markers, nothing ..."

"Let's look again." Kate reached for the keyboard and relaunched the video.

The three watched in silence. When they were done the location of the door in the forest remained as big a mystery as what lay beyond it.

Chapter 19

MOONLIGHT FILTERED THROUGH the thin layer of passing clouds, casting silvery highlights on the skeletal outlines of the unfinished house. The structure stood out in blinding detail under the piercing gaze of the sedan's high beams.

With her weapon pointed safely at the ground, Kate made her way around the perimeter of the foundation to a large pile of two by fours. Within less than a minute she had rounded the stack. No one was there.

Preparing to holster her weapon, she idly wondered whether she would ever feel comfortable exercising at the construction site again. The sound of an approaching car destroyed the speculation as well as the newly discovered sense of ease.

Since moving into the rental cottage, Flaherty and the sheriff had been the only two visitors who had ever ventured to the end of the private drive. Ducking behind the woodpile, she peered through the gap between two pieces of wood. The approaching vehicle slowed then pulled in next to her car.

With the rental's high beams still blaring, the only thing she could make out about the new vehicle was the fact it was an SUV. She tightened her grip on the Glock. The driver's side door opened. Tony walked into the light.

Shaking her head, she reached back and tucked the weapon neatly into her waistband. The sight of the sheriff so close to her doorstep was both a relief and an irritation.

"Looking for me?" she asked.

He raised his chin in the general direction of her voice.

She emerged, squinting into the blinding light. "What are you doing here?"

"I was on my way to your place when I saw your car parked here."

She gestured toward the cul-de-sac. "Considering recent events, I thought it would be smart to take a look around the neighborhood first. And you?"

"I don't want to sound weird, but I came here because I didn't want to go home." He raked a hand through his hair. "Those skulls ... the video. We got to see where the girls are being held, but we have no fucking clue as to where the hell it is!" The last words tripped over themselves in an angry rush to assault the night air.

"You sent the video to ...?"

"Everyone! ICE, Forestry, National Parks, Police, Fire, Coast Guard, Border Patrol, you name it. Victoria Island is only a two-hour ferry ride from Port Angeles so I sent it to the Canadians, too.

"We've got to hope someone recognizes the area."

"Come on! You saw the video. There is nothing in it! No markers, nothing!" As if suddenly aware he was preaching to the choir, he looked off awkwardly into the darkness.

Kate watched as futility and frustration fought for command of his expression. The same war was being waged within the chambers of her own heart. It had been four and a half hours since her counseling session with Chloe. Certainly not enough time to process what Kate had heard from her mother, nor enough time to figure out how she felt about it. Throw in an attack from a raccoon, the discovery of two skulls, and Kate was on the verge of surrendering to both sides.

As it turned out, her stomach won the day. The organ roared to life in a series of vicious hunger pangs, prompting her next words before she could weigh their implication. "Have you eaten, yet?"

He turned back to her as if she had addressed him in ancient Sumerian. "No."

She stiffened at the irritation in his tone.

The sharp edges of his expression melted. "Shit, I'm sorry. This whole thing is …"

"I know."

His eyes probed hers as if he were searching for a spot where he might curl up and hide away within their depths.

The raw openness in his expression snatched hold of Kate's heart, dragging her down through an emotional whirlpool with the weight of an aircraft carrier's anchor. Hoping to break the connection, she headed toward her car.

"Where are you going?" he called after her.

"Food … remember?"

He pulled out his phone. "Forget it. I know a place that'll deliver." Noting the uncertainty in her expression, he sweetened the pot. "I'll trade you a perimeter search of your cottage for a place to hang out and eat."

She regarded him critically.

He took a step toward her. "Okay, forget the trade. The truth is I owe you for being such a dick the other night at the lake. But I do think it would do us both some good to grab a meal right now. And I know someone who will deliver. Even at this hour."

"Anyone who can admit when he's a dick is welcome at my place."

Half an hour later, she stood in the cottage's tiny bathroom wincing at the sting of hydrogen peroxide as it bubbled up across the length of the wound inflicted by the anxious mother racoon. A loud knock at the front door made her jump. Swearing to herself, she grabbed one of the discolored bandages from the ratty looking box she'd found under the sink and hastily applied it before heading for the door.

Tony smiled into the peephole proudly holding up a brown paper bag. She pulled the door open.

"Francesca's son met me in the street." The aroma coming from the large brown bag bearing the restauranteur's name sent her appetite into overload. She ushered him inside, leading him through the small hallway, past the bedroom, and into the kitchen. Removing the gun from her waistband, she laid it on the counter. His eyes rested on the weapon. If he recognized it was different from the one she had wielded at Delford's house, he did not comment.

A musty smell crept out of the cupboard as she retrieved plates patterned with some of the ugliest flowers ever to have defiled dishware. She laid them on the counter near her Glock.

"I hope you don't mind 70's floral," she said, referring to the garish pattern.

He had already begun packing the food onto the antiquated oak bistro set. "As long as I can eat off it, I don't care what it looks like."

Kate set out two amber colored glasses and grabbed a bottle of Cabernet.

"You okay with Italian food?" Tony said as he pulled a wad of napkins from the bag.

Fiddling with the stubborn cork, her eyes suddenly went wide. "Italian is one of my favorites." She turned in time to catch the seductive smile spreading across his face. Titling her head to the side, she waited until the expression faded.

"We've got chicken parmesan and spaghetti and meatballs. Pick your poison."

The wine cork finally gave way. She poured two generous glasses. "Chicken."

"You're gonna love Francesca's." He finished plating the food and dropped onto one of the unforgiving wooden chairs. "I was a little worried about finding good Italian when I moved out here, but this place is about as authentic as it gets."

"And a Luchasettti would be an aficionado, right?"

"Italian through and through." He retrieved a cardboard box from the bag and opened it.

A fragrant mixture of garlic and olive oil wafted toward Kate from some of the thickest focaccia bread she had ever seen.

Pulling out a long, rectangular slice, she closed her eyes and bit into the warm dough. For a split second the simple pleasure blocked out everything she felt was crashing down around her. A small purr of contentment escaped her throat.

When she opened her eyes again, she found Tony's eyes riveted upon her face. He wore the same passion-filled expression that had nearly swept her away during his first visit to the cottage. Memories began to well up inside of her, replacing one hunger for another.

Before the need became too great, a far fresher recollection chased it away. The glint of metal securing tooth to bone. The vivid appearance of eyeless skulls, followed by the devastating notion it was too late to fulfill her vow, because one of them might belong to Zamira.

Kate dropped the bread onto her plate. "What did the county prosecutor say about the new video?"

Tony downed a bite of pasta and answered from behind his hand. "Hasn't returned my calls yet. This one has got to light a fire under the judge's ass—we need those subpoenas for Wells' phone records as well as for Aaru. Last time I talked to Steve he gave me some crap about jurisdiction and whether the county courts were the appropriate venue for obtaining it."

Happy to abandon the twisted images from the warehouse to focus on the banal details of criminal justice administration, she paused with a large forkful in front of her mouth. "If a bracelet made from the bones of six different victims didn't motivate them, what makes you think this video will?"

He waited for her to take the bite before continuing. "Because it comes with two skulls, and if isn't enough, I may have to remind him of the ugly scrutiny he'd get if any of this became public."

Kate recoiled as if she'd been struck.

"I'm not saying I would, I'm saying reminders about what can happen can be helpful. Honestly, I can't blame him for the pushback. Technically everything should be under the FBI now. Which reminds me—how about Fuentes? He call you back yet?"

"Their tech guys are really backed up right now. If the state lab can get to it sooner, he's happy to let them have it."

They sat in companionable silence for the next few minutes, each focused on their respective meals. Tony finished first. Reaching for his wine glass, he watched Kate swallow her last bite.

"How is the reunion with your mother going?"

The words struck with the ferocity of a newly exposed nerve. Leaning back in her seat, Kate crossed her arms over her chest. "I invited you into my home to share a meal—it did not include a carte blanche invitation into my private life."

He held up his hands. "Hold on! I didn't mean to pry. Whether I like it or not, all small-town gossip reaches me eventually. Hell, half the time it's about me."

Kate thought about the gossip chain which had revealed the leak in Tony's department. Another in a long string of reminders she was not in the big city anymore.

Dropping her hands into her lap, she settled her gaze on the nearby refrigerator. "What's the rumor mill reporting?"

"You and your mom haven't spoken in years. You came here to see her."

"Point for the mill."

"Look, you're right. It really is none of my business. But I want to let you know I'm here for you if you need me."

Kate took another sip of her wine. "Let's flip the magnifying glass in your direction."

"What do you want to know?"

"Tell me about your family."

He smiled. "That particular topic could go on for days."

"I'm running low on sleep. Try the abridged version."

Weaving together story after story from his childhood, he created a picture of boisterous laughter and love. The warm tone shifted drastically with the recollection of his father's tragic passing from lung cancer.

With more than a hint of sadness in his voice, Tony explained, "At sixteen I was suddenly propelled into adulthood. I had become the de facto male role model for my five younger siblings—brother and dad all rolled into one. The truth is, for as much as I love them all, I couldn't wait until everyone was out of the house."

He took a long sip of wine before continuing. "My mom finally remarried two years ago. With everyone settled, it was finally time for me to do my thing. I practically jumped at the chance to leave Arizona and move to Washington. Don't get me wrong, there were no guilt trips or anything. It was exactly the opposite. I think they thought by moving here I'd finally settle down and start adding to the Luchasetti clan."

"But that hasn't happened."

"Hell no."

"Will it?"

He tried to read her face, but it was completely blank. "I don't honestly know. I'd like to think it might."

She grabbed the wine bottle and refilled their glasses. "I guess it's easier to see such a future when you've already seen it work." Kate had dodged bullets, plunged into a lake and learned a cruel gang rape was the reason her mother had finally found sobriety. Added to her recent face-to-face confrontation with the scant remains of two young girls and the combined pressure was forming major fissures in the walls behind which Kate had been piling a mountain of emotional fallout.

Before she could stop it, the past began to slip through the unwanted openings. "You heard me tell Wyman I had a younger sister who died young."

He nodded.

"Her name was Candace. She was born with a rare bone disease. I don't think she had one day close to anything like a normal childhood, but I tried to do what I could for her."

Empathy blossomed in Tony's eyes but he remained silent.

"My dad was always at work and my mom ... let's just say she was more interested in her prescriptions than her two kids. I was a few years older. Everything fell to me.

"As bad as things were, Candace was an amazing and imaginative person. No matter what happened, she always managed to stay so positive. She died when she was ten and I was thirteen. My mother blamed me for it every day for the next five years."

Tony raised his hand, intending to lay it atop hers. Catching a glimpse of the wild shadows haunting her eyes he raked it through his hair instead. "Losing my dad was the toughest thing I've ever gone through. As hard as it was to lose a parent, I cannot imagine how it would have been to lose a sibling, especially at that age."

The sharpness in her gaze sliced through him like a razor as her walls became impenetrable once again.

"Don't be sorry for me. Be sorry for Zamira and those girls out there. And don't forget about the others who are already dead." Eyes suddenly wild, she jumped from her chair sending it crashing against the nearby counter. "I can't believe I'm sitting here crying to you about old shit when those girls are ..." She slammed her fist down on the counter with a resounding thud, shaking two magnets off the refrigerator door. "I am wasting our time!"

He was out of his seat and had enveloped her in a deep hug before she could respond. To their combined surprise, she did not fight against the contact. He held her gently for the next few minutes as she fought back sobs, completely unaware it was the first time anyone had ever held her while she cried.

Resting his lips against her crown, he spoke in the barest whisper. "You are a very good person, Kate. As bad as your childhood was, it made you who you are."

She gently pulled away and looked up at him. "And who is that?"

"Everything I want to be."

The words broke down what was left of her resolve. Wordlessly, he led her back to her bedroom. Settling her onto the bed, he climbed in next to her. With her hair splayed out on the pillow it took every bit of his self-control not to seize the opening. As much as he wanted to ravage her in every way possible, something inside was telling him he should be playing the long game. Ignoring the pulsing demand in his crotch, Tony pulled her into his arms.

"Did you lie about me being the only woman you've ever asked out while on duty?"

The question came out of nowhere. It took Tony a moment before he could adapt to the sudden change of topic. "I'd hope by now you'd know what kind of person I am."

He assumed she believed him because she drifted off to sleep seconds afterward. For the next twenty minutes, he studied her features as she slept, wondering how many people knew the secrets she had shared with him. Brushing a few strands of hair from her forehead, he decided it was a very short list.

Doing his best not to jar her with his movements, he reached for his cell phone and sent a text. It constituted the fifth he had sent the recipient since Kate had ventured into the mezzanine at the warehouse.

Right before midnight he the awaited response. Gently extricating himself from Kate's arms, he bent over and planted the kiss he had been denying himself for days softly on her lips. He did not linger because he did not want to be late.

May 6

Steve Felder stared at Tony over a glass of whiskey. The sheriff regarded the county prosecutor dolefully. An ex-college football star, Felder was known for having an unrelenting sense of humor akin to that of a frat boy. It was a trait Tony had found entertaining—in small doses.

A lamp sat on the desk between them. A convincing reproduction of a stack of law books, it cast a soft yellow light on the two men. Ignoring the drink before him Tony leaned forward. "Come on, Steve. I need those subpoenas. You saw the video! Those girls are out there right now and we ..."

"We do not have jurisdiction. You said it yourself. The victim was trafficked into this country. This is squarely on the FBI's shoulders."

"You know the FBI can't spare the resources. We've got to keep driving this train. At least get me the warrant to access Wells' phone records. We need to know how he got involved as Delford's attorney. His firm doesn't even specialize in criminal law."

"Look, I know it's disappointing, but Judge Nance will not budge. It's the FBI's jurisdiction." He took a swig of whiskey then eyed the sheriff carefully. After a full minute he exhaled. "You need to move on, Tony."

"I can't move on, Steve! What the hell is the matter with you anyway? We are talking about young girls who are being held captive and sexually assaulted. We have the corpse of one victim, parts of five others, and two new skulls to add to the tally! And don't forget there are others still in captivity. For shit's sake, this county is turning into a fucking horror show ..."

"Damn it, Tony!" The prosecutor slammed his hand down on the desk. The outburst was followed by a forced smile. "We've been friends ever since you came to Eagle's Nest. We play poker together every Thursday night. I'd say I've done everything I could to make you feel like you are an extension of my family."

Tony frowned. "You have, but I'm talking to you as the sheriff right now."

"I'm talking to you as the county prosecutor … and your friend." He took another sip before leveling his gaze back on Tony. "You were originally appointed to your position. The only way to keep it is through re-election."

"This has nothing to do with politics and elections."

"It sure as hell does. Elections don't happen in a vacuum, Tony. You need endorsements and you need voter confidence. If you haven't noticed, this Delford shooting has brought a lot of unwanted attention at both the state and national levels. The voters passed I-940 for a reason."

Tony scowled. The mayor and Samuelson had brought up the law governing police use of deadly force more times than he cared to remember.

Felder plowed ahead. "I've heard through the grapevine everything is going to work out for Wheaton."

"Samuelson has cleared me to return her to duty."

"She will have to tread carefully. The formal investigation won't be wrapped up for a while. Until the investigation is closed and she is publicly cleared, your deputy is not going to have the full confidence of this community. She's in a very precarious position. It also means you," he pointed directly at the sheriff, "won't have the full confidence of this community. That puts you in a very precarious position as well." He paused to let the words sink in.

"I'm not telling you to do something wrong here, Tony. I'm telling you to follow the law. This is the FBI's baby. Whether they have the bandwidth to take it on right now or not. All I'm saying is you need to walk away. Not only for yourself, but for your deputy, your department, and this entire community. All you need to do is punt the ball."

"And what about those girls? Mildred has one in a drawer at the lab who is right around your granddaughter's age. Delford went to a lot of trouble to point us in someone else's direction. Those other girls are in that son of a bitch's clutches while we sit here and argue!"

"First of all, we don't know for sure whether the bones in the bracelet or those two skulls even come from victims who were murdered in this county. Secondly, we certainly have no proof there are any more girls out there. Delford was a filthy, lying, amoral son of a bitch. He may very well have been trying to set up a game of misdirection. There may not even be another suspect …"

"Fuck, Steve! We know there is. We have the second DNA profile!"

"Doesn't mean Delford didn't kill them. If there was someone else who she had sex with …"

"Had sex with …? The girl was fucking raped!"

The prosecutor inhaled deeply and eyed Tony for a long moment.

The sheriff broke first. "And if he wasn't lying?"

The older man's expression grew distant. "Then my heart breaks for those girls, it really does. But the simple truth is girls are assaulted and killed all over this planet. It happens every minute of the day. All we can do is try to clean up our little corner of it. In this case, those girls if they exist, fall outside our little corner."

The prosecutor took a sip of whiskey while Tony rubbed a hand over his eyes.

Putting his glass back down, Steve transformed into a high school coach before the big game. "Make the announcement tomorrow. As far as this community is concerned, let it all die with Delford. Tell the public the FBI has taken over and turn the page."

"And if I don't?"

"People are talking, Tony. Important people. No one is saying you invited all of this. But it is happening under your watch. You've benched one of your deputies, another is being investigated under I-940, and the public still doesn't know what the hell is going on with the original murder. Can you imagine what would happen if the town learned about the bracelet? Or the skulls?" His next words dripped with derision. "And what are you doing? Sitting in your office putting out fires—while some California detective runs all over town as if she owns the place."

Tony sat back in his chair. "The department is low on resources. I brought in support and she happens to have a great résumé."

"A great big-city résumé and a great big city set of ti …"

Recognizing the lecherous tone he had heard all too often around the poker table, Tony surged forward. "Enough Steve!"

The prosecutor raised an eyebrow. "Oh shit! Don't tell me you're nailing her?"

The sheriff's face was unreadable.

"Shit, Tony! I mean she is a hot piece of ass and all but … you've got to know how much worse that would make everything!"

The sheriff tossed back the rest of his whiskey. Standing, he started toward the door.

"Well! Have you nailed her, or haven't you?"

Tony paused with his fingers brushing against the handle. "Thanks for the enlightening conversation, Steve."

The older man shot up from his chair and grabbed Tony's arm as he started into the hall. Whispering for the benefit of his sleeping wife, he warned, "Whether you're fucking her or not, you need to cut this whole thing loose. The investigation. The woman. Every-thing."

Tony stared down at the prosecutor's hand. Detecting a warning in the set of the younger man's jaw, Felder released his grip then raised his eyes to the sheriff's.

"Trust me, Tony. In the end it's not worth it."

"Thanks for the whiskey, Steve. I'd say thanks for the advice, but I'll be the judge of what is and what is not worth it. I am the sheriff, remember?"

"You are ... for now."

The older man's response echoed down the hall and stayed with him during the drive back to his empty house.

Chapter 20

HER MIND SWEPT ALONG by the deepest waves of sleep, Zamira moved restlessly atop her cot. Beads of sweat glistened upon her brow as she slipped deeper into a dark pool of swirling memories.

The clamor of voices was almost deafening. Undeterred by the ever-present heat and humidity, the entire village of Kampung Batai had turned out to celebrate the holy day.

Nestled at the edge of a one-hundred-and-forty-year-old rainforest on the island of Borneo, the small community in the South China Sea was a living example of its traditional Malaysian roots. Stilts elevated the simple, single-story wooden dwellings high enough to ensure the inhabitants were safe from monsoon flooding, snakes and other dangerous creatures. Lines of drying laundry decorated the yards between the structures. A series of narrow dirt roadways meandered through the village, allowing for the movement for people, livestock and the occasional moped.

By the time the sun had started to slip toward the horizon, the festival-goers had coalesced in the center of town. Standing amidst the raucous crowd, fourteen-year-old, Zamira fought the urge to cover her ears. She had been warned repeatedly about displaying such signs of outward displeasure and had no interest in incurring her mother's wrath today.

All eyes were on the main event. About thirty feet ahead, a group of young men encircled a massive wooden pole which had been greased in a thick coat of butter. Each of the would-be glory hounds had been given a chance to scale the log; each had failed to reach the flag affixed to the top.

A little over ten minutes before, the boys had come to the realization success could only be achieved by that which had sustained Kampung Batai for generations—collaboration. They were now moments away from completing the second tier of a human pyramid. If the wobbly structure could hold together long

222

enough for a third tier to be completed, the prize would soon be won.

Tearing her gaze from the lively antics, Zamira spotted her sister standing at the front of the crowd. Despite being two years older and half a foot taller, Haryati might have passed for Zamira's twin. Both girls had been blessed with perfect almond shaped eyes shaded by dark, long lashes. They also had the same thick, full lips and supple figures which had captivated the imagination of every boy in the village.

Except where Haryati always had an easy smile at the ready and rarely questioned what she was told, Zamira favored scowls over smiles and rarely did as she was bidden without a justifiable reason. The differences in their demeanors were a constant worry to their mother. She was convinced Zamira's disposition would doom her to life as an old maid.

Only Haryati understood Zamira's natural skepticism and her tendency to overanalyze. She alone had taken the time to uncover the fierce loyalty and generous heart dwelling beneath the taciturn outer shell.

Zamira watched her sister cheer for the lanky-haired young man who stood braced at the bottom of the pyramid. The difficulty of supporting the weight of the boys above him, forced his biceps to strain against the fabric of his gray cotton shirt and prompted his knees to shake below the hem of his shorts.

The crowd cheered harder, making it impossible to pick out Haryati's voice from those of the masses. Zamira wished she had arrived earlier so she could stand beside her sister. While it was far from her idea of fun, the festival would likely be the last one the girls would attend together. The boy Haryati was applauding, the one who had already been granted her hand in marriage, was a stranger to Kampung Batai. After the festival, he would return to his home across the sea on the Malay Peninsula. One month later, he would come back to marry Haryati, then she would leave and start a new life on the mainland.

It had been an easy decision for their father. The generous dowry which had been promised could not be equaled by any of the young men in Kampung Batai, or by any in the surrounding villages. Twelve years ago, the entire area had been devastated by the government's construction of a nearby expressway. Left with no alternatives but plenty of shame, their father had shuttered the family business. Had it not been for the grove of coconut and tapioca trees at the east end of the village and his occasional hunting expeditions into the rainforest, the family surely would have starved long ago. Having never slept one night without her sister beside her on their mat, Zamira's heart had gone cold at the prospect of life without Haryati.

A sudden surge from the crowd propelled her forward. Up ahead, the afternoon humidity was proving stronger than the mix of adrenaline and testosterone. The pyramid shook and pitched as if it were caught in the middle of a monsoon. Despite dire warnings from the audience, and the frenzied attempts of those at the top to regain their balance, the entire structure collapsed upon itself. The assembly screamed out in disappointment, before rushing forward to congratulate their fallen heroes.

In the commotion, Zamira slipped quietly around the corner of a nearby house. She did not wish to see her sister fawn at the feet of the stranger who was about to ruin their lives forever.

∨

The sound of creaking wood stirred Zamira from a deep sleep. Moonlight filtered through the louvered panels near the ceiling, revealing an empty place on the mat next to her. A piece of paper lay in the spot normally occupied by Haryati.

She snatched it up, squinting to make out the words which had been carefully penned in the same script they had been taught by the missionary group that ran the community school.

Beloved Bapa, Ibu, and Zamira,

My dear Junada has obtained work in Kuching and says we must leave tonight. We will be married in his village two days from now. His father will come to Kampung Batai to pay my dowry. Junada expects he will earn enough so I may send for my dearest Zamira within the year. I love you all very much and will do all that I can to bring honor to your name.

Semoga Allah memberkati anda. (May God bless you.)   - Haryati

224

The creaking returned. The sound was as familiar as the smell of her mother's recipe for tapai—someone was treading on the front stairs. Zamira leapt up from the mat.

She could not bear the thought of Harytai leaving, let alone like this. Forgoing her headscarf, she pulled a dress over her head and hurried to the main room. Her father's soft snores beat a lazy rhythm in the far corner where he lay sleeping beside her mother. Holding her breath Zamira padded across the floor to the front door.

She slipped silently out onto the small porch. The bright moonlight bathed the quiet village in a mercury glow. Across the road, she spotted a flash of red fabric waving above a petite heel just before both disappeared behind a small stand of mangroves.

Cringing, Zamira crept down the stairs. She paused after each step, praying her parents would sleep through the protests of the aging planks. The moment her right foot touched the ground she took off running.

After rounding the mangroves she glimpsed Haryati sprinting between two other dwellings on her right. A brightly woven bag bounced against her sister's back as she hurried along.

The sprint ended minutes later when Zamira reached a garden at the end of the village. She watched her sister duck behind a nearby shed and enter an open field abutting the property.

Less than two hundred yards past the field, the rainforest swallowed up the rays from the moon. Like a huge monster perched on the edge of civilization, the wild ecosystem offered a wealth of bounties, but it also offered equal amounts of danger—especially at night.

What kind of fool was Junada, expecting Haryati to meet him there? Not only was he denying their parents the opportunity to attend their daughter's wedding, but now he was creating an opportunity for them to attend her funeral.

Despite the risks, Zamira remained silent. In her pubescent mind, her sister stood a better chance against the creatures in the forest than she did against the inevitable disgrace from running away with a boy before she was properly married. Muttering under her breath, Zamira threaded her way between rows of tapioca plants before plodding into the high grasses.

She swiveled her head from left to right diligently scanning for sinuous forms. A year ago, vipers would have been her greatest concern, but a recent story from neighboring Indonesia had spread like wildfire, knocking venomous snakes from the top spot.

According to reports a grandmother had been at work in her garden when a twenty-foot python had seized her with its massive reticulating fangs, whipped its coils around her body and squeezed the life from her lungs. Witnesses claimed when the massive snake was cut open, the woman's body was found intact—evidence she had been swallowed whole. Zamira had always loved the taste of python but since hearing the story, even the smell of it cooking triggered her gag reflex.

A sudden flash of bright light drew her gaze from the ground. It originated from the tree line. Up ahead, Haryati had also spotted the beacon and began to sprint toward it.

Saying a small prayer, Zamira took off after her. She pumped her legs as hard as possible, desperately hoping her pounding footsteps would send any oversized, scaly predators slithering from her path.

She shot forward, trying to outrun her sister as well as the warning voices in her head. Unfettered by a bag of belongings, Zamira began to gain on Haryati. By the time her sibling disappeared into the foliage, she was a mere ten seconds behind her.

As Zamira neared, a narrow path became visible. Bracing herself, she plunged into the savage darkness. She slowed as her eyes adjusted to the weak moonlight spilling through the tree canopy. A mixture of verdant growth with loamy underpinnings flooded her olfactory senses.

Likely no more than a trail for the denizens of the forest, the way was extremely narrow. Branches tore at her dress, further slowing her progress to a walk. She was no more than ten meters in when an ear-piercing shriek split the night.

Stopping dead in her tracks, Zamira lifted her chin to inspect the vast network of branches above. It was impossible to make out any distinct shapes *but she soon recognized the familiar sound of a primate scurrying away.*

Letting out the breath she had been holding, Zamira started forward once again. She had barely gone another two meters before she spotted Haryati inspecting a deep scratch on her ankle.

"Sister!" Zamira exclaimed. Had she any reservations about the voracity of the warnings in her head, the sudden rustling around her reminded her how densely populated the forest was.

Haryati turned in time to be wrapped in her sister's embrace. "Zamira! I was worried you'd hear me sneaking out."

Zamira pulled away then slapped her sister softly on the arm. "How could you do this? You know it will kill Bapa and Ibu if they miss your wedding."

Haryati smiled sadly. "They sacrifice too much for us. I can't bear to watch them wasting away just so I can have food in my belly." She brightened suddenly. "Besides, I love Junada. He is my future family. Come and see."

Grabbing Zamira's hand, she circled a monstrously large, carnivorous pitcher plant and led her into a small clearing about thirty feet wide. The ground was dotted with numerous species of flora, but there was enough space between the trees to move around freely.

"What is she doing here?" Junada stood about ten feet away. A battery-powered lantern revealed a foul countenance which bore no resemblance to the good-natured young man who had won their father's approval.

Haryati's brow furrowed slightly before smoothing to accommodate a sweet smile. "Zamira only wanted to say goodbye. With your new job we will be able to save enough so she will be able to visit us soon, right Junada?"

He crossed the distance between them with lightning speed. Anticipating a kiss, she tilted her chin upward and lowered her lids. His knuckles connected with the side of Haryati's face with so much force she spun a full one-hundred-and-eighty degrees before crumpling into the brush.

Zamira screamed and dropped to her sister's side. The tangy smell of blood reached her nose as she gently lifted Haryati's face toward the light. A thick, crimson channel flowed freely from the side of her mouth, spilling over onto Zamira's fingers.

Seeing her sister was dazed but otherwise unharmed, Zamira turned to confront her attacker. She opened her mouth but was cut off by a new voice which emanated from the trees somewhere behind her.

"Shit, don't hit her in the face! What are you trying to do—drive the price down?" A heavily muscled, bald man dressed in denim pants and a canvas jacket stalked out of the underbrush and into the light.

Junada winced. "The bitch deserved it for fucking up our plans. What are we supposed to do now?"

The new arrival pointed a finely sharpened machete at Haryati. "You heard what she said about letting her sister visit. We can still make it work."

Junada turned to his fiancé, "Did you leave the note?"

Trembling with fear and confusion, Haryati nodded weakly.

The stranger turned back to Junada. "They'll assume she convinced you to let the sister tag along. Besides, you're missing the best part." The conversational tone mutated into something predatory. "This new one is as luscious as the other. We'll double our fee."

With the same casual effect, one might have while swatting a fly, he whirled around and slammed the elaborately carved, thick handle of the machete down on the back of Haryati's skull. She collapsed unconscious into Zamira's arms.

An anguished scream erupted from her throat as Haryati went limp. In the next split second Zamira was torn between wanting to cling to her sister and wanting to flee. Eyes wide with greed, Junada made the decision for her. He pulled a pistol from the back of his waistband and cracked it against the side of her head.

Zamira's field of vision collapsed like a camera shutter. In the moment before the darkness took her, regret flooded her heart. Had she encountered a python earlier, the torture certainly would have ended tonight—instead, it was only beginning.

Zamira woke with a start. A thick layer of sweat coated her body. Disentangling her arms from the thin sheet, she sat up. Other than the soft snores of one of her fellow captives, all remained silent.

Uncertain, she peered into the darkness. Something was different, and it had nothing to do with her surroundings. A feeling was welling up inside her—one so foreign it took her a moment to recognize it.

Drawing her legs up underneath her, she rose and tightened the muscles in her core. Every moment since the day she and Haryati had been kidnapped, Zamira had been living as a victim. Perhaps if Haryati had not been killed, butchered before her very eyes, Zamira would have continued the same way.

Once again, the cruel memories of her sister's death surfaced in her mind. This time Haryati's feral screams, the coppery smell of her blood and the flash of the knife produced a different response. Her face turned stony in the darkness. The whirlwind of horror and grief which had crippled her was replaced by ice cold fury.

As Haryati's final screams died out in her head, Zamira thought about the men who had defiled her sister and the one man who had ultimately murdered her. To them she had been disposable.

Eyes widening in the darkness, Zamira's consciousness collapsed into a pin prick. There were no distractions, no wants, no needs. Within the dark internal void, her soul was giving birth to the spirit of vengeance those men had sowed inside of her.

Her hands balled into tight fists. She was only vaguely aware of the damage her fingernails were causing to her palms. She finally had what she had lacked that night in the rainforest, and every moment since—a purpose.

⋁

Parked a few doors down from Beans of Mine, Kate waited for Trina to pick up the phone. After the fourth ring the younger woman's exuberant tone surged through the device, bouncing off the walls of Kate's skull.

"Hi, sorry it took so long. I had to wait for the chance to get out of the office. You were right. The name of the lawyer you gave me earlier showed up a bunch of times in our accounting records. But it was kind of weird."

"How so?"

"We've been paying him the same monthly amount for the last three years. Every time it was coded to our general and administrative overhead account."

"Why is that odd?"

"I double checked it against the name of the law firm where he works. Not only have we been paying him, but we've also been paying the firm an annual retainer for over fifteen years. It's always been paid out of the legal fees account. I don't get why we would pay the lawyer from a different account. Or why he his fees would be billed separately."

Trina continued without taking a breath. "I pulled up the invoices. They are super vague. The only description is 'consulting services.' So, I popped over to legal and asked one of the guys over there about it. They knew about the payments to the firm Wells works for, but nobody seemed to know anything about paying him directly. It makes sense though."

"Why?"

"Because none of them had approved the invoices for payment."

"Who did?"

"Cruthers."

"Unusual?"

"Very. I didn't even know he had access to our invoice system."

The implications of the statement set Kate's thoughts on fire. "What was the monthly amount?"

"Fifteen thousand dollars. Do you think …?"

"Listen Trina, I appreciate your help, but it will be best if you don't ask me any questions."

"Got it." Her voice dropped to a deeper whisper. "If Cruthers is up to something even nastier than general misogyny, I hope you nail his ass to the wall."

Suppressing a smile, Kate thanked the younger woman again and climbed out of the car.

The tantalizing aroma of espresso greeted her as she entered the coffee shop. Scanning the open seating area, she spotted her quarry perched on a barstool. Shoulders hunched; he was bent over the counter typing furiously on an open laptop.

Kate's gaze shifted behind the counter to where Fiona was pouring iced coffees for two twenty-somethings decked out in auto repair overalls. Catching the proprietor's eye, Kate nodded. The older woman responded with a tilt of the head, acknowledging Kate's thanks for letting her know Delford's attorney had shown up.

Given Beans of Mine was the only upscale coffee shop in Eagle's Nest, it had been a safe bet the big city lawyer would eventually find his way here. Kate had been surprised Fiona had contacted her so soon after Wells' last visit. Something was bringing the attorney back to town and it certainly was not his dead client.

While unexpected, the news had been welcome on the heels of repeated failures. Tony had shared with her the county prosecutor's directive to turn the case over to the FBI. Despite her furor over the prosecutor's decision, Kate had not pushed the sheriff for more details. He had seemed preoccupied on the phone, and she had felt self-conscious about having fallen apart in front of him. Having never been a big fan of moments of personal intimacy, she had yet to figure out what, if anything, it had meant.

Sliding onto the barstool immediately to the left of the one Wells occupied, Kate swung her head over to get a look at his screen. His hand shot forward and slapped the lid shut.

He scowled in her direction. "Detective Barnes. Shouldn't you be out looking for vandals?"

"I'm more interested in murderers."

He waved her off.

"What are you doing back in Eagle's Nest, Mr. Wells?"

"That is none of your business." He reached for a nearby cup of coffee. The gesture would have appeared nonchalant except for the slight tremor in his hand.

"Did you know I visited Seattle recently?"

"Good for you."

"TekPharmaCel's corporate headquarters are very impressive, don't you think?" The liquid in his cup came precipitously close to spilling down the front of his expensive oxford shirt as he raised the cup to his mouth. Sucking noisily on the drink, he looked away.

"I hear your firm has done quite a bit of work for them over the years."

"We have an extensive client list." The response was tendered to the blank space directly in front of him.

"Sure. A big-name law firm would. But why would they be paying your firm fifteen thousand a month on top of a retainer?"

He sneered at her. "Our clients pay us well because we are the best there is."

A wry smile played on Kate's lips. "You and I both know isn't for legal fees."

There was only one person she had come across in the last few days who had the money to pay for the best. She leaned forward until her mouth was inches from his ear. Her hushed tone was barely audible above the grind of the espresso machine as she threw out a statement which was more of a Hail Mary pass. "Martin Cruthers pays well for what he wants."

He pulled away as if he had been splashed with acid.

"Why are you back in town, Wells?"

"I'm checking on Mr. Delford's property."

"Do you consider teenage girls to be property?" Kate tapped on her phone pulling up the photo Agent Clayton had provided of Zamira. She thrust it toward him.

His face collapsed as he studied the image. "Delford was my client, but doesn't mean I ..." He dropped his voice to an impassioned whisper. "Fuck, I have kids of my own! You don't think there are more girls, or that I would be ...?"

Aware his increasing volume had drawn the attention of nearby patrons, he shut his mouth.

Sensing blood in the water, Kate continued quietly. "Listen, we already know about the payments. Even if you think you can get clear of criminal conspiracy charges, I can't imagine the Washington State Bar, or any other bar association in the country, would approve of what you've been up to. If you cooperate with us, we can offer ..."

Fear flashed in his eyes. "You can't offer me shit, Detective. You're playing a dangerous game."

The words were almost identical to the warning Delford had spat out during his interrogation. Memories flashed. The unmistakable sound of shattering glass. The feel of bullets whizzing past her head. Vivid reminders of exactly how prophetic his warning had been. Wells was right, she was playing a game of smoke and mirrors. And it was dangerous. "Hmm, sounds like a threat."

"Merely a statement of fact."

She eased off her barstool. Pulling a card from her back pocket, she slid it across the counter and tucked it under the corner of his laptop.

"If the game is as dangerous as you say it is, the smart move would be to get out before the shit really hits the fan. Call me when you decide your ass is worth saving."

Chapter 21

MILKY WHITE WISPS of precipitation stretched across the asphalt, lending a distinct air of isolation to the stretch of highway. Somewhere beyond the murkiness Wells' sleek Porsche was zipping along the road. By Kate's estimate he was no more than a quarter mile ahead of her, but thanks to the windy roads and weather conditions, she was safely behind his line of sight.

After leaving Beans of Mine this morning, she had followed him directly to Aaru. Given the attorney's taste for nice suits, and even nicer cars, Kate had not been surprised he did not opt for either of Eagle's Nest's two-and-a-half-star motels.

Wells had returned to the coffee shop for an early-lunch espresso, prompting another tip off from Fiona. The Porsche had been pulling onto the highway as Kate was about to pull off at the exit for the downtown. Navigating a tight U-turn, she had followed him southeast, past the town limits.

Still unsure where the attorney was headed, she glanced down at the navigation screen. The name Forks appeared beside the small arrow indicating her vehicle's position on the map. Thanks to Deputy Flaherty, Kate knew something about the community.

During the odious road trip to Port Angeles he'd tried to impress her by boasting how Forks had been a filming location for adaptation of the fantastically successful young adult book series, *Twilight*. Having never seen the movies, she had turned a deaf ear on his fanboy rant.

Highly doubting Wells was on a vampire-themed pilgrimage, she stepped on the gas. The Porsche's taillights emerged from the mist, followed by a small sign announcing her arrival in the fandom mecca.

A few minutes later, they arrived at a junction with Highway 110. She tailed him past the turn off, continuing southeast into the town proper. Eventually, he turned left onto a side street with well-spaced houses. Kate continued past, taking the next left to circle the block. She spotted Wells continuing east so she took a right, slipping in behind him at a respectable distance.

When the right turn blinker flashed ahead of her, Kate drove past Wells, driving through another stop sign before turning around. She eased into an empty spot across the street from where the attorney was knocking on the front door of a tidy, but modest, brown and white, single-story home.

Turning off the engine, she pulled out her phone. Wells stood patiently on the doorstep with his designer windbreaker zipped up against the morning cold. He looked very much like a man for whom his current environs were very familiar.

The moment the front door opened Kate snapped a series of pictures. A weathered brunette in her early thirties emerged. Arms crossed protectively over her chest, she eyed Wells cautiously as they exchanged a few words.

Nodding, she held out her hand to accept a manila envelope. Wells spoke again. The woman shook her head and looked away. He turned and headed for the Porsche. Kate followed Wells at a safe distance until he was almost out of the city limits. Pursing her lips, she pulled over to the side of the road and dialed Tony's cell.

He answered on the second ring. "Hey Kate, how is the …?"

"Hi, can you run an address for me?"

"An address? Why?"

"I'll fill you in later. Right now, I need to know who lives at 906 Eastmore Lane in Forks."

"Give me a minute. I'll call you back."

It actually took six minutes, but he did call her back. After providing the requested information he had more to add. The sharpness in his tone could not be mistaken. "Listen, you're getting this information because I trust you. But I don't appreciate being kept out of the loop. I expect a full debrief as soon as possible."

"Agreed." She hung up, the sting of the sheriff's tone still ringing in her ears. Clenching her teeth, she made a U-turn and headed back for Eastmore Lane. By the time she pulled into the spot Wells had recently vacated, she had buried the unpleasant sting of Tony's words beneath the weight of the clock still ticking down for Zamira and the other terrified girls who were with her.

∨

Kate waited across from the bank for what seemed like hours. In reality it had only been twelve minutes. The woman, whom Tony had since identified as thirty-one-year-old Lyra Johnston, emerged from the building. She started up the same faded blue sedan Kate had caught pulling out of the Eastmore address upon her return.

After another twenty-three minutes had passed, the woman had completed a brief stop at the grocery store and finally headed home. Kate parked her car and hurried over to the driveway where Lyra was busy retrieving her packages from the trunk.

"May I help you with that?"

The question drew a guarded glance. "Oh, no thanks. I've got it." The sentence finished with a partial smile, as she closed the car door with her hip and headed toward the front porch.

"Lyra, I want to introduce myself. My name is Kate Barnes. I'm working with the Eagle's Nest Sheriff's Department and I want to talk to you about your relationship with Herb Wells."

Lyra's back stiffened. "I don't know who you're talking about."

Kate followed her up the short steps and waited while the woman deposited her bags onto a small table and searched a battered leather purse for her house key. Unlocking the front door, she turned to find Kate holding her purchases.

"Please, I really don't need your help."

Kate stared at the set jaw. Above it, the woman's face was a maze of fine worry lines—ones not befitting her physical age. Without a second thought, Kate held the bags out.

"Lyra, I am trying to help a group of young women who are in serious danger."

An unreadable expression flashed across Lyra's features. She grabbed the bags and turned toward the open door.

"Please help me. One girl is dead; there may be more. If there's anything you can tell me about your relationship with Wells ..."

The woman spun around before Kate could finish the sentence. Her eyes gleamed with static energy as she glanced up and down the street before retreating into the foyer. "Come in."

Kate did as she was bidden, carefully closing the front door behind her. She was immediately struck by a familiar aroma—one which had been an indelible part of her childhood. It was the unmistakable mixture of hospital grade cleaners and those which they were meant to erase.

Following Lyra down a short hallway to the kitchen, she paused to glance into an open doorway. Inside, a young woman wearing green scrubs was diligently disposing of soiled adult diapers. Kate glanced to a hospital bed where an elderly woman lay.

Dim sunlight filtered through the room's sole window, draping its grace across the prone figure. Bony fingers clutched sterile white sheets to a frail chest. The aged brow was furrowed in what appeared to be a pained expression. Conversely, the gaping mouth remained serene. A narrow trail of spittle dripped from her lower lip to the tip of her chin.

Pictures adorned every wall. Earlier images of the woman in the bed, going all the way back to her childhood. Her smile radiated at every age, a stark contrast to the sense of withdrawal emanating from the bed.

Sympathy clawed its way through Kate's professional veneer, tearing its way straight into her heart. Ignoring the lump forming in her throat, she turned toward Lyra who was busy unloading her purchases.

"Let me just get the milk put away." Lyra gestured to one of two chairs which stood alongside a recently refinished wooden table.

Kate took a seat and waited while the other woman completed her task. The young nurse appeared in the doorway. She smiled pleasantly at Kate before addressing Lyra.

"I've changed her and she received her last dose about an hour ago. She should rest for a while. Did you pick up her new prescription?"

Lyra recoiled as if she had been struck by an arrow. "Oh God, I forgot."

The younger woman responded with practiced calm. "It's fine, Lyra. She won't need it for a couple of hours. If you want, I can run out after your guest leaves and ..."

"No, Steph. I will be fine. But I don't want to wait to get it. Here ..." She fumbled through her purse then thrust a few bills toward the nurse.

"No worries. I'll be back in a few." With a final smile, the woman exited.

Lyra turned to Kate in exasperation. "I'm sorry but I can't leave her unattended."

"You don't need to explain."

The statement did nothing to relieve the tightness around Lyra's eyes.

Kate followed Lyra as she returned to the sickroom and checked on the older woman. The nurse's ministrations must have met expectation because she joined Kate in the doorway less than two minutes later.

Lyra propped her shoulder against the frame, her eyes still glued to the unconscious visage. She addressed Kate in a hushed tone, "Francis Johnston. She's only sixty-eight and she's my mom. She's also been battling Alzheimer's for the past five years. Then last month a new front opened up. She was diagnosed with pancreatic cancer." She turned to Kate with a single tear running down her cheek. "It's a battle she's about to lose."

As if to disagree, her mother suddenly called out. It was a cross between a painful whimper and a cry of surprise.

Taking her cue from Lyra, Kate did not respond to the outburst. Instead, she plunged her hands deep into the pockets of her jeans. Knowing the woeful inadequacy of the words, Kate offered them anyway. "I'm sorry."

In the following silence Kate's heart bled for the torment in the other woman's features. She decided to give the only thing she had. "My sister was very ill when we were children. She died when she was barely ten."

Lyra brushed away the tear. "Now I'm the one who is sorry. At least my Mom had the chance to live a full life. Ten is an awful tragedy."

Kate inhaled deeply. "So is Alzheimer's and cancer."

Lyra's smile was so thin it might have been nonexistent. "Thank you. But you came here to talk about Mr. Wells, not my mother."

Kate forced herself to still the emotional turmoil inside her. One by one she shut off the input from each of her senses. By not acknowledging the smells, sights and sounds in the small chamber she could focus on the task at hand.

"As I said, one teenager has died and there are more in danger. I need to know about the nature of your relationship with Wells. I saw you accept an envelope from him a little while ago."

A disgusted sigh escaped Lyra's lips. "The envelope? It's the blood money that has kept my Mom going for the past three years." She shook her head ruefully before continuing. "When my Mom was first diagnosed, she had been working part-time, getting by with the help of social security. But when the medical bills started piling up and the insurance had capped out, I had to do something to help her. Fortunately, my suffering helps ease her pain."

"I don't understand."

"You're not meant to. No one ever is. They promised me no one would ever understand because no one would believe me. The money is an extra insurance policy—to make sure I never tell."

Kate recognized a new desperation in Lyra's face. One which had nothing to do with her mother's imminent passing.

The other woman swallowed deeply. "It was my own fault. At least that's what I've always told myself. I felt so self-important. Getting out of Forks, earning a bachelor's degree." She glanced back at the figure in the bed, her eyes searching for any substantive change in status.

Finally, she glanced back at Kate. "She was so proud of me when I graduated college. And when I got my first big job she was completely over the moon. After all, Bellevue was not too far away and …"

"Bellevue?" Kate immediately regretted the interruption.

"If you're here checking up on Wells, I'm guessing you already know where I was working."

"TekPharmaCel?"

"Yes."

The affirmation was a huge boon to the investigation, but it fell like a dead weight slamming into Kate's abdomen.

"What were you hired to do there?"

Lyra's dry chuckle slipped across her lips—the sound like heavy grit sandpaper on driftwood. "I was hired as an executive assistant to the Vice President of Purchasing. He was a dorky, older guy who couldn't keep his calendar straight. He never was a problem. But the other son of a bitch was. I never even met him until my third Christmas party at TPC."

She inhaled deeply. "The bastard invited me and my boss up to his office. Said he wanted to show us a new program the company had in mind for the purchasing department." She tilted her head and looked off into the distance. "But when we got outside his office, my boss suddenly got a call on his cell. I still don't know if he was in on it or if that monster somehow had arranged it in advance."

"Anyhow, he told me to come in. And I did. He offered me a drink. I wanted to come off as a real corporate player, so I said yes."

She frowned suddenly and swallowed. When she regained her voice, it came out in the barest whisper. "I took a seat on that damn antique couch and the next thing I knew he was all over me. He wouldn't stop, no matter what I said. The more I tried to pull away, the rougher he got. Finally, I threw my drink in his face. That was when he picked up a carved marble bookend and did this."

She reached up and parted the hair on the left side of her skull. A five-inch scar cut a jagged line across her scalp. "Compound fracture to the skull. Mom came to the ICU every day. The Alzheimer's had already started in by then. Sometimes she was more of a hindrance to the hospital staff than as a help to me. But she came every day."

Kate ventured a clarification in the same hushed tone. "How long did the recovery take?"

"You mean for the fracture?"

"Were there other injuries?"

Lyra's face crumbled and she slid slowly down the wall coming to sit on the floor with her legs drawn up around her chest.

Kate knelt beside her and gently took her hand. "Were there other injuries Lyra?"

The next words had to be knitted together between sobs. "It was eight weeks for the skull fracture. But smashing my skull wasn't enough. That son of a bitch was going to have his way whether I was conscious or bleeding out on the floor. He … raped me. My mother never knew about it. She believed I had taken a bad fall leaving the party."

"Didn't the hospital staff perform a rape kit?"

"His henchman brought me to a private hospital. I was unconscious so I have no idea what they did. All I know is by the time I was released I was pregnant, and I hadn't been with anyone for at least six months before that night."

"Did you ever tell the police what happened while you were in the hospital?"

"How could I? The bastard's private security guard was there from the moment I woke up. He lied and told them he was a family member. He also told me they had found alcohol in my system which would put my credibility in doubt. He promised to bury me, and my mom, if I ever spoke up.

"That was the stick. Then they offered the carrot. They offered to pay all my hospital bills if I kept quiet. They had dug into my mom's background and found out about her condition. They offered to pay her bills too. Hell, they even paid for the abortion. And they've kept paying right up until this morning."

Before she could prepare herself, Lyra fell forward into her arms. Not knowing what else to do, Kate began to rock her. Finally, Lyra pulled away. She raised her arms in turn, using her shirt fabric to wipe away the wash of shame, torment and humiliation trailing down her face.

"My last memory before I went unconscious was of that horrible painting. Ever since then even the sight of a deer makes me physically sick."

Recalling her recent visit to Bellevue, Kate thought about the unusual painting which had caught her eye. She stared at Lyra for a long moment testing the fragility of the bond they had formed. "I saw a painting of a stag's head recently. It hangs in Martin Cruthers' office at TekPharmaCel. Is he the one who did this to you?"

Lyra went perfectly still. "Yes, but you have to understand I will never tell anyone else." She gazed back at the hospital bed. "Not until she is safe with the angels."

Chapter 22

THE SKULLS LAY UPON a stainless-steel tray, mere feet from where Kate stood. She tore her gaze from the ghoulish countenances. The movement did little to relieve the constricted feeling in the back of her throat.

Turning away, she tried to erase the image of Zamira her mind kept trying to overlay upon the features. "I wish I could slap an arrest warrant in Martin Cruthers' face." It was the fifth such iteration of the sentiment Kate had voiced to Tony during the drive to Mildred's lab. The process of recounting the details of her meeting with Lyra had not been easy, nor had the process of smoothing Tony's ruffled feathers over her solo flight in the investigation.

The sheriff turned to Kate. "Cruthers is a multibillionaire. He's protected by extreme power and privilege. You've got to have rock-solid evidence and even then, it can get dicey. Unless, and until, Lyra wants to come forward ..."

"I know. There's no rape kit and the fetus is long gone. We've got nothing."

"Exactly. And the odds of proving ..."

Mildred breezed back into the room and stood near the counter upon which the remains lay. "The odds of proving what?"

"Proving someone is a vile son of a bitch." The words dripped like acid from Kate's lips.

"If we had proof of that, half the people on this planet would be locked up."

"An appealing notion."

Mildred narrowed her gaze. "I don't have the time or inclination to take on such a large sample size, so let's focus on the case at hand. I know there's pressure to turn this case over to the feds, but I'm glad these came my way. The state lab's backed up at least a week to two, and the FBI's even worse." Mildred settled her hip against the counter.

"How about age and gender?" Tony asked.

"Further analysis of key gender markers—size of the tympanic plates, shape of the supraorbital margins, vaults and foreheads, greater prominence of the frontal and parietal tubers, and smaller zygomatic bones—confirm my original guess. Both individuals were definitely female. And based on the fusion of the plates, the advanced phase of teeth eruption, sinus cavity formation, etc., I'd say we are looking at victims in their late teens."

"Sinus cavity formation?" Tony asked.

"Yes, researchers have determined sinus cavity formation does not happen until a certain point in the growth process. For example, the paranasal, ethmoid and sphenoid sinuses develop up until age seven or eight. The frontal sinuses are the last to develop during adolescence. And speaking of age ..." She retrieved one of the skulls from the table and held it upside down. "This is the mastoid process of the temporal region. For a young woman of this age, it should be around 130-145 millimeters, or approximately five to six inches, thick."

Kate and Tony peered at the area which had been scored by what appeared to be the marks of a tiny chisel. Kate's lips curled back in distaste. "The bracelet?"

"Exact DNA matches to the two unknown Malay profiles from the bracelet."

The fact neither was Zamira did little to alleviate the vulgarity of the discussion, or the violation and cruelty which had made it possible. Looking as if she'd reached her fill of technical details, Kate asked, "And what about the dental implants?"

"There are three present in skull one. One present in skull two." Mildred picked up a paper which lay alongside the skulls.

"Have you been able to trace them yet?"

"That's why I asked you over. If you'd like, you can have three chances to guess the manufacturer." She held the document aloft for emphasis. The printed side faced away from them.

"TekPharmaCel's subsidiary, Gerterre Industries."

"Hole-in-one. And would you like to guess where they were shipped?"

Tony fielded it. "To a certain dead dentist in Malaysia?"

Mildred nodded and turned the paper to face them. "Here's the purchase and shipping details." She tilted her head toward the skulls. "The order for these implants was fulfilled six months *before* the run we found in Haryati's mouth."

∨

The notification chime penetrated the sense of quiet desolation outside the coroner's office. Kate pulled open the car door and climbed in before checking the display—a new text from Agent Fuentes.

Skimming the briefly worded message, she slammed the car door shut. "We can't catch a damn break!"

Tony closed his door and dropped his gaze to the steering wheel. "What now?"

"The FBI lab struck out on Delford's video."

He started the engine to a tune of expletives and had barely rounded the corner of the lab when a late model silver sedan sped into the parking lot.

"Holy shit!" Tony slammed on the brakes as the car careened across the asphalt toward them causing Kate's head to snap back and forth. She raised her hand to the back of her neck where the already ravaged muscles raged to life with searing indignity.

Smoke rose from the brakes of the other car as it came to a screeching halt inches from the edge of their bumper. Tony reached for his gun, but Kate stilled his hand as Celia jumped from the driver's side of the car and sprinted for the passenger window of the SUV.

Tony rolled down the passenger window just in time for the winded woman to thrust her hand into the opening. Kate caught her wrist, stopping the black tablet Celia held less than a millimeter from Kate's nose.

Meeting the other woman's gaze, Kate noted the thick blackened rivers coursing down her cheeks. Above them, the whites of the woman's eyes were fouled by a manic maze of red lines.

"Oh my God, Oh my God! You have to see it! You have to see it!"

"See what?" Tony demanded.

Celia's manic gaze fixed on the sheriff. "That bastard! That sick bastard! He …" She continued to speak but the words were unintelligible.

Softening her grip on the woman's wrist as she gently retrieved the tablet with her free hand, Kate flashed Tony a meaningful side glance.

Taking her cue, he jumped from the vehicle and hurried around to Celia who was devolving into a writhing mess. The jumble of words had been replaced by wracking sobs of hyperventilation.

Tony laid his hands on her shoulders and turned her toward him. "Celia? Celia? I need you to look at me, Celia. It's going to be okay. You need to look at me and tell me what's wrong."

As Tony did his best to soothe the tormented woman, Kate turned her attention to the tablet. She opened the front cover prompting the screen to power up.

A photo gallery appeared. Fifteen different images of soap were featured in thumbnail. Kate scrolled through page after page of individual bars of soap, as well as bars in various stages of creation. Each had been painstakingly posed to be Instagram click-bait.

Outside the car, Celia was starting to choke out a few words. "He … he … the bastard … he …"

When Kate scrolled to the seventh page she noticed a familiar white triangle in the center of one of the images. The picture beneath it was a bar of soap into which the now familiar phrase, "Somewhere Between Heaven and Hell" had been carved.

Celia finally found her voice. "There are girls, girls in cages! Oh God, please tell me it's fake." She clutched at Tony's shirt. "Please, I beg you, tell me it's fake! If it's not, I can't … I can't … Please just kill me. If you don't I will! I will kill myself!"

"What's going on?" Mildred demanded from the corner of the building.

"Ms. Mayhew is overwrought, Mildred. Can you help us get her inside?"

"Sure."

It took Kate, Tony and Mildred to coax Celia into the backseat of the SUV. The effort was worth it. No sooner had she settled onto the seat, then she promptly fainted.

Without another word, Tony reached for his shoulder radio and called for assistance. "We've got a female requiring medical. She's fainted on scene. May qualify for a 5150."

Kate winced at the code for a forced seventy-two-hour psychiatric confinement. Without comment, she retrieved the tablet while Tony finished the call. Holding the device to her chest, she asked the coroner, "Will you stay with her Mildred? I think I found what Celia wanted us to see."

"Sure but tighten your abs before you watch it. If whatever is on there did this to her, I can't imagine it's going to be rainbows and lollipops."

Kate smiled thinly. "Will do."

Tony accompanied her about ten yards away from the vehicle where she activated the device and launched the video.

The bar of soap abruptly disappeared replaced with the image of a flat dirt surface. It bobbed along for a few moments, then stopped.

"Smile girls, smile big for the camera!" Delford's voice emerged once again from the great beyond.

The image began to move, skipping along and angling up off of what was clearly a dirt floor and over a metal threshold. Chain link fencing rose up on either side, creating walls which encircled a small cot. A bitter looking young woman sat upon the makeshift bed, clad in a tank top and shorts.

Kate's hold on the tablet tightened as she studied the girl's familiar features. Zamira glared back into the camera.

"I said smile!" Delford jeered in the background. "Too bad you girls don't speak English. You could tell all about the troubles you've been through. You're lucky though, you don't know what troubles are still coming your way."

The image shifted to the right where another cage ran parallel to the first, a second girl lay curled up on another cot. As the camera was about to shift further to the right, the video abruptly ended.

Kate pulled up the file's metadata. "This was taken on the day of the vigil—the day Delford died. Looks like it was an upload from another device."

"At least we know they were still alive then."

The words dropped like lead weights in Kate's heart, dragging her into a black abyss matching the exact hue of Zamira's eyes as she had stared into the camera.

V

An hour and a half later, Kate and Tony watched as Deputy Carson whisked a now cogent, albeit still tormented Celia, away in the back of his patrol vehicle.

Tony laid his hand on the top of his head and dragged it down his face. "This is about as fucked up as it gets."

The image of Lyra's scar returned, followed by the sounds, sights and smells of the sick room in her house. They were rapidly replaced by Zamira's eyes. Shutting her mind against the memories, Kate dropped back against her seat and gave Tony a sidelong glance. "Do you trust my judgement?"

His expression hardened. "You wouldn't be here if I didn't trust you."

Ignoring the serrated edge to his tone, she began tapping on her phone. "The answer has got to be in the other video."

"Of course it is, but we've made zero progress determining the location. And while this one confirms Delford's claim there are more girls out there, it doesn't give us any more to go on."

Kate began dialing.

"Who're you calling?"

A new voice spoke through her speakerphone, one entirely unfamiliar to the sheriff.

"Hi Kate! How're you doing?" The words were issued in a slightly clipped cadence, with the faintest trace of a southeast Asian accent peppering the pronunciation.

"Hey Kevin. I would be doing a lot better if you could do me a favor."

The responding chuckle was short lived. "You know I'm always up for helping you out. But the biggest favor you should be looking for is finding out how to get one of those drinks with the little umbrellas."

"In my dreams. I've got you on speaker with Tony Luchasetti. He's the sheriff for Eagle's Nest here in Washington state."

"Hello, Sheriff."

Holding Tony's eye, Kate offered a brief introduction. "Kevin is the god of all things tech-related in the San Francisco Police Department."

"Definitely the guy we need. Kate's helping me on a case, but we've hit a brick wall."

After a brief pause, Kevin's voice boomed back through the speaker. "What kind of brick wall?"

Kate leaned in. "The kind no one up here can penetrate."

"Able to reach out to the feds for help?"

"Already in on it, but they've come up empty, too."

"State?"

"Ditto."

"I'm intrigued."

"So, you'll help?"

"I'll try. What've you got?"

"Abducted girls and a video showing where they're being kept."

"If it was as simple as you made it sound, you wouldn't be calling me. The catch?"

"The video was shot in the forest. We're on the Olympic Peninsula, and we are surrounded by what seems like a billion damn acres of forest. No one's been able to pull anything useful from the audio or the video."

"Got the source device?"

"Nope. Found it on a flash drive. Metadata is sparse and no way to track back to cell towers at the point of recording."

"I don't know if there is much I can do. But email it to me and I'll take a look. Want me to get back to you, or the sheriff?"

"Either one," Tony chimed in.

"Will do."

Kate sighed. "Thanks, Kevin. Oh, and could we make sure to keep this between us?"

"Any special reason?"

She broke eye contact with Tony. "I'm on leave, and what I do with my personal time is my business."

"No worries, it stays between us. But there is one price you'll have to pay for this one."

"You name it."

"You're going to have to hear me say ..."

"Kevin ..." It was the first time she had ever used a warning note with him.

"Sorry Kate, but I have to. You were supposed to be taking this time off for yourself. I don't mind helping, but please promise me you'll walk away from this case after I respond. You need to be taking care of yourself."

She shook her head but stopped short of adding an eye roll. "All right Kevin, I listened, I appreciate it, but I'll be fine."

"You know you are a certifiable workaholic, right?"

"Takes one to know one." Amassing the last of her patience, she bid Kevin goodbye and ended the call.

Tony regarded her carefully. "He cares about you."

"He's a good guy. SFPD is lucky to have him."

Tony watched her for a moment, then nodded and looked away. "Do you think he can help us?"

"If anyone can find one specific pine needle in an entire forest, it'll be Kevin."

The sheriff turned on the ignition and headed back onto the highway. With each passing mile, Kevin's admonishment resounded in Kate's head. He was right—she should not be working this case. It was not the reason she had come to Eagle's Nest.

The little balloon of hope which had begun to rise when Kevin had promised to help, began to fall like a lead weight. *What cost, if any, would there be for failing to follow her doctor's orders?* Without giving voice to the question, she promptly banished it to the deeper recesses of her mind.

∨

While the United States Geological Survey (USGS) has offices in every state, the one in Mountain View, California is situated in the belly of the beast for seismic activity. Strategically placed, it is front and center to the activity of some of the state's most dangerous faults.

The mighty San Andreas, famed for the devastating 1906 earthquake and ensuing fire which destroyed much of San Francisco, is only one part of the story. Across the bay, the lesser known but arguably more dangerous Hayward fault snakes its way along the East Bay corridor putting billions of dollars of property and lives at risk in the event of liquefaction. These two major faults lines are part of a spiderweb of volatile geology crisscrossing the region.

The two-story, glass and steel frontage of the USGS building sat unassuming in the darkness. With most of the parking lot deserted, it had the deceiving air of a typical federal administration office.

Kevin hurried out of the lobby and headed directly for the car. Hung at a diagonal across his chest, a laptop bag slapped against his thigh as he moved. Entirely unaware of the sound, Kevin's mind was consumed with replaying highlights of the meeting he had just attended. In addition to working at the USGS the man he'd met with, Asan Demir, had the distinction of having recently been one of many victims of a cybercrime ring in San Francisco.

Before viewing the video Kate sent, Kevin had decided any solution to her problem would require employing a method outside the standard state protocols.

Kate's lamentation about the vastness of the forest planted a seed that had taken root as he watched the video. No more than thirty seconds had passed after the screen went still, before he had begun opening search bars and pulling together the pieces which had eventually prompted him to call Asan.

A firm believer in public transportation, Kevin had been

forced to borrow a vehicle to drive down the peninsula for the impromptu meeting in Mountain View. Arriving at the car, he climbed in and placed his laptop on the passenger seat. Once the phone was securely positioned in the dashboard holder, he tapped the screen, initiating a video chat call.

Kate answered on the second ring. Her hair was pulled back into a high ponytail, something he had never seen her do before. She had scrubbed her face clean of the minimal amount of makeup she usually wore at work. Something about the look made the detective seem more vulnerable than he'd ever seen her.

Her eyes bore directly into the camera, obliterating the impression. "Hi, did you get anything?"

"I might have."

She leaned closer to the screen.

"I might have a way to get what you need, but making it happen might be a bit of a longshot."

"Tell me."

"I checked out the area on Google Earth and you weren't kidding! Not only is the Olympic Peninsula covered in forest, but Vancouver Island is majorly green, too. There's the rocky outcropping near the door but no other obvious landmarks to go on. However, not being obvious and not being there at all are two different things."

"So ..."

"So, you can see how the perspective rises and falls as the camera moves through the forest. Assuming the camera is being held at a fairly steady height the whole time, we should be able to recreate a 3D image of the topography of the area."

"You'd use the contours of the ground to find the door?"

"I'm *hoping* I can create a kind of reverse-LiDAR."

Kate was familiar with the acronym for light detection and ranging technology. She'd first heard of it years ago while watching archaeology documentaries. It had earned even more fame when one of the world's leading cell phone manufacturers decided to offer it as a function in their devices. "What do you need?"

"To start, a control image for comparison."

"So, you'd take a topographical map and ..."

"And superimpose a 3D image of the topography captured in the video. I met with the USGS. They have the most extensive collection of topographical maps in the nation. We talked through the viability of using their 3D maps."

"When can you get started?"

He hated to dim the bright hope sparkling in her eyes. "The problem is getting the software. It's not an off-the-shelf thing. Geologists use comparison software, all the time, but it's custom stuff. Part of the challenge will be the relatively small area we're working with. No matter what, this will have to be a custom deal. First, we need to create a 3D model of the recorded landscape. But in order to make it accurate we'll need to know the exact height of the person who filmed it."

"No problem."

"Good, but there is another one. My contact spent time up there studying volcanic modeling for Mount Rainer. He said the Olympic Peninsula is notorious for flooding and landslides due to massive annual rainfalls. He warned me the USGS maps might not exactly match current conditions."

"There might be another problem." Kate thought about the regional maps she and Tony had pored over ever since finding Delford's first video. "Some of the land nearby belongs to the Makah tribe. It might not even be included in USGS mapping because the land is not part of the United States."

"Don't worry. We're good there. My contact mentioned the reservation. He said it wouldn't be an issue because the USGS had partnered with the Makah people as part of a joint effort to map out an epic archaeological find discovered in the 1970s."

"Anyway, the program will need to account for weathering and erosion from the date of the maps to now. Asan gave me the name of some companies and geologists who can help get me started. I think I can do this Kate, but you're going to have compromise a bit on this one."

"Meaning?"

"I'm swamped right now. But I do have a good buddy who recently lost his job. If we give this to him ..."

"Lost it how?"

Kevin shook his head. "I wouldn't hook you up with a deadbeat, Kate. He's one of the best out there and can probably turn it around in a day or so."

She closed her eyes for a long moment. "It's a tough call because it's not my investigation."

"I understand. If you want to consult the sheriff first ..."

The ever-present clock ticking down on Zamira and the other girls would not be ignored. Kate shook her head. "Forget it. We don't have the time to waste. All I need to know is when we'll have the results."

Kevin smiled. "I'll cut him loose as soon as we hang up."

"Awesome, and thanks." She ended the call.

Kevin tapped the screen again, dialing the buddy he had discussed with Kate. As he waited for his friend to answer, he considered everything he knew about the other man. Kate was right, she did not want to know any more about him, especially not the reason he had lost his job.

It was equally likely she did not want to learn about how Kevin had wrangled one of the department cars for the trip. Tyler Harding having signed out the car on his behalf would definitely set Kate's teeth on edge. Moreover, finding out what Kevin had been forced to tell Harding to get the favor, had the potential to set off an explosion that would make the power of the San Andreas look like a hiccup.

Chapter 23

May 8

EACH SUCCESSIVE TASTE BUD seemed to die a little more as the acidic liquid slid across Agent Fuentes' tongue. For all its foulness, the coffee was far less bitter to swallow than the pill his supervisor had just forced down his throat. His stomach was still roiling with the aftereffects.

Placing his mug back on his desk, he opened his laptop and began typing. Moments later, his screen filled with a real-time image of Sheriff Luchasetti's office in Eagle's Nest.

Kate and the sheriff sat side-by-side. Instead of returning their greeting he launched directly into the reason he had requested the weekend call. "I need to make you aware of two important new developments."

On screen, the pair exchanged a hopeful glance, but remained silent.

"Belovol is dead."

Kate looked like she had taken a swig of his coffee. "A hit?"

"Yes. A single gunman. Must have been a pro for hire. Was in and out before we knew what had hit us. Two agents lost."

"I'm sorry."

Fuentes remained stoic. "So am I. I've been working on Belovol for over a year. With him out of the way, the syndicate will simply pop another son-of-a-bitch into his place and move on."

Kate leaned forward. "What about his cooperation agreement? You should have enough information to shut those guys down for good."

"He was slow-playing us. Everything we got up until this point has been low hanging fruit. We've got nothing near the top branches." He sat back in his seat and glared at Kate. "I'm beginning to feel like a musical instrument. Between you and Belovol, I've been getting played a hell of a lot lately."

A frown burrowed between Kate's brows.

Before she could answer, Tony jumped in. "What the hell are you talking about?"

Fuentes eyes never left Kate's face. "I thought we had established a working relationship when we collared Belovol."

Kate leaned forward. "We did."

Fuentes glanced away. His gaze settled on one of the many awards sitting on the far set of shelves. He let a few beats pass before turning back to Kate.

"Then why the hell did you reach out to Elias Jennings?"

"Who?" Tony's eyebrows soared toward the ceiling.

"A disgraced FBI software specialist."

For a split second, Kate's expression mirrored the sheriff's. Remaining silent, she inhaled, letting her features melt into a calm reserve.

"Don't play dumb, Kate. I warned you before, I don't like being blindsided."

Tony leaned forward. "What the fuck are you ..."

"Let him finish." The command in Kate's voice was clear.

Channeling all the injury and impotence he had felt during the meeting with his supervisor, Fuentes practically spat out the next words. "Apparently Mr. Jennings thought he could access some of our databases without being noticed. He was wrong. He was also less talented than his replacement. Our new guy was able to trace the IP back and penetrate his firewalls. While they were poking around, your name came up, as well as information pertaining to this case."

He stabbed his index finger toward Tony. "You'd better not

have been involved in this, Sheriff."

"Hold on Fuentes, before you threaten me let's …"

Kate stared at Fuentes. Shadows of things the agent could not quite place coursed through her eyes so suddenly he could not quite identify any of them.

She cut Tony off. "The sheriff had nothing to do with this. It was my idea to reach outside for help."

Tony frowned. "But you didn't …"

She tilted her head in Tony's direction without bothering to look him full in the face. "You don't know what I did."

The sudden ferocity of Kate's response hit Tony like a slap to the face. He sat in mild astonishment as she turned back to the screen and addressed Fuentes in a softer tone.

"I reached out to Jennings. I thought I had come up with a possible way to determine where Delford filmed the second video."

"How?"

Kate met the agent's eyes again. "I thought we had enough topographical data on Delford's video to create a software program to match it to known coordinates on a USGS topographical maps."

The derision melted away from Fuentes' features. Left in its place was the seed of begrudging respect. "Why Jennings?"

"No special reason. I asked around. His name came up."

"Fuck, Kate! Jennings is not the type of resource you reach out to. He's the kind of guy who will tank your entire fucking case! He was drummed out of the FBI for shit's sake!"

"I didn't know anything about the guy, other than he's supposed to be a top-notch software guy. I needed one. It was as simple as that. Frankly, I don't give a damn why he was kicked out of the FBI. I just want to save those girls." Kate crossed her arms and scowled at the screen.

Fuentes opened his mouth but immediately clamped it shut. His gaze bore into the screen for five seconds before he tried again. "The Bureau certainly dodged a bullet when you refused the offer to join us. We're not here to get the answers at any cost. Our job is to get the answers the right fucking way."

"Bullshit, Fuentes. Like an FBI badge is evidence of moral authority. There are good cops and bad cops, the same way there are good FBI agents and bad FBI agents."

He shook his head. "Well fuck me, because I had to learn the hard way that you, Kate Barnes, are a bad cop."

Face reddening, Kate grabbed for the arm rests and was about to propel herself out of her seat when Tony put a hand over hers.

Turning back to the screen, the sheriff fixed Fuentes with a withering stare. "Enough! Do I need to remind you we are trying to save innocent girls? We are on the same damn team here. There's no fucking reason to fight among ourselves."

The agent slowly tore his gaze from Kate's face. By the time his eyes met Tony's, the feral fire in them had dimmed to a weak ember. "Jennings has pissed off a lot of people. Not only in the Bureau, but in the Department of Justice as well. I'm taking serious shit for this. Barnes put her name on the top of a very bad list."

Kate took a deep breath. Gradually her features contorted into something resembling contrition. "You're right. I waded deep into a shit pool. I should have asked more questions, and ..."

"*And* protected both the team and the investigation. Bottom line, you are off this case."

She tilted her head to the side, studying him as if he were an alien creature.

Tony glanced at her, then back at the screen. "I am the one who brought Kate in as a consultant; I think I should be the one who ..."

"What you should be doing is regretting your decision, Sheriff.

This case is still under FBI jurisdiction and …"

"Fuck jurisdiction, Fuentes! This isn't some television show."

"Fuck you, Luchasetti! This decision was made above my pay grade. Kate had already stepped onto shaky ground when she overstepped with the federal prosecutor during Belovol's interrogation. Strike one. In this game you don't usually get a second. Bringing Jennings in was the last straw."

"How dead set are they on getting rid of Kate?"

"Consider her a political grenade which has already detonated. No offense, but I don't know her well enough to put my job on the line to fight for her. At this point I'll do my best to keep them from reporting this to her captain at the SFPD."

Tony opened his mouth again but Kate held up her hand. Her rigid posture collapsed. "Fuentes is right. When you start hurting instead of helping, it's time to go."

"I'm glad you understand, Kate. Tony, I'll circle back with you tomorrow to regroup."

He ended the call without waiting for a response.

Ⅴ

A melancholy folk tune grated through ancient, stereo speakers mounted at the four corners of the ceiling. The diners in Harry's Place seemed inured to the underlying screech of static. For Kate, whose nerves were already frayed, the music was its own watered-down form of torture.

Situated one block down from Beans of Mine, the restaurant offered a limited fare of classic American favorites in a setting charitably considered shabby chic. Kate glanced around at the mismatched furniture and broken-down odds and ends adorning the walls. Ruefully, she decided it leaned more shabby than chic.

The unforgiving bench beneath her seemed to be colluding with the music. Ignoring her aching backside, Kate eyed the graveyard of salty spuds scattered across the tabletop. Holding her hand in midair, she searched the stack of fries piled high on the plate before her for a point of structural integrity.

Tony smiled at her from across the table. "It's a bit like playing Jenga. If you pull the wrong one, the whole thing will fall apart."

Her eyes lingered on his lips, tracing the sensuous curves around his mouth. Regret threw a roadblock in front of the wayward turn in her thoughts. Had she not been so damn needy after everything that had happened in San Francisco, she might have ignored his initial overture on the side of the road. If the ill-fated meeting had never occurred, she wouldn't be sitting in abject misery.

Shaking off the recriminations, she reached for her pint of cheap beer. After a long drink, she put down the glass and forced a weak smile. "The stack of fries won't be the first thing I've screwed up since coming to Eagle's Nest. And it certainly won't be the worst."

Sympathy dragged at the corners of Tony's mouth. As she watched, they pulled back into a straight line.

"Why didn't you mention Kevin to Fuentes?" he inquired.

Giving up on the potatoes, she straightened her shoulders. "There was no reason to. Kevin wanted to help us get the software fast. He doesn't need the FBI coming down on him because he tried to help me."

"Sounds to me like Kevin keeps some unsavory company. Are you sure ...?"

"I have no doubts about Kevin or his integrity."

Tony's eyes searched her features. Finally, he nodded. "All right. Let's assume Kevin made an honest mistake in reaching out to Jennings. You still should have reached out to me first." He took a sip of his pilsner.

"I know. If I could go back and change it I would."

Reading the misery on her face, he nodded and leaned back in his seat. "You admitted to making the mistake and you regret it. Good. Now we can move on. We need to find another resource who can complete the program for us." He watched her expression change as he spoke. "Why are you looking at me like that?"

"Like what?"

"Like you don't trust me."

"Trust is not the right word. Let's say I'm more curious about your motives."

His expression hardened. "Faith in each other's motives is the foundation for trust. Why are you questioning mine?"

"Because you don't want to rip me a new one, *and* because you're implying I will continue working a case after the FBI kicked me off of it."

"Let's get a few things straight. First, I'm not the one questioning your motives. When you wanted to call Kevin, I told you I trust you, and I do. Even though psychiatry isn't my area of expertise, I think it's safe to say there's a bit of projection going on. So we're clear, I don't appreciate having to carry the shit someone else crapped on you." He let the words hang in the air until she had the good sense to look away.

When he spoke again, his tone had softened considerably. "Don't get me wrong, I don't mind helping you scrape it off. But I'm not going to take the punishment for it."

Kate leaned forward, looking as if she were about to bite his head off. Then something softened in her eyes. She took another sip of beer. "You shouldn't have to. I'm sorry."

He reached for her hand. "I thought we made some progress getting to know each other at your place the other night." His fingers brushing against her for a split second before she withdrew from the contact.

"We did, but I don't want to feel like I have to ..."

"Do you really think I'm willing to go to war with Fuentes to keep you on this case because I want to hook up with you?" He looked down at the table and shook his head before raising his gaze once again.

"Don't flatter yourself, Kate. As attracted as I am to you, those girls' lives are way more important to me. By the way, this kind of bullshit projection is making you less attractive by the moment."

She searched his face for some sign of duplicity but was stymied by a wall of sincerity and conviction. Her shoulders fell. "I'm sorry. I don't know what the hell is wrong with me ..."

The hardness in his eyes derailed the half-hearted attempt at self-deception.

She winced. "That's not true. I do know what is wrong with me. Hell, I've spent enough hours on the psychiatrist's couch. I'm putting shit on you, old shit from my family and ... other people. Crap you don't deserve."

He appraised her for a long moment before picking up his glass. "Here's to finally getting to know the real you, Kate Barnes. And by the way, I appreciate the honesty." He winked and held up his drink.

Surprised by the warmth spreading in her abdomen, she raised her glass to his. "To honesty. Whether we like it or not."

He took a sip then put his glass down. "Let's agree we don't have to be completely honest *all* the time."

"Reneging already?"

"I can agree to check the honesty when it comes to my personal feelings toward you. You just need to promise to tell me if the time comes when you want me to step back on the field."

Kate's gaze fell down onto his broad shoulders. She stopped herself before it went any lower. "Don't tempt me."

"I'm the one who gets screwed in this deal you know. On one side, I need you on this case. On the other, working with you is an awful temptation. And the honorable boy scout routine only goes so far."

"Were you a boy scout?"

"Trying to deflect?"

Kate pulled another fry from the stack. "You sure know a lot of therapy terms."

"Do not."

"I feel sorry for your younger siblings." Kate shoved the fry into a small puddle of ketchup. "Now, let's figure out how we're going to keep Fuentes from coming out here and forcibly removing me from the case."

"Fine. I'll simply have to hang onto the dream I'll be allowed to pay you a visit in the Golden State when this is all over. Then we'll see what develops."

Kate paused in the process of retrieving the submerged potato. She looked back up at Tony with a faraway expression. "Golden State!" She glanced down at her watch. "We need to call Mildred."

"I don't think she is going to want to hear about whether or not we ..."

Kate frowned. "No! You said it yourself. The Golden State!"

Tony looked lost. "Yes, I did, but why does that concern Mildred?"

"Because Mildred is from the Golden State too. She'll remember the Golden State Killer."

∨

Mildred walked into the restaurant in a Washington Huskies sweatshirt and pair of jeans. The waitress escorted her to Tony and Kate's table, and deposited their second round of drinks. The coroner sat down beside Kate.

"What's so important it couldn't wait until tomorrow?"

"Fry?" Tony gestured to the forlorn stack which had dwindled considerably in the forty minutes since they had called her.

She eyed the remnants with disdain. "I already ate."

Kate took a sip of the second beer she had ordered. Gazing at the older woman over the rim of her glass she offered three words, "Joseph James DeAngelo."

Mildred nodded. "The Golden State Killer. Responsible for over fifty rapes and committed thirteen murders—that we know of."

Tony picked up another fry. "I got as much off Google. Kate wouldn't let me read more. She said I had to wait until you got here."

Mildred waved a hand in the direction of a passing waitress. After ordering a pint of whatever was on tap, she turned back to Kate. "The second DNA profile. You're wondering whether we could go open source for it."

"Open source?"

Mildred turned back to Tony. "The Golden State Killer terrorized the state of California for over a decade. He moved around within the state, earning himself the nicknames East Area Rapist and the Original Night Stalker before DNA evidence revealed DeAngelo was behind all of it."

"I remember hearing about it."

"You would have. When they finally caught him in 2018, the story made all the major newswires. Not only was he a prior cop, but the arrest was the result of DNA match to genetic genealogy."

"You mean those websites where you spit in a cup and they tell you where your ancestors are from?"

"Exactly. In 2001 investigators were able to match the DNA profile of the Original Night Stalker to that of the East Area rapist. The problem was the profile did not exist in CODIS, because DeAngelo had never been convicted. Thus, the cases went cold for another seventeen years.

"Finally, the decision was made to run it through a genealogy database. They got a hit for someone who was a close match to the profile, likely a relative. Investigators then obtained DeAngelo's DNA from samples extracted from both discarded tissue and the handle of his car door. It matched. The bastard was finally arrested after over four decades."

Tony turned his attention back to Kate. "We have the second DNA profile but we can't match it to anyone in CODIS. You want to see if we can go to one of these genealogy companies for a match."

"Right."

He turned back to Mildred. "Why haven't we already done it?"

She looked at him dryly. "Like much of what we do, it has received a mixed response from the public. There are some real privacy concerns out there. Even some folks on our side of the ledger don't feel overly comfortable with it."

"Nothing like politics in law enforcement."

"If there's a place where one happens without the other, buy me a ticket and I'll be on the next plane."

Tony smiled. "Do you think we can find a way to make it happen?"

Mildred's drink arrived. She nearly devoured one third of it before responding. "We'll have to jump through quite a few hoops, but I'll get on it first thing Monday morning."

Tony's reaction was the antithesis of what the coroner had expected. His features had frozen.

Kate looked from the sheriff to Mildred and back again. Based on the angle of his head it was immediately apparent that he was not looking at the coroner, but beyond her. Kate craned her neck to follow his gaze but no one stood between their table and the bar. She looked beyond to the large screen television mounted behind the bar.

Mildred made a joke to Tony about his expression but Kate

did not hear it. She was too busy staring at the screen. With the sound muted, black closed captioning boxes appeared below a photo of a man in his late twenties. According to the breaking news, the man was an ex-FBI agent who had been arrested on suspicion of selling stolen US intelligence to a foreign nation. The name of the man appeared over and over in the caption box: Elias Jennings.

Over the image, a snippet of her earlier run in with Fuentes' replayed in Kate's head. He had said Jennings was involved with serious shit. As she gazed at the screen, she knew it was serious shit indeed. Somehow, she had walked right into the middle of it.

Chapter 24

THE WOMAN SEEMED out of her element, although there was nothing in her appearance to suggest it. The low-profile hiking shoes, jeans and oversized sweater fit perfectly into the Olympic Peninsula vibe.

The disconnect arose in the way her dark eyes moved about the coffee shop. As the early morning hour wore on, they zeroed in on each new entrant with an intense scrutiny that belied the casual fashion statement. At five-nine, with aristocratic Indian features, she had attracted more than one eager male eye in return.

Having completed an intense once over of two elderly ladies headed toward the pastry counter, she turned her attention back to her laptop. A *Science Daily* article on synthetic molecular biology dominated the display. She reached out to tap at the scroll bar when the small bell above the front door sprang to life once more.

Her gaze veered back to the entrance where Kate Barnes was making her way to the register. She lingered on the new arrival's face almost half a second too long. Before Kate's eyes could happen upon hers, the woman tipped her head back down toward the screen.

The article held her interest no longer than three seconds before her attention drifted back to the register where Kate now stood placing her order. Her eyes ran up and down Kate's body, cataloging every nuance in clothing and body language. Inventory complete, she forced her attention back to the computer.

As Kate moved to the pickup counter the younger woman stood and headed in her direction. Aware of her approach, Kate stepped aside to make room at the small counter.

Shoving both of her hands deep into the back pockets of her jeans, the woman called out to Fiona. "Excuse me." A hint of British formality lingered in the easily identifiable Indian accent.

"Yes?" The proprietor looked up from the stainless-steel mug of milk she was steaming.

The woman beamed back at her. "This is my first trip to this area and my friends told me I should check out Lake Crescent. Is it hard to get there?"

Despite the mellifluent pronunciation of the location, its mention drew a severe sidelong glance from Kate. Betraying no other outward signs of interest, she waited until Fiona had finished rattling off her local travel hints before casually looking away.

Ebony lashes batted in rapid succession toward the proprietor. "Oh, thank you! My friends warned me the road work around here can set you back hours in travel time. I only have until two this afternoon. Then I have to catch the ferry back to Vancouver."

"No worries, honey." Fiona smiled back at the appreciative inquisitor.

The woman turned her ebullience on Kate. "I can't wait to see the lake, but my friends insisted I've got to do some of the trails. Are there any you recommend?"

Kate stared deeply into the woman's eyes, where a lack of certainty bobbed behind the bubbly personality. "No. I'm not from around here."

The woman placed an arm on the counter and looked at Kate with wide eyes. "Well, then you should check out the trails too. There's one in particular my friends told me about. It's right past the Ranger Station. It leads up to Marymere Falls and it's supposed to be awesome!"

She turned back to Fiona, "Thanks again! I better get going, I want to get my stuff from the hotel before I head over to the lake."

271

She spun on her heel and returned to the table. Within seconds she had packed up her laptop and made straight for the door.

Kate watched her go, then turned back to the counter. A napkin adorned with the Beans of Mine logo sat in the spot the woman's elbow had occupied moments before. Three words and a series of numbers had been printed in bold letters in the lower left corner.

As Fiona turned to pass a steaming paper cup over the counter, Kate laid her left hand casually atop the napkin, then reached for the drink with her right. Bidding the proprietor a good day, she turned and headed out of the shop.

It was not until Kate was back in her car, that she looked at the napkin she had swiped. Precise blue capital letters stood out in dark contrast in the fading morning light. If there had been any question whether the napkin had been intentionally left for her, the answer was in the first word:

BARNES TRAIL – 9 a.m.
ALONE – 14257

She picked up her phone. Nine o'clock was only twenty minutes away.

∨

At an elevation of over forty-five hundred feet, Mount Storm King stands in austere prominence over the south shore of Lake Crescent. Its ragged peak emerges majestically from the thick forest, offering the highest vista of the numerous mountains encircling the lake.

Not far from the foot of the mountain is the Storm King Ranger Station. Constructed in 1905, the two-story log cabin looks more like a dwelling out of Jack London's epic tale, The Call of the Wild, than a federal government building. It also happens to be located at Barnes Point, the popular starting point for anyone wishing to hike the Barnes Trail to Marymere Falls.

All of these facts had appeared on Kate's phone less than fifteen minutes before. The internet search had confirmed that not only did a Barnes Trail exist but that it ran right by Lake Crescent.

Identifying the destination had been easy. Thanks to unusually clear skies, the drive had progressed similarly so—until the trees along the road began to thin.

Kate compressed her lips. Seconds later, the first glimpse of the blue waters jolted her nervous system like an electric cattle prod. The response was followed by the overwhelming sensation the car was suddenly sliding across the road toward the icy depths. The ghostly scent of earthy water filled her nose, as if tens of gallons per minute were once again flooding the front seat of her car.

Tightening her grip on the steering wheel, she fixed her gaze firmly on the double yellow line dividing the two lanes of traffic. The fact the car never came too near the line did nothing to ward off the tendrils of fear slipping up through her neck, attacking both her mind and her equilibrium.

A moment later the lake disappeared behind a wall of trees. The change of scenery worked like a magic wand to dispel the debilitating illusion.

A stilted voice called out from the dashboard causing her to jump in her seat. "Take the next right. The destination is on your right."

She had to wait for an oncoming RV to pass before she could turn onto the short drive to the parking lot. The early hour had not attracted many visitors. Besides her rental, there were only two other vehicles in attendance. Neither was a black SUV.

After circling the lot twice, she parked in front of the trail head marker. Retrieving her Glock from the dashboard, she leaned forward, lifted her jacket and tucked the weapon into the rear waistband of her jeans.

Outside in the brisk air Kate scanned the lot and the surrounding trees once more. Satisfied there were no visible signs of human life, she shut the car door and approached the map displayed on the marker.

A minute later she was on the path headed toward the lake. She had traversed a relatively short distance when a huge lawn area opened up to her right. The ground began to slope gently at first, then fell more determinedly toward the water.

Straight ahead a wooden dock floated upon the practically still surface. Through the turquoise water, she could see fallen trees and branches lying on the lake floor. For a brief moment she envisioned herself lying among the botanical odds and ends.

Tearing her eyes from the lake, she followed the trail to the right. Before she knew it, she had arrived at the Ranger Station. Other than its quaint architectural style she noted no signs of human life. According to the information provided on the trail marker, the station did not open for another two hours.

Soon after passing the quaint building, she was enveloped by the forest. The temperature dropped a few degrees beneath the thick canopy. It seemed to plummet further still as the trail led her closer and closer to the water.

About twenty yards before encountering the shore, the trail doglegged to the right leading her to the mouth of a tunnel. Taking no more than another second to scan the area around the rocky exterior, Kate ducked inside. She carefully picked her way along the right wall, while the occasional car passed on the highway overhead.

When she emerged on the other side the sounds of civilization disappeared, dampened by some of the most beautiful forest she had ever seen. Vibrant green ferns and new growth volunteers sporadically dotted the forest floor. The more mature timbers towered toward heaven like organic skyscrapers. Birdsong echoed melodically in the air, balanced by the arrhythmic rustling from unseen busy bodies moving about in the underbrush. In its own way, the ambience was as vibrant as downtown San Francisco on its busiest day.

Eyes constantly scanning her environs, Kate continued at a strident clip. In less than ten minutes she arrived at the creek bearing her surname. She crossed the wide, low bridge in the same solitude which had accompanied her since leaving the parking lot. It was not until she followed the trail around and up to the foot of a very different type of bridge, that Kate found herself in the presence of human company.

The structure looked more likely to have been built by forest fairies than constructed by man. Unlike the typical manufactured plank construction, the span above the small waterfall consisted of a simple, large tree lying upon elevated supports. Handrails rose in an outward V-pattern from the surface of the tree which had been stripped of all its bark. The narrow walkway consisted of a trench appearing to be no more than a foot or two wide.

Standing midspan, with her right heel in front of her left toes, the woman from the coffee shop watched Kate with keen interest.

Without hesitation, Kate climbed the small wooden ladder which led up to the bridge. She stopped on the top rung and stared back at the woman.

"It's really not quite as bad as it looks." The stranger smiled. There was no trace of the earlier exuberance.

"It doesn't look so bad to me."

The note of challenge in Kate's voice was met with a raised eyebrow. "He said you'd come right away, but I was worried you might miss the napkin."

"I tend to notice things."

"He said that, too."

"Are we going to talk, here?"

The woman smiled again, then rolled her eyes. "You're right. We'll have more privacy at the top of the falls." She looked pointedly toward the trail behind Kate. "Give me a second to turn around. Then you can follow me."

Kate watched as the other woman carefully positioned her hands to navigate the one-hundred-and-eighty-degree turn on the narrow surface. Waiting until the way was clear, Kate stepped onto the bridge. Proceeding step-over-step and hand-by-hand, she tried to keep an intermittent eye on her companion. In less than a minute she had made it safely across and down the far ladder.

Without a word, the woman led her up a steep series of switchbacks. Nearing the top of the mountainside, they turned sharply to the right. They made their way into a narrow opening between the hills.

The sound of falling water drew Kate's attention upward. The lovely cascade spilling out from the forest floor above earned nothing more than a glance. Instead, she focused on the fact the trail dead-ended at a sheer rock wall.

A series of roughly hewn logs served as guardrails, protecting visitors from plummeting more than seventy feet to the rocks below. Kate turned back to her guide who suddenly swung her backpack around.

Dropping back a step, Kate reached for her weapon. She stopped midmotion when the woman pulled out two cell phones.

"By the way, I'm Natalie. I know this must be weird but I'm assuming he has his reasons."

"And I'm assuming you have your reasons for doing this for Kevin." Kate uttered the name with authority. While she still had no idea how he fit into this, she had immediately recognized the numbers 14257 from the note as being the file designation for the

Tower Torturer case.

Not long after they had started working together Kate had discovered Kevin's penchant for referring to every case by its file number. The habit had driven her crazy for six solid months until she had finally convinced him to stop.

Natalie's expression turned wistful. "Kevin and I have been friends since I came here from India at thirteen. He was an immigrant, too, and we hit it off immediately. I moved from the Bay Area to Vancouver after med school, so we haven't seen each other as much in person over the last few years."

Under any other circumstances Kate might have dug deeper, but girls were missing and the ever-present clock in her head continued to tick down.

The woman passed her the smaller of the two devices. "It won't work out here. He wants you to call as soon as you get back to the parking lot. You'll have cell service there. He said you should only call him once, then toss the phone."

"Did he say why all this was necessary?" She gestured to the waterfall.

"No. Trust me, I wouldn't have done something like this for anyone but Kevin. Great work on the Torturer case, by the way."

Kate shoved the phone into the pocket of her jacket. "It was a team effort. Kevin was an important part of it."

"I can believe it. He's a bright guy."

"And a good one."

"Definitely a good one." Natalie glanced down at the ground as if worried her eyes might betray more than she wished to convey. Looking back at Kate, she held up her phone. "He asked me to wait for thirty minutes after you leave, so I might as well get some pictures."

Kate extended her hand. "It was nice to meet you Natalie. And thank you for ... for whatever this is."

The woman's handshake was warm and firm. "Be sure to tell him I followed his directions."

"I will." Kate turned and hurried back along the path, her head buzzing with questions to which she would soon have answers.

V

Kate backed the rental car into a stall in the far corner of the lot before turning on the phone. A text appeared. It included a phone number, along with the words "call me."

Kevin answered on the first ring.

"Are you alone?"

"Yes. What the hell happened with Jennings and what the hell is with the spy games?" Anger and a hint of betrayal dripped between her words.

"This is way bigger than Elias." His tone was equally unpleasant.

"He hacked the U.S. government! Do you realize what position this has put me in?"

"It's all bullshit! Would you listen? We don't have much time." The vehemence in the admonition shocked her into silence.

"Elias was booted from the FBI for hacking a social media site that puts people on one-way blast. His sister's ex posted nudes of her on the site to get back at her for dumping him. If he hadn't bragged about it to a coworker, he'd still be at the FBI today."

Kate frowned but remained silent.

"The only thing Elias is guilty of is being a protective younger brother."

"Look, I don't know why you'd ever believe this guy, but ...?"

"Shit, Kate! You're the one who started all this. Elias is in jail because of you!"

"What?"

"Whatever shit you're into, you need to get the hell away from it, and fast."

"Did the feds talk to you, or anyone at SFPD about this?"

"No."

"Well hopefully they won't, and you won't get dragged into this any further."

"I was dragged six feet under from the time you called me. You know how good my personal tech security is, right?"

An oily heaviness began to roil in Kate's stomach. "Of course."

"Since the shit hit the fan I went back and ran some diagnostics. Before Elias was arrested someone tried to attack my laptop. It was a coordinated hit, reaching out to all of my linked devices. My cell phone was the targeted point of entry."

"Okay."

"It took a while, but I was able to trace the file back to its transmission source. It was launched from an IP mirroring the cell phone number of someone who I had already accepted as a trusted caller on my phone."

"Whose number was it?"

His long sigh made the anticipation worse. "It was yours."

The fact there had been a second assault on her, albeit a technological one, chilled her to the core. "Someone hacked my phone?"

"And whoever did it was no joke. We're talking major skills. And don't freak out but there's something else I need to tell you."

He waited through the ensuing silence. "I reached out to your laptop last night."

"Reached out?" The note of warning in her tone was even harsher than she had anticipated.

"You know me, Kate. I swear I didn't get into your business. But I did find what I was afraid of."

"They got into my laptop, too?"

"Yep. I got in by pretending to be a major retailer. I ghosted in through your backdoor to track your search activities. I didn't want to attract attention but I was able to stay around long enough to trace the signal back through all the proxies to the point of origination. It came from a laptop located at a company in Bellevue, Washington."

"TekPharmaCel?"

"No, but you're close. It was one of their subsidiaries. Does TPC has something to do with your investigation? Wait, don't tell me. I don't want to know any more than I do."

Kate glanced out the window, trying to put the swarm of emotions in check long enough to clearly see the pieces on the chess board. *A cyberattack on his own computer even Kevin couldn't trace. Delford's devices expertly wiped clean.*

Staring intently into the forest, but not seeing anything beyond the hood of the car, Kate apologized for the second time in as many days. "I'm sorry to have gotten you into this, Kevin, and I appreciate the lengths you've gone to for me. But I need you to walk away from this. I can handle it."

"I don't think you understand, Kate. Not only were you hacked by those guys, I think they set up Elias, too."

"You're wrong, Kevin. I do understand, and I know exactly how to deal with it."

Another long sigh. "Look, Kate, I don't know what the hell is going on up there, but I've got some sick time coming if you need me to …"

"No, I mean it. I can handle this."

Indecision weighted his tone. "How about if I tell Harding, he'll definitely want to …"

The response was reflexive, a knee jerk to both the discomfort of knowing how much he cared and the need to protect him. "No way! I told you at the beginning of this, I don't need you discussing this with anyone."

"But Harding isn't anyone and he …"

"He has enough work to do without worrying about me. Like I said, I'll be fine. The most important thing you can do for me right now is to lie low and forget about this. I'll call you when it's over." She hung up before he could say another word.

Mind racing, she turned on the engine. Halfway across the lot, she pulled alongside a large brown trash bin. Leaving the car running she hopped out and dropped the phone inside it.

Moments later, she turned onto the highway. The momentary fear she had felt upon learning she had been hacked was long gone. It had been replaced by a need to even the odds.

She glanced at the clock. It would take a few hours, but she was going to punch back.

Chapter 25

TRINA CHEN TOOK A DEEP BREATH before opening the door to the office. She walked in, aware feigned confidence was her only shield against the wrath she was about to draw from the man sitting behind the desk.

Martin Cruthers glared at his assistant. "What do you want?"

In answer to his question, Kate appeared behind Trina. "I thought we should talk."

He stood and gestured for her to take a seat in one of the chairs opposite his desk. She crossed the room, stopping short of the desk and took a seat on one of the couches.

The executive cut a scathing glance at his assistant, "Get out."

Trina glanced from her boss to their visitor. Kate responded with a nod. With a slight smile the younger woman turned and exited the room.

Cruthers crossed to the bar and began pouring himself a whiskey. "Drink?" he asked over his shoulder.

"No."

He turned from the bar and gestured to her with his glass. "The first time you came here, you were able to get a meeting with less than twenty-four hours' notice. This time you breeze in with no notice. Right past my extensive security. Points for getting what you want, but it was a bit selfish. You must know this will cost Trina her job."

"Not a big loss from where I'm sitting."

Anger flashed in his eyes. After taking a long drink, he dropped onto the couch next to her. He threw his left arm over the backrest, his hand coming to lay within inches of her neck.

Seemingly unphased by the intimate proximity, Kate raised her chin. "I'm merely wondering how your family is going to react."

Something nearing rage contorted his features. Taking another sip, he looked away. When his eyes found hers again, the maelstrom within had calmed to placid pools.

"React to what?"

"Sex trafficking, rape, murder … it might be a bit overwhelming to process."

"I'm sorry, but I don't follow."

The floor suddenly caught her interest. "I was going to commend your janitorial team for cleaning the carpet so well. But then I realized you probably had it replaced."

The practiced smile took longer than it should have to reemerge on his face. "You came here to discuss my décor and housekeeping? No wonder you have not made any real progress on the case you were working on."

"It is really hard to get blood out of carpet, isn't it?"

"Detective Barnes, I'm afraid you're not making much sense. No wonder the San Francisco Police Department put you on leave. You really should go back and let Dr. Wissel help you with your mental issues."

At the mention of the doctor's name, Kate's lips tightened into a thin line. She turned her head and eyed him steadily. "What I have is an idea about how to solve this case."

"Really? Well, I don't know anyone should trust your ideas right now. Now I see why you were removed from the investigation. I think it's far past time for you to return to California."

Kate tilted her head to the side. "You seem to know a lot about me and the investigation."

"You came here before to warn me TekPharmaCel was potentially under threat. I take it as a personal responsibility to monitor any such threats to the company or its employees. And I am extremely skilled at finding out what I want to know."

She tapped her hand against the top of her thigh. "Finally, something we have in common. Since you know so much about the case, you may also know we had hit a brick wall identifying the second DNA profile."

His expression neither confirmed nor denied the charge.

Turning her head, she gazed at the painting on the far wall. "It's a stag's head, right?"

"What?"

"The subject of the painting. I mean, it looks like a basic circle with a bunch of sticks floating above it, but it's meant to be the head of a deer, right?"

He followed her gaze. "Yes, it is."

"If I hadn't gone through the rear lobby to get here, I would have missed the large mural of the Puget Sound. In the nature context it could represent the head and the antlers of a deer."

"Good for you, Detective. But as entertaining as this little visit has been ..."

She turned back to him. "Context, Mr. Cruthers. Like the type of context familial DNA can provide."

He took another sip of his drink. "Your mental state is very troubling. Your mind seems to be jumbled and your thoughts are quite nonsensical. None of my family members would submit to DNA testing, and no one has cause to try to compel it."

"You're right about the compelling part. But where you're entirely wrong is on the idea we would have to obtain it now. A very important fad has been sweeping the globe over the past ten years. People seem to be red hot on the idea of tracking down their ancestry. Practically everyone is sending in samples. Did you know the companies who collect the samples keep records of the profiles? That is how they build the database allowing you to identify potential relatives."

His lips twisted into a sneer. "I can't imagine you have time for such things. You should dedicate your time to more worthwhile pursuits. Swimming, for example." He looked across the room and to the glass wall and the view of Bellevue beyond.

When he spoke, his tone was velvety. "You ought to be careful about doing it at night, though. Sometimes the waters are a lot deeper than you think." The fingers of his left hand brushed against a few strands of her hair before suddenly tightening into a fist. "It could be very dangerous."

The corners of Kate's mouth drew down in false sympathy. She stood and stared down at him. "It's common for people to become more fearful as they get old."

He looked back toward the window. "It's also sad when someone doesn't know it is time to throw in the towel." Rising from the couch, he did nothing to hide the distaste from his expression. "You believe in justice, Detective Barnes. One day soon you'll learn justice is simply a word we use to pretty up the exercise of power."

Kate smiled. "Sometimes true, but not always. In this case you'd do well to recognize who holds the power."

She strode to the door and pulled it open. Trina Chen stood waiting silently on the other side of the threshold. Worry clouded her expression.

Kate pulled the door behind her. It shut just as the glass of whiskey shattered against it.

∨

Mildred took off her reading glasses and rubbed her eyes. It had been an unusually long day and it was way past time for it to end. Closing the binder she had been reading from, she tucked it away on the shelf above the worksurface and grabbed her glasses.

Crossing the lab, she paused long enough at the threshold to turn off the lights before closing the door behind her. Making her way down the short corridor to her office, she thought back to the long roundtrip to Seattle she had made earlier. The visit to the Washington State Crime Lab had been worth it on more than one front.

Over the past few years, she had often reached out to the state for support. The preponderance of correspondence had been virtual. Today merited an in-person visit. It had paid off in ways she had never imagined.

Darren Holcum, her contact at the CODIS lab, happened to be a vocal proponent for the use of open-source DNA. He also happened to be very handsome. After a failed marriage in her early thirties, and a string of ill-fated relationships thereafter, Mildred had resigned herself to the idea of ending her days alone.

Only two years her junior, Darren's twinkling blue eyes had sparked an ember of hope in the charcoal ashes of her personal life. Their meeting had lasted an hour, but in accepting his invitation for lunch, she ended up delaying her return trip by another hour and forty-five minutes. She had not laughed so much in ages.

One of the biggest surprises of the visit was learning the man actually shared her passion for art. He preferred paint to pottery, but the appreciation for transforming the basic into the profound was there, nonetheless.

She crossed to her desk and turned off the computer. Tucking two files into her bag, she shouldered it and headed for the hall. The heating and air system had cycled off half an hour earlier, leaving the building preternaturally quiet.

She flipped off the light switch and was about to step into the hall when a metallic crack reverberated off the walls. The muscles in her arms and legs froze. For a split second it seemed as if her heart had joined the bandwagon. Her mind searched for an explanation for the sound. It did not take long to find it.

The amount of air exchange capacity required in the lab was

very different than that in the office area. The resultant negative air pressure often created a vacuum in the narrow hall which could cause any of the metal doors left unsecured to slam shut in their frames.

Shaking her head, she continued down the hall. Passing the door to the lab, she confirmed it was now properly closed. As she continued on her way, her thoughts drifted back to Darren and whether she should text him tomorrow.

Lost in internal debate about how fast to respond to his offer to visit Eagle's Nest, she reached the end of the hall. Opening the door to the rear service exit, she paused abruptly.

On the far wall, the fire alarm panel hung open. A black electronic device hung from a wire affixed to one of the open ports inside. Green lights blinked at the edge of the gadget.

She started toward the panel, her brain racing for an explanation. The fire monitoring company was not due out for maintenance for another two months. *Had she been so preoccupied with Darren's charms she had not noticed the open panel earlier? But why would ...?*

The thoughts were interrupted by a cruel blow to the back of her skull. The coroner crashed to the floor.

Clad head-to-toe in black, the man who had struck Mildred stepped over her as if he were stepping across a pile of discarded laundry. Dark eyes glittered from inside a plain black mask as he stopped and considered her inert form. Lifting the gun he had used to knock her on the back of the head, he aimed and fired a single shot into her chest.

Mildred's body recoiled from the impact, but she did not make a sound. Neither did the silently growing pool of dark blood seeping out onto the concrete floor.

He hurried back down the hall to the lab. Retrieving a canvas bag from the storage closet where he had been forced to hide when she had returned earlier, he pulled out a space heater and checked the cord. He bent it outward until the wires were visible inside the plastic casing.

Working quickly, he plugged it into the power strip under the worktable. He straightened and tucked the gun safely into one of the bag's side compartments. A few moments later, he returned to where the coroner's body lay, and began attending to the open alarm panel. Seizing the device he had affixed earlier, he counted the sequence of flashing lights before removing it and stowing it back in the bag.

Closing the panel, he turned and cast one last look around the room. His eyes flitted over a stack of tall gray canisters with copper valves. They stood along the entrance to the hall. Not one to leave room for error, he paced off the short distance between the fallen form and the stockpile. His instructions explicitly stated she must be within four feet of the cannisters so when the flames enveloped them, the woman's body would be well within the full force of the blast radius, eliminating any potential concern about bullet retrieval.

Satisfied, he cast one last look at the coroner before heading out to the parking lot. Pulling the satellite phone from his bag, he stalked straight to the edge of the woods.

He typed two short words and hit the send button as he disappeared into the darkness. The simple two-word message transmitted into the night:

It's done.

Chapter 26

JENNA PRACTICALLY DISLOCATED her right shoulder trying to roll the gate to the impound lot closed. By the time she had secured it firmly in place, it felt as if every ligament had been ripped from its moorings.

Gingerly working the joint around, she grabbed the chain and wrapped it around the stationary pole. It was her own fault for chasing off the tow truck driver who had delivered the broken-down Toyota to the empty lot. Even though he had exhibited a nasty habit of hocking his phlegm as he spoke, the guy had been a good foot taller than her. More important, he had the build of a gym rat. Had she simply asked for help, she would already be on her way home.

Another bad decision to add to the growing tally. Since the incident with Delford, it felt as if she had done nothing but lie to everyone, including herself. The truth was she had never actually killed someone before and the reality of it had knocked her for a loop.

It wasn't like she regretted what had happened that night. The guy had been a scumbag. She had said as much to the Port Angeles therapist Tony had required her to see. While the woman had cleared Jenna to return to duty, she had done nothing to stop the late-night vigils she'd begun keeping at her son's bedroom door. Hour after hour, she had stood watching him sleep, wondering the same thing. *Am I worthy to be his Mom? Would he be better off with a different family who could keep him safe?*

Donning the uniform again had done little to alleviate the feelings of inadequacy and self-doubt. If anything, it made her feel she needed to go out of her way to prove she deserved to be wearing it. Tonight, was a perfect example. As menial a task as it was to check the vehicle into impound, she could not bring herself to accept the least bit of help.

Pursing her lips, she pushed the ends of the padlock together with all her might. The shackle slammed home into the lock bar with a loud click.

Her eyes registered the blood before her nerves registered the pain. A small section of skin on the inside of her palm had gotten caught in the lock. Blood welled to the surface. As it began to pour, the pain lit up her hand, and raced up her arm all the way to her elbow.

Casting an explicative into the empty night air, she turned around and headed toward her patrol car. By the time she opened the driver's side door blood was dripping freely from her hand. Trying to staunch a growing anger already disproportionate to the problem, she rifled through the car, searching the stash of wipes she kept in the center console. Discovering it had been raided by her colleagues, who hadn't even bothered to remove the empty package, she swore again.

Resigning herself to the prospect of a messy ride back to the sheriff's office, she started the ignition. The headlights blazed through the night, pointing directly across to the neighboring property. Beyond their reach, a single security light mounted near the roof of the coroner's lab shone onto the rear yard where Mildred's car was parked.

Anxious for the chance to save what was left of her uniform, Jenna drove over and parked alongside the coroner's vehicle. Thick droplets of blood slipped between her clenched fist as she walked to the door.

Reaching for the doorbell, she detected the faint smell of smoke. With more than a bit of jealousy, she imagined one of the nearby residents settling in to enjoy a cozy evening by the fire. The thought was a reminder of the flagrant holes in Jenna's life—holes she was unlikely to ever fill in Eagle's Nest.

After two full minutes, irritation began to get the better of her. She drummed on the bell once again. As her gaze fell away from the button, she noticed an odd shadow between the door and the frame.

She reached out with her left hand and seized the handle. The door swung open easily. Muted light spilled through the open doorway, limiting her view of the room beyond.

Something sharp and uncomfortable awakened in her gut. Mildred would not leave the door open at any hour, let alone at night. Equally indifferent to the potential damage to her uniform, she hastily wiped her bleeding hand against her thigh and reached for her gun.

"Mildred?" The name echoed beyond the door.

Hoping the coroner was merely out of earshot, she called out again.

Silence.

Jenna took a step inside and flipped the nearby light switch. The body on the floor drew her gaze like a magnet. Noting the crimson corona around the fallen form, she rushed across the chamber. Dropping to the coroner's side, Jenna was immediately overwhelmed by the coppery scent of blood.

Grabbing her radio, she called for an ambulance. As she spoke, an icy cold realization dawned. The smell of smoke inside the building was much stronger than it had been outside.

May 11

The acrid stench of smoke seemed to permeate every square inch of the building but was most severe in the lab where the fire had originated. Two freestanding, battery-powered work lights illuminated the room where Kate and Tony stood side-by-side surveying the damage.

Three of the room's four walls were completely charred. The row of shelves and the counter mounted to the far wall had been almost entirely burned away. The Port Angeles Fire Chief had just walked out of the lab, leaving them to ruminate in silence on the preliminary result of his investigation.

The older man had pointed out the remains of the compromised space heater and the power strip which had been used to start the blaze. He had also detailed how the fire monitoring system had been bypassed, how the fire suppression system had been deactivated, and the how the security system had been hacked. In over two and half decades of arson investigation, he'd never seen anything as sophisticated as what had occurred the night before.

"This is all my fault," Kate said in a hushed tone.

Tony shrugged. He'd arrived when the blaze was still burning and had watched the fire department put it out. When the last embers were out and the building had been deemed safe to reenter, Tony had called to apprise her of what had transpired.

News of the fire had hit her like a fistfull of brass knuckles. She had raced from the cottage with her stomach in knots.

Still smoldering over her decision to confront Cruthers without a warning phone call, the sheriff braced his hands on his hips. "I would try to make you feel better by arguing, but this was no coincidence. The lab was targeted by a sophisticated adversary."

Kate's voice was husky. "I never should have pushed Cruthers so hard yesterday. If it wasn't for me, Mildred would be sculpting right now instead of ..."

Noting the pained expression on her face, he crossed the distance between them coming to stand within a foot of her. She readied herself for the lecture she knew she deserved, but the sound of footsteps in the hall froze his lips.

Jenna Wheaton appeared in the doorway. Her haggard expression morphed into something more pointed as she studied the lack of personal space between the room's other inhabitants.

Reading the deputy's face, Kate took two steps back.

Tony shifted his gaze to the new arrival. "How's your hand?"

She waved the comment away with the bandaged appendage. "It's fine. I heard from the hospital. Mildred is out of surgery."

"She's going to be okay?" The hope in his tone was mirrored on his face.

Jenna winced. "They don't know. She's in critical care. They said the next twenty-four hours will tell."

He nodded. "Thanks to you she has a fighting chance."

"I told you, it was purely accidental."

"You may have saved her life," Kate said.

The deputy stared at the other woman, trying to divine the motive behind her words.

Watching the odd exchange, Tony stepped into the silence. "Go home, Wheaton. Your shift should have ended …" He checked his watch. "Six hours ago."

She looked from Tony to Kate and back again. "I guess I could use a shower."

"We're all gonna need a shower to get this smell off." Deputy Nolan adjusted his glasses as he made his way into the room. "Shit, that asshole could have burned down the entire forest! Do you guys have any ideas who did this?"

The question had been directed at Kate, but Tony fielded it. "We're working on it. What would really help is if you could hold off getting back to Port Angeles long enough to make sure Deputy Wheaton gets home okay."

Wheaton crossed her arms over her chest. "I'm perfectly capable of driving myself home, Sheriff."

Nolan's gaze shifted to Kate. He studied her for a long moment during the awkward silence. When he finally looked at Wheaton, his expression shifted dramatically. "Hey, Wheaton, it's no big deal. Besides, I still owe you for the time you helped us with traffic control for that head-on, remember?"

Casting one last rueful glance at her boss, Wheaton headed for the exit.

Tony called out as she reached the threshold. "And Wheaton?"

Her weary eyes found his once again. "Yes?"

"We're glad to have you back. And I'm grateful to have you on my team."

A hint of emotion flashed in the woman's eyes before she nodded and turned away. Kate waited until the sound of both deputies' footsteps disappeared down the hall before turning back to Tony.

"That meant a lot to her."

"I meant what I said to her as much as what I'm about to say to you. Going to see Cruthers without talking to me first was a dumbass move. But this …" he gestured to the mess around them, "… was not your fault."

She took a step back. "You just admitted I provoked him. If I hadn't told him about the open-source DNA, he would never have targeted Mildred."

"Bullshit. While you were in Bellevue yesterday, Mildred was in Seattle at the state's CODIS lab. If Cruthers had the power to tap your phone and manipulate the FBI, it's not unreasonable to assume he has been watching Mildred as well. It's a safe bet he's watching me too."

She turned and started walking toward the open door.

"Where are you going?" He called out.

Kate stopped at the threshold. "I'm leaving."

Something in the set of her jaw sparked a tightness around his eyes. "This building or Eagle's Nest?"

"The entire state of Washington."

He looked like he was about to protest but seemed to think better of it. His shoulders dropped a bit as he nodded.

"I'm going back to San Francisco to see Kevin. We need to find those girls. No more screwing around. We've got to find that door." Before she knew it, she had reached out and grabbed his arm.

His eyes fell to her hand. When he looked back at her the corresponding wave of emotion was more than she could handle.

She let go and continued in a deliberate tone. "The only way this will work from here on out is if it looks like we're giving up. Don't mention a word of what happened here to Fuentes. Stay quiet and let it appear like you think it was a random accident."

"You think he's in on this?"

Kate thought back to the human auction in Seattle. "No. But I've been wrong about FBI agents before. Either way, Cruthers has long talons." She thought back to the photos of ex-presidents, senators and other world leaders she had seen in his office. "At this point we need to go completely quiet. Especially when it comes to your buddy, the county prosecutor."

Wincing at the allegation, Tony nodded anyway.

"I'll leave town this afternoon. Pick up a disposable cell. I'll get one, too."

"Will you give me your new number before you leave?"

"No, I don't want to take any more chances. Let them think this was my last straw." She thought for a moment. "Start your morning with coffee at Beans of Mine tomorrow. Fiona will have my new number."

"Okay, but ... when do you think you'll be back?"

The look in his eyes made it clear the question was about more than the case, Kate gave the only answer she could think of. "I'll do whatever it takes to save those girls. I don't have time to think about anything else." She turned and hurried out of the building before he could press her any further.

∨

The walnut dresser creaked as Kate tugged the bottom drawer open. She pulled out two pairs of jeans as the doorbell rang.

Placing the clothes on top of the dresser she crossed to the nightstand. Trusting Tony to abide by their agreement to let her leave Eagle's Nest with no further interaction, Kate retrieved her Glock from the top drawer. Releasing the safety, she carefully made her way into the hall. Instead of continuing toward the front door, she slipped into the kitchen and through the back exit.

A pair of cotton leggings, a flimsy cotton T-shirt and a pair of thin socks were no match for the biting cold, or the puddles from an early morning rainstorm. Ignoring the unpleasant sensations, she paused at the corner of the cottage.

Poking her head around the side of the house revealed no one in sight. Right shoulder skimming the wall of the house, she hurried along, with the Glock pointed toward the ground. The sudden sound of a voice brought her to a standstill.

"Yes, Jacob … I will … I wanted to drop this off with Kate before I go to the grocery. I'll see you soon. Love you."

Kate risked a peek around the corner. Chloe stood at the doorstep waiting with a foil covered baking dish in her hands. A blue Volvo was parked alongside Kate's rental. No other vehicles or people were in sight.

Rolling her eyes skyward, Kate reengaged the safety on her weapon and jogged back to the rear of the house. She had opened the door and was busy peeling her off her soggy socks when the doorbell rang again.

"I'm coming!" Kate called.

Arriving at the door, she paused to collect herself before

yanking it open. "Chloe, what are you doing here?"

Chloe held up the dish. "I made scones ... to let you know how much I appreciated your compassion during our session with Pastor Brian. I don't expect you to make time for me today. I truly wanted to thank you."

Compassion was not an attribute Kate would have thought she could feel for her mother. Chloe was right. Yet, hearing her mother's story had cut through the sizeable ramparts the woman had helped build around Kate's heart.

Thinking about all she had learned about Chloe since coming to Washington, Kate was struck by one fact in particular. The addict she had known had been a recluse. But the sober version of Chloe was a veritable social butterfly.

Kate made the decision in a split second. "It's cold outside. Why don't you come in ..." Retreating inside, she held the door open wide. "For a minute."

Chloe lit up. "Oh, I really wasn't expecting an invitation. But it would be nice to get warm for a minute. Thank you!"

She entered, placing the dish on the coffee table next to Kate's laptop while her host shut and locked the door.

"Is it alright?" The older woman gestured to the couch.

"Yes."

Kate took a seat in the chair opposite her mother. "You still haven't told me how you found out where I've been staying."

"You know Joyce Turndale ...?"

Kate nodded at the mention of her landlord.

"Well, she is one of the faith ministers at the church. Earlier this morning, I remembered how she had been so thrilled when she had found someone to rent this cottage."

She looked pointedly at the dated décor. "Joyce has never bothered to do anything to update this place. I figured anyone who would be willing to tolerate it at this time of year couldn't be a regular tourist. So, I got curious and called her. She confirmed you've been renting from her for the past few weeks."

Ignoring the implicit breach of privacy, Kate replied, "Funny you mention Joyce. I need to call her today."

"Is everything okay?"

"Everything has been fine. I need to let her know my stay here is over. I'll be catching an early morning flight out of SeaTac tomorrow. I'm staying in Tacoma so I won't be late in the morning."

Chloe's face fell. "Oh."

"Yes, I've stayed much longer than I anticipated. I need to get back to my life in the City." Kate did not need to make any further explanation. Her mother was a Bay Area native. She understood the reference to "the City" meant San Francisco.

Chloe cast her gaze about as if she might stumble across the right response somewhere in the room. "Well, I had hoped we ..." She stopped and stared Kate straight in the eyes. "Never mind. I understand. I hope you had a nice visit to Eagle's Nest."

"Thank you." Kate stood.

Her mother rose and began to follow her daughter to the front door. On the way, her knee struck the corner of Kate's laptop sending it sliding off the table and onto the floor. It bounced once before settling onto the thick shag carpet. The impact had popped open the lid, waking it from sleep mode.

"I'm so sorry!" Chloe plucked the computer off the floor. "If it's broken, I'll be happy to replace it. I cannot believe I did that!"

She stared down at the screen which displayed the last file Kate had opened. Celia's bracelet was displayed in vivid detail ...

Chloe passed the device to Kate. "It looks like it's still working. But you should check to make sure it's okay."

Kate accepted the device, closing the lid and placing it back on the table. "I'm sure it's fine. It wasn't a long drop and this carpet might be ugly but it is pretty thick."

"Okay. Well, you've my number. Please call me if you discover it isn't working right. Or, if you ever want to talk again …"

Memories laden with some of her deepest and darkest emotions threatened to push Kate off course. Corralling her feelings, she succeeded in stopping the flow of all but the smallest ones through the floodgate.

"We did make progress the other night. I still don't know what it means going forward but I was able to invite you into my house. That must count for something."

"Yes, yes it does." Looking as if she had just won the lottery, Chloe opened the door and walked onto the front porch. She turned and smiled back at her daughter. "Save travels, Kate. And thank you for coming here."

Kate nodded and was about to close the door when Chloe spoke again. "By the way, I love the orca bracelet."

"Orca?"

"The shapes of the bracelet—on your laptop."

"Those are orcas?" Kate thought of the odd shaped medallions which had been carved from human bone. Now that Chloe had provided the context, Kate begrudgingly agreed they did resemble rudimentary carvings of one of the great local sea mammals.

"I think so. In fact, if it weren't for the English inscription, I would have thought it came from the dig."

"The dig?"

Kate listened as Chloe elaborated. Fifteen minutes later, she bid her mother goodbye and hurried back into the house.

In the bedroom she exchanged her leggings for jeans and finished packing. When she was done, she checked her watch again. Thanks to Chloe she was going to make a detour before starting out for Tacoma.

Chapter 27

THE TWO-LANE HIGHWAY between Seiku and Neah Bay is equal parts beauty and danger. It's serpentine twists and turns, as well as the risk of washouts, falling rocks, and other natural hazards, have been detailed in harrowing detail by numerous travel sites. Some have even whispered about the impatient loggers whose penchant for tailgating and cutting wide corners could make the journey an exercise in terror.

To Kate's infinite surprise, the coastal drive along the Strait of San Juan de Fuca proved far less vexing than the drive around Lake Crescent. The difference was likely the fact she had been shot at and run off the later, but not the former.

It also didn't hurt that Mother Nature had been on Kate's side. The goddess had shown up in splendid fashion, keeping the strait free from clouds to show off the rugged tree-lined vistas of Victoria Island in the distance. Whatever the reason, Kate had navigated the coastal road at a speed sure to earn appreciation from the locals.

Spotting a long chain link fence running along the right side of the road, she eased on the brakes. The massive U.S. Coast Guard sign hanging on the barrier was exactly as Chloe had described. Within a few hundred feet, she crossed from the United States of America into the sovereign tribal lands of the Makah people and the town of Neah Bay.

The small community had been named for the breathtaking body of water which served as the main point for commerce and fishing. From a bird's eye view, the bay loosely resembled a fish-hook notched out of the northwest corner of the Olympic Peninsula right before the landmass abruptly ended at the Pacific Ocean.

A lovely array of tall totems heralded Kate's arrival at the Makah Cultural and Research Center. She pulled into the parking lot and made her way to a building with gray siding. Kate paused to examine the two whales swimming in yin and yang positions across the front doors before heading in.

Inside, the space was beautifully appointed with vaulted wood ceilings. It was lit by the readily welcoming type of soft lighting that encouraged learning.

An attractive gentleman in his early seventies was manning the admittance desk to her left. Long silver hair pulled into a braid, he was busy collecting entrance fees from a young couple decked out in matching hiking gear. A gift shop opened up behind the desk, offering an array of products produced by local craft workers, sprinkled with the occasional standard souvenir fare.

Kate lined up behind the couple. As she waited, her gaze drifted to well-crafted verses adorning the wall which led into the museum. The more she read, the more she sensed there were a great many things to be learned from the Makah. Things Dr. Wissel, despite all his good intentions, had never been able to properly convey to her.

When the couple finished their transaction, Kate approached the desk. She was greeted with a broad smile.

"Hello, my name is James. Welcome to the Makah Cultural and Research Center. Have you come to visit the museum today or just the gift shop?"

Kate pulled her iPad out of her backpack and placed it on the desk. "Hi, James. My name is Kate, and I'm here on a research project."

"The museum it is then. You certainly won't be disappointed. The archaeological dig near Lake Ozette uncovered one of our coastal villages. It had been buried in a landslide hundreds of years ago. Much like Pompeii in Italy, the buried city gave up all sorts of examples of daily life including many incredible works. Art has always been part of our traditions. Our people incorporated it into our tools, our boats and of course, our jewelry."

Kate perked up. "Jewelry is what I'm here for. Bracelets, to be specific."

"Inside the museum, we have a perfect replica of one of the longhouses my ancestors lived in. Right across from it is a large display of everyday items including beauty products and jewelry. Nearly all of them are adorned with the creatures who have lived among us since time began."

"Like orcas?" Kate asked.

"Of course."

She tapped the screen of her iPad. Celia's bracelet appeared. She turned the screen toward him. "Ones like this?"

Bending over, he squinted at the image, then waved to a petite female docent who was making her way into the gift shop. "Martha knows jewelry far better than I do."

The woman came around the desk and waited while the older man explained Kate's question. He passed the tablet to her. She studied the picture for a moment and nodded. "It does resemble some of the carvings in our collection, although it is obviously a crude modern copy."

"But it is an orca?"

She handed the iPad back to Kate. "An orca or some other type of whale. Blue and humpback whales are also indigenous to this area. You'll find they're a recurring theme in our artwork. I'd say whoever created that piece was definitely inspired by one of ours. The portrayal of the dorsal fin is uncannily similar to one on display in front of the longhouse."

"And the dig site was down near Lake Ozette?"

"Yes. It was an active dig site during the nineteen seventies."

The older man smiled again. "Our people were very involved

in the process. I was lucky enough to be part of it. There was day upon day of hard work, but I cannot tell you the joy it brought or the pride I felt in helping to support the excavation."

"You spent a lot of time in the area?"

"During the dig and throughout my life. The site is near the northern tip of Lake Ozette. It's south of here."

Kate tapped at the screen again. Careful to mute the sound, she turned the device around so they could both see the display. "Is there any way you can tell whether this video was recorded there?" She tapped the screen again, launching Delford's video.

When it ended James shook his head.

Kate could not keep the disappointment from dripping into her voice. "You don't recognize the area."

The older man fixed her with a keen gaze. "I can tell you it definitely wasn't filmed at the dig site."

"Do you know where it was filmed?"

He pursed his lips and looked off over her head. "The last part at the end seems familiar, but I can't place it. What do you think?" He looked to his colleague, who shook her head.

"Sorry, James. You know me. I'm more bookworm than outdoor enthusiast. I have no idea. I do recognize the man though."

Kate restarted the video. She paused it when Delford appeared. "This man?"

"Yes. He was here recently and he was definitely a handful. The workshop cancellation set him off."

"Workshop?"

"Yes, we offer classes on carving and basket weaving. But when he arrived for our carving class, he found out the instructor had called in sick. He was extremely annoyed, but eventually decided to buy an admission ticket to the museum.

"Later I found him sitting in front of the display I told you about. I informed him we were closing up, but he didn't want to leave. He had bought a notepad from the souvenir shop and was trying to sketch some of our pieces. He got kind of nasty so I had to get a couple of the guys to come over and escort him out."

Kate nodded. "Thank you. You've been very helpful." She began to return the device to her bag when James put out a hand.

"Wait a minute. I really do think the last part seemed familiar. Mind if I take another look?"

∨

The dirt fire road was fairly well maintained given the abundant amount of rainfall which annually inundated the Olympic Peninsula. Having made the trek back from Neah Bay, Kate was less than ten miles from Eagle's Nest, putting the rental car's shocks through their paces.

Thanks to James, this would be her second outing in the woods in as many hours. Rewatching the video had helped jog his memory. He'd recalled a similar rocky outcropping where he and his buddies had once constructed a makeshift fort, but the intervening decades had muted his memory of the actual location. She'd asked if any of his old friends might be around, but only one was still living in the area. According to the docent, the man was not a fan of unannounced visitors—especially outsiders.

A folded map rested on the passenger seat. Three areas had been circled in a wavering line of blue ink. James had indicated the sites after Kate had shown him the video a third time. He had warned her they were only possibilities.

The decision to investigate the locations had meant delaying her departure for Tacoma yet again. Were she to come up empty on all three locations, she would risk calling Tony on the way to Tacoma. Even if she had to risk calling Tony, it would be worth it for him to visit Neah Bay. If James could not remember the location where he had played as a kid, perhaps his antisocial friend might be encouraged to recall it.

The first location had been a complete bust. She had not found anything remotely close to the rock outcropping in the video. Luckily, it had been a short walk from the highway and had not eaten much time off the clock.

Up ahead, the road split. Kate pulled over and reached for her backpack. She tucked the map inside between her Glock and her compromised cell phone. The battery had been stored in a separate compartment to ensure no one would be tracking her movements. She planned to give the device to Kevin for a more thorough analysis.

From another compartment, she withdrew the small compass she had bought at the general store in Neah Bay. Climbing out of the car, she locked the door and glanced up at the sky. The sun was starting to grow weary of the long day. Within another two hours it would retire for the night. James had told her this location was only a twenty-minute walk from the road.

It took her a full minute to spot the unmarked trail James had described. During the first fifty yards into the forest, she dedicated her time to searching the ground for a suitable walking stick. James had warned her this desolate section of the forest was prone to bear and elk. While the elk were not as great a concern outside of mating season, she did not want to risk startling representatives of either species.

Finally, she spotted a four-and-a-half-foot branch that fit the bill. Stepping off the trail, she planted her foot against two extraneous smaller branches growing midspan. She pulled upward with all her might. Two satisfying cracks echoed through late afternoon.

Peeling off the bark around the top, she found a comfortable grip, and began to drum the opposite end into the ground. Mud and leaves fell away, leaving her with something half-decent.

Within thirty yards she fell into an easy rhythm with the stick. In another quarter mile, her new tool saved her from taking a nasty spill while traveling downhill over some exposed roots.

Sobered by what might have been a catastrophe, she stopped and checked the map. James had warned there was no cellular service in the area. While it prohibited her from using the GPS on her cell, she pacified herself with the knowledge whomever had hacked the device, would not be able to track her. Yet another reason the walking stick had been a lifesaver.

Getting her bearings, she caught the unmistakable fresh scent of the ocean. According to the map she had been working her way toward it, but the aroma was fleeting and the knowledge felt disjointed without the accompanying roar of the waves.

Kate closed her eyes and thought about Delford. *Had the girls been brought here? Had he detected the briny scent when he walked this trail?* Shaking her head, she tucked the map back into her bag.

The wind rustled through the trees. Carried on its currents, a phantom memory resurfaced from a voice she hoped never to hear again. *"The more you focus on yourself, your own feelings and perceptions, the more you'll stay locked up in your own head—thus ensuring you'll stay out of his."* The recollection brought the bitter taste of bile to the back of her throat. Once again, she had failed to heed the warning from Special Agent Benjamin Fraye.

If he were here now, he'd say ever since coming here she had approached the case with divided focus. One leg stuck in the dysfunction she had shared with Chloe and one leg stuck in the traumas of battling the Tower Torturer.

It was an unpleasant pill to swallow, but she could not ignore it. Over the next quarter mile, she restricted all thoughts to Delford. With each step she catalogued everything she had learned about him from their first meeting at his house, to the moment she found him dead at Detective Wheaton's hands.

Her pace was unconsciously increasing as her thoughts progressed. The aggression with which she attacked the trail grew more ferocious. Despite her best efforts, Fraye's words and the recriminations which emanated from them began to resurface. At first, they were merely peppered throughout her thoughts. Within the next few breaths, they began to pop up so frequently it became hard to hold onto any thread for longer than a moment or two.

Her pulse climbed with the added exertion, taking her frustration level with it. Try as she might, she could not fill her head with anything but those damn words.

Her feet moved, keeping pace with her thoughts. It seemed as if her brain had been dropped into a centrifuge which had been placed on the highest setting. For a split second the earthy sights and smells of the forest seemed to disappear. The vibrant hues of brown and green drained to white—white tile walls, white tile floors and a woman in a chair …

Before she knew it, Kate had dropped the stick and was sprinting full tilt through the woods. Her pack slapped against her back as she ran, the heavy weight of the Glock falling into a steady rhythm as it struck her spine.

It was the rhythm that helped her regain control of her thoughts. Eight steps. Five steps. Three steps. She came to a stumbling halt. Placing her hands on her knees she struggled to get her breath.

When she raised her head again, Kate realized she had left the trail far behind. She raised her hands to her head and plunged them deep into her hair. *What the hell had she been thinking? Running like a madwoman further into the forest?*

Still breathing heavily, she pulled the compass from her backpack and tried to make sense of where she was and how to get back to where she needed to be. Since she had been traveling southwest for the majority of her journey, the short sprint could not have taken her too far from the trail. If she headed back in a north-eastern direction ...

Kate began to spin around trying to get a true bearing. When she had her course, she looked up and forgot all about the trail.

Not forty feet ahead of her, the ground sloped upward into a hill. Her eyes followed the crest to the right where the entire elevation was covered by a rocky outcropping. Despite the dim sunlight filtering through the trees, she spotted a door tucked between the large boulders at its base.

The fleeting scent of the ocean teased her nostrils once more. The sensation never had the chance to fully register. She was too busy reaching into her pack. There was no way she wanted to do this on her own.

Kate pulled out her cell phone and reinserted the battery. A whirling pinwheel appeared on the screen as the device went through its startup protocols. When it finally disappeared, it took her confidence with it. The icon in the upper right-hand corner of the screen confirmed James' warning. There was no detectable cellular signal.

Replacing the device, she withdrew her gun. As she shouldered her bag, the words Delford had spoken on the video rang out crystal clear in her memory.

"I approached from this angle so I'd be outside of the camera range. I'm not as stupid as you think."

Kate was painfully aware she had not approached from the same angle. She was about to find out if she had been too stupid for her own good.

Chapter 28

THE DEVICE WAS DEAD. No matter how many buttons Hyland pressed, or how hard he stabbed at them, the green light would not illuminate.

Forcing a smile tempered with exactly the right mix of competency and contrition, he turned to face his newest guest. "My apologies, sir. It appears we have run out of batteries."

Tall and slender, the older man stood with his back to Hyland. With his shoulders held high and his hands clasped behind his back, he exuded all the dignity of a statesman. Beyond the glass wall, the clouds hung low over the Pacific Ocean. The space between was filled by a narrow thread of waning sunlight.

Turning, the CEO of the world's second-largest online retailer smiled genially. "I'm sure y'all will have it set right for us, Hyland."

The affable southern drawl almost lulled Hyland into believing the oversight would be forgiven. "I will do so right now." He strode over to a built-in bookshelf made of Brazilian cherrywood. The second drawer from the top held his lifeline.

Aware of the other man's eyes on his back, he pulled the panel off the remote control and replaced the batteries. Bracing for impact, he closed his eyes and pressed the power button. When he opened them again, he was greeted with a small green light.

"Power restored, sir." He held up the device.

"Fine, fine. It was a long trip from D.C. If y'all don't mind, I'd like to relax now."

Like all the guests attending Oceana Week, the business mogul had come alone. The purpose of the annual event was to rejuvenate and inspire the guests, without the added distraction of familial concerns.

"Of course. As I said before, the staff will be ready to unpack your belongings at a moment's notice. All you have to do is press the housekeeping button on the remote device."

"There's no rush. I'll look forward to someone comin' out in a bit. For now, I want a lil' privacy."

"I understand, sir. Please do not hesitate to contact me if you need anything further. I am available to assist you with any concerns, twenty-four/seven."

The older man chuckled. "I can't think of any reason I might have to call. Everyone knows Aaru has a reputation for bein' the best of the best."

"Yes, sir." With a slight bow, Hyland turned and let himself out the front door.

Leaving his guest to get settled in, Hyland pranced down a short set of stone steps set in a tasteful open fan pattern into the hillside. His eyes moved at the speed of light, scanning for any sign of imperfection.

By the time he reached the last step he felt a small sense of satisfaction. Not one stray pine needle littered the path. Everything appeared as perfect as it had when he had performed a quality assurance review on the villa precisely one hour before the billionaire's arrival.

The knowledge was not enough to balance out his fury over the battery failure. After drilling for two solid weeks about the importance of paying attention to the details, verbally warning them countless times, and providing detailed checklists, one staff member had still come up short.

Despite his Herculean efforts, he'd been forced to stand in disgrace before a guest. He had personally reviewed each and every checklist and performed spot inspections of each villa. But he had missed one damn remote. Oceana Week was off to ignominious start.

As he reached the vehicle, his phone rang. Hyland's blood ran cold. With so many high-profile guests at Aaru, all operations had to hum along with precision. Hyland did not want to consider his fate if he failed to meet expectations during the resort's most important annual event.

He pulled out his phone and checked the display. An alert had popped. He tapped the screen, causing another prompt to appear. This one required an additional password before the application would open. His heart began to race. This was the last thing he needed right now.

As soon as he entered the required series of digits, the screen filled with a security camera feed of the forest. According to the banner, the alert had been activated by a motion sensor. The feed drew from a set of cameras which were not linked to the standard system—the one set for his eyes only.

A female hiker appeared in the background. She fumbled with a compass, appearing to be searching for her bearings.

He tapped on her face, zooming in on her features. After a few seconds, she turned and stared directly into the camera. A familiar pang of distaste soured his stomach. As he glowered at the screen, the feeling morphed into something darker. He minimized the view, leaving it open while he activated a video call.

Due to the nature of their clientele, Hyland's standard security team was comprised of elite industry professionals. Despite their extraordinary discretion, none were as uniquely suited for the task as the gentleman who was staying in the Veritas Suite.

Blood boiling, he climbed inside his electric cart. Placing the phone in the dashboard holder, he turned on the engine. On his way back along the coastal path, he reached over and tapped the screen once again. The phone began to ring ...

V

It was not until Kate was within ten feet of the door that she spied the cameras. As far as she could tell there were two of them. One, concealed in a false stone set into the outcropping on the right, trained directly on the door. About twenty feet above the portal, another was concealed between two boulders, facing the open area where she now stood.

Her mind raced from thought to thought. She had lost the element of surprise. Anyone monitoring the cameras knew she was armed. Crossing the remaining distance to the entrance, she stepped into the natural alcove created by the surrounding boulders.

The camouflage paint on the door appeared far less convincing up close. In two small areas near the frame, the underlining steel glowed dully in the fading light. Kate eyed the handle. No exterior lock. Merely a narrow horizontal slot some kind of key card.

The incongruity of technology operating in the middle of an uninhabited part of the forest was oddly disconcerting. With no visible cords available, she reasoned the wireless transmissions had to be going through some sort of local broadcast hub.

Glock in her right hand, she reached for the door handle with her left. As expected, it did not budge. She leaned back against one of the large boulders.

By the time she hiked back to the car and drove far enough out to get a cell signal, it would be too late. If the girls were still alive, whoever was on the other side of the door would have killed them and escaped long before reinforcements could arrive.

She had to get inside, and she had to get inside now. The question was how.

In the next moment, the answer revealed itself. A soft whirling sound emanated from the door handle. It was followed by a loud whooshing noise, as the door began to swing outward.

Running from the alcove, Kate took cover behind the rock

wall. Training the sights of her weapon on the door frame, she held her breath and waited.

One second passed. Then another, and another. After a full minute had gone by, the adrenaline pumping through her veins began to run thick with anticipation. The open door was an open invitation. Someone wanted to lure her inside.

As the seconds ticked by, one certainty played over and over in her head. If any of the girls were still alive, she might only have moments to get to them. Despite the obvious risk, the decision to enter was an easy one. She crept back into the alcove.

Holding her gun before her in a dual grip, she used her right foot to toe the door the rest of the way open. She peered into what looked like a natural extension of the chasm into which the door had been installed. The waning sunlight only penetrated about six feet into the corridor before being swallowed up by the darkness. Kate crossed the threshold, and the world changed.

Soft blue LED light illuminated the corridor beyond. The accessway appeared to continue for another twenty feet before making a ninety-degree turn to the right.

Other than the track of lights mounted overhead, there was nothing but the stone walls and the earthen floor. A white power cord ran from the lights through a series of intermittently spaced hooks to the end of the corridor.

She hurried forward, keeping her stride tight. When she approached the turn, she leaned her hip against the wall. After a few seconds of silence, she ventured a quick look around the corner. The passageway continued for about ten more yards before splitting in two. Each branch was secured by a plain steel door. If there were any cameras on the doors, they were so well concealed Kate could not detect them.

Taking a deep breath, she made her way around the corner. She tried the right door handle first. It was unlocked. Casting one last look at the door on the left, Kate pushed the door open with her foot. She pointed her gun into the darkness. Aware of presenting a backlit target in the open doorway, she hurried across the threshold.

Another set of LED lights sprang to life. With only a plastic table and single accompanying chair, the room had no occupants. What it did have was supplies.

Boxes of bottled water had been stacked from floor to ceiling in the left corner. Along the right wall a row of cheap laminate cabinets stood alongside a mini refrigerator. Two economy size boxes of cereal and three large bags of bread lay atop the appliance.

Set dead center in the far wall, was another steel door. Heart pounding with the knowledge a predator was about to spring upon her at any moment, she risked crossing to the refrigerator and picking up one of the loaves. The printed expiration date was six days in the future. Delford had been dead for almost two weeks. Assuming an average shelf life, someone had to have brought the food here since his passing.

Kate replaced the bread and turned to head for the door. Something caught her eye, causing her to turn back. Peeking out from beneath one of the loaves, was a flat piece of turquoise blue plastic.

Pulling out the plastic card, she discovered it was attached to a canvas lanyard. Holding it up to the light, she recognized the face of Rick Delford in the small picture on the front. The backside bore the Aaru logo.

Recalling the card slot at the outside entrance, Kate stuffed the badge into the front pocket of her shirt. Moving to the nearby door, she paused to listen at the frame. Detecting no sounds, she tried the handle. It was unlocked.

Wondering how many doors she could pass through before her luck ran out, she breached the threshold. When the lights came on, she was standing directly across from a series of chain link cages running all the way to the wall on the right. There was a ten-foot gap between the exterior wall of the first cage and the wall on the left. A lone wooden bench had been shoved up against the rock wall.

Each of the narrow metal prison cells was comprised of a metal cot and a camping toilet. A single teenage girl stood in each pen. Besides the prisoners, the room was empty.

The same nausea and rage which had threatened to overwhelm her at Belovol's auction swelled inside Kate. Biting back the emotions, she raced to the nearest cage. She was in the process of examining the padlock when a thought struck her.

Raising her head, she looked from girl to girl. Each stood with their head down and their eyes fixed firmly on the ground. Not one had reacted to her arrival.

The thought was followed by a sudden stinging sensation in the right side of her neck. Releasing the lock, she tried to reach for the source of the pain, but her arm would not do as she had bidden. Within less than a second, reality began to fade away. The bones in her legs shifted from solid state to liquid and Kate crumpled to the ground.

As her field of view collapsed, paralysis fixed her eyes on the one object immediately before her. Having been jarred loose from her pocket as she fell, Delford's badge had settled against the foot of the cage. It lay upside down, resting at an angle.

As her sight collapsed to a pinprick, the image of the resort's logo set off an inner alarm bell. Whatever was coursing through her system had made it too difficult to hold onto the idea for very long. Her vision disappeared, taking her consciousness with it.

Chapter 29

THE FIERY BURN SOARED up her nerves and pierced her brain. For a split second the world disappeared. Only the pain remained. Chloe turned away from the counter, choosing to suffer in silence rather than make a scene. The roof of her mouth was already going numb from the scalding latte.

The last thing she wanted to do was to offend Fiona. After all, she was one of the kindest people in Eagle's Nest and Chloe was the one who had insisted both drinks be prepared extra hot. It was a precaution to ensure the drinks would be pleasantly warm by the time she made it back home to Jacob. He was preparing omelets for breakfast.

In another lifetime, Chloe had loved preparing elaborate breakfasts for her first husband. But everything had changed when Candace was born.

The memory of her dead daughter, and the guilt for the innumerable ways she had retreated from those who had needed her most, sat like an ever-present lead weight in Chloe's stomach. Some days she fared better at ignoring it. On other days, the relentless march of appalling memories convinced her there was no possible path to forgiveness for her sins.

Shelving the self-hatred, Chloe turned back to the counter and picked up a cardboard carrier. She tucked her drink in one corner, then glanced at Fiona who was steaming the decadent full-fat milk for Jacob's latte.

Working her tongue gingerly around her mouth, Chloe did her best not to wince at the searing sensation. As bad as the pain was, it was nothing more than a minor inconvenience. Nothing could take away the gratitude she felt toward the universe for bringing her oldest daughter back into her life. While she could never make it right with Candace, there was a chance Kate might not be lost to her forever.

She turned to a nearby table where a glass carafe of water sat near a stack of paper cups. Eying the slices of cucumber and ice cubes floating in the vessel, Chloe's entire life's purpose suddenly coalesced into one simple goal—getting the icy liquid into her mouth. Snatching a cup, she barely registered the sound of the bell above the front door.

"Good Morning, Sheriff!" Fiona called out brightly, as she finished pouring Jacob's drink.

Chloe took a huge swig of water and held it in her mouth. The cooling sensation lasted no more than a few seconds before the liquid began to warm.

"Hi, Fiona," The sheriff replied brightly.

The proprietor tucked Jacob's travel mug in Chloe's carrier. "Have a great day, Chloe!"

Chloe responded with a wave. Swallowing carefully, she took another drink. The water stayed cooler for a few seconds longer this time, numbing the burn a bit.

She watched as the sheriff entered into a brief exchange with Fiona. They spoke too quietly for Chloe to hear what they were saying.

Downing the remainder from the cup, Chloe tossed it into a nearby wastebasket. Oral nerves still screaming, she picked up the carrier and turned to find the sheriff standing a few feet away.

"Great way to start the day, right?" she offered. Her first impression was he looked disappointed about something, but his ready smile dispelled the notion.

"Absolutely. I'm here almost every morning."

"Fiona is a treasure! Thank goodness we're not reliant on the big chains." Her expression shifted. "By the way, I wanted to thank you for working with us on the vigil for that poor girl. Everyone really appreciated the opportunity to express the community's sadness."

Something flashed in his features, but it passed too fast for Chloe to be sure what it meant.

"Thanks again. You and your friends did a great job coordinating it."

A wave of genuine sympathy sidelined the pain in her mouth in a way the water could not. "What happened was such a tragedy. I was happy to do it." She stared at his handsome features, idly wondering whether her daughter found him equally attractive. The two had been working together since Kate arrived. But it was none of Chloe's business. Instead she asked, "Are you going to let the public know the case is closed?"

"Excuse me?" The sheriff's expression remained pleasant and open despite the irritated tone.

"I mean, I assumed so since Kate went back to San Francisco ..."

He nodded. "I owe you an apology about that."

"Why?"

"She came here to see you and the case monopolized her time."

The lead weight in Chloe's stomach did a flip flop. She wondered whether Kate had confided anything about their past to the sheriff. The thought made her feel small and horrible.

"Oh, please don't apologize to me. I'm just sorry she had to leave so soon. Hopefully she can come back up. I'd love to get the chance to show her around."

This time there was no mistaking the change in Tony's expression. The wistfulness in his features, confirmed not only was the man attracted to her daughter, but it appeared he was carrying a bit of a torch for her as well. The thought brought Chloe a level of maternal pride. The sensation was strange and wonderful all at the same time.

She beamed back at him. "Maybe we could all get together if she comes back?"

"I'd look forward to it."

Unsure how to respond, Chloe voiced the next thing that came into her mind. "At least she got the chance to visit Neah Bay before she left."

"Neah Bay?"

"Yes, I stopped by her place yesterday. She said she was going to stop there on her way to Seattle."

"But Neah Bay is in the opposite direction from Seattle."

"I told her it would take her out of her way, but once she found out about the Makah Cultural Center, she'd made her mind up. I told her about Cape Flattery as well, but she didn't seem as interested. Which was better anyway, because if she tried to squeeze in both visits, she would've been stuck driving in the dark."

"Do you know why she wanted to go to the Center?"

Chloe watched the growing intensity in his expression, wondering what she might have stepped into. "Yes. Kate had a picture of a bracelet she was interested in. I had told her I thought it looked like one of the orca bracelets made by the Makah."

"And she went there yesterday?"

"I think so."

"Have you heard from her since?"

Another maternal instinct swelled inside Chloe. Another with which she had grown unfamiliar—apprehension. The emotion twisted her features into a frown. "No, she said she was going to text me when she finished up at the reservation, but she never did. I'm sure she was just busy ..."

The uncertainty in her voice made the words sound more like

a question than a statement.

The tightness at the corners of Tony's eyes was not reassuring. "I'm sure she was. Well, it was nice to see you again."

"You too!" Chloe was not sure if he actually heard her.

He had turned and headed for the door without even waiting for his drink. Chloe forgot all about the pain in her mouth. Now it was her stomach bothering her. It was rapidly filling with dread.

∨

Kate awoke to a frigid reality of aches and pains. Opening her eyes, she found herself lying in a world of absolute darkness.

Placing her hands on the smooth metal surface beneath her, she tried to raise her head. The world tilted and pitched, making it feel as if she were at sea in a hurricane. In an instant, her stomach swapped places with her mouth. As digestive acids edged its way up her esophagus, she closed her eyes and inhaled deeply.

Easing herself back down, she rested her cheek against the cold, flat surface. Her thoughts could only be strung together in the lulls between the waves of debilitating nausea.

The cages.

The girls.

The stinging sensation in her neck …

An injection?

Who could have snuck up on her?

The lull between waves slowly began to grow in duration. After a few minutes, she felt well enough to attempt moving. Ignoring the impulse to rise, she slid her hands outward in either direction. In the inky blackness it was impossible to determine where she was, or how safe it might be to move around.

Once her arms were fully extended, she waved them in sweeping wide arcs. Nothing. She held her breath for a full minute. Her ears came up as empty as her hands and eyes.

The cold bit ever tighter, enveloping the entire surface area of her body. Instinctively, she reached for the warmth of her jean pockets. Rather than brushing against denim, her fingertips skipped over an uneven field of goosebumps before stopping at the elastic leg band of her cotton panties. The shirt and jacket she had been wearing earlier were gone as well. Only her bra remained.

Fear pierced the latent veil of disorientation, bringing the world into hyperfocus. Although blanketed in darkness, she felt as exposed as if she were standing under a thousand-watt light.

Determined not to give in to the debilitating emotion, she tried to focus her thoughts. *Was she still in the room with the other girls?*

"Hello?" she rasped. One long moment after another. Nothing but silence.

"Hello, is anyone there?" Another long wait with the same result.

"Please, is anyone there?" Minute after minute ticked by.

"Zamira? Zamira, are you there?" Kate was met with the same emptiness. "Zamira, I want to help you. I came here to help you because of your sister, Haryati."

An image of the arrest record for the doctor in Indonesia flashed in her mind. It had been completed in Malay, the language the girls likely spoke. *Were they there in the darkness? Was it they couldn't understand English, or had they been threatened not to make a sound?*

It might have been a latent effect of the drug, but she grew increasingly certain she was alone in the darkness. The conviction was accompanied by a sense of utter desperation.

The world seemed to shift again. She could feel the bite of rusty, phantom handcuffs. In the next moment, an equally irrational fear seized her mind. Although he was safely behind bars, Kate held her breath, fully expecting to hear the familiar voice of the Tower Torturer.

Rolling onto her side she squeezed her eyes shut and curled

herself into a tight ball. The defensive position had no calming effect. In fact, she felt weaker and more vulnerable.

Her heart pounded painfully in her chest. Adrenaline spurred her thoughts to fly by with the chaotic panic of forest creatures fleeing a wildfire. The vile smells and grisly images of so many crime scenes—images of corpses, pain … fear …

One thought moved a little slower than the rest. It wound its way in and around every recollection, whispering to Kate as it worked its way deeper and deeper into her heart. It could be summed up in one word: victim.

Starting with her sister Candace, there had been so many victims. Some she had saved, and a whole host of others she had not. The word took shape around the edges of other memories, bringing each failure into vivid detail. The three girls the Tower Torturer had killed. The unimaginable horrors each victim had experienced before they died. The grisly image of Haryati's ravaged body hanging limply in the pit. The grim faceless stares of the two unnamed skulls she had recovered. The bone fragments from six different victims in Celia's bracelet.

She retreated further inward, feeling she was now taking her long-awaited turn. The belief manifested with a physical brutality, prompting her to gasp for air.

The issuance from her throat was a mix between a hoarse choke and a wheeze. The foreignness of it struck like a slap to her face.

As a Special Victims Unit detective, she'd met many victims, each of whom had faced a life sentence of bearing the burden of the horrors they had suffered. She had taken it upon herself to peddle hope to them, insisting they could take their power back.

Her ragged breathing melted away in the face of those past promises. The words she had uttered so many times were not meaningless. Kate had truly believed them. She had looked up to each and every person who carried such a burden, because each of them had actually given her hope. Their example proved no matter what came your way, you could persevere.

The epiphany she had found illusory in the comfort of Dr. Wissel's office in San Francisco now revealed itself in the infinite emptiness of this nameless place. The real reason she had been drawn to law enforcement was not simply because she wanted to help people. She desperately needed them as much as they needed her. She had been on a subconscious quest—hoping to learn the secret to triumphing over cruelty from those who had been blessed with the ability to endure. Beyond pain. Beyond suffering.

Her work allowed her to experience what she never seemed to get enough of—the indominable human spirit. It could not be demeaned or diminished by mere experiences. It was not transitory, nor was it a commodity. It could not be bought, sold or stolen. No matter what, it endured. Even in death. Like her little sister Candace.

Opening her eyes in the darkness, Kate stared into a growing certainty. This was not about whatever might happen to her. It was about finding justice for Haryati and saving the girls. No matter how Kate's fate was about to play out, she had to continue to fight.

Clenching her teeth, she rose to her knees. Resolve building, she reached out blindly. With nothing before her, she inched forward. Right knee, left knee. Right. Left. Right.

A loud metallic squeaking sound, akin to a rusty door hinge opening, reverberated through the emptiness. At the same time, the surface beneath her began to dip forward.

She came to an immediate stop.

The sound petered away and eventually went silent. Pulse pounding, she pulled her right knee backward then the left. The sound rang out again, as the surface drew level once again.

She was on something, but what it was and how much

immediate danger she was in, had to be determined. Kate dropped onto her rear end.

Perhaps if her arms were not long enough …

She gently raised her right leg and probed the air in front of her. Just as she was about to extend the limb completely, her toes made contact with cold metal. Keeping an isometric hold on her muscles, she carefully probed the obstruction. It was almost the full width of her foot and ran vertically. The edges were smooth and rounded, like a pole.

Moving her foot to the right, it slipped off the poll, encountered dead air, then hit another pole. This time she worked her way up and down the length of the obstruction. It had been fitted into the surface upon which she was balanced.

Shifting her weight, Kate repeated the motion over and over again. Each time she moved to the right she encountered the exact same situation. When she was confident, she had made a full three-hundred-and-sixty-degree rotation, her suspicions were confirmed. She was in a cage, but one entirely different than those the girls were held in. She had not seen anything like it in their room.

A faint scent reached her nostrils—entirely unpleasant, but distinctive. Oil. Like the kind used to fuel lamps. She raised her chin to try to confirm it, but the aroma disappeared as quickly as it had come.

Rising to her knees, she placed her hands on the floor and carefully stood. With no idea what might trigger the platform to move, she inched her feet apart until they were separated by an arm's width. Confident in her balance, she extended her arms upward. A metal roof hung about two feet above her head. Kate braced her hands against it, worried any imbalance might shift the platform beneath her.

With her arms separated in a V-pattern above her, and her legs positioned similarly below, a more recent memory came to the fore. The sight of Delford's security badge as it had lain against the cage right before she blacked out.

Frowning, she pictured the Aaru logo as it had appeared in its topsy-turvy state. The sun which normally shone at the apex of the pyramid, had rested at the base of the inverted triangle. The exact opposite of the way she had seen it represented on Delford's jacket, his badge, or the resort's entry gates.

As she focused, her mind superimposed a bold outline over each of the geometric shapes. In a split second, the hypotenuse of the triangle disappeared. With only two sides remaining, it now resembled the letter "V" hovering above a circle.

The familiarity of the image seized hold of her consciousness. If only she could remember …

Calming her mind, Kate slipped into detective mode. Methodically, she started retracing the places she had been over the past few days. The Makah Cultural Center, the rental cottage, the coroner's office, TekPharmaCel …

Kate's heart dropped as the memory of Martin's Cruther's penthouse office took hold in her mind. Their last conversation, about context … she had mentioned the painting on his wall …

The stag's head—interpreted loosely by the artist as a circle with a "V" over it. Memories flooded her head.

The first time she had arrived at the security gate at Aaru. The guard … who had moved with the precision of ex-military.

The meeting with Hyland at the motor pool … discussion of the upcoming annual event—Oceana Week. His nearly ballistic response to their request to search the grounds.

Walking into the room with the cages … there had been far more girls than Kate had ever imagined. *Why so many? Surely not for one man?*

Cruthers' last words to her … his use of the pronoun "we."

And a longer memory … the research she had done into psychopaths during the Tower Torturer case. The fact they gravitated toward powerful positions where their lack of guilt, remorse and empathy formed a guaranteed recipe for success.

A malignant thought seeped out of the darkness into the base of Kate's spine. It crept upward with excruciating deliberation into her brain. It was a name familiar to most San Francisco Bay Area natives—Bohemian Grove.

Kate winced at the enormity of what lay before her. If she was right, it meant certain tragedy for her and every one of the girls in those cages.

Chapter 30

FOOTSTEPS SOMEWHERE IN THE DISTANCE. Kate's head snapped upward. Heart pounding, she peered into the inky blackness.

A dim beam of light appeared about fifteen feet ahead. As she watched, the luminosity expanded to reveal a corridor. The passageway had been hollowed out of natural stone, identical to the ones she had traversed.

Plowing through mounting fear, she stared intently at the blue-tinged light. A second later, a man stepped into view, illuminated by the backwash. He abruptly turned right and started toward her.

With the beam now pointed directly in her face, Kate held up a hand to shield her eyes.

"Hold on, hold on!" The familiar voice was laced with a note of annoyance.

A new sound—a match being struck. A hand elevated the flame, lifting it upward along the a nearby wall. It lingered for a moment before igniting a bright blaze inside a round, iron wall sconce.

Squinting against the brightness, Kate watched the man make his way along the perimeter of the room. A moment later, he lit another match, and reached up to ignite another sconce. The process continued five more times.

When he was done, her prison was revealed in vivid detail. The thirty-foot-wide chamber was perfectly round. Twelve arches were spaced evenly throughout, supporting the vaulted ceiling. Each arch was comprised of large stones tightly wedged together in the medieval style.

Two of the archways led to corridors. The other ten framed

small alcoves. Black velvet curtains draped the entrance to each room. Identical stone tables stood at the center of each mini chamber.

Kate's cage hung in the dead center of the room. Constructed of iron and cylindrical in shape, it was tethered from floor to ceiling by two thick steel chains. Above it, painted in red, a large reproduction of the painting from the CEO's office at TekPharmaCel sprawled across the ceiling.

Martin Cruthers turned off the flashlight and walked over to her. Appearing completely at ease, he wore a blue track suit and a pair of vividly white tennis shoes.

"I didn't figure you for a party-crasher, Detective. You arrived one night early and then slept the day away. The festivities are not scheduled to get underway for another couple of hours." His eyes dropped down to her nipples. The cold had forced them to strain against the thin fabric of her bra.

Kate glared at him. "Let me out of here!"

His eyes traveled up and down her body, twisting his expression into something far more lascivious. "You know that's not going to happen. "It is a shame. You don't fit this year's theme … I mean I don't mind, but the others would."

Ignoring the bait, Kate straightened her shoulders. "I know what you've been doing here. The perfect five-star resort, with the perfect five-star girls."

"Perfect?"

"Yes, perfect girls with perfect smiles, courtesy of dental implants from one of your subsidiaries." She pointed to the ceiling. "The same as the painting in your office. I should have seen the similarity with the Aaru logo earlier. And the number of girls—far too many for one man. Oceana Week is your twisted version of Bohemian Grove."

He regarded her with something approaching respect. "What

do you know about Bohemian Grove?"

"It's a private property about an hour's drive from San Francisco. A men's only group called the Bohemian Club owns it and has been having their annual gathering there since the 1870s. It's said to be comprised of the world's most powerful business magnates, scientists and politicians. Security is top tier—provided by elite ex-military personnel. Extreme secrecy about what goes on there has given birth to all sorts of conspiracy theories and rumors. The fringe whisper about extremely illicit behavior."

He nodded. "Their membership roster has included Presidents and global dignitaries. In fact, the United States can thank the group for hosting a Manhattan Project meeting which ultimately led to the creation of the atomic bomb."

"Nice plug, but I'm guessing your group's tastes run a little darker than those guys who put on plays at Bohemian Grove." Kate thought back to an eighteenth century sketch she had come across while researching the Tower Torturer case. It had depicted men dancing about in various stages of sexual debauchery. "More like those of the Hellfire Club …?"

Moving with all the pomp and circumstance of a Victorian nobleman out for an evening stroll, he began to circle the cage. "A much earlier men's club, comprised strictly of powerful politicians."

She shifted her feet as he moved, ensuring he could not get behind her. "Who were known for mocking societal norms and morals. They were said to have held meetings in caves where they engaged in all manner of sexual perversion up to, and including, murder."

"So judgmental, Detective! I'll have you know Benjamin Franklin attended their meetings while he lived in England." When no response was forthcoming, he continued. "No, we are not a modern-day chapter of the Hellfire Club. There are no politicians among us. We are titans of commerce and industry. But we were definitely inspired by those early pioneers."

He turned the flashlight back on and pointed at the back wall of the nearest alcove. Hung from a series of iron hooks was a wicked-looking, two-foot recurve blade. He moved the light to the next alcove where a hand-held, double-sided axe was similarly suspended. In the next, was a noose. And so the pattern progressed until he had illuminated a different weapon in each of the niches.

He tipped the light toward the ceiling. "And as our logo, we adopted one of the world's oldest symbols of male power and sexuality—the stag's head. Hence, the namesake of our group— The Stag."

Kate pursed her lips. "The horns are disproportionately large compared to the head. Reminds me of men with little dicks who buy big cars."

"Ah, the embittered tones of a frustrated feminist." He shook his head. "Let's start with the basics. Most of the people in this world are not worth the air they breathe. They blindly plod along well-traveled paths laid out for them by the masses who have gone before them. Whether it is the choice of careers, decision to have children, own a home … such apathy breeds generations of malleable followers. Thereby leaving the job of leadership up to a select few."

Her chin dropped a fraction of an inch. "Delford wasn't so malleable, was he? If not for him, no one might have ever discovered your dirty little secrets."

"Delford was incompetent."

"He left enough evidence to expose your pathetic band of rapists and murders."

Turning off the flashlight, he took a step closer. "None of our members were responsible for the deaths of those you have recovered. You must understand. If any of us were to kill every time the impulse struck, there would be no excitement to it. Really,

Detective. In your line of work, I'd think you'd know all about the dangers of desensitization."

"Then who killed them?"

He shrugged his shoulders. "The first fancied herself an escape artist. An ill-conceived attempt which was poorly executed. It became a teachable moment for the rest of the girls."

"Doesn't answer my question."

"As trite as it may sound, we have someone for that. He was there in the forest behind Delford's house the night after the vigil. He was supposed to get rid of Delford for us, but luckily the sheriff's department saved him the trouble."

Kate recalled the scurrying sounds she had heard after Wheaton's gun had gone off. Her thoughts shifted to the next piece of the puzzle. "And the two skulls?"

"An unfortunate case of dual suicide. The girls were entertaining one of our newer members who came into town a while back to sample our new acquisitions. He made the mistake of allowing them to fall asleep with him afterward. When he awoke, he discovered they had gotten into drain cleaner. We were forced to replenish our inventory sooner than expected."

Kate's stomach roiled, her imagination supplying all manner of sensory terrors one might experience from consuming the corrosive chemical. Allowing the thoughts to pass out of her brain as soon as they had entered, she cast another quick gaze around the room. "What about the others?"

He drew his jaw back. "There were no others from the Malaysian shipment."

She stared at him for a long moment thinking about the two bones whose DNA did not match the others in Celia's bracelet. Kate didn't need to repeat the question. Her brain was linking the facts as she voiced them. "You said I don't fit this year's theme, which is obviously Malaysia. Which Scandinavian country was it last year?"

The corner of his mouth lifted, but he didn't miss a beat. "Norway."

Kate's hands balled into fists. With the two bones, Delford had provided a mere sample of the girls who had been killed last year. She spat out the next words between clenched teeth. "Why here? Why not do it at Aaru?"

A dark shadow crossed his face, but Cruthers brushed it aside with another smile. "To celebrate another year of success! You must understand, every member wields a tremendous amount of power in our daily lives. In this setting, we can indulge in the ultimate expression of that power.

"Here, we are the arbiters of life and death. The givers of pleasure and pain. And here, as nature intended, we bathe in our own glory. The girls are kept in rotation for visiting members throughout the year. But once per annum, we up the ante."

"Power is demonstrated by overcoming a superior foe, not one who is weaker. Like I said before, men with little dicks ..." Kate looked pointedly at his crotch.

He crossed to the cage in a split second. Before Kate could respond, he reached out. Dropping the flashlight, he seized the cage bars and jerked downward. The edge of the surface beneath her feet tipped precipitously toward the floor.

Kate dropped onto her buttocks with a bone-jarring thud. Between gravity and the smooth surface, there was no way to stop herself from sliding against the bars.

Cruthers reached between the bars with his free hand and snatched her chin. His fingers bit into her flesh, the tips curled around her jawbone, threatening to dislodge her molars.

Ignoring the feral glimmer in his eyes, she stared back at him. Without a word, she eased her right hand onto her left wrist. Locking out her elbow she used all her might to shove her left forearm upward. The unexpected force dislodged the CEO's grip. His arm flipped back with breakneck speed into the unyielding force of a nearby bar. Kate raised up onto her knees, pinning the arm with her full weight.

His high-pitched scream surprised even Kate.

"Mr. Cruthers!" The exclamation came from the passageway entrance.

Without relaxing her grip, Kate glanced toward the archway.

Hyland Fairborne stood with a look of abject horror on his face. In the next moment, the resort manager sprinted across to the cage. Standing to the right of the CEO, he retrieved a gun from inside his jacket. Rather than pointing it at the compromised captor, he turned it on the aggressive captive.

"Release Mr. Cruthers."

Kate looked at the gun. "So, the man who donated his kidney for free has no problem selling his soul."

Smugness dripped from his features. "We are all more than the sum of our parts, Ms. Barnes. Oceana Week VIPs are our clients and investors. Aaru was designed to be their refuge from an increasingly demanding world. Here we attend to serving their *every* need. Now, let … him … go."

Nodding, she began to lean back. A split second before breaking contact with Cruthers, she lunged forward again, eliciting another cry from the CEO.

"Release him!" He made a show of disengaging the safety on the gun.

Kate met Hyland's gaze. Tilting her head to the side, she studied him for a long moment. Finally, she did as she was bidden.

Cruthers retracted his arm.

"Are you okay, sir?" Pocketing the gun, Hyland regarded Cruthers with the eyes of a supplicant.

The CEO waved him away. "I'm fine, Fairbourne."

"But sir, if you require …"

"What I require, is for you to get rid of this bitch once and for all!"

"Yes, sir. I have taken all the necessary steps." He reached into another pocket and passed a taser gun to Cruthers.

"Perfect." He turned back to Kate. "Had you not stumbled into the investigation, this would have all blown over in a week. But instead, you had to keep pushing. You brought in the FBI and fueled public sentiment with that damn vigil. You went after Delford and Belovol. You even had the balls to confront me. It is long past-time for you to leave this world, Detective."

"People will look for me."

"You still have no idea how omnipresent our power is. Despite your recent experiences, we do know how to cover up our mistakes. Look at your new friend, Lyra. Although she is relatively young, she will not outlive her mother."

Kate blanched. "Don't you dare!"

"You really are not in a position to be demanding anything. But you should be grateful. Tonight, you'll have the honor of providing a pregame show of sorts for our members. In your final dying moments, I hope you think of me."

Before she could respond, he pressed the trigger. The barbs shot forward through the bars. The moment they made contact with her abdomen a crackling sound filled the air. Kate's body seized as thousands of volts of electricity attacked her nervous system.

∨

The speedometer edged up near ninety as the sheriff's SUV sped along the highway under dark skies. His roof lights scrolled across the passing trees. They looked on in silence, like rows of jaded nightclub goers for whom the bright dancing colors no longer held any meaning.

Behind the steering wheel, Tony grimaced. He was well aware he was breaking the very safety laws he was meant to enforce. The worst part was he had no good reason for doing so—at least no reason based on proof. What he had were a series of coincidences, and none of them were good.

After his visit to Beans of Mine, Tony had returned to the office with a sinking feeling. Given the early hour, he had been forced to wait for two hours before he could reach out to the Cultural Center.

The call confirmed Kate had visited the prior afternoon. According to the woman with whom he had spoken, Kate had learned Delford had been a recent visitor. She had also obtained directions to three different locations where Delford might have recorded the video.

Unfortunately, the docent who had provided the directions was off for the day and could not be reached. Tony had responded by calling his counterpart with the Makah Tribal Police. It took the better part of the day to track down the older staff member who had gone on a fishing trip with his son.

In the meantime, he'd called the rental car company in Port Angeles where Kate had rented the sedan. They confirmed Kate was supposed to have dropped off her rental at their location at SeaTac but had never done so. A second call to the airlines confirmed Kate had checked in for her flight online, but she had never actually boarded it.

Within an hour, Tony had received a follow-up call from the car rental agency. They stated Kate had called to extend her rental by three more days. She had also changed the drop-off location from SeaTac to one of their facilities in San Francisco.

Part of him had wanted to believe Kate had simply decided to forgo the plane trip for a scenic drive. Yet, while Kate had not bemoaned her recent roundtrips to Seattle, he had seen the toll they had taken on her. He could not imagine she would trade a two-hour flight for a fourteen-hour road trip.

Taken on its own, Tony might have disregarded the unlikely change in itinerary. Yet, Mildred was still battling for her life in the hospital and Kate had been shot at and had almost drowned. Not long afterward, someone had gone out of their way to get her kicked off the case. That same someone had been monitoring their every move.

As soon as the docent's boat had pulled into the Makah Tribal Marina, Tony had been there to meet him. Luckily the older man's memory had sharpened since the day before. He was now able to identify the exact location out of the three possible ones he had given Kate.

"According to the GPS we're still about thirty minutes out," Tony announced to his passenger.

James nodded and glanced out the window. Not willing to take any more chances, Tony had persuaded the docent to serve as his guide through the forest.

The sheriff checked the clock again. Every minute that ticked by would prove to be one of two things—either a waste of his department's resources or a precious moment lost.

Chapter 31

ICY AIR BARGED IN through the open door. Hyland shoved Kate out into the biting cold. She managed a couple of unsteady steps before promptly collapsing to the ground. Her bra and panties were as useless against the frigid nighttime temperatures as they were against the rocks and branches littering the forest floor.

Hyland frowned. "You'd better get going!"

Kate looked down at her left wrist. A set of zip ties had been fastened to her so tightly the skin had welled up on either side of them. Between them, was a small black device.

Following her gaze, Hyland offered, "You won't be able to get those off without scissors." He looked pointedly into the forest. "And you're not likely to find those out here."

"Tra ... tracking device?" Kate managed through the echoing sting to her nervous system.

He rolled his eyes. "No. Can't you see the damn lens? It's a high resolution, night-vision-enabled camera—courtesy of our security department. It will catalog the entire hunt from start to finish. It was my idea, you know. As Mr. Cruthers said, you're going to be the pregame show for this evening's festivities. I decided to make it a literal show, camera and all."

Kate's eyes went wide. "You're going to hunt me?"

He recoiled. "Of course, not. You will be pursued by the most elite member of our security detail. A rematch of sorts—he is more than eager to redeem himself for his failure at the lake."

Hyland pulled out his phone as Kate struggled to get to her feet. Holding it in front of his face he activated the camera and smiled. He spoke into the device with all the fake exuberance of a reality TV show host.

"Welcome Honored Guests! The hunt will commence now. The prey will have a five-minute head start. From here on, you will be watching live feeds from both the hunter and the prey. Enjoy!"

Tapping the screen, Hyland dropped the device into his pocket. The veil of vivaciousness was discarded as easily as it had been adopted. His eyes met hers for a brief moment before he tore them away. "I advise you to run. As fast as you can." He scurried into the doorway, pulling the door shut behind him.

She lunged after him, but she was a split second too late. The door slammed firmly in his wake. The echo set off a flurry of activity. Snapping branches, and other sounds of frenzied commotion erupted from the underbrush surrounding the clearing. Luckily, all of the sounds seemed to be tracking away from Kate.

Eyes still trying to adjust to the darkness, Kate glanced about, simultaneously trying to process the reality of what was about to happen. Stabbing, shooting ... all made sense, but *hunting a human for entertainment?*

An image flashed. Haryati's corpse lying in the coroner's lab. Her skin had been a patchwork of small bruises and lacerations, most of which had been incurred in this very forest. But it was the numerous traumas she had endured after being captured that had made her corpse a terror to behold.

Kate had caused The Stag far greater grief than Haryati had. Who knew what they had instructed the hunter to do to her.

Despite her best efforts, Kate's breathing grew more and more shallow. With no shoes, no weapon, minimal light, and only a five-minute lead, there was virtually no chance she would ever make it to her car. Assuming her car was still where she had left it.

She had to think, but the last vestiges of the shots from the stun gun were still zinging through her brain. With the additional challenge that over twenty-four hours had passed since she had last had food or water, every thought felt as if it had been fitted with a fifty-pound anchor.

The image stuck in her head and stayed long enough to spark an idea. Ignoring the barrage of fatalistic thoughts peppering her mind, she dropped her head and started to run. Successful or not, it was the only idea she had. And she was running out of time.

∨

Martin Cruthers swished the fresh pour of five-hundred-dollar brandy around in his glass. Still in his tracksuit, he reclined in solitude on a sofa in his chalet at Aaru. Like his fellow club members, he had just finished watching Hyland open the hunt.

As recommended by the resort manager, the impromptu pregame show was to be enjoyed individually. The communal elements of the festivities would start soon enough.

Completely unaware of the ridiculously expensive gold leaf frame into which the large, flat screen television had been mounted, he glared at the appliance, "Go, you stupid bitch!"

The same way professional football players would never hear the vehement castigations from Monday morning quarterbacks, Kate had no way of hearing Cruthers' decree. The camera feed was one way, as was the audio.

As if intuiting his will, the camera angle slowly swung from left to right. "Trying to assess the landscape?" He wondered aloud.

He suddenly wished they had outfitted the detective with a heart monitor. It would have been so much more enjoyable to watch her heart rate climb. He took a sip, deciding it would be a good feature to add if they brought back the hunt next year.

The camera suddenly bounced to life. She had finally started running. Smiling, he sank back into the soft cushions.

If only the world knew the woman who had brought the world's most feared serial killer to justice was now running for her life in the forest. He wondered idly if she could even feel the cold, or if the combination of adrenaline and fear had made her impervious to it.

Tearing his gaze from the pitching landscape, he zeroed in on the clock in the right-hand corner of the screen: four minutes and forty-five seconds.

As he watched, the seconds continued to tick down. Suddenly, the image on the screen split in two. The feed from Kate's camera moved to the right. A new feed appeared on the left. An AR-15 rifle was in the process of being loaded. The calm, deliberate movements were diametrically opposed to the wild rush on the other side of the screen.

Hyland had told him the hunter would be outfitted with a helmet camera, as opposed to the wrist mounted one, they had improvised for Kate.

He took another sip of brandy. Relishing the complex flavors in his mouth, as much as his own certainty, he rejoiced in the affirmation life was exactly as he had described to Kate earlier. Power was everything.

∨

Bushes, branches, rocks, trees, branches, trees, rocks, branches. Kate's eyes darted back and forth over the landscape as she ran, cataloging every potential obstacle and making split second decisions to evade them when necessary.

Her heart pounded out of her chest. An image of it bursting took hold in her mind's eye. For a split second, she wished it would.

A five-minute head start meant nothing against a trained hunter. Especially when the hunted was suffering the early stages of dehydration and starvation compounded with the added fear of hypothermia.

So far, she had done a decent job of keeping herself upright in the weak moonlight. But it had come at a cost. Caution was slowing her down.

In the next heartbeat, her world changed. Her right foot landed heavily in thick mud. Unable to find purchase, it went out from under her. Tucking her head, she tried to roll into the fall.

She hit the ground hard and slid to a stop. What felt like thousands of small cuts set her skin on fire. Screaming above each of those wounds was a searing pain across her right ankle.

The moonlight filtering through the thick tree canopy was too weak for a proper inspection. Her survival instinct kicked into gear. All that mattered was to keep moving.

Scrambling to her feet, Kate tested her weight on the ankle. Pain erupted along every one of her nerve endings, but the joint held. Bending over, her fingers probed the affected area. A nauseatingly thick roll of skin … beneath it a slippery mess. The contact prompted a whole new bout of pain as well as an added sense of despair.

Even the most inexperienced tracker would be able to follow a trail of blood. Her eyes moved to the camera on her wrist. The recollection of Martin Cruthers' smug expression when he had bid her goodbye …

The image reached inside her soul and stabbed at her sense of indignation. Knowing the odds for survival were not in her favor, she held onto the image of the CEO. Silencing the clock counting down in her head, she dropped to her knees.

It took no more than a second to find the source of her injury. Two feet behind her, a jagged rock protruded from the mud. Digging her fingers into the terrain, she tugged with all her might. She was rewarded with a foul sucking sound. In the next moment, the rock came free. She turned it until the blunt edge faced outward.

Raising her right wrist to her face, she glared directly into the camera.

"Fuck you, assholes! The show is over."

Kate laid her right forearm on the ground. Without the slightest hesitation, she raised the rock in her left hand, and slammed it into the device. The ensuing crunch was accompanied by shockwaves of pain radiating through her right wrist.

A single ribbon of blood snaked its way around the broken bits of lens. The sight of it brought the hint of a smile to her lips.

Flexing her wrist muscles, Kate rose to her feet. Fueled by a newly found sense of dignity, she set out at a decidedly faster clip.

A few moments later she confronted a massive group of trees. On the other side of the copse, a familiar scent filled her nostrils. It was the same crisp odor she had detected during her hike to the hidden door—except it was much stronger.

A minute later, the sound of crashing waves joined the briny aroma of sea air. After two more minutes she emerged from the forest onto a high bluff overlooking the Pacific. The full moon hung low over the ocean. Its vivid light bounced off the tumultuous waves, creating a broken kaleidoscope of bright light.

She ventured to the edge of the bluff and peered over the side. The roar of the surf was almost deafening. The success of the world's largest ocean's age-old campaign against the continent was evident in the dense number of craggy outcroppings and eroded cliffs below.

Looking back over her shoulder, Kate studied the tree line. No perceivable movement, but there soon would be. Her gaze followed the trail of bloody footprints she had left. A series of thoughts occurred to her in rapid succession.

The hunter would soon be upon her.

There was nowhere to hide.

She turned back to the water. The upwelling air currents whipped her hair around her face with cruel indifference.

The decision was easier than she had thought it would be. Like destroying the camera, she would rob Cruthers and his twisted cronies of any pleasure in her demise. Most of all, she would rob them of what they really wanted—the illusion of having any power over her.

Pursing her lips, she turned around and dropped to her hands and knees. Muscles straining, she dropped her legs backward over the edge.

For a moment, her limbs swung free. In the next second, the persistent updraft in air currents shifted to a downdraft. Feeling as if she were being sucked into a maelstrom, she clung closer to the bluff and began lowering herself inch by inch. Her face disappeared below the edge, as her left foot made contact with a small, slippery outcropping.

She dropped another inch. Her right foot made contact with a similar feature, albeit slightly lower than the first. The next question was whether she had the guts to test if the separate ledges would bear her weight.

The toe of a boot suddenly appeared in the space between her hands.

Time had run out.

"Well, what have we here …?" The voice was almost indiscernible above the ferocious surf.

Heart racing so fast no beat was distinguishable from another, she watched as a camera came into view. It was strapped to the top of a helmet.

There was not even time for a small prayer. In one deft movement, Kate seized hold of the boot with both hands, then dropped as if her entire body was a dead weight.

Heaving with all of her might, she dragged the boot away from the earth. Loose dirt rained down on her from above, stinging her eyes.

A split second later, the second boot appeared. Kate caught

sight of an assault rifle just before the man came teetering over the edge.

Releasing her quarry, Kate threw her body flat against the jagged rocks in the cliff wall. A flailing boot connected sharply with her left thigh. The impact bounced her against the wall.

In the same moment, the downdrafts returned. It took every muscle in her core to retain her balance on the improbable perch.

The ensuing splash was almost impossible to pick out from the ongoing cacophony below. Panting, Kate reached for the lip of the cliff and started to climb.

Her head had cleared the edge allowing a glimpse of the tree line, when the last of her reserves gave way. Arm muscles trembling, she began to sink slowly back down. If she did not have the strength to climb out, she certainly did not have the strength to cling to the improvised perch.

The darkness pulled at her, whispering it was finally time to let go.

Tears pouring out the sides of her eyes, she thought once more of Martin Cruthers' smug visage. Hatred for everything the group stood for, and every victim it had claimed, flooded her veins.

"Son of a ... fucking ... bitch!" The scream tore through her throat with animal rawness. With it came the last bit of adrenalin. It was all she needed. Her head rose above the bluff once more. It was followed by her chest and then her waist.

She kicked her right leg up over the edge, letting momentum carry her forward. Rolling onto her back, she panted for air, grateful for the feel of the small loose rocks biting into her flesh. When her breathing finally slowed, she rolled back to the edge and peered over.

The waters raged below. There was no sign of human life.

There was also no way of knowing how much those watching had seen on the camera feed from the hunter's helmet. At the very least, they would send someone to check it out.

She was on her feet in the next moment doing exactly what she hoped they would not expect. Rather than running from the steel door, she made a beeline straight back to it.

Approaching the edge of the clearing minutes later, she crouched down and started skirting the perimeter. It was paramount she avoid the mistake she had made during her earlier arrival. Having watched Delford's video so many times, it was easy enough to follow the route he had taken to stay out of the view of the cameras.

When she reached the hill on the far-right side of the entrance, she clambered up to the top in less than a minute. Not pausing to catch her breath, she began picking her way down over the rocks toward the top of the entrance.

Nearing the bottom, she slipped into a gap between the two boulders which formed a natural lintel over the doorway. Wedged between the stones, she waited for the sound she had most wanted to hear.

The door opened and two men emerged. Clad in Kevlar vests and toting AR-15 rifles, they headed directly toward the sea. Kate waited until they had reached the far end of the clearing before climbing out of her hiding spot.

She had traversed over forty percent of the distance to the ground, when her left hand slid at light speed across a thick patch of mud trapped between two smaller rocks. Blood roaring in her ears, she teetered back and forth before regaining her balance. Kate dropped to her rear end to wipe the wet dirt from her skin but stopped herself in mid-movement.

Staring at the slick substance smeared across her hand, Kate reached back and scooped out a handful of the wet dirt. She briskly made her way around to each of the cameras. In less than a minute she had thoroughly obscured the lenses of each device. A minute later, she was back on the ground standing before the entrance.

The odds she had been running in her head ever since taking off from the cliff proved to be in her favor. Expecting the men to return soon, no one had bothered to lock the door.

∨

Hyland Fairbourne emerged from the tunnel with the weight of the world on his shoulders. Things were not proceeding the way he had planned.

He closed the door behind him, waiting to hear it lock before continuing. Unlike the entry Kate had stumbled upon, this entrance consisted of a pair of doors set into the forest floor.

The route had been excavated by an international team who had been flown in to construct the ceremonial chamber. It ran underground for a full mile before emerging into the open area which served as a mini-parking lot. Martin Cruthers had spearheaded much of the design. For Hyland, it was nothing but a maintenance nightmare.

He hurried past the row of electric vehicles parked along the perimeter of the path. With the pregame show ending early, the guests had abandoned their plush accommodations at Aaru for the unique venue.

The destruction of the Barnes woman's camera had created the first wrinkle in the show. Luckily, the remaining feed from the hunter's camera had more than made up for it. Knowing her pathetic attempt at rebellion was about to be brutally eliminated had made the show more engrossing than expected.

Unfortunately, the hunter's feed had gone dead right when he discovered Kate's attempted hiding place. Hyland had been forced to cut into the live stream, broadcasting a lie that would hopefully buy him enough time to figure out what the hell had gone wrong.

He had told his guests the camera signal had been dropped—a

minor technical glitch. Hyland had offered his sincerest apologies, promising the hunter would record Kate's execution in detail, but they would have to wait until he returned and manually uploaded the file from his camera.

This was his second-year hosting Oceana Week. He had never inquired into the details of what exactly had transpired last year, and other than fulfilling those logistical requests related to the year's events, he expected to know as little by tomorrow morning. If they kept to the same schedule as last year, the guests would not be returning to Aaru until the near dawn hours. They would then sleep for the rest of the day, giving him time to dispose of the girls. The grisly duty had fallen to him after Delford's failure.

Tomorrow's responsibilities could wait. Tonight, he had to figure out what the hell had happened in those final moments of Kate Barnes' life. The need to know had grown in the pit of his stomach ever since the second feed went dead. Whatever had gone wrong, it must have been more than a minor glitch. The hunter had not responded to one of his numerous radio calls.

Hyland's next call had been to his technology specialist. Known as one of the top technical experts in Europe, Hyland had every reason to trust his word the radio signals, cell phone jamming systems and secured Wi-Fi transmission were all operating perfectly. If the hunter was not communicating, there had to be some other reason.

Arriving at his vehicle, he climbed in and started the engine. He was halfway back to Aaru when his cell phone began to ring.

The sound sent his temper soaring. The only sound he had wanted to hear was from his radio. The two security operatives he had dispatched had left the caves over ten minutes ago. Neither had reported in yet.

Glancing at the screen, Hyland felt as if the world were suddenly spinning out of control. The simple text from his IT specialist added a new host of fears to those already rending his abdomen.

Cameras at Entrance 2 have been compromised.

For the first time since accepting his position at Aaru, Hyland's cocksure opinion of himself began to falter. Snarling into the darkness, he vowed to make as many people pay for the moment of uncertainty as possible.

Chapter 32

KATE'S HEART RACED as she hurried along the corridor. There was no way of knowing how much time she had before someone investigated the cameras and drew the obvious conclusions. Moreover, she still had no idea how she would get the girls, let alone herself, out of this alive. It was all about sheer faith and instinct.

Arriving back at the two doors, she pressed her ear against the one on the left. She could not hear anything, but presumed it led to the room where she had been held captive. By now, whatever Cruthers and Fairbourne planned to do in that bizarre playroom was either underway, or about to start.

She put her ear to the door on the right. Silence. Kate bolted through the door back into the kitchen. Her luck was holding—the room was still empty.

Darting to the opposite door, Kate paused for a breath. Cracking it open, she peered inside. Other than the girls trapped in the cages, no one else was in sight. Kate rushed in and pulled the door shut behind her.

Clad in identical black satin robes cinched tightly at the waist, with long hoods hanging down their backs, the girls eyed Kate with open interest. Their gazes flitted over her multitude of abrasions and lacerations, to the bits of dirt and branches in her hair, then settled on the tattered vestiges of her bra and panties. The resulting expressions told her what a mirror could not. She did not look like anyone's hero.

One by one, they made up their minds. Deciding Kate was yet another victim, they began to turn away. Only one girl came to stand at the door to her cage. Unlike the others, her eyes sparkled with dark passion.

Kate was familiar with the look. She had seen it often enough in the eyes of domestic violence victims who had faced murder charges after having been pushed too far. She had also seen it on the face of Maria Torres in the Tower Torturer's lair. It was simple and primal—the need for revenge.

Kate approached the cage. She studied the girl's familiar features—the same ones she had first glimpsed in a photo during her meeting with the FBI. "Zamira?"

"You know my name?" The words were issued with a thick Malay accent.

"You speak English?"

"Christian school." She narrowed her gaze. "How do you know my name?"

"I am here to help you."

"Me?" Zamira raised an eyebrow. "Looks like you need help, too."

"Maybe we can help each other."

Zamira pointed to the far wall. Above the wooden bench a set of keys now hung from a small iron peg. "Maybe."

Dropping her gaze back down to the bench and recognizing what lay upon it, Kate nodded again, then turned back to Haryati's younger sister. It was time to do for Zamira what her older sister could not.

Kate laid her hand against the chain link fence. "We don't have much time."

V

Martin Cruthers gazed across the room at his fellow club members. Each man stood inside his chosen alcove. Having been designed to appeal to the voyeurs in the group, the room offered perfect lines of sight for those who derived exquisite pleasure from seeing and being seen.

The men, whose ages ranged from late thirties to early sixties, were bare chested. Each member had reproduced a crude version of the stag's head symbol in red body paint upon his chest. They wore identical black satin kilts. All went barefoot.

The soundtrack to one of Wagner's operas played softly on hidden speakers. He could feel the anticipation in the air. Their collective patience was about to pay off.

As the music built, one of Hyland's most trusted employees appeared at the main entrance. Wearing a monochromatic black suit, the employee paused to nod at each man in the assembly.

When he had paid his respects, he stepped to the side. A female appeared behind him. Martin smiled, pleased to see Hyland had followed his instructions to the letter.

The girl was dressed in a black satin robe, the hood of which had been pulled down low over her face. Only the bottom of her chin was visible. Like the men, she was barefoot.

She proceeded into the room with the slow, measured pace of a bride walking down the altar. Five paces behind her, another identically dressed girl appeared. She was followed by another who arrived at the same interval. And so, the process continued girl after girl.

They made their way to the center of the room, coming to stand in a wide circle around the hanging cage. Spaced evenly apart, with their backs to the cage the detective had occupied earlier, they did not make a sound.

Martin turned to Hyland's assistant and nodded. The man bowed briefly, then turned and retreated into the corridor.

Satisfied, Martin turned his gaze back on the girls. He expected to be overwhelmed by dark stirrings. Instead, as he shifted his gaze from girl to girl, he experienced a totally different feeling. Something about them seemed off.

It was not their clothing. Nor was it their demeanors. Each girl stood with head bowed in supplication as they had been instructed. Martin's gaze shifted to the club's senior member, who was emerging from his designated alcove. The man's eyes sparkled with keen interest as he made his way to the first girl who had entered the room.

It was understood the rest of the club members would successively make similar choices, until one girl was left standing. She would be placed in the cage, kept in special reserve as a dessert of sorts for those who still had the stamina to go at her in the end.

As the senior member returned to his alcove, and the next member stepped forward, Martin turned back to the girls. Then it dawned on him. The number.

There should have been eleven girls. One for each alcove and one for the cage in the center of the room. But there were twelve.

It was impossible. He had reviewed the inventory with Hyland numerous times. During the last six months they had imported a total of fourteen girls from Malaysia. Having lost two to suicide and having killed the one who had tried to escape, eleven remained—the exact number required.

Thoughts racing, he performed another headcount, finishing as another member stepped up to make his claim. He had not miscounted. There were twelve females in the room.

He scrutinized each of the hooded forms. They all appeared identical … except the one on the opposite side of the cage from him. She stood almost a full head taller than the rest.

Turning, he snatched the recurve blade from its mount on the wall. Relishing the heft of the weapon in his hand, he ran out of the alcove.

Cries of outrage rang out at what his fellow members mistakenly interpreted as a breach of protocol. Moments later he stood before the figure. Reaching out, he tore the hood from her face.

Kate Barnes' eyes burned with raw hatred.

The sight of her turned his stomach. "I'm almost glad you survived. Now I have the pleasure of ending you myself."

He raised the blade over his head but faltered at the smile spreading across her features.

"I wouldn't do that if I were you." Her words were punctuated by the feel of cold steel against his bare chest.

He looked down to find the same gun they had confiscated from her when she had arrived. It had been left with her belongings in the dormitory.

Raising his eyes to hers, he found the smile had been replaced with a sneer.

"Drop the blade—now."

He did not hesitate. The weapon hit the floor with a metallic clang.

His fellow members murmured among themselves, speculating whether the tableau playing out before them was an unscripted part of the festivities.

"This isn't going to work, Detective."

"Oh, but it is. See, I have enough rounds here to take out each and every one of you."

"You're wrong." In the next moment he screamed out a single word sounding oddly like "Tahiti!"

Kate raised an eyebrow as her brain tried to make sense of the non-sequitur. Alarmed, but not sure why and certainly not willing to show it, she raised her chin and addressed the rest of the club members. "I want all of you to drop to the floor—now!"

Not one of the men made a move. "I said now!"

When another ten seconds passed with no response, she stabbed the barrel of the Glock into Martin's abdomen.

Wincing, Cruthers called out. "You forget yourself, Detective. I told you earlier. Here, we are the arbiters of life and death." He inclined his head toward the corridor which lay behind her on the right.

"I am not dumb enough to take my eyes off you."

"I recommend you do."

The sound of Hyland's voice drew Kate's gaze to the corridor. The resort's general manager stood alongside the man in the charcoal suit. Both were armed, and both had their weapons trained on Kate's head.

While there was a good chance Hyland might miss, Kate doubted the other man would. Taking a deep breath, she turned back to Cruthers and nodded slowly. "You win."

She raised her weapon toward the ceiling. Hyland and the other man rushed toward her as Cruthers reached for her gun.

His hand was about to make contact with hers, when she punched him in the throat with her left fist. Without waiting to see his response, she threw her back against the cage. Bullets ricocheted off the bars as she spun around and dropped to a knee.

The assembly cried out as she squeezed off two shots, hitting each of the new arrivals in the legs. As they fell, she shot again and again. Both men hit the floor. Hyland did not move, but the man in the suit tried to raise his gun once more.

He never had the chance. A robed figure appeared at his side and kicked the weapon from his grip. It flew across the floor. One of The Stag members bent to retrieve it.

In the next moment, Kate was at the man's side, whipping her gun against the side of his head and knocking him unconscious. From the corner of her eye, she spotted another reaching around for one of the weapons on the wall of his alcove.

He screamed as her next bullet tore a vast hole through his hand.

A voice called out what sounded like a command in Malay. Two of the girls flew into motion. Within seconds they had retrieved the gun from Hyland's fallen form as well as the one that had been kicked free. Both girls arrived at Kate's side. Bowing their heads, they presented her with the weapons.

She was about to take one from the girl on her left when the edge of the recurve blade suddenly popped through the girl's chest. It glistened with dark red blood. Kate watched as it suddenly retreated.

Horrified, she raised her gaze to the girl's face. Blood bubbled up through the young woman's mouth. With a soft cry she fell lifeless to the floor.

Martin Cruthers stood over the corpse, murderous glee reflecting in his eyes. He lunged for Kate. A single tear slipped from her eye as she raised her hand and calmly shot him in the face.

Another series of astonished exclamations arose from the men, but the females remained unphased. Kate plucked the gun from the other girl's hands. Raising both arms, she began to spin in a slow circle. "Face down with hands behind your backs! Now!"

The air redolent with the smell of human blood, the remaining males threw themselves to the floor.

"Zamira, tell the girls to take off their belts and use them to tie everyone's hands," Kate demanded.

Zamira pulled off her hood and repeated the instructions. As the girls set to work, Kate turned her attention to Hyland. One glance at the gaping wound in his throat confirmed he was dead.

"Do you want me to keep recording?" Zamira asked, holding up Kate's cell phone.

Besides her gun, the phone had been the only other item she had bothered to retrieve from her pack. It had been left abandoned on the bench beneath the key to the cages. Zamira had readily accepted Kate's request to surreptitiously record as much as she could, for as long as she could.

Kate cast one last look at the prone figures on the floor and nodded. "We have more than enough."

Zamira joined the rest of the girls. When they were done, she returned to Kate's side.

"I guess you didn't need us." Another male voice from the corridor.

Kate's heart fell. She knew the facility was a few miles from Aaru, but she had no idea how much of the resort's security had been deployed here. For all she knew Hyland had alerted an army.

She wheeled back toward the corridor with both guns raised.

"Whoa!" Tony held up his hands.

"I told you not to worry, Sheriff. This woman is a badass." Deputy Wheaton smiled at Kate as she entered the room along with Deputy Carson and a slew of other law enforcement officers.

Kate spotted a couple of Department of Forestry and Port Angeles Police Department badges before she wearily shifted her gaze back to Tony. Feeling as if gravity had suddenly increased by a factor of fifty, Kate lowered the gun. "How did you find us?"

Tony rushed to her side and shrugged off his jacket. "Your mother."

"My mother?" Kate could barely form the words.

He gingerly placed the coat around her shoulders. "She told us about the bracelet."

"And you went to the Cultural Center ... but how did you know about the trail?"

"Your buddy James is waiting outside. He led us here."

Kate felt a tug at her sleeve. Zamira stood at her elbow looking at her expectantly. "You said you would help me."

"Of course I will. Your parents have missed you. We'll get you back home to them as soon as we can."

"That is not the help I need."

Tony looked at the girl with abject tenderness. "It's okay, you're safe now. We'll bring all these men to justice."

Zamira regarded him with consternation, then turned back to Kate. "But not real justice for Haryati. The one who killed her has to pay."

"He's not here?" Tony asked, gazing about the room.

"No." Kate turned back to Zamira. "Do you know what he looks like?"

"Sheriff, a little help over here?" Carson was busy trying to haul up a particularly large man who had begun to bawl.

Kate scowled at the pathetic display. So easily moved to tears, when he had been so ready to torture and kill for his own amusement. It was a common theme—often those most ready to dole out cruelty to others were the least likely to take it from others.

Tony looked at Kate and rolled his eyes. "I'll be right back," he promised.

Kate pulled Zamira aside. "Can you tell me anything about the man who killed her?"

"I know what he looks like. And I know something else about him. Haryati told me …" Her eyes glazed over. For a moment she looked as if the world were shattering into subatomic elements before her. Her lower lip trembled.

In the barest whisper, Kate asked, "What did Haryati tell you?"

Zamira walked over to the body of the girl Martin Cruthers had just killed. Without a word, she dropped to her knees alongside the trail of blood snaking out from beneath the young girl's corpse.

As if it were the most natural thing in the world, Zamira dipped her finger in the trail of blood and began to draw on the floor. When she was done, the last of the puzzle pieces fell into place and Kate knew exactly how to find justice for Haryati.

May 13

The outer reception area was pitch dark. Kate flashed her

pocket light along the far wall until she spotted the door she had used when she had first visited. At the time, she had been so plagued by her past and her present she had never seen what lay right before her.

Thanks to Haryati and Zamira, Kate's vision had finally cleared. Everything now stood out to her in vivid detail. Including the aches and pains adrenaline had kept at bay for the last few hours.

Her feet and right ankle had not yet been treated. It would have to wait. There was a more immediate priority.

Minutes after Zamira had shared her secret, Tony's team had found the other entrance to the caves, as well as the hidden path to Aaru. They were getting ready to make a move on the resort but the sheriff had agreed Kate had already done more than her share.

Tony had assigned Flaherty to help her out of the forest. The deputy had strict instructions to take Kate directly to the hospital to get checked out. It took some of Kate's best flirting and the occasional not-so-accidental flash of cleavage from her open jacket to convince the deputy to take her to the sheriff's office instead.

Once there, he loaned her a pair of sweats and tennis shoes from his locker. He even went as far as to bring her to the downtown for a cup of coffee before they headed to the hospital.

She had given him the slip by climbing out of the bathroom window at Beans of Mine. That was more than ten minutes ago.

About twenty-five-feet ahead, a dim yellow light spilled into the corridor from the open office. As Kate crept along, the sound of a drawer slamming echoed down the hall. Nearing the opening she could hear what sounded like someone muttering under their breath. She paused at the doorway.

During her visit to the sheriff's office, she had placed a call to Maria Torres. The consummate journalist, Maria called Kate back within fifteen minutes with the answers to the questions burned into her mind since the moment when the hunter had plunged over the edge of the cliff.

It had been a risk coming here. There was a chance she could be wrong.

Assuming she was right, she did not think he would skip town. After all, he had no way of knowing what Haryati had told Zamira. It was more likely he would try to con his way through, the same way he had been conning people out of their life savings. People who trusted him. People like Chloe.

She strode into the room. "Looking for something?"

The man, who had told the truth about having served in the military but had lied about the capacity in which he had served, stared at her in surprise. The same man whose apparent charitable works were detailed in the photos adorning the outer reception area—works based in third world countries like Malaysia, ran a hand through his still damp hair.

"Hi, Kate." Straightening, Pastor Brian closed the drawer he had been rifling through and smiled at her warmly. "To what do I owe the unexpected pleasure?"

"I think you can guess."

"Interested in another counseling session?" He raised his hands in apology as he made his way around the desk. "I'm sorry but I can't help you tonight."

Kate waved his words away. "I understand."

Sitting on the corner of the desk, he regarded her affably. "Well, have Chloe call me tomorrow and we can set something up, okay?"

Kate scratched her head, shifting the mass of mangy locks bound together by an unforgiving rubber band she'd pinched from Flaherty's desk. According to a glance in the mirror at Beans of Mine, recent events had made it appear more akin to an unruly rat's nest than anything resembling human hair.

She shook her head. "I must admit you've disappointed me.

From the first moment I met you, you struck me as a pretty perceptive guy."

He raised his eyebrows. "You don't think so anymore?"

"How can I? You see, I just strolled in here sporting men's sweats and shoes at least four sizes too big. My skin is torn, battered and bruised. All in all, I look like I've run a gauntlet in the post-apocalypse ... But you don't seem to be shocked at all."

He blinked several times before pointedly looking her up and down. Slapping his hand to his forehead, the Pastor exclaimed, "Oh, my word! I'm so sorry, Kate! It goes to show how preoccupied I am. What in the world happened?"

Her jaw dropped. "A silly question from the man who was hunting me in the forest." She crossed her arms over her chest. "I was surprised you survived that plunge into the ocean. Must have been quite a shock to the system. I've gotta give you points for the swim. The surf looked awful."

His expression went cold. "I don't know what you're talking about."

Kate's eye was drawn to the small paperweight on his desk, sitting to the left of his hip. It was a smaller version of the upturned wing above the marquee at the church next door.

Pastor Brian had adopted the old theater's trademark sign as his church's logo. It was identical to the one Haryati and Zamira had seen at the mission school they had attended in their village. The school which had been sponsored by Faith, Hope and Light. And it was the very same one Zamira had crudely recreated from blood of yet another dead girl.

"Okay, then let's talk about who you really are. War vet, yes. But not an ex-pastor. Ex-Special Forces. Dishonorably discharged for trafficking in black market contraband, illegal arms sales, as well as ... human trafficking. A good gig while you had it. But once you came back here, you found a new one."

She gestured wide with her arms. "Built up a nice little faith racket, but the real money doesn't come from the collection basket does it? The real money comes from stealing young girls from foreign countries and selling them to rich perverts. Perverts rich enough to help you erase your past and remake it."

"Kate, I don't know where you're getting this but …"

In the next moment, the paperweight was hurtling toward her. She ducked the projectile but could not duck the lunge that followed. He appeared as if out of nowhere, slamming into her abdomen with a vicious blow that threw her backward into an enormous bookshelf. It rocked precipitously back and forth, raining books down on her head before regaining its balance.

Before she could catch her breath, he fell upon her with his full weight. His forearm clamped down across her windpipe. She could feel her trachea compress flat upon itself. Lungs burning, Kate stared into the cold depths of his eyes for what seemed like an eternity.

She did not bother to claw at his arm. He was too strong.

She simply slipped her hand into the pocket of her sweatshirt, tilted her wrist upward and pulled the trigger of her gun. At point blank range, the bullet tore through his stomach. The pain had to have been debilitating, but it only served to enrage him.

Abandoning her throat, he placed his hands on either side of her skull intent on snapping her neck. She fired again.

This time he recoiled mightily, falling off her onto the carpet. Panting, she dragged herself back toward the desk. Keeping a wary eye on his still form, she used a nearby chair to help her to stand.

Gun trained firmly on his chest, she reached over and activated the speakerphone. With the combined smell of blood, burnt gunpowder and burnt cotton, so thick in her nostrils she imagined she could taste them on her tongue, Kate informed the 9-1-1 operator there had been a shooting at Faith, Hope and Light's administrative offices. Asked about the condition of the shooting victim, she walked back to the pastor.

A quick check of his pulse confirmed what was evident from the liters of blood soaking into the carpet. The pastor was dead.

In the next few heartbeats, she recalled everything that had happened since she had gone to the sheriff's office to cancel her date. Victim after victim. Those with faces, and those without.

It was all Kate could do not to unload the rest of her rounds into his body while she waited for help to arrive.

Epilogue

June 10

HOPING IT WOULD BE the last time she would ever do so; Kate opened the door to the empty interrogation room. Memories of Rick Delford's adamant denials seemed to haunt the corners of the chamber as Kate took a seat at the table.

She was not alone for long. Muffled voices drifted in from the hallway. Clayton and Fuentes appeared in the doorway moments later. Both agents looked exhausted.

"Thanks for agreeing to meet with us again." Fuentes closed the door and took a seat next to her.

Kate watched Agent Clayton settle in across the table. "No problem. I know you guys have a huge amount of clean up on your hands." Crossing her legs, Kate leaned back in her seat. "I'm not sure there's anything I can add to what I've already told you."

The statement was nearly identical to ones she had made during two other meetings with the agents. The first had taken place in the Port Angeles hospital.

After ministering to a nasty network of cuts and bruises, the doctors had talked her into staying overnight for observation. The federal agents had arrived a few hours before discharge the next day. With the exception of a few softball questions, they had spent the majority of the time listening to Kate's version of events.

The second interview had been conducted at the rental cottage—a place to which Kate had returned without any say in the matter. Tony picked her up from the hospital. As soon as they began to drive away, he made an admission which had sent her temper through the roof.

364

The sheriff had been busy conspiring with her mother. He had asked Chloe to negotiate an open-ended lease on the cottage. She had gone further, persuading the landlord to give her an extra key so she could prepare the dwelling for Kate's return. The facts had assailed Kate's psyche in the same fashion as the gunfire at Belovol's warehouse.

At the cottage, she had found the closet and bathroom stocked with replacement goods. The day she had set out for the Makah reservation, her luggage had been locked in the trunk of the rental car. As Kate had feared the night of her flight into the woods, the vehicle had disappeared from the fire road where she had left it.

The last thing Kate had wanted was for Chloe to come to her rescue, but beggars could not be choosers. She had thanked Tony for his efforts and pled exhaustion to encourage his departure. On his way out, he'd presented her with a new cell phone into which his and Chloe's numbers had already been programmed.

Agent Clayton cleared her throat, bringing Kate back to the present. "You look much better."

"Thanks." Kate ignored the sudden itch above her left brow. The phantom sensation had almost completely faded since her doctor had removed the stitches two weeks earlier.

"I don't think I can remember the last time I've had more than four hours of sleep." Fuentes looked at his boss. "How about you?"

Clayton shook her head. "Sleep is for wimps."

Kate's lips twisted into a perfunctory smile. "Do long nights indicate progress in the investigation?"

Clayton glanced at the other agent before locking gazes with Kate. "We keep turning up more and more every day."

"That's for damn sure," Fuentes confirmed. "When you first approached us, we couldn't put together more than a few hours per week to dedicate to this case. Now it's like biblical fish."

365

Clayton tapped the end of her pen against the table. "It sure didn't help to have the video go public."

Kate nodded. Within days of the FBI taking Kate's cell phone into custody, the footage Zamira had filmed in the ceremony room had been leaked to social media. It had gone viral in less than an hour, inciting worldwide horror and outrage.

The upside was no amount of legal wrangling, political pressure or financial privilege on the part of the men in custody could ever explain away the vile behavior it depicted.

Agent Clayton watched Kate for a long moment before moving on. "Aaru wasn't exclusively a front for The Stag. It was also a profit center. We found an extensive guest list of powerful businessmen who were allowed use of Aaru's off-ledger amenities. The fees would make your head spin. So far it looks like none of them knew about the ceremony room, they only knew Aaru was a place they could have a five-star experience all the way around."

"Will the guests be harder to prosecute?" Kate asked.

"We lucked out there. Turns out Hyland Fairbourne covertly installed hidden cameras in the guest houses. Probably part of an extortion scam for after he left Aaru. There's an entire digital library of incriminating evidence."

"As bad as those bastards were, what they were doing was still small potatoes compared with Pastor Brain's operation."

"Absolutely. His missionary outreach allowed him to source girls from all over the world. Supplying to The Stag was one small drop in a very large global bucket."

"And all of it done under the guise of piety and the umbrella of a tax-exempt status."

Clayton picked up her phone. "I do have some good news for you." She tapped the screen then passed it to Kate.

On the display was an image of a smiling Zamira caught in the loving arms of her parents. Kate recognized the drab décor of the

FBI's offices in the background.

"Break the Chains worked with us to bring Zamira's parents here. They will take her back home, where she will receive ongoing counseling support as she tries to transition back into society."

Kate stared at the screen for a long moment more, trying to burn the image into her brain.

Clayton watched the intensity with which Kate looked at the screen. "I can send it to you if you'd like."

Kate handed the phone back. "I would like that very much. Thank you."

Pocketing the device, Clayton took the cap off her pen. "Why don't we start back at the Makah Cultural Center ..."

Kate played along for the next few hours, painstakingly taking them through every detail of her trip through the forest and all that had followed. They hung on every word as if they had never heard the story before.

"And then Sheriff Luchasetti showed up," Kate finished.

Fuentes leaned back in his chair and stared intently at her. "Right. Now take us through what happened when Deputy Flaherty took you back to the sheriff's office."

Kate studied the new lines etched around his eyes. Her gaze shifted to Clayton, who was holding her shoulders a little higher than normal.

In the past, the agents had voiced equal praise for her heroism and disappointment for her choice to confront Pastor Brian. According to her formal statement, Kate had thought she recognized his voice from the few words he had uttered at the cliff. She had insisted the visit to his office had merely been a fishing expedition. After all, no one but Kate and the pastor had known the roar of the surf had made such an identification impossible. And one of them was dead.

Careful to control the inflection in her tone, as well as her body language, Kate continued the story. When she was finished, she sat back in her seat and waited.

"Well, I guess that's it then," Fuentes put his pen down. "Thanks again for coming in today, Kate."

"You're welcome." Standing, she flashed a brief smile at each of the agents and began heading for the door.

"There is one more question." Clayton's words stopped her in midstride.

Kate turned. "Yes?"

"We pulled the phone records from the sheriff's office that night. There were two outgoing calls during the time you were there with Deputy Flaherty. One to the cell phone number of an old friend of yours, Maria Torres. And another to an unknown number."

Kate's expression remained passive. "I called Maria. She's a friend and I certainly needed one."

"She is also a well-known journalist. According to the records, Torres called back after about fifteen minutes. How much did you tell her about what had transpired?"

Kate returned to the table and regarded each of them. Not bothering to hide the venom from her voice, she spat out the next words. "Oh no, you don't! You don't get to accuse me because of your incompetence." She held her hand up for emphasis, ticking off each of the next points with her fingers. "Do you realize because of this case, I was shot at, run off a road into a lake, hung in a cage, and hunted like an animal?"

The agents stared back at her as if she were a stretch of grass in their front yard and they were waiting for it to grow.

Shaking her head in disgust, Kate addressed her next words to the ceiling. "You looked up Torres, so you know how we became friends—joint trauma when we were both almost killed by the Tower Torturer.

"Not that you deserve my explanation, but the call went to voicemail. I told her I wanted to know how she was doing. She understood and started telling me about her dog. Believe it or not, it helped to ground me. As for the other call I have no idea—ask Flaherty."

Clayton held her gaze for a full minute. Finally, she nodded. "Torres told us the same thing. With everything going on, we had to follow up. You understand."

Kate raised her chin. "I understand perfectly. You didn't trust me."

Fuentes interjected. "You're right. We didn't. But you can imagine the hell we're getting over the video leak. We've got to shake every tree." He stood and walked around the table to face Kate. Their eyes locked for another full minute.

Finally, the agent's features relaxed. "Flaherty claimed he didn't make any calls. He must have been mistaken. We believe you, Kate. But you understand why we had to be sure."

Kate turned and headed for the door. She had begun to cross the threshold when she stopped and turned back. "And now you understand why I said no to the FBI every time I've been asked to join."

∨

The trailhead was clearly marked. The tall wood sign welcoming visitors to the Cape Flattery Trail, had been adorned with a map as well as information on local wildlife as well as notable flora and fauna.

A dozen or so long branches, cut to near even lengths and adorned with colorful feathers and beads, were propped against the marker. According to the handwritten note stapled above them, the walking sticks had been fashioned by members of the Makah and were available for public use.

Kate pulled out a five-dollar bill and placed it in the donation box nearby. Forgoing those with brighter adornments, she selected a stick with white and pale-yellow accents. The heft was comfortable, and a natural bend in the wood allowed for the perfect grip.

She studied the map for another few moments before starting out. A few yards in, a strong breeze whispered through the forest, teasing wisps of hair free from her ponytail.

Kate decided to take it as a good omen for her first solo trek into the woods since the night of horrors. Her mother had offered to accompany her today, but Kate had declined. For as much progress as the women had made in their relationship, the wounds with Chloe were much more injurious than any of those she had incurred recently. They would require far longer to heal.

It would be a similar process for the community of Eagle's Nest. The twenty-four/seven news coverage for the first two weeks, had dwindled. The numerous news networks which had descended upon the town had all packed up and set off in search of fresher stories.

In downtown Eagle's Nest, the Faith, Hope and Light sign had been torn down. Proposals had been floated for eventually bringing the old theater back, but for now, the building remained shuttered. Aaru was also locked down tight. Public demands for it to be leveled to the ground had to wait. Both sites were crime scenes. For justice to be served, the community would be forced to remember before it could be allowed to forget.

A guttural roar tore through the quiet afternoon air. The sound of the bear call was close enough to make Kate freeze. Thirty seconds passed, then forty. Other than the thunder of her pulse in her ears, the world seemed to have gone preternaturally quiet.

After a full three minutes had passed, during which the largest creature in sight had been an energetic squirrel, Kate decided to press on. She proceeded along the trail, making as much noise as she could to avoid and accidental confrontation with any of the local denizens—big or small.

Gradually, the dirt trail gave way to an elevated walkway. Set only a few feet above the forest floor, there were no guardrails on the wooden path as it snaked its way through the woods.

Accompanied by the steady rhythm of her footfalls, Kate relished the verdant aromas of the forest and the feel of the fresh air in her lungs. Other than a few birds, she did not encounter anyone else along the trail. It was exactly as she had hoped.

In the wake of being discharged from the hospital, the unexpected outpouring of concern had been smothering. In addition to Tony and Chloe's almost constant attention, Deputy Wheaton and Fiona appeared on her doorstep a few times a week, delivering premade meals. Maria Torres called daily, as did Kevin and Harding.

She and Kevin had avoided any reference to the video leak during their calls. While it had been true Kate had not mentioned the video in her call to Maria Torres, it was also true she had mentioned it to Kevin when she had called him a few minutes later.

The falsehood was regrettable, but Kate knew all too well how fragile the justice system was. Zamira and the other girls deserved justice and the release of the video was integral to ensure they would get it.

The conversations with her ex-partner had been more complex. Harding had purchased a ticket to Seattle the minute he had heard the news. It had taken every bit of charm and coercion Kate possessed to persuade him not to come.

Having never had a large support structure, Kate was stumbling through the contradicting feelings of gratitude for the kindness of others and self-resentment for being weak enough to accept help. Tony had been helping her navigate, applying equal parts patience and brutal honesty. Thanks to him, she was beginning to understand what she had, and how not to lose it.

The smell of the ocean arrived on a light breeze. A flash of memories—the cliff, the boot, clinging to the rocks ...

Inhaling deeply, Kate shook off the remnants of anxiety and pressed on. Minutes later, she arrived at a tall, wooden viewing platform. She propped her walking stick against one of the vertical supports and reached for the ladder.

Indifferent to the achingly cold metal handrails, she climbed up and stepped onto the platform. In a moment, her world changed. The stress, pain, fear and trauma of the past weeks was swallowed by the vast expanse of the Pacific Ocean.

Dead ahead, about half a mile from shore, Tatoosh Island sat serenely beneath the rapidly clearing skies. Standing in stark confidence despite its isolation, the distant lighthouse drew her eye like a magnet.

Kate walked across the platform and grabbed hold of the guardrail. Transfixed by the building in the distance, she could only imagine the storms it had weathered.

Flashes of death peppered her thoughts in slow motion snippets. Cruthers. Fairbourne. Pastor Brian. For the past few weeks, she had not allowed herself to think about the killings, other than to acknowledge their necessity.

The rugged natural beauty enveloped her senses, chasing the unpleasant musings from her mind. Her pulse beat in rhythm with the surf, she inhaled and exhaled with the wind. The scent of the ocean tinged with hints of the forest set her senses on fire. In moments, her heart slipped into a state with which she was decidedly unfamiliar—serenity.

Subtly, her thoughts fell into a sober question and answer session with the wind and the waves. During the gentle exchange, Kate probed a host of things she had spent years avoiding.

She remained lost in the depths of introspection until the sun began to slip toward the horizon. Strengthened by the power of the honest internal dialogue, she loathed to leave the place that had facilitated it. But with the darkness, the temperature had begun to plummet.

When the cold had stiffened Kate's joints to the point it had almost become unbearable, she activated the flashlight on her cell phone and started back down the ladder. By the time she returned to the parking lot, she had made up her mind about a good many things. One of those was what to do about Tony.

The sheriff possessed every attribute that mattered to Kate—honesty, bravery, and loyalty. He was the type of person who wanted to add to the world, not take from it. Opening herself to the idea of a relationship was a scary prospect, but she had just resolved fear would no longer factor into her decision making.

The first priority was to get warm. The next was to call Tony and see if he was free tonight. She turned on the car and set the heater on high. Goal one achieved.

Goal two would have to wait. Chloe had warned her cell service was nonexistent at the Cape. On the way up to the trail, Kate recalled having wound her way more than halfway around the mountain before losing her signal. She should be able to reach out to Tony in less than six minutes. The thought warmed her in a way she had never thought one could.

Less than three minutes later, the sudden ring of her cell phone proved her estimate wrong. Eyes pinned to the road ahead, she answered the call.

"Kate?" Tyler Harding's tone was oddly grave.

"Hey, Harding. Listen, I'm doing much better. You really don't need to keep checking in ..."

"We have to talk."

Frowning, she eased up on the gas. "Everything okay?"

"Everything is fucked about eight ways from Sunday."

Checking her empty rearview mirror as a precaution, she pulled over to the shoulder. "Tell me."

"The Norse Thorn ... The Tower Torturer ... Shit! Hold on, I'll text you." She could hear him tapping on his device. In the next moment, a text appeared on her screen. She enlarged the image.

What appeared before her made her clench her eyes shut. The soft light from the screen displayed the torment in her features.

Without opening her eyes, she asked, "What do you know?"

"Not much. About ten minutes ago, the phone lines started lighting up at precincts all over the city. I'm on my way there now."

Nodding, she opened her eyes and pinned her gaze on the screen. "Give me some time to pack. I can be back in Seattle in about four hours. If I can get a ticket, I'll be at SFO in a little over two hours."

"Send me your flight information as soon as you have it. I'll meet you at the airport."

Kate ended the call and pulled back onto the road. Edging the speedometer up above the posted limit, she tried to clear the image from her mind. It was impossible.

As a native of the Bay Area, San Francisco's skyline had been an indelible part of Kate's frame of reference. Over the last decade, an economic boom had completely transformed it. More high rises had popped up out of the ground in the last ten years than should have been possible. Rising above them all to snatch the cherished title of tallest building in the city from the iconic Transamerica Pyramid, was Salesforce Tower.

Harding's photo had featured the top six floors of the building. Normally, they served as the backdrop for the projection of a massive, three-hundred-and-sixty-degree digital display of various art projects.

Tonight, instead of ballet dancers gracefully leaping about *en pointe*, the night sky was dominated by the image of a young woman—a dead young woman. Her torso had been brutally carved

374

open from the base of her neck to the top of her pubic bone in the shape of a bloody Norse thorn.

As she made her way down the mountainside, the one thing of which Kate could be certain was all which had transpired in Eagle's Nest was child's play compared to the evil awaiting her in San Francisco.

Marie Sutro is a native of the San Francisco Bay Area and a member of Sisters in Crime. Her debut novel, Dark Associations, was a bestseller for which she won the Benjamin Franklin Award for the Best New Voice in Fiction. A proponent of adult literacy, she volunteers with California Library Literacy Services, helping adults improve their reading and writing skills. Her father, grandfather and great-grandfather, grandfather and father all served in the San Francisco Police Department; collectively inspiring her stories.

She resides in Northern California and is currently at work on the next Kate Barnes thriller. To learn more about Marie, visit her website at mariesutro.com.